Old Buck

SEXUALITY, SECRETS AND THE CIVIL WAR

ROGER EVANS

HL
A
Longfellow
Book

Longfellow Publishing Company
18 Hammond Drive
Falmouth, Maine 04105

ISBN: 1-4392-0774-7
ISBN-13: 9781439207741

Visit www.booksurge.com to order additional copies.

DEDICATION

This book is dedicated to my children, Jonathan, Gillian, Carey Leigh and Skylar, in great thanks for the endless blessings, through the hand of Providence, they bring to me and others.

SNOW-FLAKES

Out of the bosom of the Air,
    Out of the cloud-folds of her garments shaken,
Over the woodlands brown and bare,
    Over the harvest-fields forsaken,
        Silent, and soft, and slow
        Descends the snow.

Even as our cloudy fancies take
    Suddenly shape in some divine expression,
Even as the troubled heart doth make
    In the white countenance confession,
        The troubled sky reveals
        The grief it feels.

This is the poem of the air,
    Slowly in silent syllables recorded;
This is the secret of despair,
    Long in its cloudy bosom hoarded,
        Now whispered and revealed
        To wood and field.

HENRY WADSWORTH LONGFELLOW, 1858

THE BEWILDERED OLD WOMAN.

MRS. J. B.—"SAKES ALIVE! I KNOW NO NORTH, NO SOUTH, NO EAST, NO WEST—NO NOTHING! AND WHO ON EARTH'S GOING TO TAKE THIS PLAGUY MESSAGE?

TABLE OF CONTENTS

PROLOGUE

Old Buck sat inside the churning coach, withered and nearly forgotten. He rested his sagging frame on the plush bench and squirmed amid the molding purple upholstery. His dull fingers traced stubby arcs slowly dissolving into the satin. On the bench's corroded pediment, the deeper outlines of an eagle rampant could still be seen, its wings carved into the sandalwood, its jagged beak dimly limned in flaked gold leaf.

Outside, the broken ribs and torn flesh of grey leaves rose above the road and descended into late fall's worm ridden decay. A surging stream of townspeople, most in breaking carts and runabouts, a few straggling on foot, traversed the corduroyed patchwork of mud and toppled trees. If it were as it should have been, Old Buck thought, there would be no battlefield at the journey's end.

Pompey's driving was informed by a half century of loyal service. He was vigilant with the brougham, mindful of the status of its occupant. Still, the voice carped at his former slave, "Pompey, dammit, go easy! You know the weariness of these bones. I've precious little padding left. Don't keep grinding me down."

Each jolt of the buggy shot through the passenger's body. Old Buck felt martyred. It was as if Age herself were baking his doughy flesh, insinuating her dry rot into his very sinews. Pompey kept his eyes forward. He did not need to turn around and look at the frayed husk of white hair squatting like last year's corn on the cocked head, the odd two-colored squinting eyes, and the tiny pursing lips to understand that it fell to him to husband the pain. He noticed, but did not mention, the solitary dog, its tongue hanging to the hardening ground, keeping pace with the carriage.

If only we had left ahead of the crowd! Pompey thought, but he knew that they had to be careful about not arriving early. Careful about not being spotted. Careful, most of all, about being able to stay on the sidelines.

In early July, 20,000 goobers and graybacks, bucktails and Yanks, perished. Scores succumbed from the scorching organ-carving upward thrusts of bayonets into gullet, gut, and groin. Hundreds fragmented from minie balls exploding into their onrushing bodies. Thousands were cannonaded. A further 20,000 expired slowly but no less certainly from gangrene, camp fever, and the diseases they called mortification and corruption.

During that carnage, Old Buck fled Wheatland, the home where he was now imprisoned, for the nation's first capital. He had burrowed into the Hotel Metropole on Broad, south of Locust. In daylight hours he crawled out only to seek the furtive pleasure of a massage and vapors at Kelsey's Oriental Bath three blocks away. At night he pinched and pounded Madeira at the Man Full of Trouble on Little Dock Creek, and scuttled along Camac, Fawn and Quince. On his way back to the Metropole, Old Buck eyed, hopefully, the alleyway behind Spruce's shuttered stores. At Rittenhouse Square he puffed a Fragrant Vanity Fair or a Bon Ton, blowing flowing broken rings into the night air. With the first insinuations of revealing light, the remaining wisps of his white topknot flattened by perspiration across his beaten brow, Old Buck retreated to his shell at the Metropole, recalling days of gin slings and brandy sours, champagne and caviar.

Of course, the memory of the young woman who rose quietly from an iron bench in what was then Southwest Square and ran shrieking through those very streets, fairly out of her mind, simply would not go away.

That was months of war ago. Now, the carriage carved nearer. The stalking brindled dog slipped through the standing dead of the climax forest and established itself in the strangle of displaced curs slinking at the crowd's edges. Its access to interred bones and remaining flesh was, briefly, denied.

No one had sought his presence at this ceremony, but Old Buck could not resist the journey to hear the words of Edward Everett roll through the bustling valleys and over the empty hillsides of his home state. Everett—Senator, Governor, Harvard President, minister and classicist—known to him and all as the greatest orator of the era. Old Buck had often been accused of pomposity in his speech. Perhaps, like Jefferson, he told himself, I am more at home with the written word. Yet if I have one grand skill as to which my pride is justified, it is my proficiency at compromise. Certainly, that sometimes implicated a bit of shading, of truth-trimming, perhaps even calculated deceit, but such was the process he learned as a boy that had, at least up to a point, served him and the nation well.

• • •

The second speaker had arrived by train at noon. As he tried to pick his way through the well-tunneled bones, their porous yellow rails split under his boots. The marrow of hundreds of horses lay leaching into the soil. Thousands of corpses more, gray and blue, crunched in the boneyard barely a dog's paw below the withered grass. The sojourner fought for long hard draughts of disordered air, knowing even then that the deep sensory recesses of his guilty brain would remain forever invaded.

He wept.

• • •

Governor Curtin's protracted introduction was rounding its halfway point as Pompey pulled gently on the reins and uttered a soft "whoa" to the bays. He negotiated a place among the swarm's outliers. Old Buck remained inside. Through the drawn shade of the veiled window he waited to hear the great man's words, and yearned for the inevitable failure of his successor.

Fathers held their littlest ones aloft. Older brothers raced, weaving their way through their elders. Well-bustled mothers in balmoral petticoats peered toward the dais under their beehive bonnets. They scurried to corral their children as bits of their undergarments snagged on tangled skeletal splinters. Torn crinoline drooped like limp flags on the bony staffs. The sounds of cracking body parts butted into the howls of the compassing dogs, the crowd's chords swelling as if they sought to defeat the mounting pounding surrounding feral rhythms. Local politicians peppered the flock, most parading toward the front. Those who knew their place—the poor, the servants, the vagrants, the dark-skinned—stood near the rear.

A rising sluice of jealousy washed over Old Buck as he observed the scene. The chief executive of West Virginia, barely a state, and even the mayor of the tiny town that stood on the outskirts of this battlefield, were seated prominently with seven other governors. No one had asked him to speak. No one had even asked him to attend. Here he was, uninvited and unacknowledged, cast by foul circumstance to the back of the crowd. What impertinent absence of gratitude had thrust him among such hoi polloi?

Curtin's rambling exposition finally ended. Everett gestured toward the more prominent politicians, nodded to the next speaker, and inaugurated his peroration. The roiling masses were accustomed to two-hour sermons. They would not be disappointed.

He began, "Standing beneath this serene sky, overlooking the broad fields now reposing from these labors of the waning year, the mighty Alleghenies towering dimly before us, the graves of our brethren beneath our feet, it is with hesitation that I raise my poor voice to break the eloquent silence of God and Nature…"

As Everett invoked Athenian history, and quoted, without attribution, Milton's "Paradise Regained" and Byron's "Second Canto," Old Buck was vaguely uncomfortable at the echoed murmuring of his mother's voice, redolent of Appalachian hollows, reading to him in Stony Batter a lifetime ago.

Everett rolled on. Old Buck recalled the pain of his pale prescriptions for the nation, his own attempts to deal with the southern cavalcade. Secession was unconstitutional, yet there were no lawful means for the northern states to stop it. It was, of course, all the fault of the one set to speak next, the one who caused all that he sought, by compromise and concession, to avoid.

Everett concluded to round after round of applause. Afternoon's shadows began to enfold the carriage. Old Buck poked his head outside and immediately recoiled. Raw smells laced his nostrils. Even at the crowd's outer reaches, he found it necessary to remove his cream handkerchief from his top pocket and press it firmly across his twitching pink nose. How could the others abide this fetid stink? His head jumped back at the sight of two boys tossing a punctured skull, one of its teeth unaccountably clinging to the soldier's lower jaw. The valley-echoing yelps of the circling hounds, chafing at exclusion from their five month feast on flesh and bone, grew louder, louder as they sought to invade the gathering. Only boots crashing into the gaping mouths of the boldest canines blunted the pack from what it had long since claimed as fully and exclusively its own.

The next speaker sat quietly, his head bowed. Old Buck snickered to himself, even from this distance, as the stovepipe hat was removed from the obviously balding head.

A singular silence descended. Drawing to a full six-feet-four, his face clawed by years of doubt and unanswered prayer, in a tenor tinged with tones of the American frontier, Abraham Lincoln began, "Four score and seven years ago, our forefathers brought forth on this continent a new nation…"

The lawyer's mind was provoked. What new nation, Old Buck quickly calculated, was "brought forth" 87 years ago, in 1776? Why, none indeed. Lincoln was certainly alluding to the signing of the Declaration of Independence, which of course established no new nation at all, only set in formal motion the very sort of rebellion that Everett so effectively denounced, and which Lincoln fathered. Would not it be more correct to say, "Four score and two," and recognize the supplanted Articles of Confederation in 1781 or, better and more properly still, "Three score and fifteen" and acknowledge the United States Constitution, ratified in 1788? Old Buck licked his little lips. He recalled the Westerner's bare 40% of the popular vote, deriving comfort from the somewhat uncertain thought that his countrymen still shared his deep disdain for the war-weary man before them.

Lincoln kept stumbling. "Dedicated to the proposition that all men are created equal." How perfectly silly. Here we are, gathered before this President who a few months ago shifted the whole focus for this unnecessary tragedy to the idea that we are fighting for the "freedom" of some negroes down South. Where were our "forefathers" on this one? Why, and constitutionally so, most of them owned slaves and would have wanted the right to do so to continue in perpetuity. What of the women whose voices were rippling across the land, questioning this President who purports to let southern coloreds break bondage, while women everywhere could not own property, could not vote, and could not run for office? Elizabeth Cady Stanton and Lucretia Mott would not stand for this, with their assertions that the Declaration of Independence's words surely applied to both genders. Cleverly, they compared England and America's relationship in 1776 to that of men and women. In fact, Mrs. Stanton declared, women were "even more like slaves" than the colonial subjects. Old Buck did not agree with her and those Quakers, but here Abe was, tossing scraps of calico their way.

Lincoln went on, advancing the concept that Union troops fought so "this nation might live." Old Buck almost sighed. Certainly, it was Northern aggression, abolitionists and other scoundrels that incited the rebellion and attacked the South, and not the other way around. The nation would survive. Not one state left the country until Lincoln's election. It was not until Old Buck was no longer even arguably on watch that the four final states departed and war began. At worst, another nation would now be created. Two countries, two democracies, if the North had not invaded. Two countries where free white men could vote.

Old Buck's satisfied face peeped through his carriage window as Lincoln ended this embarrassment with words that somehow resonated in the watcher's mind, "government of the people, by the people, and for the people, shall not perish from this earth." Where had he stolen that line?

He wished all his countrymen could hear his clever ripostes and counter-arguments. If only his dear sweet W, now over a decade in the Alabama ground, could be with him…

The abrupt ending occasioned polite applause as blankets and dishes were gathered. What was that? Certainly not a speech at all. Old Buck could not wait to see the Lancaster newspapers eviscerate the President tomorrow. Why had Lincoln bothered to show up? It seemed, to him, like further desecration, as if Lincoln were relieving himself on these young boys' graves.

Suddenly his eyes widened. Parting his way through the surging peasantry was that club-footed, wig-topped hound who yapped at his heels for nearly forty years, dogging his public and private life. Thaddeus Stevens, firebrand abolitionist, late of Gettysburg, earlier of Vermont, and for the past two decades in Lancaster, blackened all he surveyed. Old Buck's smuggery abandoned him. The dear sweet little moment of intellectual glory drained away, subverted by his tormentor's presence.

He could not allow himself to be seen and hissed loudly to Pompey, off corning with his fellow darkies. The wizened slave, once a plump pear of a man, hustled right over, spotted Stevens himself, and with a loud "giddap" pushed the horses through the penumbra of the still visiting crowd. The wild dogs were already reclaiming their carrion.

On the long trip home, winter's steel gray stirrings swept across the sunless land, oozed into the brougham and clutched at his heart. Old Buck could not shake the dripping persistence of Stevens. His knowledge of Old Buck's great secret empowered the anti-slaver for what was approaching a half century. Rumors were one thing. Proof, both old lawyers knew, was something else altogether, especially when the author of the letter that contained the evidence was beyond cross-examination. Stevens never let him see its contents, holding it out as if tantalizing a polecat. He was still required to guess at the full extent of what the letter imparted, but he had felt its force. His face flushed as he recalled the most significant time he was compelled to bow to Stevens' allusive incantation, and the decision that doomed his administration.

Why was he permitted to rise from Congressman, Minister to Russia, United States Senator, on to Secretary of State and, upon his triumphant return from England, propelled to the most august office in the land? Why hadn't Stevens stopped him? Why hadn't Stevens revealed what he had for the entire world to see? Their views were so different. Perhaps Stevens must have found ways to use him of which he was not aware?

Of late, his public life surely over, considerations of death and legacy loomed. He became consumed with removing the blot once and for all, of burying the secret for now and for all of history. How to do that?

The snow fell harder. Wheatland approached. Old Buck extended his right hand to Pompey, who led him to the back door of his empty home. Once again, he felt like the "Beobachter" the Germans who filled his hometown now called him, the weary watcher, the man on the outside, face pressed like a little boy's against the glass, an onlooker, a voyeur, in the city that was once the seedbed of his glory. He scrabbled up the frosted back steps and trudged, slipping on his own uneasiness, to his study. Above the mantle was Ann's portrait. The author of the letter, frozen forever nearly 50 years earlier, surveyed the room laden with the trappings of his life. Old Buck tried, again, to read something of forgiveness in her painted eyes.

He accepted the well-barreled Armagnac Pompey poured from the exquisitely cut crystal decanter, a gift from Prince Albert himself. The slumbering fire, as if a rogue lepidopterist acting on History's commission, pinned his ossified shadow against the sullied walls. Old Buck could not raise his gaze from the detrital coals, their once bright essence now cloaked by soot. Wind insinuated itself between the floor's knotted boards. Through cockled lips, he heavily drew a few sips. The eau de vie dribbled down his dry throat, choking its way inside. He gulped back the shards of bile that rose within him, and called on Pompey to accompany "ol' mon Vesubius" to bed before the horns of bedeviled memories of what once was and what might have been ripped him apart.

As he fought to enter the realm of another night of fitful sleep James Buchanan, fifteenth President of the United States of America, lay amid the sumptuous comforters and damask pillows draped across the French Victorian splendor of his Louis XIV bed, softly sobbing.

Ann. Ann. Ann.
Damn her still.

Chapter One
<u>A N N</u>

Snow. Gentle snow, silent snow. Snow light as fairy's dust, snow pure as the truest thing your lover ever said. Snow that surrounded Ann as she held her father's hand and looked up into what she trusted were his kind blue eyes. Snow that covers every bad thing.

It was the eve before Christmas and only five years into the new century, a generation removed from Independence. The sojourn through Lancaster proper filled the nine year old with sweet anticipation. There were, for her, no secrets greater than the gifts hidden beneath her parents' bed.

Ann's winter-white ermine muffler was a gift of the Marquis de Lafayette, straight from Paris. Her newly-fashioned wool coat, deeply blue against the dancing snow, was tightly buttoned. Yet she could not escape the cold.

Robert Coleman, in pale yellow breeches clinging tightly to his widening thighs, softened at his young daughter's obvious delight. He looked at the black curls spilling beyond her rimmed little bonnet, framing an upturned face that seemed to be all eyes. He reached down and, as if holding a trophy, cupped her chin. Who could, he thought, not love this girl?

The thin strains of a harpsichord playing *Adeste Fidelis* seeped through the mortar of St. James's Church as father and daughter drifted down the streets together, Ann peering into windows, Robert accepting the nods of passersby. A stranger approached and took her father aside. Ann pressed both hands into her muffler and tucked her face against the distorted Crown bullion squares of Widow Moore's small shop. Through the panes, she felt the warmth of the bayberry candles that sat dripping on the heartwood sills.

Ann overheard snippets of her father's conversation, "Yet you insist — boiler from James Watt — Scotland? What of John Fitch's patent? Did not William Henry—also rifles?"

She tugged at her father's long dove grey greatcoat, lifting her soft asking eyes to his. "Father, could we go into the Widow Moore's?"

"One moment more, Ann. I had planned we do so."

The conversation dragged on and she was about to ask if she could go in by herself. Her father turned from the younger man, "Come back to me, Mr. Fulton, when you can incorporate some more of my iron and get the legal questions resolved. I do not speculate on sinking ships."

As they entered the shop, the Widow's bonneted head bustled over to the man who made enormous profits supplying iron to the Continental Army from his forges and ironworks scattered about the new nation's largest inland city.

"What might I do for you, Mr. Coleman?"

"Mrs. Moore," Robert said as he slipped from Ann's hand, "please tell my daughter something about your goods." He added, unnecessarily, "Take your time."

"Why, sir, yes. Ann, do ye see these teacups and the matching plates? They were fired in English towns like Worcester and Derby, that means they were made of porcelain and clay and heated in a kiln beyond where water boils, as much as 1200 degrees, but only once. Sometimes they even put some dry and grinded bones into the mix."

Ann's head twitched. Her lower jaw pulled back and down toward her thin neck, stretching her cheeks and exposing her bottom teeth above a taut lower lip.

"No, Ann. Not from people!"

Ann's relief immediately gave birth to curiosity. She wanted to ask what animals' bones ended up in these little tea cups, but decided she would as soon not know.

Ann simply wanted to be left alone to roam the shop and its wares. Yet the Widow stayed tightly with her and droned on about the cooling process and how the porcelain was painted, continuing, "It takes eight weeks by ship across the Atlantic Ocean to deliver these to Philadelphia. Next, they were carted by wagon for two days to come here."

The proprietress closely watched as Ann picked up a teacup, perching it carefully between fingers just beginning to thaw. The little girl inspected the blue and white portraits of the odd foreign structures and the Widow began anew, "Those designs were dreamed up by China women in the Orient, all the way on the other side of the world."

Ann replaced the porcelain. Her eyes went across the room to where her father stood in the far corner talking to a woman she recognized, even in the bobbing candlelight, as Eva Hubley. Unlike her own mother, who always wore a bonnet and a long dark cloak over her somber dresses, that woman's narrow scarlet coat opened in front to reveal layers of sheer black silk with a high waistline gathered under the bust. Hints of petticoats gathered at her ankles. The Widow slid between the daughter and her view, and continued, "You know, Ann, it was your father that helped with the new tarmacadam road that brings all this here. It's the very first in the country."

Robert sensed the movement. Hastily, from across the shop, "Ann, are not these things beautiful? They come from very far away."

Eva flitted back to a small furnished room near the rear of the store. Robert shooed Ann ahead of him down the shop door steps, and whispered something to the Widow as he left. Ann drew the back of her fine-boned hand across her eyelids as King Street filled with snow. Shadow touched shadow. Buzzing above the cobbled bricks, talk about the dueling death of Alexander Hamilton at the hands of the Vice-President, and Aaron Burr's pending trial. As gossip bounced from ear to ear, German urchins scattered by, with shouts of "*macht das nicht!*" and "*Fröhliches Weihnachten!*" Ann stared into the sodden flakes as she struggled to put aside the troubling images muddling through her.

Mothers scurried about in their handmade clothes as father and daughter made their way through a parade of men prowling after her father's counsel. Still eager to see all she could before the night fell, Ann complained, "Father, you hold too tightly." Robert looked down sharply, but relaxed his grip. He knew that being alone with her father right before Christmas was very special to Ann, and it was meant to be. Each year, in a rotation not favoring his sons over his daughters, he had taken them one by one into town on Christmas Eve. It was finally Ann's turn and he was now determined she would focus only on the good.

He began to ignore, except for a slight nod or tip of his beaver tricorn, the passersby and explained, "Ann, you should know there are more than fifty crafts here in Lancaster. You can see that the shops are in the tradesmen's homes. They have their workrooms in the back and live with their families right above. When I was a boy, even when I first came to this country, there were none of these fixed shops, and everyone sold their goods in the street."

Ann imagined that must have been very loud, and quite messy. How, too, did they fit all their children in these small houses all in a row?

"Now, you can see not only the products, but how they are made, right in the same place."

Ann looked deeply through the bubbled glass into the dimly-lit shops of millers and milliners, strolled past wheelwrights and coopers, and scanned the now vacant saddleries and smiths in the row houses and chink-stoned log cabins of Lime, Lemon, Mulberry and Vine. At Gundaker's stable, she reared back as the strong black horses twisted and snorted against the darkening air, but marveled at the phaetons, barouches and other fine carriages for hire. The artistry of smells coming from Christoph Demuth's tobacconistry reminded her of the aromas of businessmen and politicians huddling in her father's library. She loved the petticoats in the next shop, all frills and eyelets, designed and sewn by Moravians who lived on farms just outside of town.

When her eye caught a silk scarf her father told her was shipped all the way from Shanghai, she turned to him. He replied to the unspoken question, "Perhaps, Ann, Father Christmas might bring you something at least as fine."

They wandered back to their carriage, past the piles of taverns with their private upstairs rooms on the Duke of Cumberland, the Prince of Wales and House of Orange, and Queen Caroline (as her father told her the streets were called before Independence) toward the former King George Street. The houses changed to German half-timber, each the same width and each placed precisely in the middle of its particular plat. Where Queen met King, grand manses flanked from Penn Square and its neoclassical courthouse. Their pediments, porticoes, and Ionic and Doric columns mimicked, as did her own, those up and down the Schuylkill in Philadelphia's Fairmount Park. Fallow gardens lay souring under crusted ice and quick bursts of flaming ashes flushed above the chimneys, turning grey and indefinite against the clouded sky.

Ann spied a few friends heading toward their homes, and saw Grace Hubley, Eva's daughter. Ann's eyes tensed as Grace approached and twitched when her father twirled his encaped arms around the girl.

While Robert was seeking the approval of Grace, Ann caught sight of the disappearing figure of Lüder Bauschulte one block down on the other side of Orange, making his way toward the row home his parents, at the end of their indentured servitude to the Colemans, rented on Ann Street. Ann called out *"Fröhliches Weihnachten!"* to Lüder through the snow, but her cry was drowned by the clattering of a carriage. The words were captured by the ample ears of a passing German Frau who exclaimed to her father, *"Sie ist solch ein schönes süsses kleines Mädchen!"* Ann blushed, as she had been taught, at being called beautiful and sweet but wished Lüder had heard her.

Father and daughter left the city of 4,000 and headed toward home, Robert at the whip. Ann still smelled the dripping heated fruit-based lye and puffing dust of the Widow Moore's. She stared into the black arch of heaven and thought back to when her family traveled to Mount Vernon as the eighteenth century, in its final December, breathed its last. How they got there and how they got back, she did not recall, and it did not matter. The sight that day, and the name she heard while her parents' fiery words traveled up the chimney and popped into the cold stagnant air, she could not forget. Part of that trip was now simply memory reinforced by family retellings. Part of it, the part that mattered, was, desperately and silently, her own.

Nelly Custis Lewis, the granddaughter of the President's wife, met them at the door and escorted the family into the front parlor past the painted pine of the central passage. Mount Vernon was not as large as Ann had thought after hearing all the talk about it being where the father of the whole country lived, but Nelly was apparently quite pretty. Ann remembered thinking she had never seen her brother Thomas smile quite so much.

"The President is very ill," Nelly related, "and my grandmother is over at Pohick Church with her pastor. I expect she may spend the day praying with him. This afternoon, the Lees will be over and Governor and Mrs. Monroe are coming tomorrow. It's a busy time, but I know the President wants to see you." She motioned to the slave, erect in the corner, "Cicero will assist you."

Nelly surveyed the seven children. The twenty year old, just married that year on her grandfather's birthday, declared from the stairs as she went up to the sickroom, "I only ask that you not all go up together."

Ann's mother replied, "Of course, perhaps the girls and baby Sarah with their father and me, and then the boys?" Robert turned to his wife, "I want some time with the General myself. Why don't you go with the others, and I will follow with Ann."

It was here, as she watched a whiteness of swans make its way toward the winter-bared arbor beyond the window, that Ann's remembrance of things past faded into a distorted conjunction. She recalled that her brothers and sisters went up the mahogany stairs with their mother, returning like stunned ghosts as Father prattled on about swamps and sickness.

Ann thought Mother gave a sharp and fearful glance as she said, "Please, Robert, do not take our Ann up there!" She was sure of her father's disgusted steel-eyed glare at Mother as he towed his daughter upward and upward while she clung to his hand, trailing a lacquered tread behind. Father and she turned left off the second floor corridor. Ann saw only hovering murky figures with slowly swinging leather bags circling, like large dark dogs, the white shrouded canopy. She had not understood Father's attempt to tell her that leeches dredged from the surrounding bogs and marshes were treating the former President. The air reeked with the full vapors of the products of emetics and clysters, and the resulting vomit lay in a tin bucket hard by an enameled bedpan that sorely needed to be emptied. Daughter went ahead of Father toward the pallid frame. The throbbing smell of nascent death overwhelmed her. Thin skin stretched over bones that looked to Ann as if they would, at any moment, poke right through.

The old general greeted her with a gap-toothed smile and reached to pat her bonneted head. Ann saw only the worms hanging from the sagging flesh of his outstretched arm. She ran shrieking from the room, down the stairs, out the front door. Father made busy apologies to the President and all present. With the strides timed to befit his stature, he started after his daughter. Ann catapulted right by the rest of the family sitting in the small parlor and ran straight into the arms of Cicero, now standing on Mount Vernon's front steps. Mother rushed toward her and Father was hurrying down the stairs, shouting the beginnings of a stern lesson in manners and propriety, when a barouche pulled to a halt and Martha Washington emerged. Robert made straight for the President's wife and the rest of the family followed, leaving the still sobbing Ann behind.

She did not remember much else about the time before she went to bed, except that Mother and Father seemed only to want to talk to Mrs. Washington and someone named Lighthorse Harry at dinner in the next room. No one seemed to notice that she pushed her food around the plate at the table she shared with Margaret and her brother Thomas. After dinner, without a good-night from anyone else, Cicero took Margaret and her up to a small bedroom on the third floor across the hall from Martha Washington. Ann's hard little bed was trundled out from her sister's and pulled in front of the stunted fire. Both parents were soon ensconced right below with her baby sister, across the second floor hallway from the President's bedroom where he now lay alone. The brothers were barracked together in the first floor bedroom, directly off the downstairs study.

Margaret flowed easily into her dreams, but Ann's little body writhed and warped against the muslin. She tried to roll into herself, clutching her knees to her chest, but her legs and arms stiffened and shook in spasms. Sweat swarmed her body, coating her bedding with rimy hoarfrost congealed by the cold. Amid images of bone white flesh and bloated leeches came those invading words, baked on the fading embers in a chimney that also opened to the room below. Her parents' voices. Mingled, swirling. Half the words she didn't know. She did know her name, and came to know another…

"Eva Hubley. On the very night Ann was born. My flesh ripping. You were putting yours in her. Then to name Ann after me. You don't care for Ann at all, scaring her with this sight!"

"Where does that nonsense come from?"

"You were with that slut, that sloven." Then, as if Mother were spitting, "Strumpet."

"Eva Hubley. At Matthias Slough's. Ruth told me. While I was in pain, giving birth to what you now have cursed."

"I was not. The damned Hell I was not!"

"You think naming Ann after me makes it better? It's worse."

"I did that for you! My wife."

Then soft mewling screams….

• • •

Ann and her father returned from their Christmas Eve trip to Lancaster. Her mother was already in bed. Father led daughter to the room she shared with her younger sister and gazed benignly as Ann and Sarah prayed together for their parents and an unsaved world. How like an Engleheart portrait miniature they each look, watercolor on opalescent glass and seed-pearled ivory, Ann's hair black and Sarah's gold, Robert thought as he went again into the night.

Her father departed and Sarah sleeping, Ann re-lit the candle and turned to the treasure she kept tucked under her eiderdown pillow. *Love Triumphant; or, Constancy Rewarded* was published when she was one year old. She always loved to read the Bible with her mother, although she did not know that certain bold passages, including the entire book of Solomon, were off limits until one was engaged. Her sister Margaret would also sometimes share Bunyan's *Grace Abounding*, and Ann delighted in learning about the Pilgrim's progress through the Slough of Despond in the similitude of a dream. Now she had her own book.

It was a wonderful, sentimental account of star-crossed lovers, Emma and the impecunious Ferdino. Anticipating the time when she would be in love, Ann's mind and spirit wrapped around the exchange of letters between Emma and her friend Fanny, the journal entries, and Emma's bitter entreaties to her father. She could not comprehend how young Emma could go against her parents' wishes and marry Ferdino. On the other hand, Emma's parents were so heartless and so in error.

Among various poems infused with Biblical images was one addressed to a yellow bird, once free. Ann read, again, how the little bird flies in through a schoolroom window and is destroyed by the "*over-carefulness*" of the schoolchildren, its life literally pawed away by grasping hands against the backdrop of murmurings of concern. The fate of the yellow bird touched Ann's soul each time she read it, and she took to heart its message that innocence and beauty are no protection in a harsh world, particularly taken by the stanzas:

> *Ye blooming fair, who fondly gaze,*
> *And with regret this victim view;*
>
> *Death in a thousand different ways,*
> *This warning lesson speaks to you*

Nor youth nor beauty can defend,
But mortal life must have an end.

The nine year old trembled at the poem and its message of the immediacy of death, the loss of parents and a mate, and the still dawning knowledge that goodness and beauty were insufficient protection from what life might have in store. She considered long and hard life without beauty, and her mind turned to what she learned in church was the presence, everywhere, of evil. What kind of evil would make life intolerable, even if beauty abounded? Ann could not answer her own question but it would be revealed, she would learn it, on her own.

It was only a few years later that Ann ran up the stairs to her new bedroom in the home the Colemans purchased in Lancaster proper. The grand house was on the first block off of Penn Square, at 42 East King Street, on the northeast corner of King and Christian. Ann now lived near her very best friends, and the Colemans resided on the same block with the very best families in Lancaster County. Only the Widow Dutchman tavern across the way marred the quiet and prominence of their new address.

The mansion had twelve large rooms, all paneled in hard ebony wood and papered with the latest French offerings showing scenes from courts, formal gardens that stretched as far as the eye could see, and stripes and paisleys that fairly danced with intrigue. Ann was excited about the enormous ballroom with its Prussian blue marble floor and intricate handmade staircase carved from a single mahogany tree in far off Borneo. Its shining balustrade would be particularly good for sliding, although perhaps better to do so when adults were away. Ann practiced pieces of her backwards descent several times, going down a few stairs' length, hopping off onto the white painted treads.

A few weeks after the family settled in, father was in the library with his whiskey and his pipe, meeting with Robert Morris, who bankrolled much of the Revolution, his good friend Edward

Hand, who as Washington's Adjutant General funneled a series of contracts from the Continental Congress to him, and several other stern looking men she did not know. She wondered what secrets were being discussed, and curiosity overwhelmed her. Ann cracked the door ever so slightly, and looked in. Her father was going on and on about his own circumstances. Ann had often heard the polished retelling of his personal history colored by an Ulster brogue, how he was born in County Donegal in 1748, how that was only technically in Ireland despite being at the country's very tip, because his family was really English, and his odd pride that he possessed no Irish blood. What always followed was his decision to come to America to better his prospects at age 16, and how he "kept his eyes and ears open" while working as a scrivener of legal records in Philadelphia before coming to Lancaster for its greater opportunities. How he learned the business, the ways costs could be cut, the way to extend credit to workmen that they could never repay, and the mechanics of the iron business and how to finance it. In 1776, wisely right when the Revolution was declared, how he rented the Elizabeth forge outside Lancaster and set, without letting the others know, to buy out the various personal shares. Then his marriage to John Olds's daughter Ann, who brought with her a substantial dowry that completed the acquisition. As always, he was ending with a full exposition on the empire he created, taking Hessian prisoners for his ironworks and petitioning the Continental Congress to let him put to work, for a small fee, conscripted Lancaster boys as labor, rather than sending them on to General Washington. Ann had heard this all before, and she knew Mr. Hand and Mr. Morris had as well. Perhaps it was solely for the others? What was her father's business with them?

Just then, however, her father noticed the outside shaft of foyer light playing against the leather-bound books flanking the fireplace. He excused himself and approached the door to investigate. Ann scampered toward the staircase. Father strode into the foyer, his voice rising, "Ann, confound you, was that you that interrupted?" Crinoline flying, Ann had already begun up the stairs when the stinging words reached her.

She turned to answer and grabbed the balustrade. Her right foot was snared by a white-enameled stanchion and she tumbled, tread by tread, finally thudding against the Prussian marble below. She lay on the blue stone for but a second, her dress torn and her shoes ripped. She looked full in her father's angry face, got up and ran from the house, out the back door to the stables. Robert considered following her, but could not keep the investors waiting. He would deal with her later. He returned to the library, this time forcing the hard black iron bolt across the inside of the oaken door.

Ann was surprised to see an unfamiliar slave grooming Devil. Little Dick, newly removed from his duties at the Elizabeth Forge, intercepted the running figure. He took a cloth, dipped a clean corner in a bucket of well water, and patted her forehead. Ann's tears grew as the red stain spread before her. She recalled her father's statement at dinner the night before, "I was compelled to let Friedrich Bauschulte go. The old German cannot keep up with the work here. I have put a negro from the Elizabeth Forge out back in the stables. He goes by Little Dick."

Ann sat down on a bale of hay and watched Dick stroke and curry the steeds. She noticed he paid special attention to the ebony-colored Canadian Warmblood Devil who, at 18 hands, was the largest horse in his charge and her favorite. Ann remembered how she used to sneak some soot out of one of the family's fireplaces and coat the lone white spot on Devil's forehead with the ashes to confuse Friedrich, thinking this would make him believe a neighbor's horse somehow made its way into their stable. She thought, even as the blood on her hands stopped flowing, "What a silly girl I used to be!"

As Ann started to tell Dick the old trick, she spotted a well-worn copy of "Poor Richard's Almanack" lying against the coarse straw where he slept. Startled, "Little Dick, can you read?"

The space between Dick's eyebrows closed and his head dropped, "Perhaps a bit, Miss Ann."

"How can that be?"

"It was from de Germans at Cornwall. Dey taught me a bit."

"Well then, let me hear you."

Dick haltingly read to Ann as much as he could about the best times to harvest and what had been predicted for a winter now seven years in the past. He moved to the part he liked best, and his lips danced over the aphorisms and adages, "Setting too good an example is a kind of slander seldom forgiven." Another quickly followed, "Dost thou love life? Then do not squander time; for that's the stuff life is made of." A few others, pausing and looking away from Ann, "Where there's Marriage without Love, there will be Love without Marriage."

Ann was amazed. She had never known slaves could possibly read, and said so. Dick looked at her squarely and sought her promise, "Miss Ann, you will not be tellin' anyone will you?"

Ann considered the power of the secret, and replied, "Of course not, Little Dick. But you must have Devil ready to ride any time I wish."

Little Dick agreed, and Ann spent many afternoons on Devil, sometimes sharing with the slave long canters toward Mannheim, forays through Lancaster while Dick waited outside as she poked into various shops, and later hard driving rides on the paths that led to the Susquehanna. Ann particularly liked coursing through the wild fields that lined the road to Marietta. On their rides, as with her other activities, they stayed away from the "back parts" of the city more than a few blocks away from Penn Square, "the skirts" where the poor lived, Wolf's Hill, with its population of day laborers, and the colored people's Adam's Town.

Ann would sometimes relate to him that Grace was mean to her, or one of the housemaids required her to eat some German food of indefinable origin. Dick responded with a listening ear, good advice, and usually some aphorism of Poor Richard's. The sayings did not necessarily mesh in her mind, and she was never sure that she knew what "A cat in gloves catches no mice" meant, exactly. When she asked her mother to explain, all she received was a terse, "Ask your father. He long ago took his off."

It was not completely lost on Ann's mother that her daughter was spending many hours out back with the slave, but with the birth every two years or so of another child and approaching middle age, she did not have time between church work and the other children to be anything but relieved.

On December nights, wounding winds and stiff shards of straw pierced Dick as he slept. Snow stacked in steep shivering drifts around the stables. Ann would sometimes gaze from her room heated by the Franklin stove that Dick stoked each morning. She wondered, as she drifted off to sleep under her colorful Amish quilts with patterns of interlocking wedding rings, how he and the negresses, who slept at the other end four, five or six on one large horsehair mat, could survive this weather.

Dick tended the horses, daily thrusting steel blades under dreck and excrement, and strewing straw across stable floors that always remained befouled. His life was lightened only in his eyes by his companionship with Ann, who became his special charge. The slave did not know where or when he was born, nor who his parents were. His own three children were taken from him and their now dead mother and resold by the Colemans a decade earlier. "In dis hard life," he repeated to Gertrude who helped in the kitchen, "all I hab to look forward be Ann's visits and de afterlife."

As Ann grew from a trusting child, she even discussed with Dick the difficulties with her parents, how her mother always seemed to be off visiting someone else's house or at the church, and her father's nocturnal absences and months-long trips. The slave held his tongue tightly in his scattered teeth, only muttering, "Ann, de difference tween reality and expectation, dat be disappointment."

Dick nodded, but also did not respond, when Ann told him that she overheard Gertrude, preparing the family dinner, complaining about how she had to go about the house, scraping up wax and sanding down where toppled candles burned the floor, "Frau Coleman, she wanders all night, room to room, carrying that single white candle, like she is searching for something or someone who is never there."

When she provided exhaustive reports about spats with her girlfriends, Little Dick would respond, "Annie, you be a special girl. Special girls semmentimes hab to rise above others. You need to see it all from der eyes, too." Ann would think long and hard about this, about putting the hurt away somewhere else. If the dispute involved a boy or an unthinking remark, she was the one that patched the relationship together, even if it cost her what otherwise would have been her pride. Anytime a lie was involved, however, Ann found she was unable to forgive.

Dick was careful never to let his touch rest on Ann, even when she sought comfort. On her next birthday, Ann ran into the stables and wrapped her arms around Little Dick's broad black shoulders, intending to tell him of the special frock from Paris that Father brought back with him. Dick pushed her away, his eyes fixed on the figure entering the barn.

"Get away from here, Ann!" her father barked.

Ann whirled and saw her father's eyes burning at Little Dick. "Why, Daddy, what is wrong?"

Her father did not answer. He did not go to the horsewhip that was used to goad the stallions but pulled, from a ledge above the door, a longer, darker implement studded with the heads of ha'penny nails that Ann had never seen. His hand, now six decades old, flared high above his head while Little Dick fell to his knees and adopted a position too familiar to him. Ann scurried around the corner. She hid behind a rick of seasoned hardwood, tightly clasping her ears. Even then, she knew nothing would ever drown the sounds rising from the bloodied straw. Ann considered going out late that night with butter and oils purloined from the family larder but thought of her father's image and instead curled knees to chest and rocked herself to sleep.

After that, Dick was permitted to remain on the property but forbidden to speak to Ann except when absolutely necessary, and only if she spoke to him first. Robert instructed, "Ann, you are never to be alone with Little Dick again."

When tears broke at this news, she was sent to her room with her half-finished sampler, not to come downstairs until it was completed. The epigram she was stitching on the small cloth, which she later learned also came from the Almanack, was, "Three may keep a secret, if two of them are dead."

Ann knew that her destiny differed from her brothers' and that she would not have the opportunity to run the family business, or be a lawyer, or go to college in Philadelphia or New Jersey. Sedulous in her studies, she learned all that was appropriate, read well, and used basic arithmetic. Her fluency in French set her apart from many of her girlfriends whose language studies began and ended with Latin. Ann knew this was all to prepare her to be someone's wife, and she accepted that even while imagining the world that lay beyond Lancaster's skirts and the shores of the Republic.

Mrs. Coleman, by now a daily visitor to St. James and a volunteer on seemingly every committee the church constituted, was walking with Ann a few months after they moved to King Street, exploring Penn Square near the City Hall. She appraised her daughter, and thought to herself that Ann was showing none of that gawky awkwardness that bedevils girls of her age. Already, on their trips to Baltimore and Philadelphia, she was attracting a great deal of young male attention, and female envy. Mrs. Coleman again considered, with her flowing ebony locks and snow white skin, I need to watch out for this girl.

While her mother was lost in this reflection, Ann, still inspired at living in the city after a lifetime in distant Mannheim, with its lack of shops and few tradesmen, was admiring dresses and petticoats, reaching for a maternal arm as they hovered before each shop, begging to go in. Mrs. Coleman was about to protest that they did not need to go in *every* store when she was arrested by the sidelong glance of a young man coming from behind a booth at the Central Market, tucking in his shirt. In contrast with his rough companions clad in muslin and thick cotton, he was fastidiously dressed in full cut trousers, tapering to the ankle, his still crisp white shirt buttoned in silver along the length of the placket. Around his neck was a white stock finished in a neat bow.

The lad's head, as he squinted about through one eye, was cocked to the side. He appeared to be about 19, and stood apart from what the mother viewed as the soaplocks with whom he was gadding about, not only in dress but also in manner. Something about him gave her pause, but she kept her own counsel even as he stared too boldly at her young daughter. Ann eyed the confections in Frau Bauschulte's sweetshop, oblivious to the fact that the young man across the way bowed and, with great fanfare, described a 90-degree arc with his top hat.

It was not until a few months later that Mrs. Coleman saw the tilted head again, in the rear pews at St. James's. Once again, on King Street, this time riding in an imperial looking barouche that was most certainly hired. At first uncertain, she soon became convinced that it was the same coxcomb whose presence caused her such uneasiness on market day. She made a note to be aware of him. Her husband, unrevealed to her, was already monitoring the young man whose recent situation was familiar to him.

Ann spent the balance of her teen years preparing for her inevitable marriage. She knew she would soon have to exercise cheerful self-denial, and give up her childish pursuits to meet a husband's needs but how she loved to talk to her friends about boys, and books, and clothes. Would she have to give up trips to Philadelphia? Her mother never went anywhere, but her father spent long months abroad on business, and many nights out late. She did not believe what Grace Hubley said about "a woman's gaiety terminating with marriage," or that "home life was the grave of freedom and enjoyment" but her mother's empty look made her wonder. Still, she vowed, with the right husband by her side, she would in true meekness obey him in all respects.

As summer approached in 1814, Ann's mother let her know that there would be a grand soiree at the Coleman mansion for her eighteenth birthday. Her father had long promised her a voyage to the Continent, and she looked forward to that as well.

She was surprised by a visit a few days before the party from the Marquis and his handsome son, George Washington de Lafayette. "*Pouvez-vous rester pour mon anniversaire? Vous le ferez?*" she asked eagerly. The president's namesake turned to his father, who shook his head.

"*Ann, je suis désolé,*" the Marquis began, and continued in English, "George cannot stay for your birthday. We must go to Easton, as they are talking about a college there and seek my involvement, and George has other obligations in New York."

George saw Ann's disappointment, and took her aside. He began to tell her some of the places she absolutely had to see in Paris, and all across the continent. Ann coyly turned the conversation, "Now, how old was your father when he came here as a colonel in the Revolution, not even speaking any English? Nineteen I believe. And already married?" George, single and now entering his thirties, had to acknowledge the truth of those statements, but countered that those times were different, and decided to give the young girl some other advice about her pending trip across the Atlantic.

"I don't mean to set any fear in you, Ann, but I want you to be well-armed as you travel. This is not like you are used to, good horses on hard land. Especially if you go during summer season with its storms springing up from nowhere."

George related how scurvy, dysentery, typhoid and smallpox might overtake those in the lower reaches of a ship, and that impure water and decaying food were sometimes all that stood against starvation. Ann knew of the waves of diseases that rolled through Lancaster. She lost her brother Stephen as soon as he was born and baby sister Harriet to smallpox at age seven. Disease was a constant companion, and even the wealthy were constrained to live in the midst of their own waste, oblivious to any connection between germs and disease. Water was polluted by excrement of cows, swine, chickens, and humans. Food spoiled. Salt simply shrouded its decay.

George continued, "This time, a favorable wind, and there were no storms until we drifted toward the Carolinas about six weeks from port. One night, a few weeks ago, although it seems like yesterday, I woke up to the screams of those quartered below. They were muffled, but I could not sleep for their wailing. Winds were howling about, and great waves washed over the ship's beams."

Ann locked on his eyes, which now seemed calm enough.

"The storm soon passed, but it was only then that I came to understand that this was one place where all could share the same ending, regardless of class or wealth or privilege. A sinking ship would take us all."

George told Ann of discussions among his fellow travelers of tossing the people locked down in steerage overboard, like so much jetsam, if supplies ran low. First, the sick and old and disabled would be sacrificed, and then pregnant women. Ann was surprised at this talk of death and sacrifice and a bit of fear crept into her face.

He caught her look, "Ann, I am sure your voyage will go well. Almost everyone crosses without incident."

Ann was not thinking as much of the dangers of the trip as she was thinking about how people were treated differently based on whether they had money or position or not, and her thoughts were not only to Gertrude and the other German maids and cooks working off their passage to America but to what she heard from Little Dick about his childhood passage to America, as Africans lay in a great heap, unable to relieve themselves except upon one another, great iron collars around their necks, fighting over bowls of rancid slop while more than half of them died, their bodies often left for days before being tossed overboard. How horrible for them, she thought, and how grateful I am to Father that I am not among those people.

Her party looming, days were spent by the *Zimmerleuten* cooking apple dumplings; making bimbo punch of brandy and sugar; splashing together wine, sugar, and fruit for "drinking cobbler;" crafting peanut brittle and taffy; and molding various pies and cheesecakes. The Colemans' new wooden brass-plated ice box, patented a few years earlier, held last winter's chunks carved out of the backyard pond and cellared deeply beneath the house in an ever-dwindling supply. Hand-cranked ice cream would be kept firm enough within its confines, set to be served with tea cakes. Champagne, direct from France for the occasion, was long since ordered and lardered next to the bottles of

Monongahela whiskey. Sour crout, though no favorite of Ann's, was chopped and curdled by the German help.

All of her parents' friends, and hers, were invited. For the most part, that required no extension of the guest list other than the inclusion of the teenagers from the same families, the Ellicots, the Sehners, the Whartons, the Mifflins, Judge Jasper Yeats, the newly eligible Captain Stephen Chambers, Mr. and Mrs. Shippen, and the recently widowed Mrs. Hand whose last name was little Sarah Coleman's middle. The Shippens' daughter, Peggy Arnold, was in England with her husband Benedict, as she had been since early in the Revolution when he fled to escape the hangman's noose. Even old Gotthilf Muhlenberg, pastor of the Lutheran church, was present, although he was careful to take his flask out of the light before he raised it to his lips, certain never to be with drink in hand as he gazed at the young men parading on the dance floor.

Exceptions were made to the guest list with the additions Robert suggested, as he sought to use the opportunity to forge firmer connections with some of the younger generation of businessmen, clerics and lawyers who were increasingly attracted to do business in Lancaster in the wake of the War of 1812. Invited were a doctor, a young editor of the weekly *Intelligencer* and a recently admitted lawyer whom he had not yet formally met. Mr. Shippen advised him that this attorney was someone to watch, someone who was lightly able to turn a phrase and ingratiate himself by comportment barely south of pure unction. Some thought he would turn out to be a leading citizen of Lancaster despite his rural background. Robert knew the type, young men who were more comfortable with words than hard work, and whose business skills depended more on sharp practices than honor. He did not reveal that their paths had already crossed.

The party commenced as night fell. Parents looked at the couples tripping across the floor to a mélange of jigs and reels and remarked how "it was just yesterday" that they were "mere children."

Fiddling strings filled the air, starting with the sprightly, "Come O'er the Stream Charlie" and sliding into one reel after the other, the "Maid Behind the Bar" and then the venerable "Banks of Spey." The players finished "The Young Widow," a rare American tune. The jig, "Bolt the Door" started, but the band jolted to a stop the moment its lone horn player saw the young woman on the stair landing above.

Every bustling sound, every whispered word ceased. It was if clouds parted as Ann shimmered down the stairs lined by the same carved mahogany from which she had earlier tumbled, embraced by pale blue silks of bombazine and sarsanet that flowed beyond the body caged in a corset of canvas and whalebone. Her delicate frame seemed scarcely able to support the ocean of gossamer submerging it, from the daringly low neckline to the fully gored skirt. A lightly embroidered indigo pelerine danced on her shoulders and fell over the fair white skin below her graceful throat. Coiled black rivulets flowed as if carving fresh channels tumbling down a proud new mountain, framing her strong little nose, full lips and dark eyes. Soft little calfskin shoes danced from under the weightier trim of the hemline. A deep red ruby with enameled accents highlighted the first finger of her left hand. Ann's eyes were cast coyly down, but she well knew everyone was watching.

She moved through the parted sea straight to Lüder Bauschulte, the servant's boy who worked his way up to foreman at her father's Cornwall works before he headed off to the war against the British two years earlier. Ann had been forbidden to consider him as a suitor on account of his class and race. He was here for only a short while, to bury his father before he returned to General Jackson's command.

Ann reserved the first spot on her silver dance card for him and also the last. Lüder guided her with an unpracticed hand, but Ann's grace rescued his awkward steps. Ann danced "as they did in France, not like the English lofty manner" with boys she knew growing up and others newly moved to town, all under her parents' purview.

The dancing moved from the jigs and reels to swings and allemandes and quadrilles, with an homage to the century past by virtue of a minuet. At mid-evening, all moved through a decorous Sir Roger de Coverley. Ann liked the reels far better. Her father plucked her for "Merrily Kiss the Quaker's Wife," precisely promenading his daughter. He followed up with a turn with Grace Hubley while "Nine Points of Roguery" played. Ann overheard some boys joking about the origin of the "Baker's Widow" involving, as it did, the exchange of partners, with intimations of early morning departures and assignations. She blushed. Despite game efforts by her dance partners, their prating conversation about how nice the room looked and how much food there was, bored her.

In the corner, behind a spreading ice sculpture of Cupid carved for the occasion, Robert spied the town's recent addition, now earnestly engaged with Jasper Slaymaker, or was it Amos Ellmaker, now running for Congress? This next generation was beginning to look all alike.

The newcomer stood apart from the other young men. Clad in a tailcoat with a wide rolled collar, with full sleeves and a short tail, covering two different waistcoats in contrasting colors with a second pair of gloves evident in his breast pocket, the visitor was certainly *au courant*. Mr. Coleman made his way over and presented himself. The ironmaster sized him up anew but with the secreted memory of the young man's past. This young chap might make his way here, Robert thought, but something wet and damp crept up one's spine as you spoke to him. A little too eager to please, a little too much in possession of personal information.

Mrs. Coleman glided over to see how her husband was faring. She was introduced to the new lawyer in town, an eligible bachelor. His head tilted to the side and cocked in apparent deference toward her. Ann's mother met those eyes, one surprisingly blue, and the other limply hazel. This was the young man she saw in the pews of her church, in front of her house and, before that, at market bandying with those rowdy fellows. Jimmy Buchanan's soft hand was cold as it clasped hers, and his kiss slopped over her as he dipped down to meet her fingers. Mrs. Coleman's head snapped back. Robert gave his wife a hasty look as the strings of the "Scolding Wives of Abertarf" wandered through the room, but was soon in serious discussion with Edward Shippen about the likely Federalist nominee in the race to succeed President Madison in the next election. Both agreed that it should be New York's Rufus King, but each feared that the early Federalist opposition to the current war with Britain "would doom their party."

Mrs. Coleman retreated. The dance floor began to reel with "Pigeon on a Gate" and the young man sidled toward her next to youngest surviving daughter. Mother hurried across the dance floor to intervene, but Eva Hubley intercepted her and began to tell her how wonderful Ann looked, to boast the same about Grace, and to thank her for the invitation. Mrs. Coleman could only watch helplessly while her daughter's sparkling eyes reflected a seemingly earnest gaze.

The young man Ann was already calling Jamie confidently spun what was to her the first of his many tales. When, much later, Mrs. Coleman next saw Ann again, all others had already danced the evening's last dance.

Chapter Two
JAMIE

"Biting blazes, Jimmy! You throw like a girl!" bawled Joseph Ryan. The strong black-capped Irish lad stood fixed at the second post. The thin blond boy with the curling hair scurried to pick up the ball that had rolled to a stop, standing white against the outfield grass short of the runner's path. Jimmy didn't trust himself to try to reach Joseph even with a second throw. He held the ball high above his head and scampered to the infield. Joseph snatched it from Jimmy and turned away while the throng of German teammates swarmed around the striker, Hab Geheim, now scoring the winning rounder. Jimmy shot a glance at the feeder, hung his head and fought back the tears. He did not like these rough games. He would much rather play hide and seek or blind man's buff with his little sisters, watch the other boys play, or simply escape into the woods alone.

Jimmy was born on the very western edge of civilization. Life was hard. The outpost of Stony Batter, buried in the Cove Gap a short ways down the trail to the settlement recently named Pittsburgh, was his father's alone, and the senior James Buchanan was increasingly prosperous. Quite well, indeed, the 30-year-old father thought, for someone who emigrated from County Donegal less than a decade earlier. The elder Buchanan's own father abandoned him after his mother died. James Senior was raised, with his bevy of sisters, by maternal grandparents. At six feet two and 15 stone, and with a well-developed sharpness in business, Jimmy's father took care of the traders, transients, and assorted ruffians who traveled through the Appalachian gap, advantageously swapping fur for food, food for metal implements, and tools for salt. When not at the trading post, he farmed the small plot in the back for tomatoes, corn and squash.

James met Elizabeth Speer on the road from Philadelphia to Franklin County as the Revolutionary War ended. The young wife deferred in all respects to the older man. She was as small as he was large, and was soon made to know her place. James relied on her to keep house, bear children, and help as demanded in field and post.

Jamie, as his mother called him, was born in their one-room log cabin in 1791, the year his older sister Mary died, and therefore became the oldest of what grew to eleven children, counting the living and the dead. There were tasks to be done, and chores to handle. Jimmy followed his father about at first, a short handled hoe dragging behind him as he sought to match the steps striding in front.

By four, little Jimmy already revealed a propensity to hide when there was work to be done, to wander off in search of his mother or toddle off into the woods that engulfed their cabin. One day, Jimmy bent over in the middle of a patch of weeds he was supposed to pull, all the while surreptitiously moving out of the circle like a shrub retreating from the Birnam wood. Jimmy turned to look up at the unscaleable castle of his father just as James shoved him, once but hard, with the heel of his large black boot. Elizabeth raced up from the trickle of a creek where she was pounding the family's clothes and saw her son writhing in the scrabbled rocks and Duffield silt, surrounded by small carefully catalogued hillocks of quackgrass, shepherd's purse and velvetleaf, his blond hair mingled with red and dirt. He watched as his mother's head bowed and half-whispered in her lilting Appalachian, "James, the boy, he does try. Perhaps if ye would shew him some affection. He reaches out his little arms for ye, and ye pull away. He will suredly learn not to love nor trust ye." James said nothing and mother turned back to her tasks.

The father believed his efforts were designed to make a man of young Jimmy, someone who would be God-fearing, but well versed in the craft of business. Whether he grew to be a storekeeper, a tradesman or a farmer, it was all difficult. His soft little son's early proclivity for avoiding anything that required serious effort, and the odd, unmanly tilting of his head and the queer squinting mismatch of his eyes, one blue and the other hazel, troubled the father. He repeatedly asked his wife, "What kind of a son have you given me, a cussed parrot?" Elizabeth learned not to respond.

The necessity for hard physical work continued when the family moved five miles east nearer Mercersburg, to the Dunwoodie Farm in West Conococheague Settlement. Their new home was surrounded by 300 acres of orchard and farmland. Plenty of room to play, to melt beyond the apples into the foothills and crannies. Jimmy's mother was already busy with the succession of sisters born to the Buchanan family, and could not work the farm, cook and clean and keep a constant eye on them all. Jane, Maria, Sarah, and soon Elizabeth and Harriet, although his mother's namesake died before her first birthday. Jimmy took full advantage of the preoccupation caused by his mother's burgeoning duties. He did not mind trading a cudgeling from his father for the opportunity to be alone, away from the unrelenting demands of raking and hoeing and digging, feeding and milking, and cleaning up after the horse. He loathed the dirt. He loathed his sisters' bawling. Several hours with only his own thoughts was a good trade, Jimmy calculated, for a few bruises.

Jimmy was pleased to leave farm life altogether a little more than a year later when his father yet again moved the family, this time to the town of Mercersburg, full of Scots-Irish and the beginnings of German infiltration. Almost all 300 townspeople congregated at the same Presbyterian church, the only house of worship in town. The quiet village was dominated by the shadow of the punctuation point of the Appalachian range, the same majestic Tuscarora Mountain that towered over the previous Buchanan farmsteads, and was surrounded by verdant farmland swept by favorable winds, broad limestone valleys, and rushing mountain springs.

Jimmy fared better in Mercersburg. At his father's proud new store in the downstairs of their Main Street home, the nine year old sidled up to the middle-aged woman examining the hats on the far side of the store, "Why, Mrs. Crawford, it is so fine to see you on this excellent day. Your dress is especially flattering to you, and you could perhaps use this bonnet in our new color on Sundays? It came all the way from Philadelphia this morning, and it seems to me that it must have been made for you."

As he did so, he ran his little fingers over the bolts of satin set at the back of the store. He loved the colors, and especially the sweet softness, of the material.

Farmers and tradesmen, and especially their wives, increasingly shopped at the Buchanan store, many traveling from Shimpstown or Webster's Mill or even Fort Loudon, a full seven miles distant and the site of the first armed colonial uprising against the British.

"I so love to see the people parade in, Mother. This feels like home."

Elizabeth was delighted to hear those words, and listened with some satisfaction when her husband noted, "He is certainly right skilled with the women, particularly the older ones. He suggests to them what to be buying, and mostly they do. He is now even telling the farmers and the cooper and the smith what they should order. It seems my son Jim has found his place." James Senior also appreciated Jimmy's newly learned neat handwriting and careful rows of figures he made. The boy might not amount to much on the farm, thought James, but he is doing right well now.

Jimmy watched his father closely, noting the times he might short weigh some produce with a heavy thumb on the scale, or claim to one of the store's suppliers on the next round that he had delivered one item too few the week before, or assert to a customer that an item was bombazine or sarsanet when it was only some inferior silk sent over from Carlisle.

Jimmy challenged, "You know, father, that Catherine Schuyler did not get her full three yards of cotton. I saw you stretch it hard beyond its usable length."

Father looked at son and evaluated for a moment, "Jim, you should know by now how hard I work to make a living for the family. Everyone expects that there will be a little sliding. I have to tell you, I actually have shortened that measuring stick by a bit, and I also counterweight the scales with a few more pieces of shot."

Jimmy's face lifted toward his father's. It must be that everyone does this, or else why would his father be held so high in town? How could this be right?

"What you must do, howso," James continued, "is always make sure the pennies is right. People get to thinking you are treating them righteous because you are careful with making change. People respect you if you get the pennies right even if the pounds are staying inside your door."

Well, this must be. Jimmy soon developed his own little trick. Every so often, he shortchanged a customer by a nickel or a few pennies, then chased after them as they made their way down Main Street. "Mrs. McDonough, I am so sorry. I have discovered a mistake in your favor. I owe you seven cents. Here, please take it."

Jimmy played checkers with the men and listened closely to their discussions of politics. By the time the clever boy reached 10, he sometimes entered in these talks on his father's Federalist side. He shared, in his childlike way, the townspeople's hopes for the country that was only a few years older than he was. Steven Donahue, the town's cooper, remarked, "James, that laddie of yours has a gey sharp head for politics. He kens the game, how she is played. I would keep me eye on him."

Father, a rare bit of pride welling, never told son of this evaluation but congratulated himself for the fine job he was doing raising the boy. James's own world view was widening as he saw the ways to power and control in the emerging democracy. "We might be voting for these men," he told Donahue, "but once in they act like bloody kings, intruding into our livelihood and seeking one tax after another."

Donahue started, "I agree, James. We have to seek to limit their power..." when the shopkeeper responded, "Sam Hill no, Donahue. We have to figure out how to get part of it!"

Reflecting on his son's manner with the townspeople, his sharpening practices, and the fine reports from the school, James began to think that the boy might possibly even become one of those lawyers who were beginning to dominate the offices of government. Jimmy, for his part, was content to contemplate himself as a man of success and leisure, all grown up, in a big house surrounded by beautiful countryside, even as he began to imagine living in one of those cities of which he had heard, more than a thousand people all in one place.

Although unschooled herself, Elizabeth Speer as a young girl was given several books of poetry, an unlikely benefaction for a farm girl, even one from a prosperous family, in the harsh colonial wilderness. She devoured them.

Elizabeth spent hour after hour reading to her son from the works of John Milton, Alexander Pope, and William Cowper, and told him stories of men named Swift and Gay. "I so love these tales of far off lands of big ideas and deep romance. I want ye to treasure them as well."

"I will, Mother, I will."

Jimmy's earliest memories included his mother's soft Appalachian tones lulling him to sleep as he rested his head close to her bosom. Jimmy would turn to Elizabeth as she read, "Mother, you look so beautiful, even almost holy, when you read to me." Mother would smile back at her boy and give him her ring finger, "Jamie, I am so grateful for a kindred soul. Ye are just a little cherub, and will be a Godly man, I am 'sured."

Jimmy remained mystified and a bit scared by most of Milton, and studiously avoided the poet the rest of his life. If his father had understood the apparent misspellings and Bacchanalian appeal of such poems as *L'Allegro*, doubtless he would have forbidden their reading:

> *Hence loathed Melancholy*
> *Of Cerberus, and blackest midnight born,*
> *In Stygian Cave forlorn*
> *'Mongst horrid shapes, and shreiks, and sights unholy,*

> *Find out som uncouth cell,*
> *Wher brooding darknes spreads his jealous wings,*
> *And the night-Raven sings;*
> *There under Ebon shades, and low-brow'd Rocks,*
> *As ragged as thy Locks,*
> *In dark Cimmerian desert ever dwell.*

"Jamie, it is not only these poems, but hymns that ye be needing to learn. Hymns be like God's poetry."

She told her son about the church songs William Cowper wrote, including *God moves in a mysterious way*. Elizabeth gathered her children about her and raised her arms toward heaven, spreading them like an eagle over her aerie, and sang *Amazing Grace*. "That not be the eldest of all the hymns, children, but it is become my favorite."

"How old is it, Mommy?" asked her eight-year-old.

"Twenty years ago this year, back in 1779, and I but a young girl when I heerd it down near Scott's Old Fields in Bel Air, and issued by that same Mr. Cowper for his friend John Newton."

Elizabeth was not aware of the poet's periodic fits of madness, nor the greater secret Cowper carried within him, the "stricken deer" of his poem *The Task*.

Jimmy knew that his mother reserved this time together for evenings. "So Daddy can not hear us?"

"That be right," his mother said as she placed her finger into Jimmy's mouth. He sucked it rhythmically, squeezing his lips around the digit and moving his tongue over his mother's knuckles. "Your father has no ear for such things." More softly, "He does love the tavern."

The muffled intimacy of mother and young son continued as Jimmy grew. Elizabeth, her pronunciation giving way to the poet's Georgian English, read the heroic couplets of the deformed little Pope's satirical *Rape of the Lock* to her eleven year old detailing the clandestine purloining of a young lady's tress:

> *Say what strange motive, Goddess! could compel*
> *A well-bred lord t' assault a gentle belle?*
>
> *O say what stranger cause, yet unexplor'd,*
> *Could make a gentle belle reject a lord?*
>
> *In tasks so bold, can little men engage,*
> *And in soft bosoms dwells such mighty rage?*

Jimmy could not imagine why any proud nobleman could harm a gentle belle. "Mother," he asked as she gently withdrew her finger, "what's a 'stranger cause'? Why would a young woman reject someone who was a lord? What's a soft bosom?"

"It's as eef something bad has happened, but it really had not," Elizabeth tried to explain. "It were just a leetle thing that did come between a young man and a girl for whom he had affection. It were a misunderstanding over something wee, but then eet became a problem and there ne'er was the marriage that should have been."

Jimmy still didn't understand, and knew his questions had not been answered. Perhaps he would ask his teacher.

Jimmy was pondering how to formulate his questions as he sat in Latin class at Old Stone Academy, his eyes wandering to the beloved isolation of his woods as the teacher droned on about the proper use of the ablative absolute.

A lecture on Pennsylvania history followed. "Most of your parents remember when George Washington slept at the Russell Tavern here in town on his way to crush the Whiskey Rebellion," John Cass, newly out of the Princeton Theological Seminary in the first graduating class after its split with the College of New Jersey. He arrived that fall and was the town's only teacher, although he preferred to look at himself as the headmaster of the single-roomed academy.

He related how Westerners near old Fort Pitt protested the federal excise taxes levied on distilled spirits by the politicians in Philadelphia, the nation's capital, to pay for the Revolutionary War. These taxes did not hurt the large Eastern producers, but for single-still operations in most frontier farmsteads the tax was almost confiscatory, up to nine cents on a flask they could only sell for less than a quarter dollar.

His classmates were already beginning to fidget, idly curious about what "confiscatory" meant, but Jimmy's interest was piqued as Cass continued, explaining how these western protesters, wearing faces blackened with coal, or dressed as Indians, stripped the tax collectors, burned their clothes, shaved their heads and tarred and feathered them, leaving their naked black and white bodies in the woods.

The teacher looked at Jimmy and thought, at least young Buchanan is paying attention. He had counted on the fact that he was talking about whiskey to sustain a little more interest. "The angry farmers did not stop there. Sporadic gun battles erupted, and the dissenters burned at least one tax collector's house to the ground. Mail was intercepted and torn open. Worse, there were no federal judges in western Pennsylvania and the distillers' claims could only be litigated in far-off Philadelphia , several days' ride away."

Hab Geheim was reaching for the last inkless tresses of Colleen O'Brien's blond hair and Joseph Ryan appeared to be counting the number of leaves on the oak right outside the classroom window. Mr. Cass rushed to get to the substance of the saga.

"This internal tax collection was the first test of the strength of the government and its new Constitution. President Washington had to enforce the law passed by the very first Congress, in 1791."

Jimmy raised his hand. "Yes, Jimmy?"

"That was the year I was born!"

The headmaster was startled at this superfluous information, but it did seem to galvanize the class's attention. Hab shouted, "Me, too" and Joseph responded, "I'm older." Several others commence a debate whose only resolution appeared to be determining their exact birth order. Colleen reached around to the back of her neck and was alternately looking with dismay at her now blue tresses and glaring at Joseph.

"All of you, quiet!" Cass barked. Looking at Jimmy, "I would not have expected you to be the one to incite a riot." Jimmy's head bowed over his small wooden desk smeared with the initials of Mercersburg's youth and scattered deposits of his mother's raspberry jam.

The class settled down and the teacher cleared his throat and continued. "Governor Mifflin improvidently allowed this breaking of the law, or at least that was the view in the federal offices in Philadelphia. A farmer named Daniel Shay revolted against taxes a few years earlier, and many feared that the New England states would leave the Union."

Cass went on for what seemed like hours to the children who just wanted to roll into the last strands of autumn sunshine. He related how the emerging anti-Federalists, soon to become the Democratic Party, watched to see how the federal government, spurred by Secretary of the Treasury Alexander Hamilton, would react to this conduct on the nation's frontier. President Washington was obliged to suppress the defiant Westerners, for the good of the party and the country. A large military force of nearly 13,000 troops from Pennsylvania and the neighboring states of Virginia, Maryland, and New Jersey was summoned to quell the rebellion, including a Lancaster contingent captained by Robert Coleman.

Did the class know who he was? No hands went up. The teacher informed them that he owned "a dozen factories" and was "the richest man in America."

No child seemed interested and he hurried to a close. Virginia Governor Lighthorse Harry Lee. Twenty farmers seized and chained. President Jefferson repealed the tax.

Cass drew a worn paper from his vest pocket. "Class, the fact that the President could assemble citizens and armies from several states to enforce federal law against the citizens of a wayward state established a clear precedent, the constitutional use of federal power to preserve the union. It is in the Constitution, a document I hope all of you will re-read."

Jimmy had already joined his classmates in their collective reverie and missed the thrust of the lesson. The teacher read the words of General Washington:

I am mortified beyond expression when I view the clouds that have spread over the brightest morn that ever dawned in any country... What a triumph for the advocates of despotism, to find that we are incapable of governing ourselves and that systems founded on the basis of equal liberty are merely ideal and fallacious.

"That's it," announced as the Presbyterian bell rang three times. Finally! Lessons were over. The rest of the boys joined together and walked down Main Street, kicking rocks at each other on their way to playing rounders. Jimmy, as usual, did not go with them.

He heard the men yesterday in his father's store, "There's goin' to be a fowl pulling on Fort Loudon Road, James. Round dusk. Tomorrow." He knew the goose would be hung with hard leather straps to the large oak tree around the bend. Jimmy assembled a soft bed of leaves and needles from nearby pines and spread himself under the tree as evening approached. He saw Johann Stenger tie the goose's legs and watched as it squawked and struggled, beating its head hard at the wet leather even as the slowly drying bonds stretched tighter, cutting into its belly. Villager after villager stormed by on horseback. Jimmy felt revulsion and deep appeal as the successful townsman grabbed the gander's neck, twisting off its head as blood spurted into the swallowing Pennsylvania soil.

"Jimmy, dig that pit, only this time do it right!" his father commanded a few days later. Once again, at night, his father's friends were gathering for a ratting in the storekeeper's basement. Jimmy's job was to shovel 18 inches deep and six feet wide and make sure the sides were even. Herr Geheim, Hab's father, let loose a trap holding a dozen rodents into the pit. The elder Buchanan unleashed the weasel. Everyone placed bets on how long it would take the animal to rip the flesh and strip the intestines. Jimmy looked through his darker eye at the blazing frenzied faces of his father and the townsmen transfixed on the poor brown-coated stoat and the yet more unfortunate rodents. He watched as the red remnants of life flooded the excavation. Father joined in the loud cries and backslapping while whiskey coated his throat.

Surrounded by the acrid smell of tearing flesh, Jimmy could not suppress the rush of excitement and he hated himself for it. In the dank cellar as the rat blood spattered his pants' legs, that same goose-killing feeling wormed through him until he almost shuddered. He wondered at his father. Confused, and then repulsed, he marveled that this man could go to church on Sunday, sit in the pew, worship an almighty God, and then scuttle down with these screeching Irish and Germans. Jimmy hated, too, his father's belching reminder to gather the mangled carcasses from the feculence, rat flesh still sticking to the bones, and cover the already rotting remains with dreck from the cellar floor. The boy would sometimes also have to bury his last few meals after they spewed from his gut, slithered through his teeth, and exploded past his lips.

Despite his efforts at the store, at home, and at the First Presbyterian Church, where he was adept at memorization of Bible verses, Jimmy knew he continued to disappoint his father. Although he positively radiated piety, with his neat appearance and flowing yellow locks, the in-store clothes, red roundabout jacket, starched white shirt, muslin pants held up by gallowses, and buckled high-lows, that public finery hid what was now happening at home. Mother's protection only seemed to fuel Father's attacks. The old man whipped and cudgeled Jimmy for the smallest infraction. Once, the boy tried to fight back. Still a foot taller than his son, Father simply extended the heel of his large hand and cupped Jimmy's twisted chin, cackling as the boy's wildly whipping arms fell a half foot short of their mark.

Father's evenings at the tavern grew more frequent and longer, and he often returned drenched with drink. A voice shattered the dark.

"Elizabeth, woman, where's my stew!"

Jimmy and his sisters watched as Mother lit a candle and scurried to the wood-fired stove, carrying a bundle of logs she split that day in one arm and the candle in the other. Mother stoked the fire, but either the logs did not catch as they should, or perhaps there were too many, or too few. It did not really matter. Even if the dinner were perfectly warm, it would have too much salt or too little. Perhaps the shirt Mother ironed that morning with a hot stone against the pine dining table was now wrinkled.

His sisters would wake and Jimmy would rush to their room and try to quiet them, and at least make certain they did not go downstairs. For himself, he could not keep from descending halfway down, just out of eyeshot. Father raised his closed hands and began, slowly at first and then faster, and faster yet, to beat Mother. Elizabeth had learned not to whimper. Words that the girls never heard elsewhere floated on angry wings and spilled down all around them, quivering like venomous asps on the oaken floor.

Jimmy watched as Father towered above Mother, slobbering and shrieking. She hunched, murmuring her prayers in a tiny quaking softly blowing voice as the fists began to fall. Jimmy saw how she rolled her shoulders together with hands on the opposite blades, as if to protect not only her little body but her gentle soul. Son felt his own hands curling into balls, his fingers so tight that the nails dug into the skin of his palms and formed small pools of blood. Desperately, desperately he wanted to come to Mother's aid, but could not risk the pounding.

The crashing fists of Father on Mother only foreshadowed what happened, brutal and quick, after each fight. Father would forget about dinner, or rip off the offending wrinkled shirt, or kick over the log pile with the same black boots that once sent Jimmy sprawling. Again, it did not matter. While Jimmy scurried out of view of the advancing forms, Father dragged Mother up the stairs, bump after bump after bump, to their room across the hall. Jimmy again could not stay away. He peered through the crack between jamb and frame or nudged the door open just a bit, and saw what he saw. Father pressed Mother against the long knotted wood wall of the room, shoving her face away from him with his scabrous hands. To Jimmy, they seemed like an ape's, misshapen and thickly forested with sweating matted hair, as Father dismembered Mother's dress. With one paw, he raised the skirt while drunkenly unbuttoning the top of his trousers with the other.

Mother's worn tiny fingers drew tightly over her shuddering lips. Her little cries echoed across the room and traveled deeply into her son. Jimmy's bloody palms went to his ears. He tried to stanch the moans but he could not turn his eyes as Father banged banged banged hard and fast against Mother, her head scraped raw by the pine knots of the bedroom wall while Father pushed her face against it.

Should I, can I rescue her? I could pull him off. I don't care if he hits me. I don't care. I can't care. Mother and I could run away. There are so many places to go? What about baby Harriet, and Sarah, and Maria? I can't leave them here. How would we travel? Who would provide for us?

In the end, every time, he could only watch.

At last, with his mother whimpering on the marital bed and his father spent and snoring, Jimmy crept back to his room, slid under the comforter, and lay on his stomach, silently tattooing the pillow with both fists until he himself faded to sleep.

The next day in a downstairs corner, Jimmy as the father, Jane his wife, and Sarah and Harriet their babies, the children pretended to cook and sew. Sometimes, overheard grunts and murmured forgiveness reached them, but they all learned to distrust the painful dance of false apology and constrained Biblical response. They never spoke to one another about what they had seen. For Jimmy, a lifetime of bilious reaction to trouble, controversy or violence was confirmed. The fevered light-headedness stole across him each time he witnessed his mother's pain. He had to flee and he had to vomit. It became his response to any form of anger, violence or confrontation. If he could not easily resolve a dispute, he sought to avoid controversy and its physical pain at almost any cost.

While Jimmy learned his lessons, James Senior became one of Mercersburg's leading citizens, serving for many years as Justice of the Peace. Jimmy kept his knowledge of his father's character in bedroom and basement hidden within himself. The young teenager, nearing six feet but still hairless except for his blond locks, wandered into the surrounding trees, stumbling across dark green moss-ridden logs and worn stone outcroppings, shouting when he was certain no one could hear, "I hate him. I hate that old man. I tell you all, plants and birds and all living things, I hate him!"

Jimmy's secret defiance was only made worse by reflection on the difference between the public man and the private one. His father's hard practices made him, by the standards of this small town in the skirts, wealthy. The elder Buchanan refused to extend credit at the store, and even declined to loan to his friends unless the collateral dwarfed the consideration advanced. Always suspicious of others, Father later wrote his twenty year old son, *The more you know of mankind, the more you will distrust them.*

Jimmy was now almost 16, and his mother was determined to help him make something of himself away from his father and their little world. There was nothing left to learn at the local academy.

"Dr. King, please help my boy," Elizabeth begged after a spring's Sunday service as she visited with her pastor. "Jamie is right bright and a good learner. The other boys they don't give him his due. He could be a minister like you. He has in his heart the very soul of goodness."

"Elizabeth, I will see what I can accomplish."

John King, the Presbyterian pastor, knew that the father would not easily agree to college. He stopped by the Buchanan house on an afternoon a few days after his conversation with Elizabeth.

"James, you know there is no room for Jimmy at the store now that he's approaching manhood. He will want to start a family in a few years. He is an able student. I have some influence at the college over in Carlisle and he could benefit from guidance and learning there."

The elder Buchanan shifted in his leather chair and motioned the pastor to sit down across from him.

"Would you be wanting some whiskey, Rev'rand? I have some fine rye, brought up from Kentucky."

"No thank you, but you go right ahead."

"I have done right well without no education. I arrived in this country with nothing, didn't have any parents growin' up and was just surrounded by sisters. I grew as the country did."

"No one is arguing with you on that. This is now a new nation. You came to a little colony. There won't always be Washingtons and Jeffersons. The quality of our leaders will fall unless they are raised right. There will be lots of room for educated men, and I am sure you would want that for your eldest."

The minister sensed little softening in the father, and brought his best argument, appealing to the father's interests while speaking on Elizabeth's behalf, "Without the education, Jimmy will likely be a burden to you. I have seen how he flees from hard work, but then how he tries to compromise anything. That's his great skill. He seeks the middle between two points and gets the people there. That's what it's going to take in the future. There's waves after waves of immigrants still coming. I worry about his tactics sometimes, and we need to have him guided right. You and Elizabeth have done a good job, but he is moving beyond you."

James's eyes clouded and he started his second glass, warming it between his palms before lifting it to his lips. King hurried on, "You are siring a large brood of children, and it will be necessary for someone to make some money and help in raising the younger children, including that boy who has newly been born."

The father reflected as King paused. There was not only the new survivor, "after that infernal procession of sisters," but there was yet another child in his wife's belly. There would be children to these children and not all could be expected to work out well. Surely, he thought, I do not want any of them coming back to me after they have gone. Jimmy was badly suited for farm life, and there was room for only one store in town. Someone will have to take care of my offspring. James quickly calculated the burden of the $18.00 annual tuition, and figured it was not much worse than the food the boy ate. He looked into the Reverend's troubled eyes and seemed to concede, "All right, but I look to you to make sure he ends up as something after all this."

• • •

Away from his father's attacks and his mother's comfort, Jimmy entered Dickinson College in late September 1807. Unlike the more prominent self-proclaimed University to the east in Philadelphia or the well-established schools in New England, Dickinson was a backwater institution composed almost exclusively of local lads. Anyone exposed to a smattering of the classics was well ahead of his classmates. Jimmy was placed in the junior year. There was no sophomore class whatsoever and the gaggle of students wandering about were young boys in the institution's Grammar School. The school needed every dollar of tuition it could obtain. As a further goad to fund-raising, it had almost as many trustees, 29, as students, 42. Jimmy felt some comfort that he was now away from the rough attacks of the boys in his town. He vowed that, among students at this little college with no knowledge of his raising, he would bury the past and make of himself a new creature.

Dickinson consisted of one dilapidated building, the other having burned to the ground four years earlier when a winter wind reached into its basement and toppled an orphan candle. The entire faculty consisted of three professors. Courses were limited to history, geography, so-called philosophy, some scattered languages, and elementary mathematics. None of the literature so loved by his mother was taught, nor would the students likely have been able to comprehend its nuances. The acting principal, Dr. Robert Davidson, required that all students purchase his self-authored geography text, rendered in weak iambic pentameter, and memorize it. Jimmy had not realized that the ritual of committing Bible verses to memory would now find its exposition in such lines from *Geography Epitomiz'd* as:

> *In the ancient and glorious Peru,*
> *Lived both llamas and Incas too.*

Students boarded in and around Carlisle, a town laid out and developed, as was Lancaster 50 miles to the east, by James Hamilton at the instance of William Penn. It was dismissed by a Dickinson stalwart as a "trifling place," and the townspeople resented the college boys. By the time Jimmy set foot in the county seat, it teemed with "high life, of parade, of the table & ball chamber," according to Jeremiah Atwater, the educator who arrived to succeed Davidson as principal of the school in 1809 as Jimmy departed. Educated at Yale and the first President of Vermont's Middlebury College, Atwater was a man of deep religious conviction. His first view of wobbly little Dickinson

College and the surrounding community led him to complain that "drunkenness, swearing, lewdness & dueling" were the "court of the day." He wrote trustee Benjamin Rush, son of the eponymous signer of the Declaration of Independence, *I hope that as God has visited the other states, he will yet visit Pennsylvania.*

Jimmy nearly jumped out of his seat the first day of class. Dr. Davidson employed his annual interrogatory designed to assess where the new boys stood academically. He asked, "In ancient times, how many countries made up what is now France?" The blond student in the front row flung up his hand, arm waggling in the air. Without being acknowledged, he stood up and faced the teacher, responding "Omnia Gallia est divisa in partes tres!"

Davidson looked at him, and the lad tilted his head about 30 degrees to the side, staring for approval. When Davidson did not move to congratulate him, Jimmy added, "That's from Caesar, before he crossed the Rubicon. It's Latin."

The professor observed for a few seconds more. Jimmy began to get frustrated and sought to add something else. Davidson cut him short, "Mr. Buchanan, I believe? A simple response containing the simple answer is all that was necessary. You need not shoot up from your chair like a rocket and spout the answer. By the way, I *am* somewhat familiar with Caesar. And Horace. And Ovid. And Virgil. Further, the accurate quote from *Bellum Gallicum* is, 'Gallia est omnis divisa in partes tres.'" Jimmy slunk into his chair amid the titters of his 19 classmates, including his new roommate, Robert Grier.

"You look like you were born in the woods and scared by an owl," Jimmy crowed at a group that included Robert, Powhatan Ellis and Jasper Slaymaker in the back room of the Grey Boar as he rolled another cigar amid the talk of quims and snatches. Despite his somewhat prim attire, with what was becoming his signature white scarf pinned around his neck, Jimmy was on his way to becoming a regular b'hoy, as long as the professors or other "big bugs" were not in view. He took another drink of the anti-fogmatic before Robert joined him outside with the rest of the flask of Old Orchard, the rough whiskey carted up from Kentucky, smuggled under his coat. They exhausted that bottle reeling in the snow, staggered toward another rum-hole, finally scuffling back to their room only a few hours ahead of the next day's lessons. Jimmy slurred to Robert before they tumbled into bed, "I am goin' to face down those idiot refugee so-called professors who could'n make it in New England."

Jimmy was actually more interested in pedagogy than the substance of the lessons, and delighted in analyzing how lessons were delivered. "Why, thank you Dr. Davidson. That wonderful elucidation has led me to understand that it was, in fact, the Roman Church's belief that the Reformation was a human-generated materialistic philosophical reaction to the church's spiritual beliefs that occasioned their intransigence."

Davidson could only nod. Jimmy routinely corrected Professor McCormick on matters of mathematics, and had the temerity to challenge Davidson's poetical geography text and its dislocation of the Isle of Madeira, known for its Sherry, premised on Jimmy's own correct calculations. After class, he confided to all within earshot, "What a fool Davidson is. I take him where he has never been and tell him he was the one that drove me there. If these professors would read more than one chapter ahead of us, or let us study from some book other than their dancing little poems, maybe we could get a real education."

Davidson's throat stiffened as he walked the other way to his lodgings, his rent unpaid pending receipt of wages already three months in arrears.

The faculty's resentment of this upstart student, led by Davidson, soon led to reprisal. Although the Board of Trustees and its chair, Robert Coleman, the Lancaster ironmaster, heatedly debated the prospective loss of revenue, something had to be done. There were good reports about young Buchanan's scholarship, but his attitude and the new innuendos of scurrilous conduct, supported by Davidson's report that Buchanan was seen leaving, at dawn, a certain building in Carlisle proper, made the decision unavoidable.

On the first Saturday morning in October 1808, as Jimmy was preparing to return to Dickinson, a rider brought a letter to the Buchanan household. Father read slowly and silently. Uncharacteristically, there was no beating, no verbal assault. Mr. Buchanan simply handed the document to his son, and never spoke of it again.

The Principal of the college wrote:

Carlisle 21st September 1808

Dear Sir:

It is with profound dismay that I must inform you that it is the unanimous decision of the Trustees of Dickinson College as of September the twenty-first, in the year of our Lord 1808 that your son, James, not be permitted to return to this institution. His opprobrious conduct has far exceeded that of any of the other scholars at the College, and there are perhaps aspects of his dissolute behavior and the exuberant flow of unchecked animal spirits as to which honor and decorum do not permit revelation.

This decision is joined with dismay by all the trustees. We regret this expulsion is irrevocable.

To the Honorable James Buchanan, Senior
Dr. Robert Davidson, Acting Principal

Jimmy did not know where to turn. His father was certainly not the right source for sympathy, and it was far too discomfiting to go to his mother. It would break her heart! I must, Jimmy considered, go right to the Reverend Dr. King. Dr. King recommended me for the college and he is important there. I cannot believe he would now cast me out.

Approaching the parsonage, Jimmy formulated his plan. When Dr. King's wife opened the rectory door, he was already dabbing tears from his eyes. He asked to see his family's pastor. "Dr. King, you do know I was asked not to return to Dickinson College?"

"Yes. I have so heard."

"You know, sir, and you being a Godly man and watched me raised, I had little awareness of the things of the world. There were many there who, more ill bred than I, misled me."

Despite a deeper knowledge, Dr. King sought some sign of honest repentance. "Jimmy, do you before God swear there was no good basis for this action?"

Jimmy hesitated and his head tilted down and to the side. Ridges of thought appeared on his brow, then cleared. "None, as I search my conscience, that would lead to this. I was perhaps too impertinent at times and I followed some of the boys along wrong and bitter paths, but I can cure those deficiencies, and you know my scholarship was at the highest level."

The pastor remembered the late snow of the baby's May baptism, Elizabeth's smile and James's pride, and told himself he trusted what he believed to be honest contrition in young Buchanan's face. Most of all, he respected the Godly character of both of Jimmy's parents, and realized the embarrassment that this would cause his father, and the deep hurt to Elizabeth if she were ever to learn that the trustees expelled her son. Recognizing he risked the wrath of the other trustees, and especially Coleman, who had made the motion for expulsion, the pastor moved toward Jimmy and touched his shoulder, "I will do this for you. It was conditioned as irrevocable and so I must provide some justification to the trustees. Wait here a moment."

As he retreated to his study for prayer and a pen, King considered. My tenure as President of the Board of Trustees has newly commenced and I am putting that position, and my sacred word and office, on the line. May Buchanan prove my faith justified.

Dr. King returned. "This is sealed with the mark of the church. It cannot be opened without everyone then knowing."

Jimmy carried what he viewed as his exoneration with him as he vanished by horseback that afternoon for college. He so wanted to read the letter, but could not determine a way. Night fell. Jimmy approached the house of Dr. Davidson. He slipped the envelope under the Acting Principal's door, and showed up for classes the next day as if nothing transpired. The College, in desperate need of his monthly tuition and out of respect for Dr. King, let him stay.

Jimmy made a great show of taking his studies more seriously and kept his mockery to a minimum, risking his roommate Robert's chiding of his "Sabberday ways" when he now stayed away from Carlisle's groggeries. At the end of the second school year, it was rumored that only fifteen of his class of twenty were presented for graduation. The five left behind would be dwarfed by the preceding year's thirteen, and the class of 1807, which had no graduates at all. Jimmy began to fear that he might have been stabbed in the back once again by his inferiors. He raced to the list as soon as it was posted, pushed Robert Grier aside, and was relieved to find his name included.

Now it was time to hatch the plan brooding ever since his readmission. He slid into the graces of not one but both rival college literary societies, the Union Philosophical Society and the Belles-

Lettres. Jimmy secretly smirked at the ostentation of these names for memberships of less than a dozen rustics. Nonetheless, he needed to gain their approval.

The standing custom at Dickinson was that each society nominated one of its own for honors, and the faculty chose between the two nominees, granting one first class honors, and the other second honors. Jimmy considered that his best chance was to cast his lot with the Philosophicals and ensure his own nomination. He arranged his selection as his society's candidate for first class honors, and anointed a classmate, Robert Laverty, for second class. He told Grier, now a member of the rival society, that no Belles-Lettres candidate should be presented, "lest certain activities of their members be disclosed."

The faculty would not have it. Instead, they chose Alfred Foster from Belles-Lettres and designated Laverty to receive second honors.

Jimmy wrote to his father and to Dr. King, *It was only the narrow-minded ways and petty prejudices of the faculty that have led to this scandalous result. Is there not anything you, as my Father and my Pastor, can do? I refuse to accept this decision!* He kept on polishing his valedictory, confident that Dr. King or his father would obtain for him the honor rightfully his.

When Dr. King received the entreaty, he tore it into a score of pieces, crumpled each, and carefully, as he took another sip of Sherry, tossed them slowly into a raging fire.

Father wrote, after scolding his son for sending an undated letter, that he was *not disposed to censure your conduct in being ambitious to have the first honors of the college.* He also offered some additional fatalism, *often when people have the greatest prospects of temporal honor and aggrandizement, they are blasted in a moment by a fatality connected with men and things.* The senior Buchanan declined to intercede in the faculty's decision.

Jimmy ultimately extracted permission from the faculty to speak at graduation, without honors, sandwiched between Foster and Laverty. No one bothered to record, and his parents were not present to hear, his rambling address on "The Utility of Philosophy" that extended the graduation ceremony for nearly two additional hours.

Jimmy still had not revealed to his mother that it was behind a large oak desk on a deep-seated leather chair, and not in the pulpit, where his tactics and character could find their fullness. Where to practice law? He had never traveled farther from home than Carlisle. Philadelphia, recently eclipsed by New York as the nation's largest city, would be too daunting, full of many who were, he conceded even to himself, at least equally adept and certainly better schooled. Baltimore, with 63,000 residents third in population, did not have quite the caliber of young professional men as did the Quaker city, but was also a bit too crowded at the starting line for Jimmy's blood.

The community of Lancaster, not far across the Susquehanna from Carlisle, might do. Jimmy knew from his friend Jasper Slaymaker that the so-called "Dutch" in Lancaster were of course Germans, and they did not come here until the English and the Scots were well-established and servants and tradesmen were needed. He understood that the Swissers and Dunkers and Germans knew their place and that, although they outnumbered the native English speakers, most of the men were not permitted to vote. In addition, although it straddled two swamps and had no navigable waterway, its road to Philadelphia was the finest and most direct in the entire country, and its Conestoga wagons and Lancaster rifles were known far and wide. The speculative product of a 1730's land grant from William Penn now had 6,000 citizens, and it was still the largest city not on America's seaboard.

Lancaster, importantly, was the state capital and a Federalist town. The politics accorded with those he knew growing up in Mercersburg. He considered, few others with skill and ambition would choose it over the great cities of the East. In addition to opportunities for lawyering, he could engage in land speculation and other means to achieve wealth and prominence that had now become his great goal. While he might miss his mother, Lancaster was comfortably distant from his father, and offered yet another chance to start afresh.

With these prospects in mind, young Jimmy traveled to his adopted town on June 16, 1809 in the company of Jasper, who graduated a year earlier, and Robert Grier. He still did not shave, and had no body hair. They met up with a friend of Jasper's, Andy Noel. It was there he saw the obviously wealthy and obviously pretty young girl outside the Central Market to whose mother he so grandly doffed his hat. Jimmy did not yet know that Ann was only 14, or that she was an heiress to Pennsylvania's largest fortune, or that her father was the Dickinson trustee who had urged his ouster. Soon, he would.

Chapter Three
LAWYER

Now, this is a city, thought James Buchanan, Esq.

As far as Jimmy could see, animals stared and beckoned. Not to mention the carved European kings and Indian chiefs. Twenty times larger than Mercersburg and full of far more than twenty times as many taverns behind these wooden totems. Up and down every street that led toward the courthouse in Penn Center were three-story buildings and one of the roads was covered with some hard flat substance.

Jimmy sought out James Hopkins, for whom he was slated to clerk. I can get ahead here, Jimmy resolved, but I need to learn what Hopkins knows, not only the law but the *being* a lawyer. He took to his studies with vigor never before displayed, reading all the books Mr. Hopkins set before him, devouring Coke and Blackstone. All fed a love of precision, precedent, and detail that spoke to his soul. Mr. Hopkins said to him after his first few weeks, "Buchanan, some people are accused of not seeing the forest for the trees."

The clerk looked at him expectantly, but was not convinced what he heard next was the compliment he was certain it was intended to be. "You, young sir, are a leaf man."

He read enough of Thomas Paine, once himself a citizen of Lancaster, to agree that Law was King in a democracy. "Jasper," he said to his college mate, "That man was a radical, and I know they expelled him from the country. It was naïve of him to think that a democracy is always better than a monarchy, but old Tom Paine was surely correct about one thing. If you can learn and use the law, you can really get ahead."

Slaymaker nodded, but said, "Here in Lancaster, Jimmy, I know a bit about how this all works. It's not as easy as it was where you grew up, or in school. You want to enter into Lancaster society by being a lawyer? The real power in this town is with the ironmasters. They don't pay attention to the likes of us."

Jimmy lodged the information, but told himself Jasper does not yet know the power the law can have. It's incarcerated in ancient languages, and it has its own peculiar jargon and impenetrable symbols. That is power, that is power as well.

Finding lodging above the Widow Dutchman's Inn at 43 East King, Jimmy was pleased to learn that this was not only near the courthouse, and Jasper's lodgings, but was on the very block that the Governor of Pennsylvania, Simon Snyder, lived. In fact, the town's leading citizen, the ironmaster Robert Coleman, was right across the street.

One night at the Leopard tavern, he feigned more ignorance than truth would compel. "What do you know," he asked Jasper, "about this Robert Coleman?"

"Only that he is probably the richest man in all America and the most important man in town. You know he was head of the trustees at Dickinson. What else would you want to know?"

Jimmy's eyebrows drew together and his little tongue ran over first his lower lip, and then deeply around his mouth, dragging slowly across the backs of his wisdom teeth. He had, in fact, paid attention in Cass's class to the lesson that included the estimation of Coleman's wealth. He also knew Coleman's role in his expulsion. "Well, Jasper, I guess everything. If he is as important here as you say, don't you think it would be best to have all the goods on him?"

Jasper had not thought of it in quite this way. It was simply indisputably a fact that ironmasters were the power, and Coleman was at their center. He paused for a moment and said, "I know a fair amount about him. He has a good reputation, hard but fair. He came over from Ireland, County Donegal I think, with very little, but makes a show of not being Irish. Married into a family that owned some works. Knows everyone who is anyone in Philadelphia, and most of New York besides. Got rich in the war. Perhaps has over-invested in property here and elsewhere. Has several daughters. Prettiest is Ann, tho' she's but a little girl. Most important, built an empire and protects it with all of his breath."

Jimmy thought, that's enough for now, enough to really get me started. Jasper had confirmed what he knew, and added some powerful information besides.

He could look across the street at the Coleman house and down the street, both ways, and see the grand mansions. I am huddled in a room over a tavern, he thought, but this is as close to wealth and power as I can be for now. I am going to crack that society. I am going to do it through the law. The law is going to be my shield, and it is going to be my sword.

Hopkins proved to be a good mentor. Jimmy watched as his preceptor interviewed clients, and studied the business of law as he was researching its finer points. When George Hubley came in for marital advice, Jimmy sat in the back of the office and took notes. To his dismay, Mr. Hubley was circumspect as to the identity of the other party, and Jimmy was disappointed as Hopkins advised him of the difficulties of proving adultery, and the pitfalls of divorce.

Jimmy reaffirmed that his odd ocular disability, his blue eye was near-sighted and the hazel far-sighted, worked well to his advantage in conversation. A tilt of his head and an earnest gaze polished the pretense.

After watching Hopkins at work, and wandering the corridors and courtrooms of the Lancaster County Court, he remarked, "Jasper, more deals are made in the hallways than rulings by those black cloaked figures behind the bench. You simply have to admire the law's seamless nature, how it anticipates problems because it knows what happened before. In particular, how it can be worked and twisted to achieve almost any outcome."

At night Jimmy often headed beyond the edge of town via the Marietta Road, considering the prospect of possessing a suitable house amid its woods and fields. He elocuted grandly, like Demosthenes on the Aegean he proudly thought, practicing speeches to courts and juries, and working on his bedside manner for the prominent people and wealthy widows he targeted as clients. Jimmy had not actually read Plutarch, nor anyone else, on Demosthenes and was not familiar with the Ancient's aphorism, *All speech is vain and empty unless it be accompanied by action,* nor the Greek's prescient view that one should, *Beware lest in your anxiety to avoid war you obtain a master.*

In the two years Jimmy was studying with Hopkins, he never traveled the ninety miles to Mercersburg, even when his youngest brother Edward was born, joining three- year old George Washington Buchanan in the late spate of boys. It was as if all the roads west of the Susquehanna were washed away from his personal landscape. Rarely, he would wander as far as Wright's Ferry, and gaze over the river toward Mercersburg. From a distance, the steel drum of the Coleman iron works beat against his ears. My mother truly does love me, she does truly. He stared into the slowly moving Susquehanna and his thoughts turned to the nights he saw what his father did to his mother. He pushed that from his mind. I was a boy. I could not protect her. Just a boy. He hurt her. He hurt her. Is that what husbands do? He slowly unbuttoned his pants and urinated in the direction of Mercersburg.

First on some nights, and then on most, Jimmy visited the taverns that stood on nearly every corner, and many parts in between.

He sipped on a series of Sherries at the Grape, near Penn Square, as he realized that this was where the ironmasters drank. Thereafter, Jimmy often pulled Jasper in there, rather than into the Leopard, full of cobblers, wheelwrights and storekeepers.

Jimmy did not confide it to Jasper, but he wanted to study the mannerisms of the town's elite, overhear their speech, and build the belief that he could one day insinuate himself into their circle. As he went by their tables, Mr. Coleman, Mr. Shippen, and Mr. Hand never even acknowledged him, nor did they ever seem to include Hopkins or any other lawyer in their evening activities, despite the fact that his mentor owned a small ironwork at Conowingo near the Buck Tavern. "It is unfair to regard me," he said to Jasper, "as nothing other than one of the broad band of Scots-Irish and Germans who constitute the trades class in Lancaster. I will crack their little cluster."

His clerkship concluded in 1812. Jimmy and Jasper, who had failed the year before, were two of four young lawyers to pass the bar. Only a few months later, Jimmy ignored the calls to come to his country's defense. "This war, what an absurd sideshow," he declared to Jasper. "It's purely the product of rabble-rousers and firebrands like John Calhoun of South Carolina and Henry Clay of Kentucky. I am damned if I am going to risk my neck for someone in Philadelphia, or New York, let alone those hayseeds. I need to find now how my own future is best served."

Jimmy decided to visit Mercersburg for the first time since he moved to Lancaster, finally to see his mother again and to meet his now two-year old brother Edward. He tossed a grey coat about his shoulders to disguise the impending paunch already pressing against his vest's pearl buttons and place a top hat on his lap as he settled among the passengers.

The jostling of his coach, and inextinguishable thoughts of his father, began to make Jimmy uneasy. As the coach's wheels hit each

76   ROGER EVANS

rut of the rough road, the old nausea grew worse. Finally, as they neared Mercersburg, Jimmy pulled the leather cord that rang a bell up front, "Please sir, please please please stop," He choked out the words, pressing his lips together as he almost reached the large dead oak at the roadside. Eva Hubley and her daughter turned away as he lost last night's meal and a lot more besides. Jimmy rode at the driver's side up top until the coach halted at his boyhood home. Mother greeted him on the street, ignoring the smell that now bathed her son. Her embrace flooded Jimmy with childhood memories awash with scenes of bedtime readings and shared intimacies, but he could not shake the less comfortable memories. He was glad his father stayed behind the store counter until supper time, and that he had time to change for dinner.

"Why have not you not come here, barely even written, Jim? I could have used your help here with the store, and these children."

His father's hand waved over the brood of siblings assembled at the table. They all looked at their older brother for a reply.

"Father, I have simply been too busy with my studies. I am now a lawyer, and a member of the bar. It took all my time, and I could not be away from the demands of Mr. Hopkins' clients, and now my own."

Father grunted. His sisters looked at their brother, the lawyer, and wondered if he had become the same kind of man as their father. Little George and Edward were simply happy to meet the stranger. It was a relief to Jimmy that no one spoke the rest of dinner. At the age of 21, he was glad he was now too large to be cudgeled.

After dinner, James Senior retired to the study with his hand rolled cigar and Monongahela whiskey. Jimmy went to the front room where his brothers and sisters, clustered with half-read books and nearly-finished samplers, stared at him expectantly. His mother sat rocking in the corner, knitting and purling. Jane and Maria gave him hugs and Sarah kissed him lightly on his cheek. Edward knew he was supposed to do something, but the toddler still was not sure who this stranger was. Big brother declared, "I have something to tell all of you. I am already successful, and I am going to be rich." Then, under his breath, "richer than father."

He looked around for a response, but received none. "All I want to say, if anyone of you is ever in trouble, money trouble or any other kind, you can come to me." George and Edward had no idea what that meant but his sisters nodded and, Jimmy thought, seemed to appreciate the gesture.

Jimmy's eyes moistened as he contemplated the promise he had made. Careful not to dampen the stylized "JB" that was embossed in the corner of the cream handkerchief he removed from the pocket of his cream vest, he patted the tops of his round cheeks.

"Come walk with me, Jamie."

Mother and son made their way down Seminary toward Park. Elizabeth reached with her hand and softly stroked the back of his neck. "Ye still be a good boy. I am so glad you like what you are doing. Thank you for that offer to your sisters and brothers. I am so veery sorry I could not help ye more…"

Jimmy turned and put both his hands on her shoulders. He searched her face, the eyes whose brilliance had faded into a watery blue shaded by drooping eyelids, her remaining teeth rising and descending at twisted angles, "Mother, you have given me wonderful gifts, an acquaintance with the great poets, an understanding how to get people to like me, and so much more."

Through tears, but directly, "I have always loved you."

"I know you have. I wanted to be there for you. I really did."

Elizabeth looked away and drew her hand to her own eyes. She spoke into the trees. "There be nothing you could do. Your father be a good man, jes' when he is a-drinking…"

Her voice trailed. Jimmy took firmer hold of her shoulders and turned her towards him. "At least the beatings have stopped? I am bigger. I could protect you now!"

As the words left his mouth, the voice, "Get back here, Elizabeth. Bring your son."

Elizabeth looked back at the house. Hurriedly to Jimmy, "I am fine. I will be fine."

Jimmy could not get her to return his gaze. They both did not want to risk the next summons and scurried to obey.

His mother squeezed out, "Promise me this, Jamie! You will honor that promise to care for your brothers and sisters, no matter what perils life may bring?"

Jimmy nodded. "I will do that. I will."

Jimmy followed his mother across the threshold and Father pulled Son aside, "What were you and your mother talking about?"

Jimmy looked back at the old man, his wrinkles, his softening arms and his belly going to fat. "Nothing Father. Just admiring the trees, and your fine house."

James looked hard, and paused before saying, "There is something you might finally do for your family. I have purchased a bit of property in Kentucky, near Frankfort. Some infernal fool is challenging my title to it, and I might lose it. I don' know if you are good enough to do it, but I don' relish the idea of paying some backwoods swindler lawyer to stand for me."

Jimmy thought to himself, this will give me a good reason to cut my teeth out west and perhaps obtain some paternal praise. "Of course, Father, and you will pay me?" No response.

That night, Jimmy listened for his mother's screams, but heard none before he drifted to sleep. He was too old to be peeping through doors, and did not trust what he would do if he saw what still infected his mind.

On the trip to Kentucky's capital, Jimmy began to reflect on a lawyer's life in Lancaster. *I have to acknowledge my frustration. The ironmasters seem out to get me, and no lawyers ever get ahead except by politics. Even they become wealthy far too late in life. I want what they have, but I want it now.* The stage wheels seemed to clack, "Go West."

Two days in Frankfort and he could not even get a court's attention as its judges wrestled with a flood of similar claims. Trying to figure out how he could avoid failure, Jimmy determined, as he wrote to Jasper, he was a "pygmy among legal giants." The quality of lawyering in Kentucky, even in this city of barely a thousand, actually far outstripped what he had seen in the courts and chanceries of his native state. He had thought opportunities would be more open and the competition less qualified. He considered the lure of the West. It made sense. In this burgeoning country, if one did not spring from some old line Eastern family, your best chance was out here, in the newer states of Kentucky, Tennessee, and Ohio, or perhaps even the territories beyond, Indiana or even as far west as Illinois.

I don't come from those families, I'm not some Adams or some Lee or some Dutch, what are they called, poltroons? I can't compete with them in the big cities. Here it's as bad, and in a different way. These are the people with the stuff to make it. Like Henry Clay, displaced here from Virginia where his family had nothing. They are starting all even, and apparently do not fear that.

Jimmy comforted himself. *I do have some talents. I am craftier than most. I pay attention to details. I can get people to like me. If only women controlled the purse strings… Well, anyway, at least for now, there are higher fees in eastern Pennsylvania. I already understand the hierarchy. Now,* he concluded, *I simply have to pierce it.*

While the lawyers impressed him, the rough sorts coming into the courthouse seemed benighted by comparison, and far too reminiscent of the types he fled in Mercersburg. He prowled about the courthouse and noticed a random rustic sizing him up. Jimmy looked at the backwoodsman and was not reminded of anything as much as his own father. The farmer approached him. His wife tailed two steps behind, holding what appeared to be a girl, ill and wrapped in tattered muslin. Behind them both, a lanky, dark-haired three year old.

Hand extended, "Tom Lincoln."

"Mr. Lincoln, what might I possibly do for you?"

"Your name, sir?"

"James Buchanan, Esq."

"Mr. Buchanan, I am but a wandering labor boy grown into a carpenter, but I have bought three farms in Hardin County. They've made a claim against the Knob Creek place I own in Hodgenville, about 60 hard miles away. I would pay you three dollars if you would take this to court for me."

Jimmy almost laughed. "Lincoln, you offer but a pittance. I am worth far more than that. Anyway, I am not admitted in this court, though even if I were, I would hardly do this for you. "Why not," as a parting shot, "get Henry Clay."

He was walking away as he overheard the words of the young mother comforting her son, "Abraham, my sweet boy. Just you shush. We will be having supper soon."

Jimmy finally had to go into his own pocket to hire Kentucky counsel to resolve his father's claim. *I worried about going home empty-handed,* he thought, *and now I have had to pay so I don't and make my father believe I could at least do this on my own.*

Fighting through November snow, he returned to the city that had lost its eleven year reign as Pennsylvania's state capital. Several of the lawyers whose business revolved around the legislature moved their practices from Lancaster across the Susquehanna to Harrisburg. Jimmy concluded a letter to his college roommate, Robert Grier, now also an émigré to the state capital, about his travels, *The next day, I packed my trunk and came back to Lancaster; that was big enough for me. Kentucky was too big.*

Jimmy established his office within his living quarters above the Widow. A good Federalist, he still felt no need to serve in the war with Britain now raging, even as the enemy forces secured American soil. Lancaster, he thought, was well enough inland and occupation of New York or even Philadelphia would not alter his focus.

Business was slower than anticipated. Even when he managed to wangle an appointment as a deputy prosecutor the following February, he only earned $938 in 1813, barely sufficient to keep him in drink and laws books, and not enough for anything else. His reputation as a lawyer was soon that of a "plugger," someone adequate with the books and the drafting of contracts and codicils, but far from a rising star even in Lancaster. Judge Mannliebe did, however, describe him to a colleague as a "fine, imposing figure, with a large well-formed head, a clear complexion, beautiful skin, large eyes, one blue and one brown, which he turned obliquely on those he addressed, looking as honest and earnest as to engage their sympathy by his gaze alone; then his voice was strong, resonant and not unmusical, and his elocution, though very deliberate, flowed on like a full river in a constant current."

Jimmy no longer bothered to go to the Grape but his drinking creeped into ever earlier hours. As the crowd thinned and men returned to their homes, Jimmy's legs often merrily sped on one of the Leopard's back tables until the Irish jig that apparently raced only through his head stopped playing. More than once, his bobbing blonde head was also seen parallel with his knees down the adjoining alley.

Each and every next morning, Jimmy would chide himself. What was he doing, all his talent and all his hopes, what was in store for him? Still, the strong pull of the tavern would not go away. The prodigal son soon was compelled to turn to his father for a loan, grudgingly provided and not on favorable terms. The next year was shaping up similarly, until events conspired to propel his fortune forward.

June 16, 1814 marked the birthday of a young lady Jimmy first saw on his maiden trip to the city on that date in 1809. He remembered her more for her mother's reaction than any particular aspect of her visage or demeanor. He only learned upon his arrival in Lancaster that she was part of the Coleman family, and daughter of the man he saw infrequently at the Grape and in passing on the street. It was not only Coleman's prominence and his own relative obscurity, but also the remembrance of her father's role in the Dickinson expulsion that kept Jimmy at bay. Whenever in the Grape, he was more careful about what he imbibed, and did not end the evening dancing and puking.

Jimmy was raised a Presbyterian but had not joined the church in Lancaster. Nevertheless, on those days he woke up early enough, he went to the First Presbyterian Church at the corner of Orange and Cherry. The Colemans, and most of their friends, attended St. James across the street. Jimmy sometimes slipped into the Episcopalian sanctuary. He watched from the rear as the ironmasters and local aristocracy worshipped the only being they acknowledged as greater than themselves. To those who purchased pews toward the front of the sanctuary, and the Colemans proudly held not only the first pew, but also the third, of the nave's 84 numbered rows, even that deference seemed begrudging. Jimmy was not used to the liturgy, or the gymnastics, of the Episcopal service, but learned to mimic their mannerisms. In church as elsewhere, he kept his place and never approached the Colemans.

The newly-minted lawyer was therefore surprised when he opened an invitation to the Colemans' party for their eighteen-year-old daughter, Ann. The opportunity soon seemed obvious. *I can meet*

Mr. Coleman, ingratiate myself with the mother, and perhaps entice the daughter into a courtship that could thrust me upward. I have no ties to any young ladies, and who better to woo than the daughter of the wealthiest man in Pennsylvania? This party could be my ticket.

He made sure to dress in his finest, the new purchase funded by the monies advanced by his father.

Saturday arrived. Jimmy was careful not to show up too early, but made certain that he was there soon enough to evaluate every opportunity. He emerged at seven from the phaeton that he leased from Gundaker's, although the Coleman residence was just across the cobblestones. Jimmy had never been in any of the stately mansions that lined King Street, never even securing an invitation to Mr. Hopkins's house. He was amazed by what he saw inside. The paintings, the gilded furniture, the expanse of marble, and the roomfuls of acquisitions and appurtenances captivated him. It was as if he had stepped into another world. The night went as he calculated, despite the fact that several groups of men, otherwise deep in conversation, appeared to disperse as he sought to join them.

He deemed the evening an unqualified success. He was able to engage the host in conversation, which he thought went quite well, and to sidle over to the birthday honoree about halfway through the party. He had always been successful in the company of women, young and old, in groups and one on one. His sisters had taught him a great deal about this in the course of growing up, and at his father's store and thereafter he studied the ways in which older women, especially, could be smoothly flattered into a feeling of great intimacy. Little Ann certainly seemed smitten with his quick wit and well-turned phrases. He talked to her for what seemed half the night and went a time or two with her out of order on the dance floor. They had even slipped away to an upstairs balcony, returning to sit out the last dance together, with Ann only remembering as the music ended that she had promised the last dance to some German friend. At evening's close, she did seem a bit unsettled, but there was certainly at least the implicit promise of further courting.

A sharp knock woke Jimmy on Monday. He peered with his good eye at the Carpenter clock hanging in the corner but could not make out the position of its hands. Although the tavern had closed at Sunday's early time, he and Jasper had punished the whiskey quite badly afterwards, and Jimmy strained to remember where the empty bottles were. Grabbing the silk robe from its perch on the mahogany post, he pulled its gray and ruby oriental figures around him and ran his plump fingers through his thinning hair. He laced a white scarf about his neck. No time for the top knot. After fumbling for the key while trying to avoid yesterday's clothes strewn about the floor, Jimmy stuck his finger through the key's open hole, and then realized that he had again forgotten to lock the door. Only its brass chain guarded it from opening more than a few inches. He pulled the chain's knob from its resting place on the door jamb. On the doorstep stood a gentleman whom he recognized immediately. Robert Coleman stepped across the threshold.

"Mr. Buchanan," he began, "I expect you remember who I am."

Jimmy was still a bit groggy as he replied, "Of course, sir. I am so grateful for your gracious invitation to your daughter's party! To what do I owe this visit's honor?" *Could I already be in line for some portion of the ironmaster's business?*

Robert looked around the lodgings, "Mr. Buchanan, you had at my party the occasion to make my daughter's acquaintance, did you not?"

"Yes, sir. She is a fine young woman and, if I may add, quite lovely."

This line was failing, he began to realize, as the older man continued to assess him, last night's stained underwear and not one, but two, empty bottles of Old Orchard.

The lawyer stumbled, "I hope, sir, I did not offend—either her or you?"

"Mr. Buchanan, I am, as I believe you appreciate, not only suspect of the motives of young men such as yourself, but have the remembrance of your expulsion, and the good reason therefor, sharply in mind. You do recall that, do you not, Mr. Buchanan?"

Jimmy's eyes narrowed and he averted the head now pounded by the tiny hammers of a hundred concerns.

Coleman followed, "You can therefore understand, sir, why I would request that you not pursue any relationship with my daughter. She is a bit impetuous, and appears, for whatever ill-conceived notion, to have been somehow taken by you. It falls upon me to advise you not to see her again, and to stay clear of my house and family."

Jimmy's mind quivered and his stomach began to churn. He was not certain that the road to fortune and prominence ran through Ann, but it had seemed his best avenue. Now, it was not only taken away from him, but he was apparently being forced toward a different route altogether. What had begun as a most propitious encounter had suddenly, awfully, turned sour.

"Sir, I am appalled that you would believe that I would be the sort who would try to wheedle his way into your family by such means. I was simply courteous to your daughter and, by the way, your most gracious wife. I do not understand this prohibition!"

Coleman was prepared. "Mr. Buchanan, I have something by way of exchange. I am aware of your financial struggles, and your limited prospects, as you now may have seen those aspects dwindle farther as the result of your current importunacy. I am therefore prepared to make a proposition."

Jimmy's head tilted forward a bit more, and his tongue began to move between slightly parted lips.

"You have, I expect, some understanding of politics?" said the older man.

He nodded.

"You are, I believe, of course a Federalist. For someone of your bent, entry into the state legislature would greatly enhance your career and your income. I am prepared to facilitate that, on the necessary condition that you adhere to my directive to stay away from my daughter. I do not expect to see someone not of my church in its sanctuary, and someone not of my station in my house, except upon invitation which, I can well assure you, will not be forthcoming. Do you, sir, agree?"

Again, he could only nod. Jimmy was already conceiving that this plan, although not what he prospected, was potentially satisfactory.

Coleman set it all forth. He would have Peter Diller nominate the young lawyer as the Federalist candidate two months hence. In the interim, Jimmy was of course to abide by the strictures set down, and make at least some reasonable effort to visit with those who needed to approve his candidacy. Robert would provide the necessary introductions, and Jimmy would make the appropriate rounds at the gentlemen's offices. "You, also, will refrain from spirits at least to the extent that you do not appear as a public debauch until your nomination is secured?"

Jimmy assented.

It was thus put in motion. Introductions made and supplications endured, Jimmy received the party's blessing on August 24, 1814.

That same day the British burned Washington. The Madisons fled the President's House moments ahead of the fire. The picture of Dolley in exile, carrying Gilbert Stuart's portrait of Washington under her arm, became instant myth. Even the Federalists, who in Congress had to a man voted against the war, now realized that opposition to fighting the British, with flames licking the capital, was not a politically advantageous place to be.

Jimmy understood he must quickly change his position. Honor (and politics) demanded no less. The newly anointed Federalist candidate quickly volunteered for a hastily formed unit of the Pennsylvania militia composed of Lancaster's finest young gentlemen. They gathered under the direction of Henry Shippen, whose lineage as the scion of a family that had produced a Philadelphia mayor over a century earlier and a state Supreme Court justice enabled him to overcome rumors and gossip flowing from the fact that he was Benedict Arnold's brother-in-law. The soldiers gathered in refulgent array, clad in stiff white linen top-shirts and black trousers with twilled piping down the side. They wore high-crowned deep blue hats and the officers sported large white plumes. Enlisted men had simple black cockades on the left side, each about two inches in diameter, with small silver eagles centered on each cockade.

Swaggering in their full regalia and toting Lancaster rifles over their left shoulders with swords glinting at their sides, the young men mounted horses to traverse the Baltimore highway to secure the capital in the event that the British headed north. Most of the town, including Robert and his daughter Ann, gathered on the Marietta road to see them off. Jimmy was not selected to be an officer. He was compelled to enlist as a private and was required to ride near the back, a fact noted with some satisfaction by the elder Coleman as he watched the little eagle glisten in the sun as Buchanan rode out of town.

Arriving in Baltimore, the lads were delighted when they were assigned a "secret mission." Directed to go toward the harbor, with sealed orders, Jimmy and his comrades only imagined the glory that might await them. When they got into the city, the seal was broken and orders were unveiled. Jimmy's face fell. Their task was not to advance, nor to protect, but simply to obtain some mounts for other soldiers charged with those tasks. They were conscripted to be horse thieves! Jimmy was at first inclined to ignore the orders and simply return to Lancaster. He soon came to a clearer judgment, realizing how that could appear as he faced the election and sought to advance his nascent political career.

The novice soldiers asked directions of an old woman on Charles Street and were directed to a horse stable at the corner of High and Gay streets, behind the Bel Air market that opened but the year before. They did not know the horses belonged to John Eager Howard, the former Federalist Governor and United States Senator from Maryland. The steeds were spirited away under an eclipsing moon and tied to trees. The small battalion bivouacked in the bushes.

Rain came, and came harder. Jimmy was pushed to the edge of the tent by the pressure of three other lads. His body crowded against the canvas and his belly created a conduit for the night's downpour. Jimmy soon became the delta for the tributary which spread throughout the tent. Soaked and miserable, the reluctant soldier endured that night and the next. They were herding the horses to deliver them to the federal army encamped near the Potomac in Montgomery County when a hard-riding messenger handed Colonel Shippen a message:

To the commander of the Lancaster County, Penna. troops. Please sir be advised forthwith to return my property, that being 43 Arabian and other horses, to my stablery in Baltimore proper. I shall expect this to be accomplished by tomorrow at dawn.

John Eager Howard, Governor, Senator from Maryland, etc., etc.

Colonel Shippen started furiously barking orders. The soldiers reversed course, traveling into the night. Shippen personally ensured the safe return of the mares and stallions to Howard's stables, and left the panoply of privates, including Jimmy, to feed, bathe and curry the mounts. Jimmy had not been forced to work his way through horse dung and dirty straw and to tote buckets of oats since he left his father's, and did not like it one bit. A fine place, he thought, for a lawyer and a future Assemblyman, here in some Baltimore outbuilding tending to someone else's horses surrounded by the steamy smell of "crap and offal-in-the-making" as he remarked to Joel Schenk, a Lancaster cup cheese maker also privatized for the war effort. Colonel Shippen delivered that morning a note of deep apology over the signatures of all the officers of the Lancaster regiment.

By the time they marched back to Lancaster less than a week after departing with such fanfare, the war veterans had all agreed among themselves that it would be best not to disclose the exact nature of their mission.

Jimmy's service to his country thus concluded, he hurtled into his campaign with an oration trumpeting patriotism on the steps of Penn Square, providing handbills to passersby that touted his recent soldiering. He was victorious in November's voting, and headed off to the new capital, Harrisburg. I am now, he thought, finally garnering some of the respect and prominence so deservedly mine. It's a bit surprising it bothers me so little not to see Ann. I certainly do not want to go where I am not wanted! Jimmy was also pleased that Harrisburg afforded the renewed opportunity for his tavern visits after the enforced dry spell.

Politics was a bit more complex, Jimmy soon learned, than he contemplated. His maiden speech almost derailed his political career. On the second day of the session, he addressed his fellow Assemblymen. Flustered at the onset, his confidence grew as he spoke, "Those youths who are to be conscripted into this war should rightfully be conscripted from where danger lies largest. That is to say, Philadelphia and its immediate environs. With the greatest risk comes the greatest sacrifice. It is only fair that the burden not fall on Lancaster and points west, on the smaller cities where lads are needed for farms and industry and which stand little chance of British incursion."

While this might have played in Lancaster, it was at immediate odds with the interests of the cadre of Federalists in the largest city in the East. His side of the aisle loudly booed. Worse, while still on the Assembly floor, he was invited by William Beale of Mifflin County to "come on over" and join the Democrats. Shame-faced, he declined.

The new legislator learned, for at least a short while, his lesson. He thereafter spoke rarely and carefully, and only in support of doctrinaire Federalist legislation, including a proposal to put the property of habitual drunkards in trusteeship and its somewhat ironic counterpart, a reduction in the tax on whiskey. *This last vote*, thought Jimmy, *shows what a great deal I learned from Mr. Cass a decade ago. There will be no Whiskey Rebellion here!*

Fortunately, peace with England slowed the political carnage from his position on conscription. Jimmy recovered enough within the party to secure a place on the judiciary committee. It would prove to be an important springboard.

Partisanship became the Buchanan mantra in the 1815 re-election campaign. On the Fourth of July, he attacked the Democrats as "demagogues," "functionaries," and, in a particularly vituperative accusation, "friends of the French." Warming up, he followed this diatribe with aspersions of the opposing party's "blackest ingratitude" and "diabolic passions," without specifying about what they were ungrateful for, or how those passions were Satanic. Madison was a degenerate. "He orchestrated the War of 1812, which could have been averted by timely compromise. The President and his silly wife abandoned Washington to the enemy as the President's House was set afire." While the rabble reveled in the address, the severity of the attack on the Democratic Party would not be forgotten, in Lancaster and elsewhere.

Jimmy had earned only $1096 in 1814 but, as Mr. Coleman had promised, his income jumped as soon as he was elected. The following year, his compensation doubled. By 1818, he entered the rarefied sum of $8000 in his account books, enough to buy most homes on King Street for cash, *if I do not drink it up*, he reminded himself. He traveled to Baltimore and purchased a slave, Pompey, two years his junior, pudgy and an inch shy of average height. Pompey lodged in the Widow's basement and assisted in cleaning the tavern and, occasionally, Jimmy's office and lodgings. Jimmy's ardor for politics cooled in inverse proportion to his income. That was not at all a bad pact with the ironmaster. His practice was successful, in fact it neared his fondest hopes, even if he had not yet slithered into the upper reaches of Lancaster society.

With his financial goals achieved and the path seemingly clear, Jimmy resolved to give up his Assembly post. It was typical only to serve for a term or two in any event, and he now wanted to devote himself fully to the law and social machinations. Jasper Slaymaker gladly took his place in Harrisburg.

Even when Jimmy lost three pieces of land to his new law partner, Molton Rogers, on a side bet when James Monroe defeated Rufus King for President he was not dissuaded. *A man has to drink, and a little gambling was no harm.* Prudently, he thought, but perhaps simply to save on his steadily increasing bar bills, Jimmy also purchased the Widow Dutchman, including his lodging and upstairs law office. His companion in the venture was the 450-pound Prothonotary John Passmore, the head clerk of the Lancaster County courts and later the county seat's first mayor. Night after seamless night, Jimmy joined John in regaling the fellows. He felt free to punish spirits to his heart's content, knowing he simply had to stumble a few feet to the respite of his bed.

Jimmy was now viewed as one of the most eligible bachelors in town, but between his law practice during the day and drinking at night, he did not have much time for courting. Besides, only a few young women in town could aid his next step, and one was off limits, at least for now. Although he enjoyed the company of both the young men and wenches who partied with him at the Widow and elsewhere, Jimmy still frequently danced alone on the tabletops as midnight passed. He knew he was right where he needed to be before he made his next move.

Chapter Four
COURTSHIP

The city staggered in disarray. Clients clamored for Jimmy's help without, however, offering the immediate prospect of payment. He embraced Mr. Hopkins's dictum that any dereliction of the duty to pay a lawyer's fee was tantamount to treason. Mutiny, in his legal practice, abounded. Jimmy had also been dragooned into drafting a resolution reflecting local sentiment on the Missouri slavery question. It was causing him no end of anguish.

Jimmy told Jasper, back from the last legislative session, "I cannot stand any more nights like this" as his friend watched the results of his tumbling stomach. Of course, Jimmy thought, Jasper knows only of the financial despair and the political upheaval, and not what else reconquers me. He must find this quite peculiar. Jimmy could not eat or drink for days, his head would not stop bobbing and weaving, and the damned dry heaving which followed the bouts of vomiting simply exhausted him.

Monroe's presidency enjoyed some foreign policy successes, but the Panic of 1819, the first serious economic crisis of the new nation, was in full swing. The costs of the War of 1812 and the shenanigans with the First National Bank had come home to roost, and the business and trade classes were scrambling to preserve what they had, all the way up to the wealthiest in town, the Colemans.

As he emerged from the Widow on an overcast Saturday in late June, Jimmy almost stumbled over Ann Coleman, now 22. Her beauty surprised him and he blurted, "How are your father's iron works doing?"

Ann's smile turned cold. What an odd, and almost offensive, thing to say. She expected her father was right, that he had only been after her money, and that her mother was right, that he was merely a social climber, and an inconsiderate one at that. Ann responded, "I am sure they are doing perfectly fine. My father is away right now, in London."

They stood awkwardly in front of the tavern. Ann realized she was angry with herself for carrying something of a torch for this young man ever since that birthday party nearly five years ago. He seemed so attentive and so full of fun and so sincere yet never called on her, never even sent a card. She had asked her friends, even Grace Hubley, whether the young lawyer at the party ever inquired after her, and they allowed as he had not.

Jimmy correctly read the iciness of the reply and realized the opportunity that short, vital bit of information presented. He recovered, "I apologize for the impersonality of my greeting. I was taken quite unawares by your beauty."

Scarcely better, Ann thought, was I not beautiful before?

Head inclined and his eyes directly on hers, he was a bit flustered, but tumbled out the most solicitous questions he could conjure, "Did you know I was named for my father, as you were for your mother?"

"No, I did not."

"Did you know your father was born in the same county in Ireland as my father, and in fact my ancestral homestead is but 20 miles from your father's?"

Ann wondered at these rather personal, but also quite silly inquiries. Still, there was something engaging about his manner, and she still loved the look of his curly yellow hair flowing beyond the cute little topknot that appeared actually to be tied with some sort of bow, and his eyes, his eyes. Quite enchanting to her in their combination of colors!

He was now obviously straining to remember the names of her siblings, "How, Ann, is your mother? How are little Sarah, and Edward, and Thomas?"

"Fine, all of them." Would he ever get to a point? It looked like rain, and it would not only soak through her felt hat, but ruin her dress.

After some talk about a new playhouse and some string quartet, the lawyer moved to the goal that had been growing. "Might I, Miss Coleman, come calling?" His head tilted farther, "Please call me Jamie, as my mother did."

Ann paused, and blushed a bit, "Why Mr. Buchanan, I expect that would be alright, as I once before have called you that," unable to resist the quick jab but still concerned about her father's possible reaction. Then again, her father had never actually forbidden her to see him. Besides, he was out of the country, and unlikely to return for several months.

At parties, through church, and in visits to her home, Ann thought she had seen many—too many—suitors. All stodgy and self-absorbed, each was rejected. The only one who ever interested her at all was her childhood friend Lüder Bauschulte, whose lowborn origin and prospects were unsatisfactory in both her parents' views. Besides, he was both Lutheran and German and she was not going to wed outside of her faith and race, as well as her class. Yet his soft brown eyes, full lips and wonderfully curly dark hair, thicker than her own... He had never held her close, but she could imagine, after his employment at the Cornwall works, how his strong arms would feel around her.

Now quite a bit older, and Lüder no longer a possibility, Ann considered her options. "That would be agreeable," and, after a hint of a pause, "Jamie." The rain began to tickle her nose. "Couldn't we step into the hallway?"

Jimmy had not noticed the change in the weather. "Ann, of course. I am so sorry." He held the door for her.

In the short entrance hall, tavern to one side and stairs to his lodgings and office behind them, Jimmy noticed Ann looking past him. A few tradesmen were drinking ale at a battered pine table, elbowing one another and shouting nonsense, and a lone frocked figure sat in the back with a Sherry. Jimmy started to apologize, but caught something in Ann's look.

Perhaps he had misapprehended her interests. Could he risk showing her a side of life that most of her townspeople reveled in, but that was certainly beyond Ann's experience? Never, in all his evenings, had he seen her nor any Coleman except her father and older brothers, and always at the Grape. "Would you like to visit the Leopard with me tonight?"

Ann had of course often walked by taverns during the day and a few times at night. She had even peered through their open doors. No one else had ever invited her actually to go in.

"Why, yes, Jamie, I expect I would enjoy that!" She hesitated, "It would be better if it were tomorrow evening." In parting, she whispered, "My mother will be gone by six o'clock."

That was all Jimmy needed to hear. He determined to lead Ann on an exploration of Lancaster's taverns and dance halls. The visit to the Leopard would be only her first stop on the maiden voyage into the nightlife of Lancaster.

Ann went home under the shelter of a gallantly offered cape. Her time for marriage was at hand. Not only did she well remember the young man from her birthday celebration, she had followed his career, and seen his growing success. Her willfulness in dismissing suitor after suitor pained her parents, but she was not going to settle for some dawdler who was "appropriate" only because of his family name. She wanted someone going places, and this Jamie appeared to be it.

That night, her bed covers twisted about her. First, her head, then her back, then her feet, pressed against the arabesque headboard. Its carved trefoils, quatrefoils, and squandrels provided no defense to the waves of anxiety and regret. Ann remembered reading about men being drawn and quartered. She knew that treasonous women were simply burned at the stake, but it was the image of being taken apart that throbbed through her. As she sought to sleep, she felt as if she were tied to the crockets and pinnacles of the four-poster and they were slowly, inexorably marching away from one another, rending her body.

She could not not think of Lüder that evening as she tossed on her bed. Lüder had been doing so well at Father's Cornwall works. He was perhaps in line to run the works…father said so…said he reminded him of himself….I am sure we could have wed….had he only not enlisted. Of course, he had written, but those letters came months after their dates….and the strange places….victories at Emuckfau Creek, and Enotochopo, and talk of that pirate, Jean Lafitte…and General Jackson, Horseshoe Bend, Red Sticks, Pensacola. How happy I was when he came to my party…how broken I was when I could not find him after the last dance…and then that argument…that argument…. how he had simply set his mouth and turned away….and not stopping by on his way back to war… Finally on the day before Christmas… from a place called New Orleans, the only letter after my party, seeking forgiveness…I had long ago forgiven him! Did he never get my letters?

Then came other, terrible news. Frau Bauschulte had come right over to our house….and she broke into tears…and shared that horrid letter with me….five weeks after peace but only three weeks after that battle, that damned battle…..I still remember it…and all its misspellings, even his mother's name…as if he didn't really care…..

My dear Mrs. Bashulte:

Your son Luder was a brave and nobel soldier. There was a rare sothern snow in Neworleans, in the battle for Chalmette Plantation and Luder tried to save another soldier from a bayonet but went it through his Adams apple. Luder was one of only eight Americans to die in the battle, tho' the enemy lost 700 with another 1400 grievesly wounded. He was buried with proper honours and his service was nobel and a cause of pride for us all.

Yours most sincerely,

Andrew Jackson, General, United States Army January 12, 1815

The tears would simply not stop......

• • •

The next evening, Jimmy rented a phaeton and came for Ann at five minutes past six o'clock, camping behind a poplar until he spied Mrs. Coleman strolling down King in the direction of St. James Church. Younger sister Sarah watched as this new man came to the door, and knocked respectfully. She ran upstairs to fetch Ann, who had woken from her long afternoon nap only minutes before. Mr. Buchanan waited downstairs. How grand he looks, Sarah thought. What a fine carriage. Jimmy took her arm down the front steps and leaned close enough to revel in Ann's fluttering scent. "What is that wonderful smell?"

"Why, I am so glad you noticed. It is from Jean-Francois Houbigant, in Paris. He made all of the *parfum* for Marie Antoinette. She even tried to smuggle some out before the guillotine struck. At least, that's what Father says. This one is called *'Quelques Fleurs'*, and it is all the rage in Paris. Father brought it for me on his last trip to the continent."

"Well, it is lovely." Jimmy sniffed a bit harder while also considering that it might take a good deal of money to make this girl happy.

At the Leopard, Ann tried Sherry, and a small quaff of Monongahela whiskey, which caused her to choke and sputter, but which she finally swallowed. The new suitor went with her to Matthias Slough's hotel where they shared raw oysters on Limoges plates the proprietor had specially shipped from the Haviland works in France. Finally, of course, the Widow right under his own lodgings. "Ann, you know I now own this establishment?" Ann did not, but was not disappointed at the news. She was increasingly arguing with her mother and father about their restrictions on her and was enthralled to spend the evening caught up in a world which she had only been permitted to imagine.

Ann pretended to be appalled as Jimmy leapt up, obviously intoxicated, on a table at the Widow. He shouted, "Come on up and join with me!" Ann looked about, thinking she had never done *anything* like this! Jimmy continued to challenge her, but Ann probably would not have joined him even with the whiskey and Sherry lacing through their bodies had he not reached down and grabbed her. She stumbled at first but then swung and twirled with the best of them, black curls flying as all those around looked up and cheered her ever more wild turns.

By night's end, Ann was thinking she now knew what the word "smitten" meant. Finally, someone with both prospects and a propensity for fun, even if the quality of his parentage was lacking. She hoped her father would see the light emanating from this rising star, and smiling at what seemed to her to be a quite wonderfully poetic twist of thought. She had to admit she also liked the fact that Jimmy was an *innkeeper*. It was an honest business, yet how deliciously repugnant... He could certainly drink, Ann marveled. He'd slammed back, as he would phrase it, not only most of a bottle of Madeira, but nearly a quart of whiskey besides. Ann's thoughts as she drifted to sleep began to turn to a clandestine courtship, romantic late night visits with one another in the town's skirts, daring meetings in dangerous Adam's Town, frequenting taverns.

"Ann!" her mother called the next morning. "What were you doing last night, and who were you doing it with?"

Did her mother know? How?

"I have already had two visitors this morning, Eva Hubley and Jane Hill."

How did Patricia's mother and, drat it, Grace's, know anything?

Ann sought to speak, but her mother stopped her protestations.

"My dear daughter, what were you thinking? Dancing in public. *Drinking* in public. On a table. At a tavern!"

How had word gotten to her mother, unless they were there themselves?

"You can go right back upstairs, and think about this. If your father knew...."

Ann spun around to head back upstairs. Her mother's voice softened. "Ann, I know you have chafed a bit. You are certainly getting up in years, nearing 23 and not betrothed. You cannot do this to our family. With that man!"

Ann looked at her mother. How to counter this? "Mother, you are right. I am getting older. I do want to get married. There are not many boys in this town that have as good prospects as Mr. Buchanan, and none that are appealing to me. He comes from humble roots, but so did father. He works hard and has made it on his own. He's already been to the Assembly, and has a very good income as a lawyer."

Mother stared at daughter.

Ann continued, "Mother, if I promise not to go into any more taverns, or dance in public, might he—might I— have another chance?"

It was the mother's turn to consider. What Ann said was true. She had not shown any spark toward any others eligible in town, and there were not many unmarried and older who could by any stretch be considered suitable anymore. Perhaps she should give the Buchanan boy another chance. He had kept his nose clean, as far as she knew, since those curious events five years ago. He had not even bothered Ann or any of the family since that night. He was with her husband's political party, and did show signs of getting ahead. Ann might be headstrong and rebellious at times, but underneath she was gentle, even shy, always sensitive, and usually sensible.

"All right, Ann," she relented a bit, "if you promise not to do those things, and not sneak about again, and let me assess this young man myself, you can see him some more."

Ann smiled, more to herself than to her mother. As appealing as impropriety might be to break from her sheltered upbringing, and maybe get her father's attention, she also realized her desire for her parents' approval was far stronger than any rebellious inclinations she harbored. Besides, it would test Jamie a bit.

When her suitor called that afternoon, she explained that they were "found out" and that her mother insisted that there be no more of such activities, and that Jimmy needed to be mindful of appealing to her. Jimmy did know they were keeping anything secret and, as far as getting Mrs. Coleman to like him, that is the very aspect where he shone. "That is of course agreeable. I am sorry to have caused you any problems and I am delighted to come to know your mother better." He certainly did not want to cause any misstep on the march to the altar.

Seeing how far he had already proceeded with Ann, he realized that the best way to defeat his prior pact with Ann's father would be to induce an engagement before Robert's return. It was far harder to backtrack, Jimmy reasoned, after a betrothal was public knowledge.

He therefore conducted his courtship with Ann by the book, but sought to beat the uncertain deadline. He had a particular object in mind, and Ann was certainly the key. He called on Ann at least twice each week, and they visited in the parlor under the intermittent, but always watchful, eye of Mrs. Coleman. The mother occasionally clucked her disapproval, but relented as she continued to see how much her daughter desired this relationship. In any event, it was high time for Ann to be married off. The couple went to the theater with Mrs. Coleman or, alone, to well chaperoned church socials at St. James Episcopal, with either Pompey or Little Dick driving.

Ann and Jimmy always took one of Mr. Coleman's carriages, as they had since that first night. They snuggled under a pile of rare buffalo robes, traded in Pittsburgh by some visiting Shawnees and received by the Widow Moore in exchange for several pieces of Chinese porcelain. Ann thought she should be thinking how much she appreciated that Jamie, unlike some others in the past, was keeping his hands to himself under the covers. Though Mother never discussed it, she knew that many new marriages seemed to spawn children before nine months passed. She certainly did not want that! Yet Ann felt herself wishing that the good night kissing that commenced as September ended might spark a little more of a response in the man she was intending to marry. Whenever she sought to linger on Jamie's lips, he would pull them away a little too abruptly. She could hardly tell the man she wanted to be kissed more and longer. Surely, she was giving him enough hints.

Jimmy went on and on the next night. "That Ann, she is certainly in hot pursuit of me. If I were to tell you what that little puss and I did last evening…." He looked around at the faces beaming at him around the full table in the rear of the Widow, "Why, of course, honor forbids it!" "Well, you know what Magellan did around the world? Just imagine a cotton sea…." Everyone roared, and Jimmy beamed.

As they watched him carve a Virginia fence in the sleet on King Street later that night, Robert Grier said to Amos Ellmaker, "That Jimmy can sure knock them back. I certainly have to admit, that Coleman girl was not as obliging with me." Amos nodded in agreement.

Ann's thoughts flew to her cultivated image of a grand wedding at St. James ("My patron saint, may he bless our union!" Jamie had teased) and the reception at the corner of King and Christian, complete with the new concept of bridesmaids and groomsmen. Although she remembered what George Lafayette had said about ocean voyages, and had some concern about the wedding tour to Europe she was certain Father would provide despite his earlier broken promise to let her go abroad, all else was sailing smoothly. If only Jamie would propose!

"Jamie, Father should be back in the country in the next few days," Ann reported that evening. "His last letter said his ship was set to leave London in late August." Her beau grew silent, as if considering something quite complicated.

On the first Saturday in October, she and Jamie set out on a carriage ride with Little Dick at the reins. It was icy and the streets were slick, but there was the clean smell of autumn in the air, a sea of leaves blowing about the carriage as the fallen remnants of summer were parted by the coach's wheels. They headed to the play in the cool blue of the evening. Jamie strayed to the top of her crinoline-covered thigh. She reached to remove his hand and he clung to hers, and held it all the way to the theater. Ann looked sharply at him, but Jamie stared straight ahead.

On the way home, flakes from an early snow made a chiaroscuro of the harvest moon. They moved from Manor to Water to King. The streets were beginning to go to white. Jamie gallantly pulled her closer. Alighting from the carriage, with a superfluous instruction to Dick to take the Coleman carriage to the back and secure it, Jamie asked if he might come into the parlor. "Why, yes, of course."

They entered the house as the snow grew heavier. Jimmy nearly slipped, and Ann grabbed his arm.

Jimmy brushed the snow off his dark woolen topcoat and set it carefully down on a red and gold lacquered oriental box to the side of the door. He turned to Ann, "Sit down, my dearest."

Ann sat primly on the long yellow settee that graced the wall under the parlor's front windows. He went to her, and kneeled. Ann's eyes widened. Jamie put his hand to his front watch pocket and began to fiddle with a small black box that he had placed there earlier that day. He embarked on an explanation of the history of engagement rings, invoking the names of popes, Mary of Burgundy, and assorted other facts he had learned that day in the Free Library. Ann smiled but had to work to hide the annoyance. "Jamie, please!"

His head shook like a spaniel emerging from a stream as his prattle was interrupted. He reached in his vest and fished out the box. Cupping it in his soft white hand, he extended the simple gold band engraved, in French script, "A.C." Ann lent the ring finger of her ready hand.

She gave him a big hug and a huge kiss. This time, Jimmy did not pull away. He smiled with satisfaction. They were engaged. The ironmaster's daughter would marry him. He vowed not to let Robert derail him this time.

Ann told her mother in the morning and secured her still-reluctant blessing. She was not prepared for the vehemence of her father's reaction when he returned the next week from Mayfair and Knightsbridge. "Father," she cajoled, "I know he is not from our circle, but he has a grand future. Wait until he is part of our family, and has your help! You weren't wealthy when you married mother, and if her father had not owned that business…"

Her father's look summarily staunched that line of argument. Robert suppressed the desire to parry the point. He thought he had taken care of this with that young Buchanan, but would finish the job now.

That night, Ann remembered the tale of Emma, and the unjustified opposition to her union with Ferdino, the brokenness of the mother and the ultimate hopelessness of the father. Was her daddy going to be like this? Why was he so upset about the man she loved? What did Father think, she silently scoffed as she fell asleep, that he was going to ship me off to some island?

The next morning, Ann announced to her father's astonishment and her mother's chagrin that she would simply move to Philadelphia and never come back if he did not approve. "See if you can stop me!" Ann exclaimed. She argued, "Jamie makes a fine salary! He has been to the Assembly!" Even, "He is a good Federalist!" Surely, she circled back, he can do yet better when he is part of the Coleman family.

Robert could not wait to get out of the house that morning.

The 71-year-old patriarch appeared again at the law office across the way, this time weary from his months in Europe and his complicated efforts to save his empire. He found, too, a much different man from the tyronic lawyer he stood down five years earlier. Buchanan, Esq., was ready for him.

A well-tailored figure came to the office door and greeted, "Good morning, Mr. Coleman. I expected you."

Mr. Coleman took in the rows of numbered books and the mahogany Jefferson cases. A pair of pens rose from a black and white striated marble holder. A silver inkwell sat in front of the pens. Both holder and inkwell rested to the right of a leather writing pad that protected the well burnished oak. Aside from these writing tools, the desk was bare and clean. A small table to the side held three neat short stacks of paper. No clothes on the floor and not a bottle to be seen.

Before Robert could say anything, "Sir, out of deepest respect, of course, and before you commence…"

Robert could stand it no longer, "Mr. Buchanan, we had a bargain. I am sure you recall?"

"I abided by it! I went to the Assembly and stayed away from you and your whole family."

"You are now on your way forward, are you not? Much business was sent your way and yet you have pursued my daughter."

"Sir, I acknowledged your assistance. You simply asked that I stay away. It was, in fact, Ann who has pursued me, and not I her."

Robert's eyes narrowed. As he looked at Jimmy, his own head tilted a bit to the side. His lips tightly drew downwards, but his eyes stayed sharp amid his wrinkling skin.

Jimmy continued, "It was wholly by accident, sir, that we met again. Outside my business and lodgings. Our two hearts simply found each other."

Now it was Robert's turn to feel he was about to bequeath his breakfast and his eyes searched for a toilette.

Jimmy hurried on, "I am not the objectionable sort I may have been before. I know you are strong willed, some would even say vindictive, but do not be suspicious of me. I will be an estimable son-in-law!"

Robert considered his usual objections to those who sought to intrude into his wealth or trade on his social status. There was also an overhanging, potent question that had to be resolved.

"Mr. Buchanan, you know that I was the moving force behind your expulsion from Dickinson, do you not?

Jimmy nodded.

"You know that it was not solely for your exfluncticating, your carousing and your insolence?"

Jimmy, this time with a greater show of pain, again twitched his head affirmatively.

"My one last question, then sir, is whether that is who you are?"

Like a small mouth bass going after a crankbait, Jimmy swallowed the question he so long anticipated. "Why sir, of course not! Such conduct as you suggest is anathema to me now, as it was then. Although I was induced in that direction by that pastor, and he a Christian, I never went there. It was there that you all had it wrong. Such conduct was and is truly abhorrent to me!"

Robert stared, assessing. He did not trust this scalawag, but Ann wanted him, and she was getting older. Despite her rebellious display she had shown sound judgment in the past. He was aging in a way that was beginning to feel as if it were some horrible geometric progression of infirmity upon infirmity. He had stood in the way of his daughter and young Lüder and should not do so again.

"Understand, Buchanan, I do not like you, nor do I trust you. If any activity, any at all, reaches my ear of which I do not approve, this wedding is off. I will not hesitate to cut you and your law license to pieces."

"Yet I have your blessing?' asked Jimmy.

"No, sir, you do not, but you have my assent." And, he thought ruefully, a good shot at my assets.

With that, the proud ironmaster turned and walked on newly unsteady legs. It was only as Robert was out the Widow's door and crunching his way through the early fall snow that Jimmy let the smile cross his lips.

Robert told his daughter and wife that he would not block the union, and averted further drama over this issue at home. "Ann, you will keep this secret. I need to advise some people, here in Lancaster and over in Carlisle, and perhaps elsewhere, about this development."

Ann considered her father's directive. She did not trust his turnabout and immediately called on Patricia Hill and arranged a tea for that afternoon. "Patricia, will you invite Leticia and Rebekah?" Patricia agreed, and at four o'clock, the four met at the White Swan's tea room. Beck Ellis came alone but Leticia Hand arrived with Grace Hubley in tow. Leticia whispered a quick apology to Ann as Grace took off her cape, "She just wouldn't leave this morning. What could I do?"

The four of them sat down. Ann announced, "Jamie and I are to be married!" Congratulations from all, though Grace's seemed, to Ann, to be squeezed between her teeth. Ann calculated that she did hold Patricia and Rebekah very dear, but even they, and certainly Grace, would reveal her news as fast as their legs and lips would travel. It would not be long, she thought, before a series of loosely guarded "secret conversations" spread this news to all in their circle. Of course, it would percolate to her parents' friends. Jamie would be so proud of me for this tactic. Father cannot backtrack now.

Ann proceeded with a fury to finalize the wedding plans. She targeted the next June, when Lancaster weather finally headed toward summer, as the wedding date. Jamie would insist, she knew, not only on lemonade and tea, but whiskey and wine. She expected her father would agree, as she anticipated he might need a stiff drink, or several, to survive the ceremony. They would even have that new social custom at all the best weddings in Philadelphia, a white cake for all to have a small slice. She would wear a flowing lace dress, whiter than white, with a wreath of flowers over her brow. Although she scolded herself for the thought, *people will say it sets off my fair skin and pure black cascading hair.*

While Ann was preparing for the wedding, Mr. Coleman continued to struggle with the impact of the Panic on all aspects of his business. He remained particularly concerned about the potential loss of several of his iron works. The cadre of Federalist lawyers in Lancaster on whom he relied had not doctored his papers in a way sufficient to protect his holdings, and the waning influence of the Federalist Party on the national scene was further cause for concern.

Despite their antithetical politics, Robert therefore turned to the town of Gettysburg, and tapped a young lawyer with an already strong reputation for legal counsel.

Thaddeus Stevens had moved to Pennsylvania only four years earlier, in 1815, but was already known to be the attorney one relied upon for sound judgment, wise counsel and, if necessary, effective advocacy. His strong-willed reputation reached Robert early on, and the time had come for him to seek the Gettysburg Whig.

Not wishing to be seen, for practical, personal and political reasons, counseling with an out-of-town lawyer of another party, Coleman met with Stevens mostly in Gettysburg as they worked to resurrect his fortunes and reconstruct his domain. Their efforts were bearing fruit.

As autumn faded, he was confronted with a crisis. One of his lenders called the note on the Caledonia property, which he had placed under mortgage to bail out some of his other, now lamented, ventures into Lancaster real estate. He had to see Stevens immediately, this day if possible.

Robert sent a messenger on horseback to Gettysburg. The rider pulled up before noon as Thaddeus was ushering a client out the door. The messenger stared at the colored man, and handed the lawyer the short directive from Lancaster.

"Mr. Stevens, come now, and quickly!" His large brow furrowed, and he ran his fingers through a tangle of red hair. Damn that Coleman, he thought, thinking I will jump like one of his toadies. Still, he was a good client, and the work was interesting. Of course, he paid well. Thaddeus lifted his long thick wrestler's body on top of Cobbler, and headed over the river.

The lawyer arrived at half past two, just as Robert was finishing his mid-day meal. Ushered into Robert's study, the two men worked through the balance of the afternoon and were able to refashion, at least on paper but in a way the lender could not resist, his financing and solve the immediate issue. They discussed the approach to take in the next General Assembly session to ensure ongoing tax benefits for Mr. Coleman's iron works.

The evening was unusually warm for December, and Ann was rocking on her backyard swing, Jamie having departed, when a dark presence emerged from the canopy of the house and marched into the approaching evening. The figure moved to retrieve the horse hitched out back by Little Dick and nearly missed her and would have, but for the floral scent trailing through the air. Ann called to him with a smile.

"Why hello, sir. It is a clear and quite comfortable evening, is it not?"

He searched for the speaker and saw a lissome girl suspended by rope and wood from a large chestnut tree, swaying slowly back and forth as twilight gathered. "Why yes, it is," adding, "Quite unusual for December," wishing immediately he had not said something so obvious.

Smiling again, "I am Ann Coleman. Who are you?"

"Thaddeus Stevens. From Gettysburg."

"You were here to see my father?"

"Yes."

"You must be the lawyer."

Thad nodded.

"Father has had some troubles lately. I know he is grateful for your help."

"That is what I do," Thad declared, adding, "It is a pleasure to work for him."

A little smile again creased Ann's lips. She started to say something, but withdrew it.

"Well, I must be back to Gettysburg. It's getting dark."

"Mr. Stevens, I do have a favor to ask you. Before you go. If it's not too much trouble."

"Of course, if I can."

"If I should ever need legal counsel, would you be my lawyer?"

Now it was Thad's turn to smile. Women did not have business relationships, and he could not imagine where this question came from. "Miss Coleman, I do not think you are the sort to get into trouble."

"Mr. Stevens, one never knows," yet again with lips parted, although this time more tightly than before.

"Well, Miss Coleman, of course I would be pleased to do so," with all the easy gallantry he could muster at what seemed an absurd proposition. What kind of mischief could this girl ever create? She was scarcely the criminal type, all tumbling curls and petticoats splayed in the evening air. Perhaps some had found her…

He decided to take her more seriously. "Any trouble at this time?"

"No, sir. I am, if nothing else, prudent." She pressed a York shilling into his large, rough palm.

"That makes you my lawyer, Mr. Stevens, doesn't it?" Ann asked, "If I should ever need your judgment or to tell you something in confidence, you would honor that request?"

He wondered again if this was simply a schoolgirl's jest, but her question seemed heartfelt.

Thaddeus nodded as he searched her eyes, "I will be your lawyer, though I cannot imagine that you should ever require my services. I am, however, honored."

He took his leave, vowing to look after this fragile, bright, and quite beautiful young girl if the need ever were to arise. Ann watched as Thaddeus moved his lapidary body toward his horse, only then noticing how his foot dragged behind him. How painful that must be! She realized that this made him, in some odd fashion she did not understand, even more absurdly captivating as she watched him ride swiftly off into the vanishing light.

Chapter Five
D E A T H

Jimmy Buchanan sat in his office above the Widow, his feet propped on his large oak desk, his hands clasped and resting on his soft belly. Work could wait.

He looked at the prints on the wall. Pictures of little girls on horses being led by darkies into forested glades. Reproductions of English barnyards and Cotswold cottages. The verdant majesty of the Tuscarora Mountain deeply cut by scattered brooks and rills as they initiated their winding way into the Susquehanna. His diploma from Dickinson (which should, as he thought each time he saw it, be with honors) and certificate of admission into the Pennsylvania bar. The satisfied lawyer smiled into the mirror across the room as he looked forward to a positively Cartesian vortex of streaming clients and circling parties, and of course the opportunity to preside over a wife and family, sipping Sherry and smoking cigars.

Unaware, between tradesmen, housewives, members of the bar, and up and down King Street, of the words "fortune hunter" and harsher offerings rippling through the Lancaster air, Jimmy wrote his mother, *With the Coleman family fortune sailing in a better direction and me along for the ride, my future is just as bright as it could be.*

In nearby Columbia, on the river's bank, bonds issued for the Columbia Bridge Works had failed, threatening local speculators with the total loss of their investments. Allegations of fraud were, in turn, leveled against the issuing banks, clients bequeathed to Jimmy by his future father-in-law.

Jimmy thought he would be able to wrap up matters relating to the bonds in a day, or perhaps with an overnight stay in the small community. Winter dragged bitterly across eastern Pennsylvania as he left town the morning of Friday December 3rd. A few rolls of rusting wheels outside of town, Jimmy realized he had forgotten to let Ann know that he was going to be gone. Briefly, he considered sending word, then decided against it. Let her miss me a bit. It will be good for her.

The coach pulled up to the small law office near the courthouse in the river town of Columbia. There is no way, Jimmy thought, he needed to let this one go to trial. He had made sufficient fees off of it, and trial can only mean more work, and perhaps a bad result. Jonathan Gilliam, the local lawyer, seemed quite willing to broker his clients' interests.

Jimmy patted the soft leather briefcase holding the document that disposed of the case quite favorably. This should surely suffice, with no word changes or paragraph warping needed. Jimmy acknowledged to himself that he had not spent as much time on the documents as perhaps he should have, but dismissed the thought. Anything unresolved by errors planted by his own draftsmanship would not stop the deal from being put to bed. He could ignore the seeds of self-destruction planted in the documentation; they will simply mean more legal fees when they sprout some later day.

When he showed up at Gilliam's office, Jimmy saw a new face in the chair beside his adversary's desk. Gilliam presented the lawyer, "Mr. Buchanan, may I introduce Andrew Noel?"

Jimmy remembered the companion from his first visit to Lancaster. Reaching out his hand, "Why Andy, I had not known you were a lawyer. Where did you study?"

"In Philadelphia. At the university."

Nothing to worry about there, thought Jimmy, as he reflected on the small school that claimed to be founded by Benjamin Franklin, housed in the residence in which President Adams declined to live. Jimmy had been there, and was unimpressed.

"After four years' study, I clerked with Roger Taney."

A cool stare coupled those words. Jimmy's handshake went limp. Taney was well known as an acerbic, and superb, trial lawyer right across the Maryland border. Anyone he had selected would share those characteristics.

"Well, then, you do not practice here?" Jimmy asked hopefully.

"That is true," Noel responded, "but I will spend whatever time is necessary in Columbia if this matter is not resolved."

Quickly, "Oh, but that is why I am here. I have taken the liberty of drafting a possible settlement document. Of course," addressing Noel only, "if you think anything else is necessary on behalf of Mr. Gilliam's clients, I am sure that can be accommodated."

"Thank you. I expected that might be the case. By the way," Noel continued, "congratulations on your putative entry into the ironmaster's circle."

Jimmy's hesitant nod was meant to hide his concern at this odd phrasing. Noel must know a good deal of his reputation. Gilliam, rooted in the torpid community of Columbia, had up to this point been quite intimidated by the lawyer from Lancaster, and should have been more so now. While Jimmy was pleased he had not had to bring his victorious engagement to their attention, he thought, with a rueful grin at his own imagery, this Noel might not so easily snow.

That night, Jimmy headed for the Hung, Drawn and Quartered on the Susquehanna banks. He sat alone, his hands caressing the Monongahela, staring at the heavy uncaring water and the more-than-a-mile-long new covered bridge to Wrightsville, his back to the door. There was little more that could be done at this point. He had to wait for Noel's redraft and try to sell it to his clients, a consortium of Lancaster and Chester banks. No point in getting together with anyone tonight. No bankers lived in this backwater.

By their dress, Jimmy estimated that the tavern was full mostly of shopkeepers and clerks, although three quite rough sorts, appearing to Jimmy to be about his own age, sat at a table several feet away. Jimmy unconsciously edged a bit more towards the tavern wall. He wondered, "Where does Columbia's elite congregate?"

While he was considering the light of the day's events through the prism of his whiskey glass, the words "Ann Coleman" and "lawyer" drifted in his direction. Jimmy's back stiffened and his chin rose. His head inclined toward the speakers, and he realized the words came from the trio he noticed as he sat down. His lower lip drew back and tightened, and he moved to a chair across his table in an effort to hear further. Had word of his engagement to Ann reached even to these lower levels at the very edge of Lancaster County, and perhaps beyond? Maybe even to his classmates from the Old Stone Academy and certainly Dickinson? What did Joseph Ryan think of me now? Joseph who now was a minister in some Virginia outpost. And those Germans, Hab Geheim and all the rest? Cobblers, wheelwrights or innkeepers all. Jimmy smirked, anticipating their reaction to the news.

Despite straining, he did not catch anything further about himself. Perhaps he had misheard. Could there be another lawyer linked in some fashion to Ann?

As he was calculating whether it would do to approach the possible speakers and confirm their conversation, they tumbled off their chairs and then righted themselves. One after another, each extended heavily muscled arms. As if responding to an unheard cue, six hands rotated ninety degrees, perpendicular to the wide pine slats. In anticipation of the effort it would take to navigate between the scattered tables and chairs pushed at odd angles, they began swinging in unison, rocking back and forth like great stones on a double-armed catapult. First one, then another, and then the last flung itself toward the tavern door. Thrusting their trunks ahead and stretching their arms and hands as far as they could, each raised what was left of its body. Two had mismatched short stumps extending a few inches, perhaps three inches on the left leg and five on the right, as if they had been strapped together on the same hand-pulled conveyor and sliced in unison by a whirling saw. Everything below the other's waistline had preceded it into the hereafter. Each again rolled forward and again extended its arms, rhythmically repeating the motion. Where the bodies landed, blood pooled and a soiled dressing worked its way off one of the wounds. It lay, yellow and black and red, on the tavern floor. The sounds of the clumping bodies thudding against the pine reverberated through the tavern as if giant forged iron cannonballs were descending through the roof. Everyone turned to watch. Some pulled their chairs in to help clear a path. Jimmy simply, but briefly, felt sick and then a bit deceived that he had not been able to overhear them. Must have lost their limbs in the last war, Jimmy thought, and turned back to his drink as the legless creatures went out into the night.

Jimmy showed up mid-morning Saturday at Gilliam's office. Noel was there. Jimmy had held a faint hope that he would be able to parlay his newly-acquired distinction into yet further concessions. By the terms proposed, that was clearly not the case. "That is our best offer, Buchanan. Accept it or we go to trial."

Jimmy made a great show of reviewing the document. The best he could do was point out one misspelling and pitch an argument on another word's orthography. "Let me sleep on it, and of course I will need my clients' consent."

"Of course, Buchanan, go ahead. Be back by nine Monday morning."

Jimmy's stomach was cartwheeling by the time he reached the Columbia Inn. No chance of going home tonight, so off to the tavern. The crowd is quite a bit more respectable tonight, Jimmy thought, as he dug into the Old Orchard. At least no one to offend the sensibilities.

"You remind me of my college days, my lubricious friend," he addressed the bottle. Yes, those were the days, Grier and Slaymaker and I, picking, as it were, apples off the tree. He wandered to his room. Despite punishing the bottle entirely, sleep would not come. Thought after thought. How would he sell this to his clients and get it behind him? How did he get in these scrapes? He lay awake and watched midnight come and go. He should have gone into banking. How can this be postured? By one o'clock, his stomach was churning. By two, the parade started.

Jimmy snuck his bedpan out himself in the early morning hours to avoid the embarrassment of revealing the floating bits and orts of several meals to the chambermaid. His hands trembled as he carried it behind the inn toward the Susquehanna and its contents shimmied and slopped over, soiling his hands. Sunday was scarcely better as he lay in bed, eating salted crackers and drinking pitcher upon pitcher of water.

When he appeared right on the mark of nine on Monday, Jimmy's face looked like the remnants of burnt paper. "My clients, after considerable deliberation and careful thought as to the costs of continued litigation and of course what is fair to all concerned, have agreed to your proposal. I appreciate, Andy, your counsel in achieving this resolution. Please give Mr. Taney my deepest personal regards."

Jimmy knew he would have to spend the rest of the day getting signatures from his own clients, justifying to some why he had given in on particular points, and touting to others the victory those same word changes meant for them.

Meanwhile, despite feeling a bit abandoned, Ann was enmeshed in wedding preparations. She had decided to move the date up, perhaps as early as the fourteenth of February, if Jamie approved. Would not that be romantic, on the Saint Valentine's day? All her friends now knew, and her father seemed at least begrudgingly at peace with her choice. There were invitations to be designed, decisions on food to serve, a dress to be chosen….Ann thought to herself if she had known that this was so much fun, she would have done it earlier!

"Mother, do you think George Lafayette will come if we give him sufficient notice? Where did Nelly Lewis and her husband live now? Still at Mount Vernon? Would it be permissible to invite Ruth Bauschulte?"

Jimmy hurried back to Lancaster the afternoon of December 6th as snow began to fall. Although he meant at some point to let Ann know of his return, and particularly to share what he was positioning as his professional triumph, first things first. He went by a client's nearby house for the final signature and then to his office at the Widow. On the way, only the occasional ragged weed poked through the clumping snow. Jimmy carefully positioned the settlement papers in the rows of documents in his iron safe, closed its heavy door, and poured an early afternoon Sherry. Nothing, he thought, can stop me now.

Ann had complained to Patricia, in confidence, after services on Sunday when her intended failed to come by the house as usual the preceding evening, "Jamie must have left town. No word and I have no idea where he might be. Why would he do this?"

Patricia agreed she also had no idea, and soon several others declared they shared that same lack of insight. It did not take long for the news of Jimmy's unexplained absence to race over to Grace Hubley.

On Monday, Grace could not wait to let Ann know who had stopped by her sister's house that morning. She hurried over to the Coleman house as soon as Jimmy obtained the needed signature from her brother-in-law Frank Graap.

"Jimmy certainly was feeling quite triumphant today. He was so handsome as he came by Jenny's house. He shared with me that he was headed to his office. I of course did not tell him you were missing him. I hope I did the right thing. Surely, he has come to call?"

Ann muttered something and said, "I am sure he will. He has much on his mind, and I am certain that he has business to attend to." Why hadn't he told her he was going, and where he went, at least sent some messenger? Now to be in town and not even a word. It had been more than three days!

Afternoon faded to evening and she was growing impatient. He is right across the street. One would think he could prance over here. If he had time to stop by Jenny Graap's house…

Ann tried to rally from her sense of betrayal. He must have to get some paper work done this evening and will surely call me in the morning. Besides, she should of course forgive him. He is, quite appropriately, putting his job first. There will be plenty of time for closeness and long evenings at home with their children at their sides, Jamie smoking a pipe and sipping Madeira. She would learn some crafts like other girls and sit comfortably with him, sewing or knitting— maybe even try some broomstick lace.

She recalled Jamie's tales of his mother reading Milton and Cowper and others when he was but a baby. Ann resolved to read to him the same way, except she would introduce him to the poets she and her friends sometimes read together, by candlelight, filled with dreams of intense emotions and forbidden conduct. Maybe that new Lord Byron, dreamily handsome despite his club foot, who was all the rage in England and Greece! She would make Jamie's tea, and bring it to him. Scarlet rose as she thought of whispered conversations and anticipated intimacy. How dear and sweet to grow old in each others' arms.

While these pictures of her impending domestic bliss stationed themselves in her mind in no particular order, a thought suddenly came to Ann. "Mother, I am going to go over and surprise Jamie while he works, spend a little time with him."

Mrs. Coleman's response was predictable, "I do not think it is right to disturb him at his work. Besides, how will it look to others that you are calling on him, particularly at this evening hour?"

Ann considered that, and affirmed her own opinion that it was very close-minded of people to hold it against her that she would go see her betrothed, "Besides, it is not late, just eight, and I will return by ten. It's right across the street."

Mrs. Coleman relented. "All right, Ann, but I must be early to bed this evening."

Within minutes, through gathering flurries, the white-caped figure tested the ice-splotched mud, crossing slickening King Street in tiny ginger steps. Ann looked in on those drinking in the Widow Dutchman and was relieved Jamie was not dancing on top of some table. Slowly and softly, she stole up the flight of stairs to her soon-to-be husband's office, the sounds of her small patent leather boots certainly obscured by the raucous revelry below. How could, an idle thought intruded, Jamie work with all that noise?

Pausing at the door, her little gloved hand pondered whether to knock or to come upon her true one more completely. She imagined him hard at work at his desk, his head tilted over some musty old law book, his one short-sighted eye reading those "whereases" and "begats" or whatever those words were. There would be a sheaf of notes in his neat little hand piling high on his desk, his writing implement confidently gripped with a full palm while his other fingers spread against his forehead in thought, his brow furrowing as he pondered a point of precedent. She decided she would really surprise him, walk right in, fling her arms about his starched neck and give him a real kiss, full on those thin little lips.

Ann reached for the brass knob. Turned it. Gently eased the door open. Just like her father's library. Darn that brass chain. She peered through the crack between door and frame. For a suspended moment, she was transfixed.

Horror carved her face. Her stomach gave up its contents, and Ann guttered down the stairs on her own vomit, sliding and slipping past the sounds rushing from the Widow. She banged into the threshold as she spewed into the street. It felt as if her insides were torn from her. She fled down King, unaware of time and space, not knowing whether she was running or tumbling, not caring how she looked, not caring where she went. Left on whatever, right on whatever, plunging on and on and on, reeling blindly. Horses neighed darkly. Carriages clattered by unconcerned. Ann did not know whether she was screaming or stone quiet.

The candles in the shops that she visited with her father on that Christmas Eve so long ago lit her way, but she paid no heed as she scudded past the Widow Moore's with its treasures from the Orient, DeMuth's tobacco shop, Gundaker's stables. Shops, saddleries and smiths; coopers and cobblers; all unseen.

At last, Ann simply sat down in the middle of Water Street. Mud seeped across her fine new frock. Blood sluiced through at the knee, and she felt the scraping burns on her hands from what must have been a million falls. Something red ran down the back of her bonnet. Her tiny boots were torn and a little toe peered crookedly out one side. Tears began to flow onto her starched collar, simply ruining it she thought.

What to do? She could never ever see that man again. What of her family and friends? She could not stay in Lancaster now. She simply had to leave. Go to New York, take in boarders. Work somehow. Do something in some big city. Go to Europe. China. Make porcelain. Walk the streets. What can I do? Where can I go? Why, Philadelphia.

Her sister would take her in. She would take care of her. She had a house, a husband.

It must have been midnight when Ann carefully opened the door to her parents' house. Mother must be so worried, but no one was about. Had he come over here? Had he seen her? If so, what lie did he tell her parents? Silence was her only answer. Mother must have gone to bed, and was Father still out? She crept up another set of stairs and carefully pulled on the door to Sarah's room, aside from Ann the only child still at home. Softly stroking her sister's cheek, "We're going to Philadelphia. We are going to see Margaret!"

"When?"

"Why, tonight. Right now. It will be a surprise. We are going to surprise Margaret. Mommy and Father already know. I wanted to surprise you as well!"

Sarah, her mind still addled by the torpor of sleep, nodded groggily.

Ann watched blankly as Sarah stumbled about quietly and packed a few things. Let's hope, Ann thought, she doesn't fully wake and start asking questions. It must seem more than passing strange to her younger sister, but she was confident that her assurances that Mother knew and Sarah's implicit trust would overcome these doubts.

The sisters slipped out the back steps into the crusted snow. The swing had long ago surrendered to the winter wind and was banging against the oak tree. The sisters entered the open stables. Little Dick's ancient black head lay hard against the straw as he softly snored. Ann, shuddering herself, gently shook him. His eyes widened. "Dick, we need to take the phaeton to Philadelphia."

"Is you sure," he started, but if Mistress Ann said they "needed" to go it was not his place to cross question any member of his master's family, and certainly not Ann, not anymore.

Little Dick hitched the horses. Deeply concerned, "Do you want I should go wid you Miss Ann?"

"No, Dick, I can do this myself."

Dick sought to point out the obvious. How dark it was, how dangerous it was, how silly it all was, but stopped himself. Sarah stepped into the carriage and formed a pillow and makeshift bed out of the buffalo robes strewn across the seat. Ann boldly hopped behind the horses and took the reins. The night's snow fell hard and fast. It would soon cover everything. She had never driven this phaeton in earnest, and certainly not in night's gloom, but pulled sharply onto King and headed for the Philadelphia road on their way to the Athens of America. Ann was grateful that it was tarmacadam and grateful that it was only two days short of a full moon. They dodged the stumps that lined the roadway, raced through the unmanned turnpikes, and sped past mile after mile of tavern upon tavern. Even as the raw air whipped her face, Ann thanked God for the benediction of the light through December's bare trees that never seemed so necessary as tonight.

It was almost morning as they came upon the Schuylkill, and the sun was rising on the snowy steps as Ann pulled up to the mansion on Chestnut Street near the river. Sarah had slept the whole way on the carriage seat, Ann realized, as her little sister rubbed the night's second set of sand out of her eyes and trailed behind her on the stairs.

Ann knocked tentatively, then passionately, on the heavy door. Her sister's housekeeper Samantha, still bundled in what looked to be her bedclothes, cracked the door, peered dubiously out, and hushed them through. She was startled, and more than a little mystified, to see the younger Coleman sisters, but continued to shoo them forward.

Margaret Hemphill was roused from her slumber. "Ann, what in heaven's name are you doing here? Why did not you write? Look at you!"

"We have simply come for a visit. We wanted to surprise you, to spend time with Joseph and you while I am still your little sister."

Ann did not even focus on the fact that the anguish, and the all-night drive, left her wild looking, but Margaret certainly did. She hustled her little sister to the spare room and watched as Ann, still clothed, tumbled onto the bed as if she had breathed her last. Margaret did not fail to note the scraped palms, the blood crusting on her frock and bonnet and the mass of a dried substance that looked like nothing other than vomit.

Margaret grilled Sarah. "Why are you here?"

"To see you."

"When did you decide to come?"

"Last night."

Importantly, "Do Mother and Father know?"

"Ann says they do."

Sarah spilled all she knew which, Margaret thought, was precious little. Before her husband awoke, the older sister hurriedly wrote a note and dispatched it to Lancaster by messenger. She would, she figured, sort it out later, but it was not at all like her parents not to know where their daughters were!

She changed her sister into bedclothes and attended to her scrapes, which were not as bad as she feared. Ann did not awake as she did so, nor as Joseph rather noisily questioned why her two sisters had shown up unannounced. Joseph bit the words off at Margaret as he left for Third Street on the other side of town, "I do not for a moment credit your sister's story. You need to get to the bottom of this dramatic little secret she is playing." Margaret assured him she would.

A little after noon, Sarah, compelled by sibling dictum to "at least try to sleep" came down and convinced Margaret that it was useless, and said that, since they were there, she surely wanted to go shopping, go see the Independence Hall, go to the theater, go looking around, or at least go somewhere. Margaret told her it was best to let Ann sleep. She promised Sarah, if she could get Joseph to agree, that they would get an additional ticket to the Philadelphia Theater the next evening. It was not going to be one play, but two, and a comic opera besides. First, the "Grecian Daughter." Then, the "Ode on the Passions." Finally, the funny highlight of the evening, "Adopted Child." In the meantime, Sarah would simply have to content herself with staying at home.

Ann screamed at about five o'clock. She screamed again minutes later. Margaret ran upstairs. Her sister had fallen back into some half dream state, and was clearly wrestling in her sleep. Margaret sent a boy to get Dr. Nathaniel Chapman, who arrived within minutes with his colleague, a Dr. P. S. Physick.

Margaret explained the situation, and Ann was stirred from images she did not understand. Her aching eyes took in the room.

She wept.

Drs. Chapman and Physick consulted, and Chapman pulled some laudanum from his bag. He gave an ounce to Ann to drink. She did as instructed, and soon quieted. The good doctors left six more ounces, with careful instructions not to administer more than an ounce a day, in tea, until Ann's sound mind returned and none at all if Ann seemed otherwise fine after a day or two.

"She is overwrought," Dr. Chapman advised in his well practiced bedside manner, "She will soon be fine, I am sure. It was only a bit of hysterics. There's a good deal of that going around in Philadelphia, and I am sure your sister got caught up in the spirit."

Joseph came home shortly after, early from his junior post at the bank his father-in-law's rival, Stephen Girard, parlayed to great wealth and prominence. "Did you find out what her situation really is?"

"I tried, but Sarah seems not to know much, and Ann has not said much. At least she is sleeping soundly."

The day passed and Ann lay in bed, stirring fitfully, but crying less often. Dr. Chapman came by again Wednesday morning, satisfied that the hysterics were abating, and prescribed some more laudanum. "Mrs. Hemphill, in our undertakings at the Medical School and our practices, there has not yet been one young woman in our care who has perished from hysterics. Ann will be fine. She simply needs time and rest." That afternoon, Ann even ventured to get out of bed and take some air down Chestnut, walking all the way to Broad. She thought she saw some familiar faces, but could not be sure.

Although she had unaccountably not heard back from her parents, Margaret's immediate anxiety for Ann was resolved. She was safe with her big sister! Sarah was so eager to go to the plays.

Despite their efforts to be quiet as they set to go to the theater, Ann awoke at the sound of the back door opening. She called out and Margaret went to comfort her.

"Will you be fine here, Ann?"

"Yes. I just wanted to be certain to say good-bye. Can you ask Sarah to come up before you go?"

"We are running late, Ann. I will be sure to have her stop in when we return."

"But," Ann started. The sentence lay unfinished, dissolving into a crooked little smile, an odd twisting of her lips that Margaret had never seen before.

Margaret fluffed her pillow and made her goodbye. Ann's fine. She should not disappoint Sarah. Besides, Ann is grown now, even if she was acting peculiarly, and certainly seems better. We'll be close by and, if the evening is not as amusing as they hoped, they would of course come home early. What could be more caring than to leave the house quiet for her?

All the way to the theater, Ann's peculiar smile itched at Margaret's conscience.

Ann made certain that all were well departed. Thank goodness, her sister's husband could not afford evening help. The laudanum had had little effect, she thought, and her mind was resolute. She carefully wrote a letter and went to her sister's stables and spied the horse with the little white star in the middle of his forehead, sent by her parents to Margaret to spend his final days.

Ann did not bother to saddle Devil, but simply leapt atop him, her legs dangling over his massive side, her torn white cloak draped about her as she headed into the evening's quickening swirl of snow.

She rode down Chestnut and found a postal office and dispatched her brief epistle to the lawyer from Gettysburg she had met as evening fell in the backyard of the house, in the town, in the world, as she had always imagined it would be. Ann turned down 20th, searched the Ionic cul de sac, and crossed Sansom. On Moravian, she found the answer she had begun to conceive while she sat in the mud and blood of Water Street.

Ann rode Devil to the open apothecary, alit, and boldly pushed the store door open.

"What would ye be needing, ma'am, this fine night?" Ebenezer Franklin inquired.

"Sir, my mother has taken to hysterics, and has a bad toothache besides. There is no doctor to be had. She has had this before and there is only one thing that works, and that I need."

"What would that be?" asked the middle-aged man whose father's long fame shadowed his illegitimate son.

"Why laudanum, of course."

"Of course," the pharmacist agreed as his eyes went to hers, "but ye be careful not too much."

Ann nodded, but pleaded, "Could I have enough if it happens again? It seems to take a full week's worth to do any good, and there is the bad tooth, and I would hate to have to come again on these cold nights to get more."

Ebenezer poured a full sixteen ounces, "Only in case it takes eight days this time to get your mother back to herself."

Ann thanked the druggist, and slipped back out the door. She made sure Devil was secured to the post, and watched as the animal clawed at the ground.

The Metropole Hotel? No, that is not proper. Better in the open air. Ann found her way on foot to the Southwest Square.

There, on a small hard bench, amid a few others huddled in the night, Ann smelled the sticky sweetness of alcohol and opium. She downed the pungent doses of laudanum she had spirited out of her sister's house, and the two full cups besides.

Reports reached Margaret and Joseph that a white-cloaked specter was last seen crashing through the Square's wooden fence. It was seen shrieking down Locust toward the river and floundering in the plague of burnt-out goldenrod and yews and tangled, piercing rubble along the Schuylkill's banks as Panama and Pine and finally South spit into nothingness. Others related that, hands cut and small black boots sodden with blood, a girl wandered slowly down the tattered bricks and cobblestones of Christian Street toward its intersection with Gray's Ferry Road.

At the end of Gray's Ferry, Ann lurched across the floating bridge once used for General Washington's triumphal entry to the nation's capital, her compromised surplice bearing rancid stains from the Schuylkill's banks as she fought and stumbled from crossbar to crossbar. Across the sky ripped the December geminids, hundreds of short arcs catching and losing light. Several people later allowed they would have sought to help but the young woman's crazed appearance and wild eyes made them think the better of it.

Ann's last thoughts, as she lay among competing fragrances of hibernating spices crushed under the winter snow, were of betrayal and lost love. Images of Lüder, the way his throat was slit, that terrifying December day in Virginia, her eighteenth birthday, her father's unfaithfulness, the horror she had witnessed the night before, floated in and out. At least, she had made certain, that last secret would not die with her. It was not until morning light that Ann was found, between an oleander and a mulberry, her head in a horse trough, ice beginning to crust about her neck, across the river in Bartram's Garden.

Chapter Six
<u>REACTION</u>

News of Ann's death reached Lancaster early Thursday afternoon, almost two days after the earlier messenger, who claimed to be a victim of highway robbers and held hostage at one of the Philadelphia road's many taverns, brought Margaret's letter advising Robert and her mother of their daughters' whereabouts and safety.

Turmoil in the Coleman house, allayed by Margaret's late-arriving epistle, roiled into a torrent of despair.

That same afternoon, Jimmy sat drinking Monongahela at a bescrawled table in the corner of the Widow. Where had Ann gone? He was beginning to get worried, and drifted back to her mother's Tuesday visit.

"Jamie, have you heard from our Ann?"

She was certainly not looking her best, Jimmy remembered thinking. "Why no, Mrs. Coleman, and I did expect to see her. I was too busy with affairs of law last evening, but had intended to stop by this afternoon."

"She said last night she was coming over to see you. I did not think it appropriate, but allowed her to do so."

"I can assure you, dear woman, that I did not see her at all, not once since I returned from my success in Columbia," said Jimmy, recalling how his mind raced over the activities of the night before.

He had been aware of Mrs. Coleman eying him as his face reddened, and imagined the thoughts going through her head, sensing the ongoing doubts about his probity and propriety clawing to the surface. Was she thinking he could somehow have something to do with her disappearance? She could see him right in front of her. He had not gone anywhere.

"I did not hear her return last night, and she now has gone. Further, little Sarah is nowhere to be found. No note. Nothing. One of our slaves, Little Dick, has vanished as well."

Mrs. Coleman had been crying. Jimmy put one soft arm around her shoulders, cocked his head and sought her eyes. "It will certainly be fine, I am sure. It is not like our Ann, but perhaps she is with some friends or relations. Are you certain there was no note?"

"Mr. Buchanan," she had repeated, "I looked all over but saw no note, no reason for her departure whatsoever."

"It must have been that slave."

Mrs. Coleman shook her head but thought, that was exactly the position Robert was taking. Why, after all these years with them, would Dick do that? Why both girls? It was all she could do to stop Robert from arming the militia and heading in all directions. Perhaps they should do that, but she did not want the news of her daughters' disappearance absolutely everywhere. Her husband had already alerted Constable Duesing and he was, discreetly to be sure, out looking for her. Even as she was meeting with this character, who had not even offered any active service in the search for her daughter, Robert was on his way to see Mayor Passmore, who should be able to find an idea of where to search someplace amid his hundreds of pounds. Certainly, that Falstaff owed Robert for his office. Anyway, Ann was a responsible girl, and there must be some reasonable explanation. Still, if no word was received this very day…

Jimmy sensed his explanations were falling unheard. "I can assure you I did not see her. I was alone all evening, working in my office. Of course, I will make inquiries and let you know what I discover."

If it was not to relatives they went, it must have been that slave.

Mrs. Coleman had made her way down the unaccountably sticky and foul smelling stairs outside his office. He was surprised at the stench in the hallway, surprised it had not invaded his room, and angry at whatever lowlife of a tradesman had come upon his stairs, retching and puking, the evening before.

Jimmy called out, "I am so sorry for the smell of this stairwell. I can assure you I will find who is responsible!"

Mrs. Coleman, who had almost slipped down the stairs on her descent, did not turn around as she went into the morning grayness, bits of spittle dotting her leather boots. As if, she thought as her eyes tightened and her breath came in short panting bursts, as if the smell in his tavern were as important as the disappearance of her daughter. What had Ann ever seen in him?

Jimmy was still slowly massaging his well used whiskey glass, recalling the conversation from two days earlier and working to overcome his developed distress, when the sight of Grace Hubley snapped him into the present. What could she want?

Grace sat down and, between tears, said, "Dear, dear boy. Have you heard the news about our poor Ann?"

Jimmy's eyes studied his fiancée's friend, "What, Grace, have you heard? I have been so deathly concerned," daubing his handkerchief into the corners of Grace's eyes, "I must say so much so that my anger has only been subsumed by my concern."

Grace looked earnestly into his blue and hazel eyes. "I fear what I have to tell you."

Jimmy set down his glass on the scarred table. Grace met his eyes. Pausing for effect, "Our dearest Ann has died."

"Oh, my God!"

Jimmy's head twitched and his eyebrows danced upward as his little mouth opened, questions tumbling, "How did this happen?" "Where did this happen?" "When did this happen?"

In response to each uttered inquiry, a silent rondo rising, "What does this mean for me? What does this mean for me? What does this mean for me?"

Soon the unspoken concern outdistanced all others. Everything had seemed so set for him, and now cruel Fate blocked his ascent. A hundred thoughts clawed at him. Grace encircled him. She stroked his top knotted little head as it rested against her breasts and told him all she knew, that Ann had gone to Philadelphia and had died suddenly, last night, and no one seemed to be quite sure how. He half-heard. Grace ended with the report that the funeral apparently was to be for family and those invited only, and not even she nor her mother had been asked to attend. Jimmy looked at her, and used words that were soft and hurt.

"Surely I, as the betrothed?"

Grace shook her head.

Jimmy debated whether to confront the issue right away, to go himself to the Coleman house. Perhaps a letter would be better. He certainly did not want to intrude. He spent most of the next day penning his remarkable entreaty over and over until it read exactly as he wished it to:

Lancaster

December 10ᵗʰ

My Dear Sir:—

You have lost a daughter. I have lost the only object of my affections—without whom life presents to me only a dreary blank. My prospects are all cut off; and I feel that my happiness will be buried with her in the grave. It is now no time for explanations, but the time will come when you will discover that she as well as I have been much abused. God forgive the authors of it. I have now one request to make. For the love of God, and of your dear departed daughter whom I loved infinitely more than any other human being could love, deny me not; afford me the melancholy pleasure of seeing her body before its interment. I would not for the world be denied this request. I would like to follow her remains to the grave as a mourner. I would like to convince you…I may sustain the shock of her death, but I feel that happiness has fled from me forever.

very respectfully,

James Buchanan, Esq.

The letter was presented to Mr. Coleman by Courtland Parker, a local messenger. He refused to accept its delivery and instructed Parker to return it to the sender with its seal unbroken.

Ann's body reached Lancaster that same day, accompanied by Margaret, Joseph, and young Sarah. Margaret shared what she knew of the details of the death only with her father, who kept his own counsel.

St. James was under reconstruction. Its toppled steeple lay awkwardly on the stripped December ground. Freezing rain, then driving snow, bludgeoned the cemetery behind the sanctuary. Adrift among and atop the graves, scantly sheltered by the wild empty branches of scattered oaks piercing the doubtful air, lay the leftovers of carpenters and masons.

On Saturday, Thomas and Edward, her older brothers, navigated Ann's remains between the warring beams, ha'penny nails, and disordered bricks. Dripping mounds of sodden sawdust froze in distorted geometries, and the tundra of the cemetery was pocked with stalagmites of discarded residue. Thick pastes of mire covered the brothers' fine black shoes as they kicked through the mud and discoloring snow. Edward banged his shin against a cracked concrete crown and stumbled, nearly losing his grip on the coffin.

Robert helped lower Ann's corpse into the bleached sepulcher, in symmetrical array with those purchased and reserved for others in the Coleman family, right behind the sacristy. The sandstone already bore the dates of her birth and death. The service was brief and, despite the familiarity of loss to the Coleman family, agonizing.

William Muhlenberg read from the 39th Psalm:

LORD, make me to know mine end, and the measure of my days, what it is; that I may know how frail I am. Behold, thou hast made my days as an handbreadth; and mine age is as nothing before thee: verily every man at his best state is altogether vanity...

and closed with this prescriptive from the Book of Common Prayer:

Man that is born of a woman hath but a short time to live, and is full of misery. He cometh up, and is cut down, like a flower; he fleeth as it were a shadow, and never continueth in one stay. In the midst of life we are in death: of whom may we seek for succour, but of thee, O Lord, who for our sins art justly displeased?... Thou most worthy Judge eternal, suffer us not at our last hour, for any pains of death, to fall from thee.

A quick assessment of the Colemans, and particularly pretty young Sarah, inspired the minister hastily to conclude the ceremony.

A large dark man hovered a discreet distance from the closed coterie of Ann's family and their invited guests as they huddled in the falling snow. While Reverend Muhlenberg lifted the final prayer, the stranger considered the awfulness of mingled death and prayer amidst the silence of the waste. He mounted his horse and rode back toward Gettysburg.

A wayfarer found the corpse of an old man, from his color and dress surely a slave, off the tarmacadam near the Philadelphia road that very night. Next to him, a white horse thrashed slowly in the snow, its bones piercing through the matted fur of its right front leg. The body was frozen through save for the weathered black hands still clinging to the animal's neck. The stranger pried the hands from the horse, and wrestled the body a bit farther into the woods. He took careful aim through the horse's forelock. The whinnying ceased as the echoes of the single shot faded into the surrounding trees. Before tossing some scrabbled dirt and dragging a pine bough over the remains, the wanderer said a short prayer for the slave's soul.

• • •

Recriminations flew in the Coleman house. Father blamed mother. Mother wept. Sarah was unbalanced with despair and wandered about the house from room to room, root cellar to attic, her red eyes angry and lost.

The rumors that surfaced as soon as the news reached Lancaster now exploded. The Coleman family, he heard second hand from Grace, blamed Jimmy for Ann's death. Talk and more talk behind the closed doors of storekeepers and ironmasters, in the taverns that he used to habituate, and among members of the bar and bench. The chords grew into a crescendo on the day of her interment and the noisy accusations soon penetrated the office above the Widow Dutchman's. This surely would not do. He was left alone to figure how to quash the whispering campaign. Certainly, this fire was kindled by Robert's vindictive spirit. Jimmy walked Lancaster's streets while the word "murderer" was being whispered. His tavern lay empty as Christ's tomb.

How could they be blaming me? I did not even see her since I left town days before her late night departure. Now no thought, apparently, no one even thinks about being solicitous for my feelings. Maybe they should be asking that Joseph Hemphill what happened. Where was that missing slave? Or even her father... I have lost my one true love. Not only she, but I, have been abused. What about my future?

Jimmy scurried to staunch the gossip. It was bad enough that the whole pattern of his unfolding life had come crumpling down upon him. He would simply suffocate if the very air adopted the belief that he was somehow responsible for Ann's death. He had to get his side of the story out before he was ruined.

The brief announcement by the Coleman family in the Lancaster *Journal* the day before simply stated:

Died, very suddenly, on Wednesday night last, whilst on a visit to Philadelphia, in the 22nd year of her age, Miss Ann Coleman, Robert Coleman, Esq., of this city.

Underneath was a glowing tribute to some 82-year-old woman named Mrs. Ann Mitchell. No one, Jimmy thought, had ever heard of her. I can do better than that.

Jimmy went to the office of the rival Lancaster *Intelligencer* and after several tries polished the following product, somewhat inconsistent in its facts, that appeared in the paper's weekly edition:

Obituary-**Miss Coleman**

Departed this life, on Thursday morning last, in the twenty-third year of her age, while on a visit to her friends in the city of

Philadelphia. Miss Anne C. Coleman, daughter of Robert Coleman, Esquire, of this city. It rarely falls to our lot to shed a tear over the mortal remains of one so much and so deservedly loved as was the deceased. She was everything which the fondest parents or fondest friends could have wished her to be. Although she was young and beautiful, and accomplished, yet her native modesty and worth made her unconscious of her own attractions. Her heart was the seat of all the softer virtues which ennoble and dignify the character of woman. She has now gone to a world where in the bosom of her God she will be happy with congenial spirits. May the memory of her virtues be ever green in the hearts of her surviving friends. May her mild spirit, which on earth still breathes peace and good-will, be their guardian angel to preserve them from the faults to which she ever was a stranger. This gifted young woman thus eulogized was betrothed to James Buchanan—

The spider's most attenuated thread
Is cord, is cable, to man's tender tie
On earthly bliss—it breaks at every breeze.

He paid the required forty cents. There, that should help stop the wagging. In addition to constituting his attempt at absolution, before he recognized the unseemly nature of the thought, Jimmy also acknowledged that it acted as something of an advertisement for him. He was particularly pleased, unlike the *Journal* announcement, he had gotten her age right, and he preferred his own spelling of her name.

Still, it would not cease. Steaming rolling surfacing words, words that tucked under the froth and burst back up hardboiled. By the following week, Jimmy simply could not bear the cauldron of gossip. He feared for his practice and his prospects. Kentucky, Indiana, Alabama, anywhere else, no matter how far away, never looked so good. Faced with controversy and under attack, he had to go into the woods.

Jimmy slithered away from Lancaster to collect his thoughts and regroup over Christmastime with the family he had not seen since the year he passed the bar. He did not pause at the cemetery behind St. James's on his way out of town. Despite his hard riding effort to outdistance them, the rumors surrounding Ann's death preceded him to Mercersburg.

His father stared him down, "Jim, what does all this folderol mean for your future? Pastor King told me the news of that girl Ann Coleman's death. What is the truth, and I mean the truth?"

Jimmy stammered. His stomach started up. Before he absolutely had to go outside to relieve himself, he fairly screamed, "Father, how can you even say that I had anything to do with this?"

James eyed his son. He had not, in fact, accused the boy of any complicity, but his shouted denial and quick rush outside certainly alerted the senses.

Jimmy leaned over the now brown-speckled snow covered soil of his youth, and glanced sideways at Father perched at the front door like a vulture calculating its carrion. Jimmy straightened a bit and stepped left foot over right to the shelter of some nearby trees. *Who is this disgusting old man, anyway, to be questioning me? Examining me about the very thing that stripped away my happiness. I never touched her. I certainly never ever never ever beat her!*

Jimmy spat from behind the trees in the general direction of the house. When he went back indoors, his mother wrapped him, weeping, in her frail arms. Father was gone to the tavern. It was good and appropriate, Jimmy thought, to be with family.

The uneasy Christmas came and went. He had not had time or foresight to purchase any presents in Lancaster and there was nowhere to shop in Mercersburg except the family store. It would hardly do to go in there and buy. His face flushed a bit as he watched his sisters open their gifts from one another and his color deepened when he unwrapped the long soft scarf and muffler on which Jane had taken the lead but all his sisters had, in turn, helped, accounting not only for its staggered mix of colors but the uncertainty of some of the knitting. What was he to do? Mother gave him a white woolen sweater knit in the pattern of the Aryan Isles, but he thought it looked foolish on him as it stretched so tightly across his belly that he could not get it to reach as far south as his belt. Besides, who would wear such a thing?

Jimmy was grateful his father reverted to his customary response to reports of unpleasantries about his son. As when the news of the expulsion from Dickinson reached him by post, he maintained his hard silence. In fact, no one discussed his fiancée's death. Mother tried to get him to express the sadness she knew he must feel, but Jimmy seemed to have more interest in wandering though the haunts of his youth and playing whist and euchre with his siblings.

He also decided, against his learned judgment, to ask for one more favor. "Father," he solicited as he was about to leave, "I simply cannot return to Lancaster. The whole town abounds in lies and accusations. Would you stake me to a law practice in Kentucky or Tennessee, or if not there, in Alabama?" It was the elder Buchanan's turn to expectorate.

He felt he had nowhere to turn. He could not go back and practice law. How could he face those people? How could he depend on them for his very livelihood? Who else could he marry to achieve his rightful place? He would go south. This weather wass hateful. He could own a plantation, start afresh.

"Mother, I am pulling up stakes, going to the Carolinas. I will come see you when I get established. I promise."

Elizabeth looked at her oldest. She traced the still soft and hairless cheeks and the unlined brow with the tips of her scarred hands, dragging her ring finger across his pursed lips as Jimmy struggled with the impulse to suckle it. "I mus' argie with ye, Jamie," she began, "I

feerst thought it might be best for ye to stay here with us now, an' I
enerstand why ye might be wishing to flee to a new place. There's a call
for why this has all happent. The Lord, he knows why and wherefore
on this. I know ye have been with uppity folks, and have taken on some
of their ways. Ye be a good boy, and know right from wrong. Ye have to
get back in there. Ye have to return. It's the ernly way."

Jimmy took stock. He was nearing thirty and his practice and
his very career, so carefully nurtured, swept from under him through
no fault of his own. Continuing his panoply of mixed metaphors, his
plans to enter the ironmaster society in Lancaster were by the boards.
Worse, the tap was turned off, and he would have to start from the first
rung of the ladder all over again. Few from the Colemans' circle would
trust him as their lawyer, and he had gladly turned his back on his
former acquaintances, the shopkeepers and craftsmen that he rounded
with before his apparent elevation to the ironmasters' stratum. Still,
he had the Widow, and he could recapture those earlier friends for the
price of a few drinks.

More importantly, Jimmy realized as the plan began to form, he
could put this notoriety to good use. He was not without his resources.
He could use the wiles that thwarted Robert Coleman not once, but
twice, the tactics that fostered his readmission to college and enabled
him to overcome objections to the prospective union with Coleman's
daughter. Although now unjustly stripped of his livelihood, Ann's
father had also earlier introduced him to an arena where his particular
skills might do yet better than in the legal profession. Perhaps, at first,
the income might not reach his previous expectations, but that could
change. He had certainly seen ample evidence in his stint in Harrisburg
of the opportunities presented to a man who kept his ears open and
his palm extended. Not that he would dishonor those offices himself.
Politics, Jimmy vowed, politics. His retreat into the woods was over.

Jimmy leaned over and kissed his mother for her righteous
advice and her ongoing faith in her oldest. The new year turned and he

headed back to Lancaster relieved of almost all law office responsibilities but with a firm purpose in mind. It is going to take more than some girl's death, he thought, to thwart my efforts. The first of several Ann stories, so useful to him now and later, was born.

He tried it out. "Dear Grace, you know of course it was Robert Coleman who banned me from the funeral. You told me so yourself. You know I wanted to go."

Grace nodded, a small smile playing behind her lips at the opportunity presenting itself. Jimmy went further, "You know, she must have been a bit unstable, I mean mentally, don't you think?"

Grace replied, "Of course. I would not have known it, but that must be so."

"You know the way her parents always felt about me. Her father against me always and her mother conniving against my interests."

Grace's eyes misted.

"Grace, how difficult all this has been for me. To lose little Ann, with my whole future tied up with her. No wife, no children. Lonely evenings by myself with no one to comfort me."

Grace agreed that it must be very trying. "Jimmy I of course would be available if you need company, and someone to speak with about our shared loss."

So far, so good. Most people agreed that Ann must have been a bit daft in her head to do what was now widely rumored, although no one seemed quite certain of the suicide's mechanism. Then there were the Colemans talking about some never to be determined illness and Ann's gently slipping into the night. The Colemans were too silent, and certainly tellingly ambiguous, about the cause of Ann's death. No one had heard she was ill before she left, and what was she doing in Philadelphia anyway? Certainly, many of those who heard thought, she must have been a little "off." It was whispered she had just up and left the house at midnight, in the snow. Who would do something like that? Why? A girl from a family like that, with her future ahead of her, surely there must have been something wrong, probably with her mind or perhaps something caused by her home life?

Some of Jimmy's acquaintances, a few fellows and yet more young women, expressed their understanding of his plight. From the men, "Tough break, old boy. You'll get over it. There's many out there still."

Jimmy would return these volleys with a pained look. Did not they know how much the loss of the tie to the Colemans meant?

Women, several of them, brought covered dish upon covered dish. Offers to help around the office. Never alone at the Widow. Cyrus Jacobs, a rival ironmaster, threw some business his way.

People began to understand how difficult this must have been for the young man who loved poor Ann. When he felt it was safe to do so, Jimmy hinted at the ways she was misused by her family. There were many who were not fond of the Colemans, Robert's power and his imperious ways, and that Mrs. Coleman strutting about, controlling all aspects of church life, nowadays always in some Parisian novelty.

A new wrinkle of a rumor surfaced. Some indicated they "had it on good authority" that Ann wanted to break off her engagement, that Jimmy was "given the mitten."

Jimmy was taken aback. He had truly never heard such a thing, but this certainly had to be countered with an additional spin on familial opposition. Jimmy filliped, "Ann never did tell me that she wanted anything other than our shared happiness. If she did want to delay our union, that would have only come from a father who never wanted me to cross into their circle or perhaps by Ann's mother. She never liked me either."

Everyone knew the Colemans and how protective of their wealth and standing they were. Probably never wanted this nice lad to be part of their family anyway and that is why their poor daughter killed herself.

Of course, not all credited Jimmy's version of events, and some even saw through his methods, but the few friends he had despite the calumnies cast his way were soon joined by others. The despairing lover, pining over the death of his betrothed, barred by the rich family from which their daughter wished to escape into the arms of her intended, the banishment of him by the cruel father, generated some real sympathy in a public always ready to believe gossip, especially if it was directed against the wealthy. Sympathy, Jimmy reckoned, that could be translated into the ballot box.

He stood for office the following fall, seeking to go to Washington as Lancaster's man in Congress. His campaign survived a letter from someone writing under the sobriquet "Colebrook" which reflected both what he was up against and, he realized, the success of his efforts. The letter began,

Allow me to congratulate you on the notoriety you have acquired of late. Formerly, the smoothness of your looks and your habitual professions of moderation led those who did not know you to suppose you mild and temperate.

The anonymous author, writing both for Jimmy's private displeasure and for public dissemination, continued,

The late incidents of your life exhibit no small degree of defect in your moral conformation.

Jimmy did not know its source, but he could guess that it was one of Ann's brothers, probably inspired by the old man. Colebrook after all was the name of one of his foundries. Would his enemies stop at nothing?

Jimmy was aided by Coleman's political foes and backed by Jacobs's money. The cadre of Democrats in town whose electoral efforts were biennially overwhelmed, and others who did so for more personal motivations, provided financial assistance, much of it under the table for fear of giving offense to the Coleman interests.

Jimmy won the October election. At the age of 29, Congressman James Buchanan began his new life, with his goal now firmly in place. He would show them all. The Colemans, the ironmongers, his father, and perhaps especially Ann. He clenched his hands so tightly the nails dug into his palms and recalled the familiar pain.

Jimmy leapt atop his office desk, kicking the inkwell over. As the dark blue began to dribble across the polished oak, and little rivers of crimson crossed his wrist, Jimmy raised his right fist high above his head. Slowly, as if seeking to lasso a trundling calf, he swung it in ever wider circles.

One day, Jimmy vowed, one day, I will be President.

Chapter Seven
T H A D D E U S

Thaddeus Stevens did not know what to do with the letter he received on December 10th, the day after its author died. Ann's writing was stunning in its revelation, but where to turn with it? His client, Robert Coleman, deserved to know, yet he was sworn to secrecy by its terms. The young woman who was so delightful as she swung to and fro that evening behind his client's house, sweetly he thought at the time, perhaps cleverly or with a sense of foreboding, had also made him her attorney. Certainly, the needs of the living trumped the requests of the dead?

He wrestled with his professional responsibilities and his conscience. Another thought crossed Thad's mind. Perhaps there could be other uses for this information that could advance the causes of his clients? He was not unaware of this fellow James Buchanan's success in Lancaster professional and political circles. Indeed, in a thought that he almost immediately dismissed as ignoble, it might give him a great advantage if he were ever to face Buchanan across a courtroom, or in politics if Buchanan ever stepped back into the arena. He had the potential to control this lawyer, potential he could bury in his pocket right now and exhume whenever he desired.

Thad reflected on his upbringing, his recent success, and the trust before him, and realized he came about his sympathies, and this dilemma, honestly.

What would his mother want him to do?

He could not have been more than 10 but the memory was still hot in his brain. Swimming alone in a hollow on Walden Mountain. A late August afternoon. Surrounded by the beginnings of the descent into winter. Sun fighting through the clouds. Water never losing its icy edge. Feeling caressed by the light. Pulling himself quivering to the quarry ledge. Standing on the granite as best he could. Shaking like a fox terrier, drops shooting into the surrounding sugar maple crimson and gold. A frog jumping. Watching the colors of the trees dance their slow liquid dance in the fluttering ripples. Taking a round flat stone, cupping it, sending it skipping one two three four times across the surface, finally folding into the water. Mist rising hesitantly from the pond, as if it were startled by the warmth of the dying day. In the distance, a loon cried. Thad looked to the sky.

From a stone outcropping above, eyes leaning over, "Mark of the Devil!" "Sinner!" "It's your punishment!" "Let me see you run!" The spitting faces. The twisting mouths. The boys, and that lone girl, her sticky blonde hair tumbling all over her face. Covering himself with one hand, reaching for his shirt and pants with the other. Where were they?

Hopping on his good foot, flinging the other over the horse's back. Riding. Riding hard. Riding naked.

"Mother, why do they hate me? Why was I born this way? I want to cut off my leg!"

Sarah wrapped her son in a homespun blanket and held him for a long, long time. She wondered at those who would mock someone because of a condition of birth, something he could not control. She wished her arms could encircle him seven times seven.

Thad was 15 when the family of boys, including an older brother with two club feet, moved off the farm. Joshua, their father and a brawling drunk, had slipped into the Vermont woods a decade earlier, and was never seen by his family again.

Despite her son's late start on formal education, Sarah provided a strong background in the classics, and Thad was able to quote long Biblical passages *in haec verba*. At the Caledonia school he did well. Trouble arose when, on the eve of graduation, Thad staged, by candlelight, a play he had written.

The school's principal and Mayor Sweatt, on behalf of his seven daughters, were furious. "Mrs. Stevens, perhaps with the absence of Joshua," Sweatt began, "you have gone astray, but ye need not be bringing the necromantic arts of Thespis to this community."

"It's only about a young man's quest for truth."

"Truth? Truth is truth. There need not be any more quest for it than beginning with Genesis and ending with Revelation."

"Aye, that is so, but he is just seeking the application of the Bible to the world about him."

Sparks exploded as Sweatt pounded a hot red horseshoe on an anvil, "Let him put his nose where it ought right to be."

Sarah went back, eyes straight ahead, to the log cabin Thad and his younger brothers had helped her build.

"I would just as soon not graduate."

"Thad, you must graduate and go forward. This town is not for you. Do you remember our trip to Boston?"

Thad nodded, recalling the bustling cow paths and federal edifices, the church that signaled the British approach and the harbor where water, once brown with heavily taxed Asian tea, flowed from all about the world.

"That is just a small bit of the world out there. You must see, and be part of the rest."

Thad strode toward Sweatt's smithery. Curtis Root, Caledonia's only teacher, was there as well. "Mayor Sweatt, Mr. Root, my mother has been shamed by my conduct. On her wishes, I apologize for the play. I will not visit anything such as this on the town again."

At graduation, he and the other boys who helped him stage the play were compelled to seek forgiveness for their conduct in front of the townspeople. Thad revealed his christening of the production in the course of his apology, "The Root of all Evil is Sweat." Sarah, and some others, tried to trap the laughter pushing between their closed fingers.

"I don't know what to do, Mother. I like to cobble, and I like to ride. I don't want to stay in this town forever."

"I have saved a bit of money a-knowing this day would come. You could go to the college down and across the river. It might better prepare you for what God has in store."

Late the following fall, Thad took a hard swing at his freshman classmate. He missed, pain shooting up his bad leg as he fell. Thomas Whipple stood over him, "Get up you cripple! Get up!"

Thad could not. It was not just the foot, he had to admit. He was stinking drunk. Dartmouth's president, John Wheelock, looked up from his table and peered through the White Mountain Inn's frosted windows. He downed his Sherry, and went into the snow. Surely as he had expected, the flailing figure was that Stevens boy.

"Stevens, first, your conduct at morning chapel, and now this."

Thad lay there, his small smile fading. The snow was merging to ice as it linked itself with his dripping perspiration, forming a crust clutching his neck. "Master Whipple," Wheelock pronounced, without offering a hand to the figure in the snow, "come join me in the tavern. I want to know what happened here. Of course, the truth."

"He made," Whipple started, his verbal struggles spawned from the same bottle of corn whiskey, "some vague allusion to loathsome spotted old men preying on young scholars and would not disgorge who he meant. I took it as a direct affront to you, sir."

Wheelock considered the figure before him. His grandfather, though not a graduate of the college, had not only signed the Declaration of Independence but served as a justice on the state supreme court. More importantly, he had been a good friend of Wheelock's father. The choice here, he thought, is obvious.

"Stay inside out of the cold, Robert. Try not to drink anything further."

The president went outside and stood over the sprawling figure, "You may get your things, Stevens, and I do not care to what corner you drag them and your foot. You are no longer at this college."

Thad took the back of his hand and brushed through the snow coating his eyes. He looked up at the soft body bent over him. From his supine position, his good leg lashed out and rammed the back of Wheelock's knees. Thad pressed his hands hard against the flattened figure and pushed himself up. Whipple, at the window watching, ran out and helped the administrator stagger to his feet. Thad slowly walked away, ignoring their spluttered shouts.

The next semester, the entrails of a cow, its splintered crust hacked by an axe, were strewn in the basement of the only building of the campus at the Universitas Viridis Montis, a private school near Lake Champlain in the Green Mountain's foothills. The animal's owner, Randal Mathis, was irate, and demanded expulsion for the culprit. Suspicion centered on Almus Pratt, the owner of the weapon that had cleaved the cow. A new student stepped forward and acknowledged guilt, impressing the farmer with his contrition. Mathis was persuaded to place the blame on passing soldiers on their way to Ticonderoga, but the school was not as forgiving. Thad, however, had the response to his petition for readmission to Dartmouth already in his pocket. Its trustees were seeking to undo every action of their founder's son as they prepared to fire him from the presidency. What better way, they thought, to undercut Mr. Wheelock than by letting the Stevens boy back in?

Thad complained as he returned to Hanover,

October 12, 1812

Dearest Mother,

I do hope this finds you well.

You have struggled to come up with the twenty-dollar yearly tuition. There are those for whom this is but a Trifle. I have split wood and cleaned stalls for my room and food. Look at these others. Allowances from parents in Boston and Windsor and Money from Uncles in Portland come flowing. I cannot even afford books & have to beg them daily from my classmates after they finish, or do not care to finish, their assignments. They still deride me, and one has anointed me "Old Clubfoot."

Still, I struggle forward, mindful of the principles you hold dear and the sure Knowledge that I must check my Passions.

Your obedient son,

Thaddeus

Sarah replied,

October 27, 1812

Most Precious Son,

You shouldst remember the world is not fair to us, in human terms. It has God's fairness. There is a greater Reward beyond. We all deserve, save for his everlasting Mercy, to be burned like spiders in the fire of Hell. Be grateful. Be grateful. Look outside yourself. Look to God and your betters for inspiration, yet mostly think of those who can not read (as you can), do not have food (as you do), and especially those in bondage to alcohol or other men. You have had it well and you can repay by doing good. I remain in the grip of the Lord.

Sarah Morrill Stevens

Thad choked as he watched others head to the tavern or into town for dinner. He felt incarcerated in his room behind the stables, the night-long whinnying disrupting his study and his sleep. Still, he persevered and graduated near the top of his class. Phi Beta Kappa was a secret society with admission by invitation only. The main criterion for entrance was supposed to be academic achievement, and not social grace or popularity among peers. When he was excluded, Thad kicked at the doors of Dartmouth Hall and cursed that they not ever be reopened.

Although without honors, he was permitted to deliver the commencement address. Thad looked at the sea of nearly twelve dozen classmates and eight faculty and began, "Beware those fawning parasites who grasp at unmerited honors, who seem to blunder into the truth that they must flatter nobility or remain in obscurity; that they must degrade themselves, or others will not exalt them."

Thad returned to Burlington to study with a Federalist lawyer. The experience confirmed his disdain for the established social structure, as well as his dislike for the snow-driven winds of Lake Champlain. When his college friend Samuel Merrill wrote and said he was giving up what he called the *Dutch wenches* and his teaching post in York, Pennsylvania to go west to Indiana, Thad gave notice and left the granite mountains and red clover forever. He replied to Samuel, *Not only will there assuredly be more opportunity in the larger state, but Vermont's weather is eight months of winter and four months of damn late fall. I need a better, and a warmer, stage. I think Pennsylvania will be it.*

Thad said good-bye to his mother, and rode hard for the fortnight it took to get to York. He arrived wearing clothes sewn by his mother and shoes he made himself. The village's neat streets and appearance of regularity and order impressed him. Upon taking the position at the York Academy, he learned of yet another hurdle he must leap that had no relevance to his qualifications. Local lawyers had determined that unless one spent a full year of uninterrupted study of the law while living in their state, the bar was closed. Thad would not be able to teach and read the law simultaneously, no matter how long he apprenticed. There was no possibility of keeping body and soul together if he had to give up his teacher's salary.

He had to find another way. One night at the Indian Queen tavern, Andrew Noel, in town to consult with a more senior lawyer, advised, "You can just go across the river and hop over the Mason-Dixon Line into Maryland. Things are a bit looser there than here. In Bel Air, they'll test you and you can have reciprocal admission that Harrisburg cannot ignore."

Thad studied diligently and on an August evening in 1816 mounted his horse, 45 dollars jingling in his pocket, and made his way to the house of Harford County Chief Justice Hopper Nicholson. Two other judges from his court, Theodoric Bland and Zebulon Hollingsworth, flanked Judge Nicholson. General William Winder, presented as a hero from the War of 1812, was also at the long pine table that took up half of the living room. Thad sat across in a hard slat-backed chair. The candles played at the sides of his inquisitors' faces, casting half of each into a dark shadow. Nicholson's mouth, only half of it visible, began, "The custom in matters of this sort is for the applicant to provide two bottles of good Madeira."

So it must be, Thad thought, and sent Cato, the Judge's slave, for the Sherry. The inquiry began.

"Have you studied the Law?"

"Yes, sir, not only Blackstone, but Gilbert and Coke on Littleton."

"Will you explain the difference between executory devises and contingent remainders?"

An easy question, followed by two more on the law of trusts and one on contracts. The gentlemen quickly conferred. Thad overheard General Winder, "I am no lawyer, but I say admit him. We need to get the evening underway!"

"Mr. Stevens," said Hopper Nicholson, "you are admitted to the august profession of the practice of law, and we hereby transform you from a colt into a Bartolist, upon one condition."

"What might that be?" Thad asked, skepticism beginning to rise.

"Why, young man, simply that you provide us with two more bottles of Madeira," chortled the Chief Justice. Thad tipped Cato another York shilling.

It was now clear why General Winder stopped by. The remainder of the evening passed in the play of poker and fiploo. By evening's end, Thad's 45 dollars were more than decimated. Concluding his legal career in the great and sovereign State of Maryland, he leapt on his horse early the next morning, $3.50 remaining, but at least with the clothes on his back and something between his legs.

Why go straight back to York? Perhaps he should explore the larger town to the east after his cool reception by the York bar. Certainly, there would also be ramifications from his late notice that he would no longer teach school.

Cato had supplied him with directions, "Go to Jarrettsville, den toward the Buck. De new bridge should be done. Den to left, about ten more miles."

Setting off at a canter, Thad pushed Cobbler hard and soon was crossing a bridge over the Susquehanna. Cobbler knew before Thad that the structure was not complete and crashed to a halt, throwing Thad who cut his bad leg and bruised himself all over. There were no warning signs, and he had almost plunged to the stones strewn 200 feet below. "Sam Hill! There ought to be a way to sue for such negligence," Thad shouted, though nothing except a passing buzzard hawk heard him. He headed north and spent the night in Wrightsville. The next morning, he took its ferry and rode with more discretion into Lancaster.

The community of 8,000 overwhelmed him. It seemed nearly as large as his childhood memories of Boston, and far too sophisticated and socially stratified for his tastes. Thad walked the length of King Street and was impressed by not only the finery, but the distance of his circumstances from it. He entered the Leopard Tavern. His large fist soon strangled a whiskey glass. What a silly sight, Thad thought, as his left eye cocked toward a figure atop the next table. Who was this fop, his topknot jiggling and scarf waving, dancing by himself? Was that a wink in my direction? My God, can't he hold his liquor? Thad downed the rest of his glass and headed to Matthias Slough's hotel for the night.

Thad trotted right through York the next day, resolved to start afresh. He set his name on a shingle at the east end of the Gettysburg Hotel where he was staying pending more permanent quarters. The carefully crafted sign promised he would "give diligent attention to all orders in the line of his profession."

This fateful town was, after his eastern foray, more to his liking. Its 1000 people were a good mix of British stock, Germans, Scots-Irish, Indians, and free negroes. Although more distant from the mighty Susquehanna, Gettysburg was at the confluence of two pikes, one from Baltimore and the other Philadelphia, that led to Pittsburgh and the west. Here, he thought, he could make his way.

Every day he woke eager to help and eager to show his competence. A few cases collecting debts, too insignificant for the town's other lawyers to handle, were tossed his way and little else. Soon, on hooks hanging from the sign outside the door, he scrawled, "Shoes Cobbled." Even that was not enough, as he found it hard to charge a fair price to most of those who came unshod to his door.

Earlier and earlier each day, he headed to the Indian Queen tavern, grumbling all the while to Sam Coates, the bartender. By the following summer, entering before noon, he railed, "Must I make my living scavenging on the leavings of others? I am two months behind at the hotel. Maybe I should have gone to Lancaster or returned to Vermont's mountains."

Coates responded by closing his tab.

It was only a week later when a simple-minded farmer, James Hunter, raised his scythe high in the air and brought it crashing down, charting a ripping traverse through the throat of his neighbor. Blood flew from the jugular and the vena cava and exploded everywhere. Hunter stumbled along the roadway and was soon apprehended.

Local passions were intense. No Gettysburg lawyer, and none from Carlisle, York, or Lancaster would defend the farmer. It was not just the waves of local anger and outrage that swept over the region that dissuaded them; Hunter had no money. A young attorney from across the river just finishing up his second stint in the General Assembly was one of the last to be offered the representation. Jimmy had just lost a series of manslaughter cases and was eager to avoid the uncertainty of court and the certainty of controversy. He immediately washed his hands of the offer. Finally, someone turned to the area's newest lawyer. It would be his first jury case, and Thad could taste the opportunity.

The hostility toward Thad and his cause was palpable as he entered the Adams County Courthouse. The lawyer did not assert that his client was not guilty. He advanced a plea not recognized in any court in the United States. First, he contended that when Hunter committed this horrific and impulsive murder, he was governed by a momentary, uncheckable passion and was unable to appreciate the wrongfulness of his action. Second, he argued simply and forcefully that Mr. Hunter's simplemindedness should preclude his execution, that it would be unfair, illegitimate, even cruel and unusual, to send someone of his client's limited faculties to his death.

The townspeople and jury eyed the hard wrought body, stinging black button eyes and volcano of red hair but mistrusted the cursed club foot dragged about their courtroom. Soon, however, Thad's arguments, not so much by their logic, but by fervor and directedness, impressed all who listened.

Instead of quoting Latin or speaking in oblique verbal flourishes, Thad rejected lawyerly histrionics that dwarfed any thread of logic and obscured the argument they sought to sew together. He appealed, "Before you is a man much like you. He has a wife. He has children. He rises at dawn and comes in at dusk."

Thad looked at each juror, slowly and in turn. It was as if the fire in his eyes was burning away the distance between sinner and fact finder.

"One hot summer night, something snapped. Perhaps it was the one time too many he was ridiculed, the one time too many he was cheated, perhaps even the one too many drinks he had. Who among us has not been there, and *thought* what James Hunter *did*?

The twelve men in the box, save a banker from York that Thad had not been able to keep off the panel, stared down at their boots.

From there, his arguments, steadily and wisely developed, had the pure ring of truth, even if they could not overcome the ghastly nature of the crime and the banker's unyielding spirit. Observers, bench and bar, local journalists and a rotating swollen gallery of onlookers, were in awe. If they were ever in trouble, they swore, this is the man they wanted in their corner.

Stevens's renown and legend quickly grew despite Hunter's ultimate hanging. Legal matters, first from Gettysburg and the surrounding countryside, then from Lancaster and Harrisburg, came his way. If a Philadelphia lawyer needed help in a western court, he also now knew where to place his client's business.

Thad delighted in the freedom to build his own practice his way, taking "hopeless" cases if the cause was right. His photographic memory was able to recall precedent without notes and he easily alluded to just the right biblical verse or story, fostering success at trial courts throughout the region. On appeal from cases lost by others, he prevailed more than 90% of the time. Thad's caustic delivery and combative manner served him well, and many a pompous lawyer fled as his burning words overflowed them. Nor was his scorn for twaddle and puffery targeted only at other attorneys. He originated a withering remark that became a staple of lawyerly humor for the next two centuries. When asked, during an acerbic exchange with an incompetent judge, whether he was manifesting his contempt for the court. "Manifest, your honor?" Stevens replied, "I am doing my utmost to conceal it."

Despite his growing success and his emergence as the largest landholder in Adams County, the club-footed and soon-to-be hairless Stevens was perpetually embarrassed and angry, emotions that seeped in bitterness, sarcasm, and satire. He spent most of his nights playing poker and whist and euchre, only occasionally sneaking to the back room at the Indian Queen to have his way secretly and forcefully in exchange for a portion of his gambling winnings. Charges of "nigger lover" grew with his prominence, not only from his skillful defense of those whom no other lawyer would represent, but as the result of a rumored backwoods relationship with a slave named "Eve." At peach time, on a dry and dusty York bluff overlooking the Susquehanna, a young boy found the tiny negress, swollen with child, in a shallow well. A hard blow on the head spawned the blood that tinged the water. In some quarters, and with some folks, whispered cries of "murderer" arose, a buzzing never extinguished.

Thad's complex nature played out in other ways.

While the next spring sought to emerge from winter, a young man due to be married the next day wandered into the Indian Queen. Infused by premarital fear and a desire for a final fling, Peter Briscoe began punishing his whiskey and soon made his way over to Thad's experienced table. The princely 200 dollars gathered for his new life soon discovered its true home in Stevens's Queenly pile.

The young man reeled out the tavern door, and Thad followed into the gloom. The figure toppled through the snow, its drifts overwhelming each step. As bitter flakes fell, Peter tumbled into an area carved to the ground and grasped at a scarred hitching post. Sliding to his knees, he lifted his arms, palms open to heaven, and murmured a prayer Thad could not overhear. He followed the man back to his room at the Gettysburg.

"Do you happen to know which young woman is set tomorrow for marriage?" Thad asked the innkeeper. Under cover of night, he found the fiancée's house and carefully wrote something that told just enough, slipped some other papers in the envelope, and slid it under a front door. That morning, the young woman's lower lip drew tightly against her teeth as she read the note. A small sigh snorted into the still Gettysburg air, a mist forming as it was embraced. In the afternoon, a chastened bridegroom and Patricia Hill were married, their future brighter owing to, as Patricia related to a groom who had struggled to confess the events of the night before, "the generosity of my rich uncle."

Two winters later, Thad traded shot after hard shot of whiskey with Josiah Wheelwright, a frequent companion. Thad cleared Josiah's stake early and the loser left the tavern, already drunk. The next morning, one hand reaching for his still locked knob, was Wheelwright's frozen body. Thad closed his offices for the day. He took his casks of Amontillado, kegs of whisky and bottles of wine and dragged them up the cellar steps to the corner of High and Baltimore. One by one, he took an axe to the assemblage. A crowd gathered and watched the caramel and crimson lace through the snow. They stayed far back as Thad sliced his hands on the smashed shards he gathered in a large grey sack. Until a doctor required it for his ailing heart at his life's end, he never touched alcohol again.

Thad considered the course that had led him here. He was now convinced what was best to do. Covering Ann's powerful epistle with his rough wrestler's hands, he folded it tenderly and placed it in a red leather pouch.

Chapter Eight
CONGRESSMAN

T he carriage's iron tire hit James Buchanan Senior on the head, hard and true, and he died a lingering death in June 1821.

Jimmy waited until after his father was interred before he went to Mercersburg and stepped in to discharge the obligations the intestate old man left behind. He did his lawyer's best to make provisions for his siblings still at home, three boys and two unmarried sisters. Finally, he could go forward without his father hawking his every move. Unintentionally bungling the dimly remembered grammar, the thought crossed his mind that it was better for all, and certainly for his mother, to be a *familias sans pater,* a family without a father. He also realized, despite his repressed but ever-growing anger, he was pleased that his father had seen him recover from the scandal that typhooned about him, make good on becoming a United States Congressman, and start on the path whose vindicating end everyone would know.

Jimmy felt let down and a bit disappointed with Washington when he arrived to secure lodgings in November. The city, barely two decades away from a swamp, offered meager accommodations and not much nightlife. Its sharp strong spokes radiated beyond competing arcs, penetrating fallow fields and fecund marshes, only to drop limply into the wilderness. Buildings appeared to be cast randomly on the Parisian-based city plan that had yet to fill in its holes, as if each edifice were one of a series of metal balls frozen in place after progressive spins of the croupier's wheel. Encroaching winter had started its intermittent work and the congealed street mud ambushed Jimmy's new suede boots. None of the infrastructure of an organic city had yet emerged, and the atmosphere was Spartan, artificial, and depressing.

Walking along Pennsylvania or Connecticut, Jimmy dodged scurrying swine and dogs whose matted fur and taut flesh bespoke of daylight marauds in the surrounding swamps and midnight forays into the open garbage cans cast behind boarding houses and inns. On the first Saturday, while wandering cats rubbed against his new trousers, he came across an auction at 15th and K.

Jimmy stared at the black bodies on the block. He turned to his companion, Andrew Govan of South Carolina, here to fill a dead Congressman's term. "I have not seen this before, Andrew. How often are these slaves sold here?'

"I believe just once a week. It's an even bigger market than back in Charleston or, I think, Richmond. People come here from all over to buy."

"Why are their bodies so deformed? They're all missing toes and fingers as if they've been broken off at the root. Look at that one over there. He must be only 30 years of age or so yet his back is twisted and that shriveled leg is all crusted and green."

"Well, he's scarcely worth anything. Just look at those young pickaninnies over there."

Jimmy trained his eyes on perhaps a dozen boys, perhaps 6 or 8 years old, who stood trembling and alone on a separate platform, moon eyes surveying the sea of white faces. "That is the age to get them," Govan continued. "They are most useful and can be well trained. They will last for many years, perhaps a decade or two, under the right overseer. Of course, young girls can be most pleasurable."

Jimmy stared, and nodded in comprehension. He was more concerned that there were precious few good restaurants and lively taverns in the nation's capital. Then again, he only needed one of each.

More importantly, he began to appreciate the encapsulated environment, more apart from America than its epicenter, as he and Andrew Govan established lodgings together under Mrs. Peyton's wandering eye, with Henry Dwight of Massachusetts at D Street and 2nd, Southeast, only a few blocks from the Capitol. Pompey was placed in a colored boarding house down the river.

Jimmy found Henry, also new to Washington, rough and unappealing and surrounded by textbooks on cattle breeding, of all things. Andrew, on the other hand, was a perfect gentleman, his sensibilities right and refined. At night, Govan would tell him of his dreams of moving out to Mississippi after his tenure was over, establishing a plantation, "Jimmy, any time you want to visit would be just fine. I already have the name chosen, "Snowdown.""

Jimmy's maiden speech, on maintaining funding for the Indian Bureau, was delivered with the aid of the stentorian orations he made in his Lancaster rambles. Fairly yelling, as did the ancient Greek when he shambled along the strand and shouted into the sea, Congressman Buchanan staked no new positions on how to control the indigenous savages. The bill was certain to pass but he catapulted an appeal to both sides of the aisle, and both sides of the aisle resignedly recognized it as such. Thomas Whipple of New Hampshire muttered to Connecticut's Ebenezer Stoddard, "Well, here's yet another wasted Federalist from eastern Pennsylvania." Jimmy's perfervid voice rose just a bit more until one could hear the very frontier echoing in the chamber, incanting "the shrieks of helpless women and children under the scalping knife."

The President's House was reconstructed after its 1814 torching and its Aquia sandstone painted white. The Capitol, similarly damaged, was not yet finished. Its gallery was simply a raised wooden platform, and many members could not see each other or the presiding officer. Words necessarily had to be shot toward the ceiling, arching ever upward until their crescendo approached the level of human auditory tolerance, only to tumble upon those in otherwise unreachable recesses. "These acoustics are laughable," Jimmy complained to Andrew, "Everyone has to shout here. My throat is dry and strained every day."

His roommate bit back the urge to joke, "That must be why you have to lubricate it so thoroughly evenings."

Remembering the lesson learned in Harrisburg, Jimmy resolved to keep a low profile on the House floor. It was in the back rooms that deals were done, and public controversy would not be his friend. After two months in Washington, he wrote to Mercersburg, *I am forcibly struck with the idea that the reputation of many of them stands higher than it deserves. With no false modesty, dearest Mother, I expect I will be able to achieve my highest dreams.*

Increasingly, he was targeted as an eligible bachelor. Jimmy enjoyed the parties on the Potomac and his tavern evenings. His whiskey-infused charm and wit went down well with pheasant and wine. Several widows pushed themselves or, at times, their daughters on him.

Mrs. George Blake, a comely young widow with a significant inheritance, often gathered in his circle. She would wangle her way to Jimmy's side and laugh at his jokes, not so discreetly touch his sleeve, and coyly, she thought, make herself available. Jimmy had not followed up on these hints, and often took French leave at these parties rather than wait to the end of the evening when an accompanying escort home would seem appropriate.

Now she approached him more directly, "Mr. Buchanan— Jimmy, I need a strong man to travel with me to Boston to see my family. I would find it very gentlemanly if you were to accompany me."

Jimmy thought of Boston, and of what he had heard of its attributes. Perhaps it would be good to see the self-anointed Hub of the Universe. "I shall be pleased to do so. Will you and I be the only ones on the journey?"

"Why, yes. Private carriage, with only my boy Cicero managing the horses. Does August comport with your schedule?"

Jimmy nodded. He headed back to Lancaster at the close of the session to attend to a few straggling legal matters. Late May's budding smells blew into his public coach. It will be good to get away from Lancaster and see New England, and thank the good Lord, Jimmy thought, that we do not have to be in that stinking Washington in summer time. He had heard the stories of its sticky August embrace and was grateful for Lancaster's weather, even if the town was now, to him, surpassingly ordinary. He would otherwise be captive in Lancaster until the following December, or November after the election if he could justify going back to the capital early. He wrote Mrs. Blake the following month, *How without distinction this little town is. How once did I think its streets were walked by those of real stature? Yet I must in all ways feign its importance so that I may return to the embrace of dear Washington.*

The date for the trip approached and Jimmy grew increasingly uncomfortable. Do I really want to spend time with this woman? What, in fact, are her designs? When Mrs. Blake's coach arrived in Lancaster, he bade her come into the Widow. His head tilted and his lips began to move, "I simply cannot go with you, dear woman. It is not only the cases I have responsibility for languishing on the courts' dockets in Pennsylvania, but I have now realized something greater still forbids my presence."

Mrs. Blake eyed her perhaps not so well suited suitor.

"I lost, not so long ago, my life's love. I struggled to return to her when I learned, while far away on business, of her father's intrusion. Perhaps you know of him, Robert Coleman, the ironmaster?"

Mrs. Blake nodded.

"In any event," Jimmy continued, "her father broke off our engagement over her wishes and she, tragically, died soon thereafter. He is now ailing himself. I cannot dishonor her memory."

"How terrible for you! When was this?" and, to herself, why did she not know this? Why was he telling her this now, after she had traveled here and informed her family?

"It was just beyond three years ago. Her memory pricks at my very being every day."

"Mr. Buchanan, that is of course very regrettable, and quite tragic, yet it is well beyond a year's mourning. Could you not go with me? I promise it will be just an opportunity to explore the museums, visit Cambridge across the Charles where my own dear departed was schooled, and partake of some fine meals."

Jimmy considered, feeling now better defended with his story of Ann as his shield. He realized he was eager to taste the Boston offerings and if the company were otherwise, he would certainly go. "Well, perhaps I could. I would enjoy the art and the meals. And your relations. And," he added with a quick wink, "you."

Jimmy viewed the trip itself as "quite grand" and enjoyed Boston, including an Oyster House near the harbor that reminded him, as he told Mrs. Blake, with moistening eyes, of an evening long ago with Ann. He wrote a man who was to become his dear friend, Thomas Kittera in Philadelphia, *I do not quite see why this town, the exporter of Franklin and historic home of hob-goblined rabble-rousers, so prides itself. It has little of the decorum and less of the society of your fair city. It will be good to escape the widow's clutches.*

"Not so much as a kiss," fumed Mrs. Blake to her sister when she returned to Washington. "All this after his letter upon letter, talking of the 'flesh-pots of Egypt' and how it would be so delightful to visit them with me. I have seen the outside of only one fleshy pot, and that is all I care of him to view."

She soon found another target for her matrimonial arrows. Jimmy was linked successively with Cora Livingston and Catherine van Rennselaer, Priscilla Cooper, sisters Julia and Matilda Caton, and others.

Plenty of young women in their early twenties came to Washington, often ostensibly on visits to relations, and there were precious few bachelors with demonstrated political achievement on their resumes. Most House and Senate members were already well married and, while there were many opportunities to be a mistress, matrimony was rarely in play. At an age and in an era where marriage was essential for even the most financially self-sufficient women, landing Jimmy would be quite a prize.

He managed to elude these efforts. When the bolder young women questioned why his ardor expressed at the previous night's party did not translate to calls afterwards, Jimmy told his tale of a broken heart, and the recovery he needed only a few years past this anguish. Dismayed at a prospective battle against a deceased idol, most were dissuaded from the hunt.

As with any new Congressman, Jimmy realized the chief objective of his two-year term was to be re-elected. He kept an eye on what was happening about him, and who was jockeying hardest for the grand mansion on Pennsylvania. With no family and plenty of time, and ample resources as the result of the money he made with Robert Coleman's earlier assistance, Jimmy devoted his energies to the maneuvers and alliances he needed to foster. Amos Ellmaker's son desired admission at the University of Pennsylvania; Edward Hand's grandson, down on his luck and with a large family, needed a public position, minor as it might be and an assistant postmaster in Lancaster was anointed; Joel Schenk, with whom he had cleaned stalls in Baltimore during their abortive foray in 1814 was now a pastor and wished a case of whiskey; a small bird fabricated in Limoges, a gift from a French legate, had flown to him and he bequeathed it to Cyrus Jacobs's widow. He pushed for dams, road projects, and canals for the Keystone State, first favoring and then opposing tolls on the Cumberland Road, and then again supporting the tolls if the states could collect them and not the federal government. He made sure his name was featured in almost every weekly edition of the Lancaster *Intelligencer*. Jimmy was pleased when the tradition of one-term Federalist Congressmen from Lancaster was broken and he was renominated for the next term.

Distinctions between parties were blurring. Federalist loyalties drifted, sectional identifications strengthened, and cults of personalities grew. Jimmy advanced one of his basic tenets on the House floor, and in doing so suggested he was looking North to Daniel Webster. "As the esteemed gentleman from Massachusetts and late of New Hampshire believes, universal suffrage is absurd. Not all men should be able to vote, but only those with property. Property rights must parade before human rights if society is to stay organized and orderly." Nodding down the aisle, "I would adopt Mr. Webster's position that representation should be proportionate to property." The jeers started and Jimmy hastened, "I of course fear those days, as so much we hold dear, are short in number." He was not sure if the subsequent applause was for him or for the disappearing Federalist ideals, but was secure that the Southern contingent would understand the message.

Politics, in the twenties, fed on the fractious nature of the still-emerging nation. Political clubs sprang up in towns and outposts across the West, and political machines were established in the major cities of the East. Political parties were in flux. With a fluid and informal political structure, personalities were important, and the quicksand tangle of allegiances provided opportunities for those positioned to profit from the disarray. This played more strongly at the local level, where state politics subsumed national allegiances.

Men headed out to the halls and debated their positions, amply fortified by alcohol, well into the night. Fights broke out, charging the blackness with epithets and challenges to duels at dawn. Literally dozens of men were shot each year in defense of political positions enhanced, or developed, under the influence of whiskey. These pistol matches were legal and, as Jimmy would learn from his soon-to-be hero's example, death to one's opponent was no certain barrier to political success.

Jimmy could now turn to what was shaping up as a most interesting Presidential race. He evaluated the contest as between John Calhoun of South Carolina and William Crawford of Georgia, writing to his old friend Jasper Slaymaker, unexpectedly ill at an early age, *I consider Adams out of the question...his disposition is as perverse and as mulish as that of his father.*

Jimmy's Federalist Party, as he now recognized, continued to lose traction. The 1824 election would be decided by the Democratic nomination. Pennsylvania was a major prize for any candidate, with 28 of the country's 250 electoral votes. Jimmy sought to align himself with the anti-New York-Virginia-Massachusetts axis. Those states had controlled every election up to that point. Four Presidents hailed from Virginia and two came from Massachusetts. New York's political machine operated in exchange for the patronage that stoked the economic engine of the Empire State and its eponymous largest city. His direction seemed easy and obvious.

Jimmy made himself available to the entreaties of minions from the other southern states, especially South Carolina and Georgia. He was particularly attracted by John Calhoun, a commanding man with thick ebony hair pushed hard back, and a patrician air befitting his large plantation, scores of slaves, and Yale education. Back home, George Mifflin Dallas of Philadelphia, wealthy and aristocratic in his own right, was marshalling adherents to something he called the "Family Party," which threw its support to Calhoun before Jimmy could announce his intentions, leaving Jimmy and his back door efforts to appeal to Calhoun's vanguard outside on the cold steps.

Jimmy's current roommate, George McDuffie of South Carolina, provided another avenue to pierce Calhoun's inner circle. A private correspondence between Jimmy and the Senator developed, and it was soon clear that the South Carolinian recognized young Buchanan as a key supporter in his presidential quest. What, Jimmy thought, can I make from this?

Complications arose. The hero of the Battle of New Orleans, the man who led his erstwhile romantic rival Lüder Bauschulte to his death, emerged from the West. Jackson appealed to the new states of the frontier, Tennessee, Kentucky, and Ohio, and was soon favored by Northerners trying to derail Calhoun. Rabid pro-Jackson demonstrations erupted at state conventions everywhere, including Pennsylvania, and Jimmy was confounded by the shifting patterns.

The only thing that did not waver was Jimmy's position on slavery. He was already a reliable northern advocate for what was coming to be known as states' rights, including the right to possess and sell blacks as chattel, certainly south of the Mason-Dixon Line as drawn across the continent and, depending on the shifts of the wind, perhaps elsewhere.

He now had the inroad to the strong slaver Calhoun, but considered his position. If Jackson is going to emerge from this fight, and if those farmers in Lancaster want him, what could he do? He could not come out in public for Calhoun, only to have his fate tied to Calhoun's anchor.

Perplexed and queasy, Jimmy relieved himself out back of his lodgings, drenching a stray rodent in the penumbra of the vomit. He must leave Washington even before the session's end. Jimmy traveled in the spring of 1824 by carriage to the Metropole Hotel in Philadelphia, registering simply as J. Buchanan, Esq. and did not emerge from his room for several days, with caviar and champagne brought by a young bellman to his door. Only his good friend Thomas Kittera visited him. Let the battle rage a while more. He could sit this one out for now, at least in public. Upon his return to his adopted town, he confirmed that Jackson had surprising strength in the Lancaster area. Any support for Senator Calhoun would need to be muted. In July 1824 the Harrisburg *Pennsylvanian* published America's first public opinion poll, surveying propertied white men across Pennsylvania and elsewhere. Its findings showed overwhelming support for Jackson.

Jimmy himself was nominated for an unprecedented third term. Standing this time in Pennsylvania's redrawn fourth district, he was ostensibly still a Federalist, yet wrapped a curious hybrid banner around himself in a cunning linguistic attempt to straddle the established and the unknown. He called himself a "Federalist-Republican," when most others not Whigs or Federalists were "Democrat-Republicans." Jimmy worked to build a base of the conservative German farmers, who remained nominal Federalists, and his own Scots-Irish, who sided with the Democrats. Jimmy let out, to a select few, that he should perhaps be considered a "Jackson man," and demonstrated the developed skill at amalgamating various efforts that success and setback afforded, all the while secure that Calhoun would not hear of his whispered conversion. Playing with patronage and promises, Jimmy brokered the compromises that began to unite the Pennsylvania political arm.

Pennsylvania's presidential voting was slated for three weeks after Jimmy's re-election. The national campaign broke through the last dam of decorum, with allegations of bigamy, adultery, and murder. Those canards set sail under the sheets of Adams's men but did not overflow Jackson, whose supporters now viewed him "as tough as a hickory stick."

Jackson, despite never siring a child, was a man's man and wildly popular with the emerging Western population, although his political career might have been stillborn had news of peace traveled more swiftly, or perhaps not simply been ignored, in New Orleans. Pennsylvania Senator Albert Gallatin, one of the chief architects of the Ghent treaty ending the War of 1812, described the man known to his Indian foes as "Sharp Knife" as "a tall, lank, uncouth looking personage, with long locks of hair hanging over his face, and a cue down his back tied in an eel skin: his dress singular, his manner and deportment that of a backwoodsman."

Jimmy had never met any man with such a presence. Jackson was not commonly attractive, yet his eyes were deeply blazing blue and, against hair once red but now stone gray, alone made him appear handsome. Jimmy's personal assessment corresponded to that of Adams, who considered Jackson, despite his frontier background and the prejudices that presumably engendered, "vigorously a gentleman."

Many viewed Jackson as ill educated and boorish. Jimmy judged that he was far more cultured than the Westerner, but was deeply attracted to Jackson and could suffer his politics. Besides, he liked being in a position of what he perceived to be intellectual and educational superiority to the autodidact when he so often felt beneath what Samuel Coleridge (or so he had heard) was calling the clerisy, schooled in what Jimmy disdained as the "News," New England, New York and New Jersey.

Jimmy was familiar with the rumors of "murderer" for Jackson's tactics in a duel on the dawn of May 30, 1806 that had its genesis in a horse racing wager gone awry. One thing led to another and Charles Dickinson called the scrawny six-footer a "poltroon and a fool." Dickinson was an excellent shot and his first bullet pierced his opponent's body, breaking two of Jackson's ribs, landing an inch from his heart. The wounded Jackson trained his pistol on his opponent and the younger Tennessean restrained himself, comporting with established rules in such matters. Old Hickory, a veteran of 103 duels, ignored those precepts. He steadied himself and, rather than firing into the morning sun as Dickinson expected, took dead aim. For this and forever, he was excoriated by some, but the duel acted as a legend-polisher with many. Perhaps, the piece of lead that festered near his heart and provoked punishing pain for the next four decades made it hard to regret his choice.

More important were the growing tales retold by Jackson himself. He and his mother perched on Hanging Rock in Lancaster County, South Carolina watching his 16-year-old brother fight the Redcoats. Or, in Jackson's version, he had joined Robert in combat against the British. In any event, the whole family was taken prisoner.

Andy, as he told it, had a temper befitting his red hair and sustained a scabbard gash across his head and upraised hand. Beset by smallpox, upon their release he trudged barefoot in the Carolina mud as Robert led his mother on a mule, like Joseph with Mary, toward home. Thunder rolled across the sky. Rain pounded. Robert died two days later. Older brother Hugh had perished at Stono Ferry two years earlier. Thirteen-year-old Andy did not recover for many months. It never profited anyone to spring from the narrow island across the sea in later dealings with him.

Behind the scenes, Jamie let it be known that he was fully divorced from Calhoun and could deliver a fair part of Pennsylvania to Jackson. Others, on board earlier, already claimed to be "original Jacksonians." Jimmy somehow got himself in with this group and when Dallas's Family Party folks finally jumped on the Jackson train they were called "Eleventh Hour Men," and relegated to the caboose.

At the end, four candidates were in the ring. Jackson's 99 votes were a plurality of the electoral votes but Massachusetts scion John Quincy Adams was close behind with 83 votes. William Crawford of Georgia had 41 and Henry Clay of Kentucky nipped at him with 37. In accordance with the Twelfth Amendment, he was constitutionally out of the running. Calhoun had swept to the Vice-Presidency. There was no majority electoral winner, although Jackson also garnered 43% of the popular vote to Adams's 30% and Crawford's and Clay's 13% a piece, establishing himself, Jackson concluded, as the people's choice. The only constitutional alternative was to throw the election into the House of Representatives. The special session would not be held until four months later, in February, right before inauguration.

Congressmen converged on Washington. Lobbying and favor swapping were intense. Pennsylvania, which Jackson carried, was indeed a keystone, although now each state counted as only one vote. All three candidates were so-called "Democrat-Republicans" or some close linguistic variant. Rumors flew. Clay, constitutionally an outsider, supposedly would throw his support to Adams if he could just be Secretary of State. State was a frequent stepping-stone to the higher office, and therefore a reasonable consolation prize. Jackson was, rumor had it, promising Adams the same post.

Neither Jimmy nor Jackson liked the bald little Adams and his old line genealogy and Harvard ways. Jimmy became the self-appointed agent in the effort to align Clay with Jackson, and longed to be credited with the votes that tipped him into the Executive Mansion. He whispered to all who would hear that Adams would not really place the Kentuckian in the leading cabinet post and that Clay had a better chance at State if he went with Old Hickory.

By December, over a month after the election, it was clear that there were strong moves by Jackson and Adams to translate the promises toward resolution of Monroe's successor.

Jimmy went to Jackson's close friend, Major John Henry Eaton, and asked what he could do. Eaton demurred. Jimmy decided to step over the aspirant's confidantes and went to call on the war hero himself. Jimmy arrived at Jackson's apartment on December 30th and waited around as the other callers departed. The man reputedly able to whip his weight in wildcats had earlier told Eaton with respect to Buchanan, "I did not think much of this fawning lickfinger, spittling up to me at every opportunity. Looks like a damn Chinese doll with a turnip top for a head, with his flowery yellow hair!"

To Jimmy's face, he was nearly as curt, "What might you want, Buchanan?"

"Let me accompany you outside, out toward the Potomac. I have the means to your Presidency."

Jackson could not ignore the bait and the two wandered down South B Street together toward its western terminus, the General inwardly cursing his bad luck, irritated as he suffered the toady's false deference. His old wounds, the jabbing legacy of wars and duels,

ached at the knowledge that his plurality caused him to have to seek
assistance from such a hotbed of smarmy conceit. Still, he resigned
himself, one sometimes had to crawl into bed with vermin to wake
with the angels.

Jimmy engaged in small talk, dancing around the point
until Jackson called him to step forward. Jimmy stated the obvious,
"General, you are losing the support of Clay and his adherents. You
have not clearly come out and said you would not reward him with
State."

Jackson, disquieted by the overfamiliarity and sorting through
the double negative, rejoined that he had not made up his mind yet,
and that he wanted his options to remain open. In any event, he was
not going to disclose his decision to this effete young man. Jimmy hid
his smile. He now possessed more information than Jackson intended,
and he could use this disavowal with both sides.

On New Year's Eve, Jimmy wangled an invitation to Clay's
private lodgings. In the presence of the more prominent politicians, he
intimated that he had some special knowledge that he was privileged
to impart. "General Jackson," Jimmy began, "is intent on establishing
the most prominent Cabinet in the nation's history."

Several of those closer to Clay began their questioning, "How
does he intend to accomplish this?"

Jimmy let drop, "The General does not intend to go beyond
this very room in his selection at State." He pronounced the news
looking into Senator Clay's deep brown eyes. The others wondered at
this intelligence, and said so. Clay took it to heart.

Jimmy felt damn good about himself. He pleased Clay, Calhoun
would remember his early support, and he had assisted Jackson's
presidential efforts. Even if Old Hickory later lost, Jimmy factored, he
had done all he could to help. Only Adams, who detested him anyway,
and Crawford, who was no longer important, were not in his debt.

Jimmy misapprehended the game. More polished players with greater skill on the political playground soon schooled Jimmy. Clay, three weeks after the confidential information so coyly delivered by Jimmy and after further consultations, announced for Adams.

When the editor of a Philadelphia paper charged that Clay was pandering his support to any candidate who would make him Secretary of State, the Senator challenged him to a duel. The newspaperman, a crack shot, proposed squirrel rifles as the weapons of choice. Clay backed down. His alacrity in doing so was no match for the hasty withdrawal of Jimmy, piqued at his inability to orchestrate the outcome.

At this same time, the Marquis de Lafayette made his last visit to America. He toured his former haunts and visited with the few ragged patriots still hanging on, but grew concerned about the political landscape of the nation for whose freedom he fought. Only a teenager when he came to America to help General Washington, he wanted to assure himself that there was indeed an American future after the War of 1812 and the sectional divisions he read of in *Le Monde*. After a stop in nearby Easton, where the college bearing his name was slated to open the next year, he came to Lancaster to visit the ailing Robert Coleman. The friends commiserated over the death of their dear little Ann and discussed the now Congressman Buchanan, whom Coleman despised more than the Marquis had ever imagined. While visiting, Lafayette learned more of the election dispute and talk of arming the militia if Jackson were not named President. "Robert, do I have to do the saddle up and corral these Americans this time?"

Coleman shook his head, "No, Marquis. I have faith our country is resilient and we have made constitutional provisions for just this event on which, I trust, we can rely."

Even as he said this, weariness born of age and uncertainty invaded his conclusion, and he again wished he had done more to prevent Buchanan's ascent. The name was forbidden in his household, but only last week he had discussed the matter with his lawyer, Thaddeus

Stevens. Stevens, quite mysteriously, had indicated that there might be some steps he could take with respect to Buchanan.

Only the top three candidates could be considered by the House of Representatives and Clay did not make the cut. Adams, who cleanly carried only the six New England states in November, ended up with the votes of 13 of the 24 states and, *mirabile dictu*, Clay became Secretary of State. Jackson's overwhelming popular plurality, his clear electoral college lead, and his election day sweep of eight states and share of four others, translated into the preference of only seven states. A week before the vote, Clay wrote to a friend, *I cannot believe that killing 2,500 Englishmen at New Orleans qualifies for the various, difficult, and complicated duties of the Chief Magistracy.*

Jackson's more vociferous supporters burned the second President's son and the Kentuckian in effigy. Jimmy was silent. He learned that it was, behind closed doors as on the House floor, better to hold one's cards closely.

Jimmy was therefore shocked to receive a letter from Calhoun's campaign manager the following October. Duff Green wrote, in essence, that Jimmy betrayed Calhoun, and sold out Jackson. Green's letter referred to the fateful conduct of the past election, the walk on which Jackson joined Jimmy, and the New Year's Eve disclosure. Wrote Green, *The part taken by you on the occasion referred to, is known to me; and only due regard for your feelings has heretofore restrained me from using your name before the public. The time, moreover, is now approaching when it will become the duty of every man to do all in his power to expose the bargain.* Jimmy was invited to, *upon the receipt of this, write to me and explain the causes which induced you to see Genl. Jackson upon the subject of the vote of Mr. Clay.*

Jimmy was trapped. He remembered something about engineers and petards, and felt fully hoisted. He anticipated the wave of gossip, and had to prevent the cresting tide from overcoming him. The only way he knew to do that was to swim with the strongest currents.

Where to go? To whom could he turn for support in the roiling waters? Clay would not likely want to have anything to do with him now, Adams was not a possibility, and Calhoun made his position clear via Duff Green.

The young Congressman labored over his response to Calhoun's manager. He had to dissimulate his role and try to mount some sort of counter-thrust if this information were disclosed. In carefully crafted correspondence, Jimmy wrote, *There is, as you may anticipate, the promise of exposure of certain corrupt bargains that peopled the last election. Calhoun and his adherents are not beyond the pale of potential obloquy.*

Jimmy was relieved when he did not immediately hear anything further about his part in the affair and began to think that the crude tools of his youth might suffice.

Jackson, however, wrote a letter accusing Henry Clay and an *"unnamed congressman"* of cheating him out of the presidency that was rightfully his. Clay, incensed, denied such a role and demanded to know who this congressman was.

Jimmy knew he was the target and saw his dilemma as either confession, or calling Jackson a liar. He embarked on what for some would be a perilous course. Pulling on his prior brushes with truth and his stomach roiling, he opted for a putative "confession," in which he would skirt the blame for Jackson, but through his long-developed skills at extrication and finger-pointing seek absolution. Trying to steer through the situation as best he could, he moved to dispel any notion that he was Clay's agent. He admitted the meeting but asserted, "I called upon General Jackson solely as his friend and with no object nor agency in mind."

Jackson appreciated that he was at least not directly implicated in the affair but was flabbergasted at the assertion of friendship. Many thought the political career of the trimmer from Pennsylvania was now at a well-deserved end. Congressmen actively distanced themselves, one writing that, *Buchanan's career was in ruins.*

Conventional wisdom held that the young Representative's weak defense of Jackson actually pointed the finger directly at the General. Those who thought so underestimated Jimmy and the lessons he now quickly learned. There was soon plenty of mud to spread around.

The Jackson press chose to see Jimmy's statement as support of Jackson's accusations of other skullduggery. Jimmy seized upon this opening, and revealed himself "firmly and forever" a Jackson man, a resolute member of the fawning claque. He was now a sufficiently sensitive sailor of the political seas to know that the future would be defined by whether one was for Jackson, or against him. Jackson did not ever trust Jimmy again, although the old warrior felt at least some exoneration from the result of the contretemps, as pallid and legalistic as the pudgy congressman's tactics might be.

Martin van Buren recognized flummery when he saw it. The Little Magician correctly divined the situation, and Jimmy's dissembling character but artful dodging, with these vatic words to Jackson, *Our friend Buchanan was evidently frightened and therefore softened and obscured the matter, still the fact of your entire aversion to all and any intrigue or arrangement is clearly established.*

Jimmy soon earned the grudging admiration of many but one of his former adherents remarked that, "If young Buchanan nods in one direction, friends and foes alike look in the other, just in case." Another, all illusion gone, went so far as to assert, "Buchanan is the personification of evasion, the embodiment of the inducement to dodge." These evaluations reached his ears and Congressman Buchanan permitted himself a small smile. Maybe not kind words for a preacher, Jimmy thought, but they reflected helpful skills for the goal that was now ever more firmly fixed...

Chapter Nine
<u>CONFRONTATION</u>

Thaddeus Stevens of Gettysburg entered the courtroom.

Jimmy had parlayed his position in Washington not only to dispense patronage, but also to foster his legal career with select cases trading on his political position. One such matter involved the Columbia Bridge Works. The same client he had represented just before Ann's death had agreed to provide some excess iron to the York Manufacturers Guild which used the metal to fabricate a variety of farm implements, including a sophisticated steam powered thresher. Whether it was the new technology or the iron that was defective, the threshers were failing in the field, causing lost business, and spawning a wave of lawsuits by farmers throughout York and Lancaster counties. The York fabricators sought restitution from the Columbia concern for the cost of the iron, and indemnification from the farmers' suits.

It was on this case that Jimmy found himself in York on the first Friday of August 1830. His reelection to Congress in less than two months, after a difficult transition to the Jackson party, seemed assured.

Why had he taken this case? He had not bargained for Stevens, whose sardonic wit and on-point precision with precedent turned lions into lambs. Thank goodness this was just a hearing and not a trial, and the judge owed his appointment to Jimmy. At least he did not have to face a jury with Stevens on the other side. Still, judge in his pocket or no, this was not going to be an easy ride.

"Counsel, you may commence."

The argument was going badly for Jimmy when Judge Tulkinghorn called for a luncheon adjournment. Would two hours be enough? The judge invited Jimmy into his chambers. The echoes of Thad's hard soles bounced about the empty courtroom as he tried to chain his fury at being excluded.

"Congressman," looking directly at Jimmy, "I am uncertain that I am going to be able to rule in your favor on this matter, at least with respect to the provision of the iron itself, and you may have to go to trial. I strongly suggest you seek whatever compromise is possible with Mr. Stevens. I will back you up with your client as necessary."

Jimmy believed he was at least astute enough to know when a far better prepared opponent was pouring him out of court like the contents of last night's bedpan.. He now wished he had researched his case a bit better. He could have prevailed on the law, which certainly disfavored plaintiffs seeking judgments for contract breaches. There was also this absurd notion of "indemnification" for the farmers' suits. Now, nothing to do other than take Judge Tulkinghorn's advice and compromise the matter in a way he could at least explain away to those whose interests he represented.

Jimmy returned to the courtroom and bloated his way over. "Mr. Stevens, we should break bread and discuss the case."

"There is nothing to discuss. In any event, I do not eat while I work."

Thad paused. He had to be concerned about what he pictured as the *in camera* deal that might have been shot in the judge's chambers. His clients' interests demanded he obtain any knowledge that might assist their cause. Buchanan was clearly unprepared, but he could not rely solely on an opponent's ineptitude, particularly at this stage of the case. Thad had been required to cast a wide net simply to find any precedent that could possibly auger the reasonable extension of contract law in this area. Finally, he had fished up one obscure case, buried in the bottom of an ocean of Blackstone's commentaries, and was flinging it about as hard as he could. His adversary had not bothered to cite any of the school of cases in his favor.

"All right, Buchanan. I will meet with you."

The two men left York proper and headed into the countryside, riding silently into flurries tracing comet runs against the blustery gray. Jimmy's salmon greatcoat billowed as he rode, making him look, Thad thought from behind, like a giant pumpkin, his topknot a stem harvested too late. When they reached the edge of Mt. Pisgah road as it approached the Susquehanna bluff near East Prospect, just southeast of York, Jimmy opened his wicker basket and removed the currant jelly, half loaf of bread and dining knife he had packed that morning. He set it delicately on a colorful Mennonite quilt, all whorls of blue and red and white. Thad took a sausage out of his pocket and peeled back the casing.

Jimmy surveyed the scattered straw fields and the half burnt trees that survived a summer's fire, and scanned, as if he were its proprietor, the tumid river below reflecting the muddy sameness of the Pennsylvania sky. Feeling very much in control of the situation, Jimmy began, "Mr. Stevens, I know you are an astute man, and you can see that my client is in the right here. To save you the trouble and embarrassment of further proceedings before this judge, I am prepared to be fair and will agree to request of my client that it provide the amount of its profit, subject to any necessary offsets, to the York Guild, and they can do with those funds what they will."

"Mr. Buchanan, you will do a lot more than that."

Jimmy looked away as he swallowed a now sandy bite of lunch. "I am not gainsaying that my client has some responsibility here, and I am acknowledging that. Do not push me too far, sir, or we will be back in Judge Tulkinghorn's court, and I will be alone with His Honor in his chambers. You might as well know he owes his position to my good offices."

Thad could stand this no longer. He had held, for nearly a full decade, the letter, withdrawing it from his safe, and its folded pouch, only twice before, although he had long since memorized its contents. Out of obligations to his client and respect to a dead young girl, and then to her father and family, he had not unleashed it. It was held for Ann's trust, and he should use it as such. Now Mr. Coleman was dead, and Ann's grave was gray with moss, yet his commitment lived on. He had been compelled to watch as this poseur parlayed precious little talent into not only a comfortable practice buttressed by Mr. Coleman, but a political career. He had suffered on the sideline as Buchanan spun a tale of sad loss and progressive duplicity into the position where he was actually being spoken of for Senator, and maybe offices of public trust beyond even that. Thad recalled the waffling self-righteous account Buchanan had planted in the Lancaster *Journal* at the end of last year concerning his Washington activities, the Congressman's accusations that Louisa Adams, the president's wife, was born out of wedlock and a whole cavalcade of truths twisted. He was steamed beyond all expectation as he began to address the cock-eyed pot of vainglory.

"Mr. Buchanan, you remember Ann Coleman, do you not?"

Jimmy nodded assent at this completely unanticipated turn. What did that have to do with anything?

"Did you know that I was in fact Mr. Coleman's attorney for the last several years of his life?"

Jimmy said no, he had not, and marveled at this news. How could he have not known that? Well, of course, he had had nothing to do with any of the Colemans. Ann's brother Thomas had crossed over King Street just two days ago so as not to be compelled to greet him. He had not seen the senior Coleman but once, and only as he was coming out of St. James after services, since Ann's death. Among the many reasons he did not like to spend time in Lancaster was the Coleman presence, although with the old man's passing it had grown a great deal more comfortable for him.

Jimmy's head began to cock a bit more, and his tongue commenced a curious trip across the back of his frozen lips, betraying all the appearance of a young squirrel massaging a nut it was afraid to trust to its immature teeth.

"Well, Mr. Congressman, I was. Not only that, I represented young Ann herself."

Jimmy's tongue became more vigorous.

"I also have sure knowledge of the reason for her demise."

Jimmy's stomach started to tumble. He had felt secure as he iterated the Ann stories that brought him consideration by voters, and sympathy and protection from fortune hunting widows and aggressive young girls. What did he mean "sure knowledge?" Ann killed herself, everyone now knew, and was dangerously unstable. Her parents stood in the young lovers' way, and his fiancée's deep sense of loss compelled her death. The vindictive father barred Jimmy from the funeral, and he simply had to plunge into the political pool in an effort to drown his grief. Everyone, everyone knew this.

Jimmy began to explain to this Stevens fellow whose bluff was going to be called. "Stevens, I have further sad but true evidence that such instability ran in the Coleman family. Sarah, Ann's younger sister—you remember her, don't you—she went with Ann on that sublunary winter journey?"

Thad stared back, let out a short nasal snort at the florid vocabulary, all the while fighting the urge to cock his head in the opposite direction.

"Well, anyway, she was courted by young Reverend Muhlenberg, the pastor of St. James's who buried her sister. You must know they had just announced their engagement. Mr. Coleman used his position as head of the vestry and engaged in some dispute with the pastor about whether evening services were appropriate. The upshot was that he forbade Sarah to see Muhlenberg and in fact drove the minister out of town a few months after the squabble."

No reply from Thad, who knew where this particular train would depot.

"Of course, the father dies. You know the kinds of things they write on headstones."

Thad of course knew. He had visited Ann's elevated tomb maybe 100 times in the past few years, seemingly casually and often at dusk as his business was done or after an early morning's ride. He was not a praying man, but he prayed there. Her father's marker was separated from Ann's only by her mother's still-empty grave. He needed only once through to recall any writing and could have recited the entire proto-biography engraved on the sandstone sepulcher. He recalled several of its phrases even as Buchanan spoke: *To his country a valuable and venerated citizen, enlarging its wealth and resources by his unremitting industry and in public trust he was vigilant and faithful...In social intercourse open unaffected and sincere...his bounties were extended with a liberal and willing hand...He will long be remembered for his public usefulness & private worth.*

Jimmy went on, "You do know, despite his laudable qualities, Mr. Coleman, just as he had barred Ann from happiness with me, also kept his hands clutched on his young daughter's throat from beyond the grave. He willed Sarah's share of the inheritance into the trust of her older brother Thomas, to be dispensed to Sarah only how and when her sibling chose, and in no event if she persisted in that foolish romance."

Thad was familiar with that proviso. He had, reluctantly, drafted it himself but did not share that information with Jimmy. Guilt over the younger sister's death still clawed at his heart like a rabid wolverine. He could not shake it off and it would not die. He was certain he was about to hear the story again but he could not permit Buchanan to see his vulnerability on this point.

Jimmy did not disappoint, "Within weeks of Robert's passing, Sarah traveled again to Philadelphia. She was now the same age as Ann when she perished. Sarah flung herself naked into the Schuylkill on the midnight of December 9th, the same day, six years removed, as Ann had died. Surely, Mr. Stevens, this is dispositive proof to you and all of my statements concerning Ann's death, and the whole family's mental disturbances?"

Dispositive proof of nothing, Stevens thought, you dissembling fool, stretching your protean story to fit on a Proscutean bed of your own making. He reached into his pocket and pulled out a now pale red pouch. Thad slowly put his thick fingers into its opening and spread the braided black cord that laced between the brass eyelets. He reached in and slowly withdrew a folded envelope.

Thad held it just closely enough for Jimmy to see his carefully inscribed address. Ann's former suitor recognized the writing as her delicate hand. Indeed, the same gentle scrawl graced the neat, satin-bowed bundle of love letters he maintained at home, tucked beneath his very bed.

Jimmy's whole body began to twitch and he choked back the taste of rising garbage in his throat. His mouth, previously dry, now felt as if it held the entire Desert of Sin. What was in this envelope? If she wrote it to Stevens, as she indeed must have, then why? When? How did she even know him? Had Stevens been Coleman's lawyer? Well, he must have been. He said so. This was proof. Unless they were lovers? No, hardly not. Ann was smitten with me. Jimmy strained to see the postmark and the date, but Stevens was holding it too far for even his good eye. What could possibly be in this letter? For years he had struggled to figure out what impelled Ann to flee to Philadelphia in such a fury. Surely, his other conduct had remained unknown to her, and to all, had it not? Had she learned of the tales he told in the tavern that compromised her integrity? Had she simply determined that he was, in fact, after her fortune? Would those have been enough for her to kill herself? Well, yes of course, he thought, comfortable with his developed belief that she was in fact simply addled. With God as his witness, the blame for her demise was appropriately and squarely at the feet of Ann's imperious father and her rapacious mother, neither of whom ever liked him anyway.

Jimmy could not unfix his eyes from the letter as Thad held the envelope slowly flapping in the now colder wind. It appeared scarlet against the foreboding York County heavens and seemed now to grow until it blocked his view of anything else. For what seemed an eternity, his antagonist brandished the aging paper, waving it back and forth, back and forth, in slow sweeping rhythms in front of him. Thad curled it back out of the air, revealing the thunder clouds it had camouflaged. He returned the letter to its faded purse. Jimmy followed it all the way into Thad's pocket.

"Mr. Buchanan," Thad continued, "suffice it to say that our relationship is forever altered. You will make this concession today. All monies paid by my client will be returned in full, and you will compensate the farmers fairly for their losses without recourse to my client. In the future, I suggest you would be wise not to accept any matters in which I am on the opposite side. You have enjoyed some imponderable success in your political career. It will come as no secret to you that your fussy Federalism and newly seized upon Jacksonian sympathies are easily seen through by me. You, sir, are a rank opportunist, a trimmer and appeaser, and do discredit to your position of public and private trust."

Jimmy could not believe what he was hearing. At the depths of the dispute over his role in the controversy with Clay and Adams and Jackson, no one dared speak to or about him in this fashion, and here was this transplanted cripple of a Vermont farmer threatening him. What could possibly be in that envelope that would bolster such effrontery?

He should, he thought, find out now. "Mr. Stevens, what possibly could you have there? How do I know this is not simply some kind of hocus-pocus?

Thad's reply did nothing but disquiet him. He barked, "I know, sir, your secret, and much more besides. Do not push me superfluously to reveal it to you."

Jimmy was stunned by the ferocity of this reply. He quickly factored his options. He could lunge at Stevens and try to wrest the pouch and its contents from him. He could negotiate further to see its contents. Neither would work. Stevens was twice as strong as he and clearly would not give up the letter, or he would have revealed its contents already. He was left within the clutches of curiosity. He had to do something, right now, to make the immediate situation go away.

"All right. I do not necessarily credit that you have anything, for I cannot divine what information such a letter should supposedly contain. Yet I will agree to report to the court that the parties have resolved all matters to their satisfaction, and that an appropriate order, drafted," he paused and looked at his adversary, "of course by you, will be forthcoming."

The two men rode separately back to the courthouse and Jimmy made his announcement to the judge, who was pleased to have the rest of the day to himself and an early start on his weekend. On the way from the courtroom, Thad placed his large paw on Jimmy's shoulder and spun him swiftly toward him. "This will not be the last, Mr. Buchanan, that I will use this information if needed. Do not step too far out of bounds or my deference to my dead clients will be exceeded by the interests of the living."

Thad looked at him with eyes as dark as the pig iron leavings from Coleman's furnaces. Jimmy had planned to return to Lancaster to complete his campaign efforts. Instead, he turned his horse Cherry toward Washington. Stevens's chilling words echoed in Jimmy's head as he labored on the hard ride. He stopped every few hundred feet at first and soon exhausted his stomach's contents. He did not even have a change of clothes, and how to explain to Robert Grier and his supporters why he had not returned? Surely, they would be gravely concerned.

Every clatter of every hoof seemed to say, "Ann. Ann. Ann." *ad nauseum*. He tried to weigh what Stevens's veiled revelation really meant. For certain, it was not to apply simply to private disputes, but to the public arena.

So Stevens knew. He knew something. What, exactly, did that damn negroist know? Would he really use this knowledge? How?

Chapter Ten
CONFUSION

"**D**avid," Jimmy was still quite breathless when he asked the hotelier, "where do you get these lobsters?"

"Why, down from Maine of course," Barnum replied. "Swimming in salt water all the way. If they die, we don't serve them."

Jimmy nodded. He had thought he would again find a welcome respite at Barnum's fine establishment on the intervening night on his way back to Washington. He had sent the proprietor's man out for garments that would at least span the rest of the trip. Barnum's had always seemed a world away. Tonight, however, even the sight of the food made his stomach tumble. He managed only to gum through the tail, leaving the red glowing claws intact, erect and grasping. Jimmy lay awake that night in his room at Barnum's, on the third floor in the back with a harbor view, and saw the same scene behind every imagined bush. Every tree in the woods. Stevens. Stevens. Stevens with that letter. Waving it, just beyond reach.

How can I trust that there was anything whatsoever in that damn letter? How did I fall under the traducer's spell? How could that daughter of a Dactyl finger me from the grave? Why didn't I just grab it from him, rip it apart, burn it, eat it, spit it into the Susquehanna. I certainly can not go back to Lancaster even with Coleman dead. My God, I am almost 40. The West? Full of hayseeds, rubes and unsophisticates, even though it disgorged the occasional Jackson. Stevens as much as told me my political career is over. As if he had the right to do so! How can I trust ever going into court again? Or even walk on Lancaster's streets. Snickers and titters, or worse, as I pass? Whatever Stevens had, whatever the letter said or might say (will I ever know?), he would surely use it, and use it hard. My God, he threatened my very professional life. What can I do? I have got to figure out a way to stay in government. I vowed to be President. Nothing else will do. How could some youthful indiscretion stymie me now? If indeed there is one, and as if Ann would know. He held the damn thing for 10 years, more than a decade. Why would I think there is anything to it?

He churned into a fitful sleep, unaware just how far from Stevens and Lancaster he was soon going to be. Floating across the cream canopy of his four-poster, Stevens's eyes burned out of his mother's kind face. Mother, you tell me "not to be afeerd" but dammit I am afraid, and it's a perfectly reasonable fear…

He thought back to how difficult the political path for his transition to the Democratic Party had been when Federalist fortunes fully faded. He had to fight hard and dirty to remain in Washington. Party partisans remembered the young Federalist Assemblyman's Fourth of July attack, and misquoted to great effect his statement on that occasion that, "if I had a drop of Democratic blood in my veins, I would let it out to bleed on the ground." Many in his new party sought to take him at his word, excoriating him at every turn.

He was firmly hitched to the first star of the American West. Could he now fully cash in on those efforts? Without him, Old Hickory might not have been able to avenge the stolen election. The notion of backdoor thievery energized the troops and, he thought, I am one of their leaders.

"The Adams administration," Jimmy asserted, "is despotic, unconstitutional, immoral, and corrupt. The Republic has no future if Adams and his ilk remain in power." A bold step for someone who supposedly learned to keep his counsel but his dubious role in the past election was already known, and the wizened little apple off the Adams tree would certainly not be useful to his future.

General Jackson marveled when he heard of Jimmy's speech from Duff Gordon, now his aide after Calhoun's defeat, "I did not anticipate such vigor from that china doll. Buchanan is showing himself as something more than weak and manipulative. At least in speech, he looks to be strong and manipulative." Jackson winked at Gordon and had another whiskey.

Slavery was beginning to take on an importance that overshadowed all else on the national stage after its earlier retreat as the result of the Missouri Compromise of 1820, only a year before Jimmy took office. He had not given the issue much thought, except that he knew the nation could not prosper unless slaves helped the South with its cotton and tobacco. He was also very much in favor of the preservation of its noble way of life. Not only was that position logically unassailable, it was constitutionally required. Besides, he was himself personally drawn to the more genteel southern way of life and the gentlemen he had met. He remarked to Robert Grier, his old classmate and now a local judge, "Slavery is of course in some ways evil, but it is such an extremely pleasant evil."

Jimmy also believed that the nation would not be able to grow unless provision was made for the extension of slavery into the new states.

Many would not go to the country's territories if owning human chattel were not at least a possibility. His views were already well known not only to his constituents, but also to southern legislators and its propertied class, who were prepared to reward their friends. A growing group of anti-slavers, from New England, across upstate New York and into the western states of Ohio and Indiana, also well knew where he stood.

Accusations that Jimmy was "in bed with the South" actually had helped him with the Scots-Irish in his home district, but many German farmers and most Quakers were well targeted with these attacks. The political became personal. Jimmy was denounced for making money at his private law practice at the expense of his Congressional duties. He got into trouble for asserting that John Quincy Adams's wife Louisa, the only first lady born outside of the United States, was the product of an illicit union. The blue-blooded Bay Stater and his supporters purported to be shocked but the scandalous suggestion dovetailed with the sniping tenor of the campaign. One newspaper ran a list of the "seven traitors of Pennsylvania." Jimmy was first on the list.

Newspapers loyal to Adams regurgitated the lurid stories of four years earlier. Old Hickory's mother was a "common prostitute," his father was a "colored man," he was an "adulterer" and his wife a "bigamist." Adams seemed to pull ahead in Pennsylvania and the country as a whole, despite the continued stench of the "corrupt bargain" of 1824. Jimmy's early support of Jackson began to seem sheer folly. He wrote to his mother, *the persecution against me in this county has exceeded all reasonable bounds. Some of the leaders of the Adams party have transferred all of their abuse from Genl. Jackson to me. The purest & most disinterested acts of my life have been misconstrued, & out of them charges have been raised to destroy my reputation.*

At rallies and dinners, Jimmy would disappear suddenly, returning with a face drained of all color except the hard blush of embarrassment. He could not recall feeling quite this bad since he was compelled to sift though the remains of weasels and rats back in his father's basement or, of course, those other sights he still fought so hard to repress.

Ultimately, Jackson managed to withstand the calumnies, and Jimmy clung tightly to his coat. Both carried Lancaster County by comfortable margins.

It was secretly a delight to him, Jimmy had to admit, when Jackson's rabble irretrievably revealed their rough ways the day of the Inauguration. Responding to the General's invitation to the American public to join in the celebration, 20,000 journeyed to the national capital from Tennessee, Indiana and all manner of rural outposts. One group rolled a 1400-pound wheel of cheese into the East Room. Within two hours, it was clawed and chunked to oblivion. Whiskey was served in bathtub-sized vats in a futile effort to entice the mob back to the White House's front lawn. The backwoods crowd clambered over Jackson's new residence, soiled the carpets, knocked over candles, dripped wax everywhere, and kicked down doors with hobnail boots. Chunks of cheese and melting mounds of ice cream were everywhere. There was, for months, a peculiar redolence to the Executive Mansion.

Jimmy made something of a show of sniffing the air when he went to see the new President. He had not been able to obtain an audience with Jackson any earlier. The General had remained at his Hermitage near Nashville to be with his wife Rachel, who had taken ill and died on the eve of Christmas. She had suffered greatly under the assaulting charges of bigamy, and Jackson blamed his political enemies for her death. "Mr. President," Jimmy said, "I am so sorry for your loss, which so parallels my great one of but a decade ago. I of course seek no reward for myself. Surely someone from Pennsylvania, however, should sit in your cabinet."

Jackson considered, ignoring the condolences, "You are of course right, Mr. Buchanan. There are so few posts, howsoever. I am set on the Secretaries of State, War, and Navy, and Attorney and Postmaster General. That leaves just Treasury. Did you have someone in mind?"

"Of course, I do not have any direct experience…"

Old Hickory cut him off, "That's of little moment. I had not considered you."

Jimmy retreated, his head tucked to his chest as he backed out of the President's office. Pennsylvania did get its cabinet position. A rival congressman from Dallas's group, Samuel Ingham, was named to Treasury. Jimmy fumed. He had extended himself, and that was his reward? How important it would have been to march off the electoral trail before Stevens's incarnation! Must he now stand for election while Stevens prowled about?

As he lay in his bed at Barnum's, up every few minutes to go to the corner bedpan and with sleep never coming, he reached the only conclusion he could. Head bent over the remnants of the half-eaten lobster, Jimmy remembered the hope he had felt as he stood atop his desk and vowed to be President. He was too weak to leap upon his bed, and too tall for its canopied top in any event. Jimmy stared down at what looked to him like a primordial soup from which his life must rise and swore softly into the leavings, "I will still find a way."

Chapter Eleven
<u>R U S S I A</u>

The Petticoat Affair had legs.

Young Peggy O'Neale's father ran one of the largest boarding houses in Washington, the Franklin House on I Street. Its tavern was a notorious hangout for congressmen and senators at the time of Jackson's election, and before. Jackson had lodged there, and gotten to know the young daughter. Peggy later acknowledged she was "something of a pet" to the assembled politicos, many of whom she saw in states of sartorial disarray not customarily viewed in the halls of Congress.

Her dark hair, deep blue eyes, and fine skin echoed the appearance of a young woman who died in the snow at Bartram's Garden.

Peggy's first marriage, to John Timberlake, a drunk and philanderer, ended with her husband's suicide in April 1828. Within days after the sudden death, Peggy was secretly engaged to John Eaton, the senior Senator from Tennessee. Eaton had been elected to the Senate at age 28, two years short of the constitutionally mandated minimum age. No one bothered to ask, and he had not told. When he learned of the engagement, Jackson urged Eaton privately to "make an honest woman of her at the earliest opportunity."

That fall the President-elect wrote his wife Rachel, *every Sunday evening Peggy entertains her pious mother with sacred music to which we are invited.* His wife was lowered into the ground the day after Christmas wearing the gown she had made for the Inauguration. Jackson alluded to the charges of adultery and bigamy which he believed had led to her death, "May God forgive her murderers, as I know she forgave them. I never can." His resolve to help "his little Peg" grew with each shovelful heaped on Rachel's coffin.

Peggy's marriage was formalized days later on January 1st. Whispers of her promiscuity and a premarital miscarriage, presumably with Eaton the father, infected a city that thrived on scandal. Eaton was nearing 40 and his new bride was 32. Louis McLane, a Jackson confidante and a Delaware's Senator, squealed, "Senator Eaton has just married his mistress—and the mistress of 11-dozen others!"

The rumored circumstances of her own birth in her immigrant father's tavern, and allegations of a pre-suicide relationship between the Senator and the saloonkeeper's daughter, did not make for an easy entry into Potomac society. Gossip surrounding Peggy included stories of self-inflicted poison by another admirer, and an elopement to a young officer aborted only when a flowerpot improvidentially fell on the floor, waking her father during a midnight escape through her bedroom window.

The President refused to allow another young woman to be pilloried by the same cluster of hard charges that drove his wife into the ground. He nominated Eaton for a cabinet post not as Secretary of the Navy, as he had first intended, but elevated his sights to Secretary of War. When Eaton asked if that were wise in the current political climate, Jackson responded, "Damn anyone who would deny me that right. I have gone through the inferno, lost my wife. I cannot but do this for you and Peggy."

Vice-President Calhoun, he of the sharp badger eyes and now graying lion's hair, made the uneasy transition as the number two man for both John Quincy Adams, whom he had despised, and now Jackson, who he thought should have known better. Calhoun's wife, the curiously monickered Floride, other cabinet wives, and most of Washington's essentially southern society would have nothing to do with Peggy, and insisted that their husbands did not either. Not only did Floride Calhoun and her cohorts snub the new couple, they ignored Presidential invitations to any state function.

The *cause celebre* grew. Instead of cleaning house as he promised to do in his campaign, the contagion that Secretary of State Martin Van Buren anointed the "Eaton Malaria" contaminated all the President's time and attention.

By the end of September, more than six months after the Inauguration, the cabinet had met only twice. The traditional social dinner welcoming all the Secretaries and their wives had been postponed to an uncertain day. Old Hickory issued a summary call to all cabinet members, sans Eaton, plus two local ministers, John N. Campbell and Ezra Stiles Ely, who were vocal pulpiteers against Peggy. Jackson marshaled evidence, with the assistance of the young Congressman from Lancaster, Jimmy Buchanan, who seemed quite adept at commandeering arguments against gossip and rumor. The picture they painted, through affidavits and recorded statements, proclaimed that Mrs. Eaton was in all things above reproach. This gloss was too much for some of the assembled, at least two of whom personally, they later asserted, knew otherwise based on shared carnal relations. The proceedings achieved humorous proportions when, in response to dissenting views, Jackson declared the mother of two was "as chaste as a virgin!"

The President finally presided over the initial cabinet dinner in November. The men attended, with Peggy hard by the President all night, again alone with a dozen men but not feeling nearly as flirtatious. All other cabinet wives sent their regrets. Government was at a standstill. Congress passed bills that were never signed. Old Hickory, the absence of Rachel painful and his wounds more piercing than ever, walked angrily through the corridors at 1600 Pennsylvania Avenue, damning Eastern bankers and anyone who came his way. He now suspected that Henry Clay orchestrated this unprecedented and ongoing diversion, the "troubles, vexations and difficulties" of the Petticoat Affair. "Calhoun, that ambitious and devious heir to nothing of mine, is complicitous with Clay. May they both rot in their own particular Hell."

Washington was still paralyzed when Jimmy arrived, emaciated, back from Barnum's and the York bluff.

He sat down on August 9, 1830, a week before his already assured renomination and wrote several drafts alternately summarizing and expanding his accomplishments in Congress, his opposition to tariffs, the roads on which Lancaster's citizenry was now privileged to travel, canals that aided commerce, and so much more. Soon, their waddings looked like icebergs on his Arctic floor. How to do what he must now do?

Finally, a letter to George Wolf, as Governor the titular head of the Pennsylvania Democrats, with a shorter, similar announcement addressed to the Lancaster *Journal*.

It has been my privilege and honor to represent the citizens of the Fourth District and all Lancastrians for five terms in the august hallways of the Capitol. I now must announce, with regret, my withdrawal from public life. I recognize that it has been once before, as I thought myself in line for a post in our President's cabinet, that I so similarly informed you. At this time, my decision is irrevocable.

I advise you so that you may assist in making adequate provision for my successor as I shall be occupied fully in matters of the greatest national interest for what would otherwise be the balance of my term, and beyond.

Governor Wolf stared at the paper. What was this about? Last December, Buchanan had written him indicating essentially the same thing. He had chosen to disregard it. The Congressman never knew his mind. This time, though, the party needed to act quickly. He dispatched a letter of his own to a recent predecessor with family connections in Lancaster politics. Joseph Hiester arranged for William

Muhlenberg Hiester, cousin of Sarah Coleman's former intended, to take Jimmy's place.

Supporters who had stuck with Jimmy in the last Congressional campaign and the difficult transition from Federalist to Democrat buzzed about Lancaster's Central Market near Penn Square for Hiester's rally. What does Buchanan mean, "After due consideration of what is best for the party, I have decided to withdraw from public life?" No one had an answer and murmurings and speculations about the precipitous withdrawal and insinuations of "private life devouring the public" grew. Jimmy did not aid his public cause by staying in Washington until after Hiester's election, returning only to retrieve some clothing and visit a few still puzzled friends.

In Gettysburg, Thad read the late-arriving announcement in the Lancaster paper. His lips tightened. He swept his hand into the autumn air and snared a passing June bug. He crushed it, slowly, in his palm.

Jimmy had to effect the rest of his plan, his short-term goal clear. He wandered White House halls, seeking a presidential audience. Old Hickory, it seemed, had no time for him. The administration was still frozen. The Eatons' situation was not only a burden to the President but also a liability to the whole party. Jackson seemed to spend all his time raving about conspiracies and paper money. The country was, as Jimmy wrote to Robert Grier before Congress began its session, *being governed only in absentia and certainly ill prepared for crisis.* How to put the President in his debt? He finally came up with a solution that, although drastic, might work.

Jimmy first had to convince Major Eaton. In addition to everything else, his paychecks would stop when the lame duck session quacked to a close in two weeks.

He tracked down Eaton in the executive office building flanking the White House to the northwest. It was February 22nd and the War

Secretary was at work despite the informal celebration of Washington's birthday, "Mr. Secretary, may I have a moment?"

"Of course, Congressman. Moments are all I have."

"There is a way to salvage your career, enable President Jackson's administration to survive and, if it would be helpful, save your marriage."

"Well, if there is, let's have it."

Jimmy outlined the plan. Martin Van Buren, Secretary of State and the cabinet's most prominent member, would resign at the same time as Eaton. This would put Jackson in the position of credibly being able to compel all others to do the same, whereas the departure of Eaton alone would be seen as caving in to public pressure. The President could choose "a cabinet that could work together," and not include Eaton and the Peggy problems. To those who balked, swift and certain political punishment was promised. In any event, all served at Jackson's pleasure, and he was not pleased.

The session ended March 3rd. Still no word as to whether Jackson approved. Jimmy stayed at the Widow as the grey days grew longer, and the thundering spring growled through Lancaster. Whether there was really any substance to the ante-mortem scribblings of an addled girl, whether or not Stevens actually had anything at all, it had done its work. His paychecks stopped and his savings better be enough to bridge him to whatever spur of the path was next. Jimmy felt like a speckled trout, pulled from a stream of its own comfort, flopping in the snow, gills panting for oxygen it knew how to obtain in its own environment but could not find here. Somehow, he had to escape the clutches of that dead girl and the gray eminence torturing him, or political death was imminent and his quest gone.

It took two months for the plan to be effectuated but at April's end the Jackson administration consisted only of Old Hickory, the disgruntled Calhoun already back on his plantation, and not a single cabinet secretary save the Postmaster General. All others, including Jimmy's rival Ingham, were out of office. Calhoun did not bother to come back to the capital, and resigned the vice-presidency late that year. The office was vacant until Van Buren was named in Jackson's second term, a selection that led to his own ascension to the nation's highest office. Calhoun was never a serious presidential contender again, spending less than a year at State under fellow Southerner John Tyler.

Press and politicians were befuddled at the unprecedented overturning of a cabinet. Soon voices were heard that the nation was going to "collapse." Toasts were raised, "To the next cabinet—may they all be bachelors—or leave their wives at home." Jackson decided to keep none of those whose "resignations" he had compelled. Eaton was appointed governor of the Florida Territory. Peggy did not like the peninsula's humid mosquito land nearly as much as her hometown's. She could not believe it had cost $5,000,000 to obtain this swampy bedlam of bedbugs, spiders and its inescapable pounding sun.

Peggy wrote the President, *Please relieve us of the drudgery of Tallahassee, which seemed as if, Andy, you are punishing me!*

Jackson recalled his own sweaty incursion into Pensacola that paved the way for the acquisition of both East and West Florida. He extended his apologies and dispatched Eaton as Minister to His Catholic Majesty. Peggy was much happier, for a while, in Madrid.

The Territorial Governor, grateful for the young Congressman's role, had told Jimmy he would seek an appropriate reward for his efforts. Still, it had been weeks and there had been no word. Jackson continued to dodge him, and he did not want to upset the negotiations on his behalf. Finally, Eaton got back to him from Tallahassee, *Would it be acceptable if I arranged for something in the nature of an ambassadorship?*

Jimmy had hoped for State or War, but those dominoes had fallen. *Perhaps, could I be a Supreme Court justice?*, he wrote back, wondering at the triangulated correspondence in his quest for a safe place to land.

A Supreme Court could be his Ararat, beyond the reach of both Stevens and the voters, deftly swooping off that perch to pluck the Presidency at a propitious time.

Week after increasingly anxious week. Finally, Eaton wrote, *I believe, Congressman, we have gotten you perhaps even more than you might have hoped.* How could that be, thought Jimmy. He had certainly hoped for something higher than anything that might be forthcoming.

Jimmy read further, *You would be sent to a European country with a stable government, and one which is vital to our nation's future. We need to develop it as a trading partner and preclude any intrusive politics into our Hemisphere.*

Jimmy digested this information. What fit that bill? Not the Court of St. James's, not the Habsburg Empire, and certainly no Parisian destination. The final sentence, *I have prevailed upon the President to dispatch you to Russia.*

Russia! In 1831, Russia was about as far away from America as Jimmy could imagine. All this because he stood up for that strumpet! He frankly hoped for something more. Jimmy pondered the proposed "reward" of Russia, and weighed that against his other prospects. He had been compelled to give up his Congressional seat, and did not know French, the language of diplomacy, and he had never been abroad. Yet being a Minister to a foreign land, and an important one, grew more appealing as he ruminated. The ability to compromise was the hallmark of an effective diplomat, Jimmy reasoned, and the shading of the truth was the very air he breathed. It was an ambassadorship, and he could make it an important one. Out of the country is a providential place to be, away from the growing rift between North and South, manufacturer and farmer, the monied and the poor. Away, most importantly, from Stevens and Lancaster.

Eaton did not reveal how hard he was required to lobby Jackson, writing, *General, I understand you don't like the fellow much yet something has to be done for him. His life is so full of carefully crafted words that are really half-truths and casual flattery that he simply fails to separate out the dishonesty. What better place to be than in international diplomacy, where chronic lying is the accepted discourse? You know from your own experience, Andy, that Buchanan's "yes" is "maybe," and his "no" is "perhaps."*

The President considered how odd a world this was where those qualities might be attributes. He did not know what else to do with Buchanan and certainly did not want him around. He had too many other ferrets to watch. Buchanan did seem peculiarly well suited to burrow into the world of counts and tsars.

Jimmy protested when Jackson finally made the formal offer on the last day of May, "Mr. President is there not something better…?"

Old Hickory's eyes seemed on fire. He restrained his words, "That is, sir, the best I can do."

Jimmy had been waiting for months for this? Hiester had already taken his place not only in Congress but was also present at Washington's parties and partisan functions. Jimmy, uninvited, now spent his time at Barnum's or in Philadelphia at the Metropole. Damned if he had to go back to Lancaster! His inclination, nevertheless, was to turn the post down and go for something better. Surely he deserved it. He took nearly two weeks, weighing his other choices, which now looked like none. On June 12th, he accepted Jackson's offer.

Old Hickory later professed to President Polk that Buchanan's ambassadorship was not only the best he was willing to do but was limited only, "because it was as far as I could send him out of my sight, and where he could do the least harm. I would have sent him to the North Pole if we had kept a minister there!"

Jackson wanted to keep the announcement under the covers for a while to let the Petticoat Affair fully stop its fluttering. Caught in the hiatus between acceptance and announcement, afraid to practice law and out of politics, Jimmy fitfully studied French. He traveled to Boston and Saratoga, billing the government on the predicate that the trips were necessary to learn more about Russian civilization, or what there was of it. Despite the considerable resources he had managed to obtain based on Coleman's early referrals to his law offices and his own side practice, Jimmy was low on funds. He begged a small honorarium from the President, *to bridge me to my future duties.*

Feeling as if he were a secret agent in his own country, he went incognito to New York to investigate what was shipped on the trading routes to the Baltic and Black Seas.

What if the Senate did not confirm his nomination? Of course, that body would not again be in session until the next year. Jimmy took to visiting men he had known in Congress and was grateful when they had him to dinner. His tab at Barnum's was nearing four figures and its proprietor was, Jimmy thought, getting a little testy about payment. Why did I decline the certain nomination for another term in the House? Should not I have risked whatever Stevens had coming out? Just some small town, small time lawyer with an envelope and look at the wandering life he had foisted on him. Here he was traveling about, forbidden to reveal his secret agreement with the President lest even it be terminated, excuses at every turn. In letters to friends he repeated the same words, *The President has something special in mind for me, but I of course cannot reveal it at this time.*

The Hero of New Orleans remained suspicious about the depth of Jimmy's loyalty and continued to defer making the announcement. Finally, after a further four months of delay, buried in the New York *Enquirer* based on reporting by James Gordon Bennett, was the brief announcement, *President names James Buchanan, former member of Congress, Minister to St. Petersburg.* His mother, taken unawares and unsure of her son's activities since she learned from her daughter Jane that he had retired from office, wrote him plaintively on October 21st, *Would it not be practicable even now to decline its acceptance? If you can consistently with the character of a gentleman & a man of honor, decline, how great a gratification it will be to me.* She added a postscript, *At what time do you intend paying us that visit, previous to your departure from the country which gave you birth, and I expect, to me, the last visit? Do not disappoint me, but certainly come.*

Even if he had a credible alternative, Jimmy was not about to follow his mother's advice. He was confirmed in January. The following March he passed into Mercersburg on his way toward the western edge of Asia. "You don't understand anything about politics or politicians. Other events have sprung to block my path, and there are great pressures under which I have labored. I really had no choice other than to accept this situation."

Elizabeth looked at her son, "Jamie, I be right pleased for ye, yet it has been hard without your father and you never even visiting. William, dead though I had such hopes out of that college over in Princeton, but George is in a good place lawyering in Pittsburgh and sees me almost every other month. You will not forget your promise to help your sisters? Edward I think will need it as well."

"Of course. That was my promise. Be well, Mother."

Elizabeth watched her son shuffle into a comfortable place on the coach for the trip back to New York, now certain she would not see him again. In her entire life, she had not even been to York or Lancaster, let alone Baltimore or New York, nor ever ridden in a carriage. Here was her son, going all the way around the world. She wished it made her prouder.

Jimmy went on to the former capital. He spent a few days among its nearly 200,000 people, many displaced New Englanders and almost all of British descent, dining in establishments on Pearl, Water and Wall. He ventured by ferry to a new area across the tidal straight called Brooklyn Heights and passed the evening with an acquaintance.

On April 8th, the Silas Richards left New York for St. Petersburg. Jimmy was seasick most of the month he bobbed across the Atlantic. Pompey had to clamber up from steerage not only to empty the urine and excrement from his master's chamber pot but also to mop the vomit that lined the stateroom's floor and walls. The trip was extended when Jimmy jumped ship in Scotland, Pompey in tow, and meandered down through Liverpool to London on a trip that included his first-ever train ride. A full month in England was followed by the sea journey to St. Petersburg via Hamburg. Jimmy was seen on deck as the ship crossed the North Sea, slobbering in ways he thought poetic about the "silber shtellar beudee" of the stars. The ship reached the Gulf of Finland the following day, and traveled up the Neva to the Tsarist capital, arriving in St. Petersburg on June 2nd.

The American Minister was wholly unprepared for what he confronted. He had presumed that he was going to find vulgar Tatar edifices splotched together, isolated in an Asiatic version of backwoods America. Instead, the architecture was astonishing, resplendent with classical themes even Jimmy recognized from Greece and Rome, and odd turnip-topped stone buildings that were tossed everywhere like gumdrops on a meringue sea. The city's devotion to the arts was clear. Why, there were museums and museums and more museums, full of such brilliant colors and icons, frescoes and mosaics, that he was overwhelmed. His house, an Italianate villa, glutted with marble and crystal, stalls for six horses, servant quarters, and a carriage house. Jimmy felt as if he had entered the realm of royalty. He toured the city, wandering through the Mikhailovsky Castle and the surrounding square. He wrote in his journal, *I saw majestic Palace Square while the sun played with the polished red granite as it was erected, what they call the Alexander Column shooting into the deep summer sun which lasts here well into the night. It must be over 80 feet long & a dozen feet thick, and thrust ever upward. I have never seen such architecture. There shall be an angel atop its French design.*

He learned from his interpreter of the structural reforms introduced by Alexander, all of which created a bureaucracy quite orderly in Jimmy's view. Indeed, the city with its precise streets and heavy military presence seemed to him to be a grander incarnation of Lancaster. His interpreter did not tell him of the Decembrist revolt designed to force Nicholas to formulate a constitution, nor the real reason for Alexander's hasty and fearful departure toward the Siberian steppes.

The new legate waited for a week to recover from his voyage for a formal presentation to the recently anointed Tsar, who already proved devoted to "orthodoxy, autocracy, and national unity." Jimmy felt acutely aware of his inexperience, and did not want to lose sight of his mission. He was to map out the first commercial treaty ever with Russia, and the road ran through Count Karl Nesselrode, the foreign minister.

He decided it was best to go slowly with any possible negotiations while he figured out his role and the new web of relationships. He went to plays and parties, took in some opera, and studied the lingua franca of diplomacy a little more earnestly than his dithering efforts stateside. Back and forth to the Winter Palace, a four-horse carriage with a Russian driver, aglitter in a scarlet and gold uniform with long black hair flowing. A chasseur stood on back, sword glinting in the long days' sun, brass buttons polished, epaulets secured in gold, tassels everywhere. Atop his head, a plumed chapeau. Jimmy loved every moment.

One disturbing sight remained with him. He was about the streets when he chanced, in early evening, to come upon a group of individuals listening to a speaker who quite rabidly, Jimmy thought, was exhorting the circle. What looked to be imperial soldiers swept in, rounded them up, and hauled them away. Hurrying back to his villa,

Jimmy wrote in his diary, *I am grateful for the freedom of speech enjoyed in America, but there are different rules governing different societies. Here in Russia, one has to play by those rules; it is unfortunate that there is such Repression & yet nowhere are such rules clearer.*

When Jimmy passed the building again the following night, wide planks of Siberian spruce hung off large spikes driven into its walls. On the door, what appeared to be an official looking placard, although of course he had no idea what it meant.

He and Nesselrode finally met in the Count's working offices at the General Staff building. A waiter brought in a delicious frozen custard mélange of chestnuts, cherries, orange peel, Marsala, currants and sultanas, topped with a dollop of whipped cream and they set to work. Jimmy outlined the desire of the United States to increase its commerce with Russia and to ensure pathways on the open seas. He soon discovered that the Foreign Minister had anticipated his intentions.

Someone was certainly intercepting the mail, as it came in large packets and spewed into his room all at once rather than in an orderly flow. Nothing, apparently, came nor went without it being transcribed, and translated as appropriate, by his counterparts. Jimmy soon decided that a cipher was necessary for secure transmission but could not communicate that code without it itself being discovered. He therefore resigned himself either to not communicating, or letting the Russians look inside his mind. Finally to be in a place where his great skill at compromise and negotiation was prized, and unable to communicate the ins and outs of his efforts, or to receive guidance as to President Jackson's exact intentions, was disarming. A bit, he thought, like crossing a faulty bridge without knowing where the weak planks were, with the other side well aware of the secret locations of the rotting wood. It was a most disagreeable situation, and certain to cause missteps if he let it.

Jimmy was excited by the collision of barbarism and Western civilization he sensed in this splendid country. At formal dinners, women were always present, and Jimmy found he could delight them with fairy stories in his faulty French, and soon became a hit with them, just as he was in America, telling of Hansel et Gretel, Rapunzel and even *Trois Petits Cochons et le grand loup sauvage.*

At a party, a woman leaned over to his ear. Even in Russian, thecourtesan'smessagewasunmistakable,"□ □ □ □ □ □ □ □ □ □ □ □ □ □ □ □ □ □ □ □?"Jimmyblushedandshookhishead.InFrench,seekingthe origin of her smell, "*Quel est cet arôme charmant?*"

From across the table, Count Nesselrode, "The Tsar has anointed the same royal perfumer as Marie Antoinette's and Napoleon's Josephine. It has a delightful bouquet, and Houbigant's perfume is well favored by all the courtesans."

"Merci, Compte." The aroma nagged at the back of his conscience, as if the scent had aroused his nostrils somewhere long ago.

Concerning the Russian women, Jimmy wrote to his friend Thomas Kittera in Philadelphia, *everywhere, they are the most special and best part of society,* although he noted that there was *little religion among the upper classes, and ignorance and suspicion in the lower classes.* He did not reveal to Thomas that he had suggested to the Count and court that he was already engaged to be married on his return to America. He could relax here, unlike in Washington where he constantly had to be wary of women's intentions and had to keep explaining the source of his sadness and his inability to be disloyal to the love he lost as a younger man.

The letter continued, *I am a bit disappointed with the relative lack of alcohol at these state occasions and the unheard of custom that women actually sat with men and talk after dinner. In only this respect, does la société du* □ □ □ □ *(that, dear Thomas, is Russian for Tsar) disappoint.*

Rather than retreating to some other room to let the stronger sex continue smoking and drinking alone, they persist in flitting about. While the Russians drink heavily, one must sometime order from the streets. There is a hot wine brandy described as being "enough to kill the Devil" and it is, but the best is this peculiar potato based potion that the lower classes seemed to favor. It is almost tasteless yet quite deliciously lethal.

Before any substantive talks were possible, Jimmy knew he had to deal with the Russian anger at what they viewed as unfair tariffs on wool, hemp, iron and other products. From a news article delivered nearly two months after its publication, Jimmy learned that a bill lowering those duties, without his knowledge or input, was almost certain of passage. Excitedly, he advised Nesselrode that he had convinced the American Congress and the President to consider the tariff reductions and he was "almost certain" they would be approved, if the Tsar agreed. Jimmy was able to reach a compromise of his nation's interests, in French and English, which "he could present to the Senate for approval. Being a man of my position," he confidentially told Nesselrode, "I am enabled to permit you to assure the Tsar that Congress will follow my recommendations."

Karl Nesselrode took it all in. The Emperor's quick assent was communicated to Jimmy by means of a translation from the Russian's French into the American's English through the newly arrived British ambassador. Jimmy found it difficult, at first, to show his face in court when he learned that the Russians received the same newspaper, had it in their hands two weeks earlier, and knew he had no role in the process. The commerce treaty was signed by all parties in December.

The late winter and early spring of 1833 were a whirligig of wonder to Jimmy. He had no other business to conclude, and only parties to attend. He danced with the Tsarina and was lauded at every event. At fete after fete, he wondered why he had become such a favorite.

Knowing that all his mail would be read, Jimmy lavishly praised the Tsar and defended his crushing of the Polish people and their subsequent enslavement. He applauded the suppression of increasing revolts by serfs as necessary for an ordered economy and sound government. Similar rebellious stirrings were reflected in copies of European newspapers Jimmy found carved up in Nesselrode's chambers. American papers seemed to support these sentiments. If Buchanan were as powerful with the President and Congress as he claimed, he could indeed get this to stop, could he not?

Jimmy squirmed. How could he now tell the Tsar that America's press was not under his control, or even the President's? He pointed out that there were articles critical of President Jackson in those same newspapers, "This is just the American way. Newspapers can write almost anything they wish."

Nesselrode, familiar with British rules on libel, did not believe him and expressed concern that these anti-Russian articles could deter Senate approval of the treaty, "A result, I am certain, you would wish to prevent?"

Jimmy realized that he had played into Nesselrode's hands all along, "I will do what I am able."

The Russians had far more information, from opened letters with all his negotiation points, and far better access to news articles from his own country. Still, he had done the best he could. If those jackasses in the State Department did not know how to get information to him, what was he to do anyway?

President Jackson wrote in March that Jimmy's mother Elizabeth was ill, and that he had permission to return if he desired. Jimmy considered. There was little he could do there and much to accomplish where he was. In early June, he left St. Petersburg and went sightseeing, visiting Moscow and some lesser cities. He saw the same disturbing social distinctions everywhere and wondered at the system that depended on serfs for its success. These were white men, just like the Russian masters, kept in servitude. He saw trains, newly introduced in Russia, carting hundreds to the East, and wondered at the purpose of transporting peasants to the Siberian tundra. At least in our county, Jimmy thought with pride, we do not enslave our own people.

Jimmy received notice of his mother's May death on July 19th. Alone, he went into the basement of his Russian residence. He had not visited it before, but only asked that things be brought up from it, things to drink, things to feed him, things to make him happy. He spread his palms on the dirt and cleaned off a small place in the corner. The must of four decades rose dank about him. Light's absence had long since strangled the soil of any life. He sat. Sadness for him, and soon not just for him. Sadness for his mother, sadness at her life. Now, she had fulfilled her implicit pledge, made on their last coming together before he left the country. She had died. Her comfort would nevermore be his. He had left her, left her where she had died long before. He had vowed to protect her. He had not! So blithely had he left her spirit, left her on the other side of the Susquehanna, left her on the other side of the great gaping cold wave cleansing departing irrevocable sea. First, his vest, then his shirt, his shoes, his pants, his socks. Face crushed on the cold floor, he plunged naked into the running mountains and moving woods, his white belly sprawled against the brown barren earth. The tears were slow to come, but when they did they came in battalions, wet mud soldiers scaling his nose and lips, wet mud soldiers descending into the craters pounded by his fists.

So this, he thought, is what the pain of a loved one's death feels like. It was a voyage he had not made before, and he did not—ever— want to go there again.

Nicholas embraced him as he departed in August, and as Jimmy wrote to Thomas, *The Russian monarch implored me to tell General Jackson to send another Minister exactly like myself. Russia could not wish for better.*

It was doubtful, Jimmy thought, that Jackson will find another place for me. All the favors I have done will no longer count toward a post in a second administration, and if one of Adams's men won... If it had not been for Ann and the threat of Stevens, I would not have had to go so far into the woods. It is now time for my next step, one that also does not involve facing the voters at the ballot box, or Stevens in a courtroom.

He dispatched a round of letters to Dickinson acquaintances, and friends of friends, offering to trade his Lancaster law practice for one in Baltimore or New York, writing Andrew Noel,

Dear Andy,

You may remember my efforts on the matter of the bonds and indentures of the Columbia Bridge Works, which I trust you found quite skillful.

His pen wavered as he recalled his more recent legal work involving the related company and the revelation that occurred in its midst.

In any event, I find myself, after an illustrious career in the United States House of Representatives, of which I am sure you know a great deal, and returning from the same Ministership once held by John Adams père, I am in the position where law practice in Baltimore would be more beneficial to my talents. I have lost my dear mother and there is but little reason for me to remain in Lancaster or Pennsylvania.

I recall you had some acquaintanceship with Justice Taney, who of course has served General Jackson with distinction as his Attorney General, and to whom I would make the direct entreaty, but for deference to you. I have to offer to you, or anyone you might recommend, my established practice, in exchange for a thriving one in Baltimore. Please advise me of such interest by return post.

Yours in sincerity & humbleness,

James Buchanan, Esq.

5. August 1833

Jimmy continued to tour the European continent, its vineyards and palaces. After two additional months of travel at government expense, including a visit to his ancestral Ramelton in the Irish Republic, of which he wrote, *I sinned much in the article of hot whiskey toddy which they term punch,* he set sail for America.

The United Kingdom had abolished slavery the month before he left its shores. "It might work for you British to outlaw the practice, as gradual as you are doing so, only letting the six year olds fully out," he told another passenger on the trip home, "but our circumstances are peculiar to us. This never would have happened if you did not start letting Quakers into Parliament. Further, I think you will regret this action. You can no longer compete with us in the Caribbean and the West Indies, you will find, are soon to be ours."

When Jimmy returned to the United States, he learned sister Harriet married without his knowing about it. George had died of tuberculosis, choking and spitting as he argued a case as the District Attorney for the Western District of Pennsylvania. How good of the President to appoint him to that post. His brother Edward, in a move he was certain greatly pleased their now dead mother, not only married but joined the ministry. All this in just over a year's absence. Jimmy, as the man of the family, felt left out. Worse, those who had bothered to respond had declined his offer to trade practices. All the letters were to the negative. They had had months to reply, and he felt as if he had practically begged. How could it be that no one wished to have his leg up in Lancaster? Well, he supposed he could do in Pennsylvania what he had intended to do from Baltimore or New York, and perhaps more swiftly.

Jimmy went back to his earlier lodgings in the Widow, Passmore now also passed away. He looked around at the quarters that had once held his dreams. This would not do. It must be sold and a more appropriate purchase made with the proceeds. That night in the Leopard, he learned of a certain residence for sale. It would not only meet his needs but its purchase would also send the clearest signal possible to all his rivals, including that pestilence across the river when he too late learned of it.

Jimmy missed the companionship of Jasper Slaymaker, who had died just a few years back. At least his old partner Molton Rogers, who had managed his finances while he was out of the country, joined him at the Widow his first night back in town. "I am going to establish my practice across the street."

"Why there? What you have here should suffice. You will have to start over a bit again, and Lancaster has changed in the decade you have been largely absent yet," Molton added quickly, "there are still opportunities."

"You have done well with my investments. These lodgings may have sufficed while I was in all effects living in the capital. I am now apparently compelled to be here in Lancaster. I am therefore going to do something that will make all take notice, and obliterate the past."

Molton considered why Buchanan felt that he could not go elsewhere, and what merited obliteration as Jimmy continued, "You are well aware of the efforts by the Colemans to destroy my happiness, and my career."

"I know of Mr. Coleman's antipathy."

"What of Ann's conduct?"

"Well I recall her death. You have often since that day told me of the love you once had."

"I have done something to make that right."

As Jimmy unwound his plans, Molton stared at him as if he had been struck mad. He listened to Jimmy's increasingly loud talk of revenge and retribution and the acquisition that he proclaimed would again propel him into the political life. "Of course, Jimmy, anything I can do to help," Molton whispered to himself as he slipped out at midnight. Jimmy was already dancing on the table.

Chapter Twelve
SENATOR

Jimmy signed, the next day, a contract to purchase the now vacant house at 42 East King Street, corner of Christian. He wrote to Robert Grier, and the same to Thomas Kittera, *I guess I have surely proved them wrong. Today I purchased the Coleman mansion. I will live there, and all will have to come see me there, my offices in Coleman's old library, my meals in their dining room, and my nights in their bedrooms.*

Pompey carried his belongings down the Widow's stairs and across the street. The first night in the Coleman house, a cold and snowy evening requiring great cords of wood in the Franklin stoves, Pompey in bed, Jimmy pondered how best to secure his practice and proceed in a way to minimize the possibility of any entanglements with Stevens.

He wandered from room to room, belly bobbing and hairless thighs rubbing against one another, several yards of woolen Buchanan clan tartan cast about his shoulders for warmth. He caressed the woodwork with his soft hands and shuffled across the polished ballroom floor. Memories of Ann flooded through him, and the damage she inflicted on him with her selfish death.

Jimmy ascended the attic steps. He rooted about until he came upon a burnished Saratoga trunk, its leather straps orange and fraying. He took out a little ball peen and rapped at the rusting lock. The metal crumbled under his short thrusts. Breaching the coffer's brittle hinges, Jimmy unearthed a trove of immense fascination.

Strewn with cedar chips but otherwise intact was Ann's ball gown from that birthday two decades past. Jimmy slowly unfolded the still bright blue silk dress and pawed the indigo pelerine. He held the gown in front of him, wrapping his arms around the soft bombazine and sarsanet. Slowly, peering into a mirror lit by the candle he placed at its side, he disrobed. First, he softly pulled off the banyan and removed the Albert from his buttonhole, setting his large gold watch on an abandoned yellow settee that he seemed to recall was once in the front parlor. Next, he undid the laces on his well polished ankle jacks, and decorously laid them next to one another. He slithered out of his pantaloons and shimmied out of what were known as inexpressibles. His cream silken shirt flowed like a parasol as he twirled about before delicately lifting it over his head, assiduously not disrupting his topknot.

Finally, he stood naked and flushed in the attic of what was once Ann's house. Surely, he could not fit into this gown but, perhaps, if he let out the gores on the skirt and did not button the back? He lanced the skirt with his small tool but could not get the waist nearly wide enough. Jimmy yanked at it, the multiple folds of the material splitting and spilling all about him. At least, he thought, he could wrap himself in it. Now drenched in Ann's silk, he tugged the pelerine about his naked shoulders while his sagging belly pressed against the gossamer. Carefully, carefully he went down the attic ladder but his small soft feet still caught some splinters. At the landing he steadied himself against the wall. He reached down, twisting his feet upward in turn and, wincing, pulled out the wooden shards. Undeterred by the droplets of blood now trailing him, he made his way to the crest of the grand staircase leading to the ballroom below. Pausing, he lowered his eyes demurely and began an ethereal descent toward an imagined audience. With great aplomb, he held the hem of his habiliment aloft with his left hand while his right fondled the balustrade. Still, he almost tripped. Recovering his balance, he fairly glided to the floor below. A small solo dance later, he sat in the midst of the cold blue marble floor, a wan smile worming its way across his wrinkling face as he remembered the night that Ann, all ebony, alabaster and silk, stood at the top of the stairs to universal, awed silence.

· · ·

He wished, the next morning, that there were an Alexander around to cut the Gordian knots in his stomach. What had this girl done to him? He felt as if he were pilloried on a cucking stool. Jimmy reached for Ann's correspondence tied with a pale silk ribbon by his bedside, this memento mori of might-have-beens, and resolved that it would be released upon his death for all to see how wronged he had been.

His practice was searching for air like a spent horse. Lancaster's legal work had been ridden hard by others and there was no fresh steed to mount. On the other hand, not a peep from Stevens. Perhaps he was just too busy acquiring land and ironworks to pay attention to anything else, thought Jimmy, not entirely without envy. He had been back for nearly two months. Time to put his plan in motion.

Jimmy had felt politically washed up before he left for Russian shores but, just as he had missed the divisive debates of the Missouri Compromise of 1820, it seemed that his absence half a world over had worked to his advantage. He had dodged controversies over the Second Bank of the United States, which Jackson opposed but which was favored by Jimmy's former Lancaster constituents and caused more than one promising career to fail. He also had the patina of foreign diplomatic expert added to his resume.

On the national stage, Jimmy was alarmed by the unilateral revocation of tariffs enacted by South Carolina and new rumors of secession and civil war, which he saw as cloaked in "shadows, clouds & darkness," but soon was able to put these thoughts behind him.

He recalled those long ago times, suckling his mother's finger as she read to him, and how far he had come. At 42, he was deservedly proud of his great successes and was not prepared to put all that aside. Had not he served, and served well, in his country's hallowed chambers? Did not all know his great success as a diplomat, validated by the Russian emperor himself? He should not have to scrabble through the crumbs of the Lancaster legal practice. It was well sliced and devoured by others. He need not sit beneath their table, hand and tongue scurrying for fallen scraps..

It was time to parlay those efforts into a grander prize, one that did not require standing in front of the voters, and one that even Stevens could not derail, so rapidly would he ascend that word would not even reach Gettysburg until all was accomplished. He would be back on track to his ultimate goal. From the ashes of his practice, thought Jimmy, what a phoenix he would be.

Senator. To accomplish that, he would have to court his erstwhile friends, and a host of newcomers, in the Pennsylvania House of Assembly. No distasteful electioneering among the body politic. No paltry seat as the prize. Just the support of the state Assemblymen whose vote could send him to Washington's upper body. In the Senate, he would be one of just 48 men from the twenty-four states. No longer would he be lost among the swarming scores of scavenging House members.

Balloting for the Senate seat was set for December 7th, and Jimmy wrote to each of the Democrats serving in Harrisburg, advising them of his interest and accomplishments. He carefully plotted his upcoming visits to the state legislators. He would seem casually to happen to be in Harrisburg *on other business* and to have just wandered over to the Assembly *to watch some of my good friends at work,* all the while knowing other heifers had plowed the ground. Many of the legislators, even those beyond his own party, owed him favors from his decade in Congress and close affiliation with a sitting President. It should be easy to convince them that he deserved to be in the United States Senate.

Jimmy arrived in Harrisburg and began to work the crowd. As he moved down the aisles he saw a large now black mane of hair snorting in the air. Its owner turned toward him. Jimmy stopped in mid-handshake. His wet hand trailed as he fled the chamber. He retreated to the newly installed commode in the back of the chamber and promptly lost his eggs and toast.

From across the Susquehanna, a familiar and startling face. The new state legislator from Gettysburg was none other than Thaddeus Stevens. Why had no one told him? Why, of course, because they did not know what it meant, that it meant everything to him.

What would this do to his plans? He could hardly solicit Stevens's vote, a man who vowed to control his very career. Had this great dark creature run for this position solely to waylay Jimmy's deserved date with the Senate? He would not put it past him.

That night, Jimmy's nocturnal wanderings led him from bedroom to bedroom, down and up staircases and foraging for fruit in the cellar. Pompey discovered him at daybreak snoring jaggedly, cloaked in the satin tartan of the clan Buchanan, a great wet stain on the crimson carpet under his deep brown horsehair chair, a rye glass tumbled across the room.

Multiple ballots were often necessary before a winner emerged in the Senate race, as factions of geography, favoritism, and political viewpoint had to be traded and the choices winnowed. Jimmy could not, just could not, return to Harrisburg and risk confronting Stevens. He had to hope that his aborted personal efforts but strong letter campaign would be sufficient. The election took only three ballots and he ended up with a paltry 5 votes of the 130 cast. Samuel McKean was the clear winner. Stevens, he was certain, had done his dirty work. Had he revealed the letter's contents? Jimmy plied his few supporters and several others. All denied, to a man, that Thad had spoken to them about any letter, much less showed it to them, although their interest was certainly piqued.

Being a senator from Pennsylvania now seemed out of reach, at least while Stevens was in the Assembly, and he could hardly restart his practice after being out of the country for the past two years, and effectively absent from Lancaster for the last decade. If only Noel or anybody had taken his offer. Now where to turn?

During the day, Jimmy puttered about the house and tried to keep it neat with part-time servants. He soon realized that if he were properly to reside in the large King Street mansion, he would require a regular housekeeper. The Colemans' slaves were dead or scattered. Zimmerleuten and other indentured German servants had all served their time and gone on to families of their own.

Jimmy usually took his meals at the White Swan hotel, still so called despite the notoriety of the 1810 raid on the eponymous London sodomite brothel. He was friends with the proprietor, and was grateful when her innkeeper uncle proposed Esther Parker, said by him to be "a bright and pretty girl," to assist him. Miss Hetty, as Jimmy anointed her, was satisfied with the arrangement he outlined. At age 28, she entered their lifelong relationship, although Jimmy did not find her pinched and mottled face, glasses plunging down her nose with her indefinitely colored hair pulled tightly back, particularly attractive. No matter. Pompey slowly adjusted to the feminine presence, although he longed for the Russian days and the time in the nation's capital. Much as his master, he still wanted to return to Washington and escape the dreary confines of Lancaster.

Jimmy did not stop there in acquiring help for his house. When visiting his sister Jane in Greensburg, he learned that her husband's Virginia family owned two slaves, girls aged 22 and 5. Jimmy promptly purchased them with the idea that they would stay with him in

Lancaster. Under Pennsylvania law, Daphne would be bound to him only until age 29, but the younger, little Ann, would belong to him until she reached 28 years in 1858. He carefully considered the politics of the property acquisition. Pennsylvanians (and other Northerners) could view his action as saving these girls from a lifetime of servitude. Southerners would see him as a slaveholder much as themselves. Besides, he had the large residence to manage, and liked the idea of owning little Ann for the next quarter century.

Once again, a woman was linked to Jimmy in prospective matrimony. This time, it was a girl just out of her teen years, Mary Kittera Snyder, granddaughter of a Pennsylvania governor. Mary and her Uncle Thomas Kittera lived in Philadelphia at 518 Walnut Street, across the city from the home of Margaret and James Hemphill that Ann and Sarah Coleman visited that December day.

He should be in the Senate now, Jimmy thought, but that hope was at least deferred. The idea of trading Lancaster for Philadelphia still appealed to him. No bar examination to pass and its society well understood. He could make a better living there, and ingratiate himself to some of these Easterners and then of course try for the Senate again.

In Lancaster and now in Philadelphia, Jimmy accepted a few cautiously chosen legal matters, careful not to involve himself with anything that might lead to court or require him to cross the river. He was nevertheless increasingly called upon to honor his promise to provide lodgings, as death and impecunity engulfed his siblings and the effects were felt by their children. He could not make room in his household without impinging in ways that were undesirable, and arranged for his niece Elizabeth, daughter of his now deceased sister Sarah, to be placed in the Kittera household. Also in the house with bachelor Thomas were Kittera's two nieces, his sister, and his widowed mother.

Jimmy frequently visited them in Philadelphia, leaving Miss Hetty in charge of what was still known as the Coleman home. He would stay overnight at the Kittera household, spend time with his 14-year-old niece, and Mary Snyder. At night, he and Thomas would make the rounds of the clubs and taverns of Philadelphia, heading up nearby Elferth's Alley, cruising the docks dotting the Delaware, or catching a play at the Walnut Street Theater. Occasionally, it being late and not wishing to disturb the household, they would stay at the Metropole for the evening. Jimmy corresponded with Thomas frequently, asking him to *give love to my intended* or *that person in whom I feel a particular interest,* but wrote no letters to young Mary herself.

Robert Coleman had been a Free Mason and Jimmy was determined to join. Robert Grier proposed him and Jimmy successively served as Junior Warden of the Local no. 43 of the Masons, and was soon Worshipful Master. As his ascent continued, the growing anti-Mason movement in the country found a new champion, the Pennsylvania Assemblyman Thaddeus Stevens. The Masons were the perfect targets for Thad, politically and emotionally. Plutocratic in politics and temperament, Masons were largely wealthy, kept their society secret, and their membership rules were exclusionary. Without the intellectual component, it was like Phi Beta Kappa, and this time Thad did not want to join. He learned of Jimmy's membership. Masonry! Even if it were not for what he did to Ann, Thad thought, yet one more reason to despise Buchanan and the very earth he scorches.

Pennsylvania's other Senator, William Wilkins, shocked everyone in the fall by taking the unexpected, and many thought barely explicable step, of vacating his Senate seat to take over the post Jimmy had just left, Minister to Russia. Jimmy grasped at the new opportunity, Stevens or not, and sought Wilkins's unexpired term even though he had not fully forged his Eastern alliances.

The path had earlier seemed so easy, but he still could not stomach, quite literally, being present on the Assembly floor if Stevens were there. He also could not abide the possible use of whatever secret knowledge he claimed to have, but Stevens had not revealed anything in Jimmy's same quest a year earlier. Either, Jimmy began to consider, Stevens had nothing, or it was not nearly what he had been led to believe on that York bluff three years earlier. In any event, he had to risk it. There were no other options that would be this heaven sent for years, given the Senate's six year terms and the providential decision of Wilkins willingly to go to Russia against all sound analysis. Jimmy had been in Moscow out of desperation yet Wilkins was foregoing the highest electoral prize short of the Presidency. It made no sense.

The three other candidates were his former friend Amos Ellmaker, now avowedly anti-Mason; Joseph Lawrence of the recently formed Whig party; and Joel Barlow Sutherland of Philadelphia, the Democratic candidate of the wealthy faction from the state's largest city. Democrats from Lancaster westward backed Jimmy, as did Governor Wolf. The anti-Masons and Whigs could have jointly put someone else over the top. Despite frequently appearing to be on the very edge of doing so, they somehow could not coalesce behind a candidate. Jimmy relied on the Governor and a host of others as surrogates. He had to get to that seat!

He dispatched Pompey to stand outside the Assembly house, respectfully search for a report from one of his supporters, and bring back news of his progress. It was a hard two-hour ride each way. Pompey came back at noon on Friday, December 5th and advised Jimmy that he had received only 25 votes on the first ballot, and just 42 on the second. While Pompey was riding back to Harrisburg, more debate. A third ballot. When Pompey pulled up to the Statehouse, he learned that his master had received 58 votes. Then a majority, 66 on the fourth, just edging the Whig and anti-Mason candidates and their combined 64 votes. Somehow, the opposition could not seem to proceed in concert. The Democrats, though fractious, were able to put aside sectional and class differences and prevailed. What role had

Stevens played? Why hadn't he been able to coalesce his anti-Masons with the Whigs?

With his two-vote margin, Jimmy became the junior United States Senator from the Commonwealth of Pennsylvania. He permitted Pompey to have a whiskey with him when he brought the news and hustled to Harrisburg to take the office the next day, a Saturday. He averted his eyes from the body as he strode out to muted applause for his swearing in. He did not look out until his status was secure. There, in the distant corner of the Assembly, eyes burned at him.

Jimmy cautiously solicited reports from Wolf and others who had seen Stevens in earnest conversations with his fellow Whigs and anti-Masons but they did not know what they might have been saying. Although he voted against him, Stevens and all his supposed power had not been able to orchestrate a way to overpower his candidacy. A year earlier he had received only five votes, and this time he prevailed by the fourth ballot. It was not as if he had done anything in the intervening year to enhance his stature. Perhaps all had finally come to recognize his worth, or was something else afoot?

Jimmy and Pompey packed up and headed to the nation's capital the very next day. Senator Buchanan took his seat a week later. Pompey found quarters at a boarding house reserved for negroes at K and 14th Streets, Southeast, within smelling distance of the Anacostia River. Pompey made certain not to venture across the Potomac to Virginia, and particularly not to Arlington where one of the country's largest slave trading operations flourished.

The newest Senator soon considered himself fortunate for having been defeated the year earlier. His absence from the Senate's prior session meant he had not had to vote on the censure of President Jackson, a losing situation for a Pennsylvania Democrat. His previously victorious counterpart, Samuel McKean, opted to condemn Jackson in the unsuccessful attempt to discipline the President. He thereby satisfied the Philadelphia faction but angered the rest of the state and never served another term. Simply being away had again worked for Jimmy. He was above the fray, could express allegiance for Jackson as needed, yet leave his listeners hearing what they wished to hear.

Nationally, parties were Democrats and Whigs but this simply meant Jackson and Jackson's men on the one hand, and those who were against the President on the other. Pennsylvania was more complicated with its political rift premised on wealth. Still, Jimmy thought, one had to continue to ride the Jackson horse. When Jackson anointed Martin Van Buren, the Red Fox of Kinderhook, as his successor, Jimmy was comfortable that he could sell the little Dutch magician to the Germans at home. The Whigs, a party that stood for nothing, would not last long. The Whig offshoot, the Anti-Masons, was loosely bound by a lone, increasingly insignificant issue.

Jimmy contemplated the curious constructs of the competing parties. Both, and not only because of that damned Stevens, but because they are against everything he stood for, his concept of public decency, the rule of law and the narrow construction of the Constitution he treasured, both made him glad to be a Democrat. Now he must preserve and protect what he had and, of course, take the next great step.

Thaddeus Stevens had chosen a different goal.

Chapter Thirteen
WHIGGERY

Typhoid fever struck Thad at the age of 39 and stripped all hair from his head and body. His black wig covered his bald pate but he felt yet more alone and, he had to admit it, even a little more freakish with this added to the Hellish shame of his club foot. Complicating his life, his younger brother Morrill died and Morrill's sons, Thaddeus and Allanson, had now come to live with him.

A bill to withdraw funding for public schools was introduced in his first legislative session, just a year after the effort to make education freely available to Pennsylvania's youth was inaugurated by the Pennsylvania School Bill. Recalling his mother Sarah's struggles to scrape together enough money to ensure that he could go to school, and become a lawyer, landowner, and legislator, Thad stood firmly on the Assembly floor, "The current patchwork system of private schools and local funding is not only more expensive, but less efficient, than the free alternative. This bill is an act for branding and marking the poor, so that they may be known from the rich and the proud."

He concluded, "Build not your monuments of brass or marble, but make them of ever living minds. When I reflect how apt hereditary wealth, hereditary influence, and perhaps as a consequence, hereditary pride, are to close the avenues and steel the hearts against the wants and rights of the poor, I am induced to thank my Creator for having, from early life, bestowed upon me the blessing of poverty."

Cheers erupted, not only cascading from the gallery but also rolling through the Assemblymen. Parliamentary rules were suspended, and a reinforced public education bill was passed by acclamation.

Pennsylvania, decades before most of the rest of the nation, reaffirmed its free public school system.

In December 1835, as the next legislative session got underway, Stevens initiated a committee to investigate the "evils of Free Masonry." Joseph Ritner, newly elected Governor, was an Anti-Mason. With the governor's support, something resembling an inquisition began. The Masons' combination of blood oaths, allegorical incantations and quasi-religious rituals repulsed Thad. In addition, some of the chapters, including Lancaster's where Buchanan was a "Worshipful Master" or whatever the Hell that was, excluded "cripples," intensifying his animosity as it brought the Masonic agenda grindingly close to home. Senator Buchanan took Stevens's crusade as if it were directed personally against him but did not know what to do other than stay in Washington, beyond Harrisburg's subpoena power.

Former Governor Wolf, the Chief Justice of the Pennsylvania Supreme Court, and a host of Democrats were summoned to Harrisburg to divulge the shady secrets of Masonry. They refused, citing their civil rights. Masons pulled on their connections in the press and on Main Streets and the public tide turned. Thad's crusade was increasingly lambasted in Pennsylvania and elsewhere in the nation and seen as the rogue act of a malcontent. The earlier charges of murder of the colored woman Eve and her baby were revived.

In winter's midst, a mob of citizens welled at the legislature's doors and spewed past the Sergeant at Arms. Into the chamber strode the six hundred, wildly charging through the chamber's aisles, assemblymen to the right and left of them, but Thad their target. "Masonry forever!" "Death to heathens!" Thad scurried to the end of the Assembly as the masses surged toward him. No outlet but a window. He flopped through the portal to the snow-specked field below. The jeers swarmed around him as he limped across the gelid Harrisburg landscape.

Jimmy chortled at his rival's downfall. How foolish, he felt in retrospect, that he credited this country lawyer and his story of some "secret." Here he was in Washington, and Stevens was dragging his clubfoot among the haystacks.

Thad brushed off the grain at a Harrisburg tavern, sipping warm water. By the third glass, he believed he had fully evaluated his party and its one-note opposition. The Whigs were simply mewling along, lapping the ever more sour milk of a dying party. Antistrophes are fine in Greek drama, Thad thought, and he was by nature an opposer. If he could not find something to be in favor of, he better find something new to be against. There was one issue that had not particularly troubled him, or many others except in New England's far recesses, until recently. He seized upon it.

His memories of defenestration still paining him, Thad had an earnest conversation with the Reverend Jonathan Blanchard. Blanchard painted a searing picture of the scourge of slavery and outlined the growing movement to eradicate it. Here was a group of people that I had never thought of particularly, Thad thought, mistreated simply because of an accident of birth. He could identify with that. Most importantly, this was an opportunity to align with a greater cause whose pestilential spread seemed inevitable. England had just abolished slavery and the abolitionists were growing in number and power not only in New England, but in Ohio and elsewhere. Besides, opposition to wealthy southern plantation owners and their simpering plutocracy, trading on the unpaid suffering of others, could be ridden to political glory. Blanchard's principles, and his reasoned and vigorous opposition to both slavery and Masonry, impressed him. While Thad rejected the minister's call for a theocracy, where "the law of God is the law of the land," he agreed that "society is perfect when the right in theory exists in fact; where practice coincides with principle." Thad did not want to be the sort of fanatic who redoubled his efforts when he forgot his aim, and he felt he reached that point with anti-Masonry. He turned his fire on the peculiar institution that was gradually fading in his home state but persisted just to the east and south, and threatened to expand with the nation.

A delegate to the Pennsylvania State Constitutional Convention in 1838, Thad was appalled when a provision to deny the right of free black men to vote was inserted. He argued in vain against the rider, and watched with anger as negro suffrage was retroactively stripped in Pennsylvania.

This stage, he thought of the Assembly, is far too small. How best to take the quest for equal rights for all men to the broader theater of an increasingly divided nation? How best to use the man whose career remained his quarry?

In 1842, Thad suddenly left the legislature, abandoned his Gettysburg law offices, and sold of much of his property.

He moved to the larger town to the east, a community that no longer intimidated him. Into his modest house on the corner of South Queen and East Vine just south of Oblender's Furniture, he invited a young black woman, just 30 years of age, and her two sons. Lydia Smith kept his house at 45-47 South Queen and, according to persistent rumors heard on every Lancaster street corner and never denied, became much more than a housekeeper. It was not because of her, however, that he had to be in Lancaster.

Chapter Fourteen
BARNUM'S

The day before the winter's solstice, on the Saturday after his swearing in, it was sunny but chill. Senator Buchanan moaned under the weight of familial obligations.

Jimmy had agreed to take Elizabeth, his sister Sarah's girl, from the Kittera household and had placed her under Hetty's care in Lancaster. At least she was now of a marriageable age. He was concerned he would need to take in other nieces and nephews whose parents had died, or were impecunious. Sister Sarah's two boys were old enough to be on their own. Sister Jane's six year old, Harriet Lane, would likely need caring. His sister Harriet was also in ill health and her husband was dead. She had a four year old, James Buchanan Henry. Jimmy figured he would soon have James under his wing and perhaps Harriet, and let Miss Hetty know of the upcoming responsibilities while wondering at the lack of inventiveness in first names among his siblings.

Tom's niece Mary was now 24 to his 44. Mary and his niece had been a good foil for his visits, but Mary now boldly hinted that it was well more than time he made good on the implicit promises of marriage over the past ten years of what she viewed as their courtship.

He therefore had written Mary the evening after his election to lay such expectations to rest. His head unconsciously tilted and he reached up to loosen his topknot,

Dearest Mary,

Time is a powerful beast and has taken from me my best years. You are well into marriageable age and should find a beau. I know you and I have shared some intimations of affection yet I trust, however, that I have not led you into a false belief. You well know my lamentations for that Precious One from my past whose grace I have not been able to forego in these now 16 years and who remains with me still in a measure that fills my cup with waxing sadness.

I assuredly wish you all that is good in life's God Blessedness. My fondest regards to your uncle Thomas.

In obedient Service,

James Buchanan

December 9, 1834

Mary thought first of hurling the letter into her bedroom fire. Instead, she found her uncle, who placed the epistle in a small box on his bed stand.

Jimmy's brother Edward was the only other surviving son. Jealous of the eldest, he buckled at his relative poverty and never ceased to remind Jimmy that he had fulfilled their mother's dying wish that one of her sons enter the ministry. He was pastor at the Episcopal church in Leacock, only seven miles from Lancaster, just east of Eden. When his congregation could only raise six dollars to endow a proposed Bible college, Jimmy sent along an extra $144 but kept the account against Edward's paternal inheritance.

Sister Maria was a further problem. She was on her third husband, although there was some doubt about the legitimacy of a previous union. Each relationship produced at least one child. Her current spouse was a doctor, ostensibly something of a catch, but Dr. Yates was so insulting to his patients that they rarely stayed with him. Yet another sibling to bail out. Maria asked Jimmy for a loan on a larger house, which he did not provide. When the doctor lost an election wager with a patient, he asked Jimmy to provide him with the $200 necessary to satisfy the bet. Jimmy instead sent him a receipt deducting the money from the amount he claimed Yates already owed him, providing little real help.

Jimmy was ruminating on these responsibilities while promenading on Bridge Street in the venerable community of Georgetown, overlooking the swamps of Washington. Stopping in front of Patricia Briscoe's gift shop and gazing at the Spanish crockery displayed in the window, a soft hand rested on his shoulder.

The new Senator turned and looked into a round face with a full wide mouth. The nose was royal and prominent, and the still dark brown hair was tied in four crimson bows, two on each side, so that it seemed to float above the ears. The dress was somewhat exotic, a deep sapphire blue satin up top under a red coat crowned by an ebony velvet half collar. All black below save suede boots the color of marlinspikes.

Jimmy's cream scarf was tied with an air of casual informality befitting the weekend day and his topknot was bound in place with a cobalt satin cord. Still, he felt underdressed in his grey frock. Jimmy cocked his head, "Senator, what a delight to see you!"

William Rufus DeVane King stared into his eyes. Jimmy had known of the Senator since he was first elected to Congress. He had always been somewhat in awe of the man five years his senior, already in the upper house when he came to Washington. There was little fraternization between Congressmen and Senators and he was delighted to encounter Senator King.

"Why are you out and about in Georgetown, Senator?" He had not yet grown accustomed to the title he now shared, and still loved to feel the word roll from his tongue.

"Well, I guess I can call you Senator now as well, and congratulations!"

Jimmy looked down and hesitated a moment, "My friends call me Jamie."

"Call me not by my far too many given names. W, simply W, will do."

He paused as well, "I often come here, away from those malarial swamps, seeking a bit of elevation and better air. The shopping is better here as well. I prefer the old and fine to the new and crass."

Jimmy's head bounced in agreement, and the pleasantries continued. He soon hoped he had earned the right to ask the Senate's new President *pro tempore*, "If you are finished here, would you care to accompany me to my humble quarters for a drink?"

Something of a prodigy and polymath, and the youngest Congressman in the nation's history, the Sampson County, North Carolina native was elected from his home state when only 24, shy of the Constitutionally-mandated minimum age of 25, which he did not achieve until more than a month after Congress was in session. A lawyer at 19, and like Ann Coleman progeny of a prominent supplier of war materials for the Revolution, he had already served two terms in the North Carolina House of Commons when he entered the halls of Congress. Still not 30, he was named secretary to the U.S. legation in Russia, accompanying William Pinckney, President James Monroe's Minister to Russia, but soon resigned. He spent the next year wandering through France, the Aegean islands of Greece, and the various duchies, regions, fiefdoms and principalities of what was later Italy. An incident in North Carolina sent tongues wagging upon his return. King quickly moved to Alabama, where he sought to become a planter, building a home and securing acreage and slaves in Cahaba, near the town of Selma, of which he became a founding father.

Acting in advance of any derailing rumors, a close friend secured him a nomination to the Alabama Constitutional Convention and, upon the Lizard State's admission in 1819, King was named its first United States Senator by virtue of his already seasoned Washington experience and foreign posts.

When King stood with Andrew Jackson as the President sought re-election in 1828, Old Hickory could not abide the bright colors, the flowing silks and flowery satins his fellow Southerner favored. To his face, Jackson would call the finely garbed Alabamian "Miss Nancy." King always responded with courtesy, and with unquestioned allegiance, and the President eventually learned to swallow some of his disdain, at least in public.

King replied to Jimmy's invitation, "It would be a mutual pleasure."

The two Senators hailed a hack and rode together to Jimmy's boarding house to continue their conversation. Jimmy offered the senior Senator a well-rolled Cuban, just over six inches long, its filler containing slowly sun-dried remnants from a new plantation near the Órganos Mountains, making it the Caribbean island's finest slave-produced crop. Jimmy went to his oaken bar. He was a bit embarrassed at its rough Amish construction, further damaged by its cartage from Lancaster, "I am sure you have something finer?"

King smiled, "It's not so much the container as the contents. What Sherry do you have?"

Here in Washington, Jimmy thought, I cannot do myself as proud. He had some uncertain ten-year-old Madeira Malvasia, stable in the warm capital climate, but not as fine as what he could larder in the depths of his Lancaster cellar. King nevertheless seemed well pleased with his first sip. As Jimmy poured his own, his hand trembled a bit and a large drop of the caramel liquid dribbled onto his hand. He quickly licked it off, his soft pink tongue flicking his thumb. "Here's to insides!"

The men talked late into the night, and shared lunch the following Wednesday in a corner of O'Neale's tavern. Jimmy pushed his food around his plate and stuttered as departed, "W, I know a fine establishment in Baltimore. David Barnum's. Excellent wine and food from all over. I know he'd take care of us."

King anticipated the question. "I would love to go with you. This Saturday. My carriage will be by at dusk."

That weekend evening, at Barnum's restaurant and hotel, Jimmy pulled up to the table. He looked across at the man he was already comfortable calling "W," and smiled. This would be a wonderful meal. How great of good Barnum to give us the far corner table. Jimmy scanned the menu, heavy on seafood, crabs from the Chesapeake and his beloved lobster from Maine. Flanking these viands, dishes of chicken, pheasant, and boar. Jimmy was oblivious to everyone around them.

What wine would the Senator like? Perhaps a tart little something from the Chablis region, Lignorelles perhaps? Jimmy enjoyed showing off his extensive knowledge of French wines, although he had to admit it was mostly dependent on the education that he received from Barnum. What he learned from his days with Nesselrode was ill remembered and antiquated. He nominated the 1829, a vintage Barnum had shared with him one night.

Senator King settled in. "Jamie," he began familiarly, "I expect it is no secret to you that I have long admired your political skills."

Jimmy's face reddened. He had not known any Senator would have kept an eye on him. "The esteem, if I can be so bold, is reciprocated."

"Let me tell you of something closer to my heart. I have another feeling that I hope might be shared as well."

Jimmy looked up from the wine list. He was not certain what to trust. He had known—or at least suspected—something as they sat by the fireplace, and again at lunch. He had heard the rumors. Most important, he felt what he felt now. Could he be sure? Was he misreading this? If he were doing so, it would surely be at his grave peril. He had never been able to share this stirring so openly with anyone and was a bit taken aback by W's apparent candor. His whole life he had had to hide what he felt, and to satisfy his urges with strangers, in alleys and, when in Russia, with men who did not even speak the same language. Here was the esteemed Southern gentleman from Alabama, a man who once challenged Senator Henry Clay to a duel, talking openly about matters that had only, always gone unspoken. It was one thing to do those things and thereafter be able to pretend they had, like some passing dream, never really happened. It was somehow more dangerous but, he had to admit, quite titillating, to talk about them.

"Yes," Jimmy finally replied, and realized startlingly that his caution was misplaced, that he had always known this about W. He had heard the scurrilous whispers in the chambers of the House and was now ashamed that he had occasionally felt compelled to partake in the joking. What else was he to do? The older man reached over and gently ran his fingers in fluid arcs over Jimmy's open palm.

"I want to tell you some things," King said. "They have to do with my philosophy and approach, the driving dream of my life, and are the result of a great deal of careful reflection. Their sum informs my whole life. I am, like Samuel Coleridge, something of a virtual library cormorant. I draw my strength not from what is presented, which is wholly prone to manipulation, but from what I know, that which invades my soul. I feel I must explain all this before we can proceed."

Jimmy looked around the shadowed restaurant. Proceed where? Were there others from Washington within earshot? Worse, were any good burghers from Lancaster dining here in Baltimore? He determined that no one, except a curiously precise bearded gentleman who spoke to the waiter in a clipped British accent, could possibly overhear. A foreigner was of no moment. Jimmy made a larger impression in his leather chair.

"There is a poem, the *'Altercatio Ganimedis et Helene,'* King said, "dating from perhaps the twelfth century that speaks of a debate between Ganymede and Helen. Helen argues that sexual contact between males inverts the order of things, is against the law of man and scripture, is sterile and barren, and withal unnatural. Ganymede, naked before the Gods who are judging the altercation, says simply and unapologetically that the very nature of same-sex love is more natural, more normal, and more pleasurable. The Gods were with him. That is where I stand, an androphile, someone who loves what is most like himself."

Jimmy stared at his expositor. His mind whirled, and his excitement was not all intellectual. His head cocked forward. How extraordinary, unabashed and almost in the open. What he heard felt like an unleashed quiver of gently feathered arrows penetrating his heart.

"Please do go on," he said. "What other support do you have for this? How can you live so without discovery?" A thousand questions competed to emerge from between his damply-tongued little lips.

"You remember how you told me the other night, as we read before the fire, of your mother's love for Pope, and Milton and William Cowper? Did she ever read you that long elegiac poem of Cowper's, the one that starts in its blank verse,

I sing the sofa. I, who lately sang
Truth, Hope, and Charity, and touched with awe
The solemn chords, and with a trembling hand,
Escaped with pain from that advent'rous flight…

Jimmy nodded at the dim remembrance of *The Task*, often read by his mother, with that curious beginning, and its allusion to living room furniture. He knew it went on for thousands upon thousands of words, maybe a 100 pages in all, and recalled the soft murmurings as mother and son went from sofa to timepiece and garden, and embarked, in literary imagination, on a succession of winter walks. What had this poem by the renowned Christian, publisher with John Newton of the Olney hymns, have to do with what was, in all Christian eyes, an abomination?

King continued, "Do you recall its description of fathers,

…whose authority, in show
When most severe, and mustering all its force,
Was but the graver countenance of love;
Whose favour, like the clouds of spring, might lower,
And utter now and then an awful voice,
But had a blessing in its darkest frown,
Threatening at once and nourishing the plant.

W could not remember the rest of the verse, except that it spoke of the father's "gentle hand" and went on to speak of that "softer friend," the mother, who might be recalled "perhaps more gladly still" at the gates of death.

Jimmy was close to tears at the sweet recited recollections of a life that had never been his except through the power of poetry. He remembered the blows that rained down on his mother, and worse, and the guttural retchings in the rat-blooded basement. His own father was fearfully removed from the Cowperian image. He had to acknowledge, "My resentment and anger at my own father still propels, and I sometimes fear, cripples me as well."

King seemed to understand, "That does not surprise me. When a little boy, I huddled in the library of our grand Georgian home, my eyes always alert for parental intrusion, my mind fixed on the illusory prospect of what it could be like to have a daddy like the one in which Cowper reveled."

Jimmy felt the shared sadness. Where was all this poetry leading? He edged closer, his face flushed, now daring at times to lock eyes with W's.

W told Jimmy how Cowper spoke of some men as *manic dancing in their chains,* and *mere vermin, worthy to be trapped/ And gibbeted, as fast as catchpole claws/ Can seize the slippery prey* and explained how men who could appreciate what about life was good and pure were beyond such fates, as they disciplined themselves in public.

It was, in fact, he now explained to Jimmy, all this that was at the core of the way he, and he dare hoped they, could live their lives. Jimmy thought of how he could never look at a woman, without seeing, under all the layers of silk and cotton, wool and satin, his own mother. Who could have Biblical knowledge of one's mother? Every time he had gotten close to a woman, beyond the jokes, the drinking, and the dancing, repulsion reared its head. Put another way, he thought, what was there about the female form, glandularly absurd in one area, and woefully deficient in another, that could be ever expected to attract one? The soft scents, the murmured confidences, yes, but the actual physiognomy, the unclothed body itself—how could that compel? Why would one want to be enfolded and submerged in that quivering female flesh, only to withdraw, shriveled and emptied, almost into oneself?

To illustrate his view, the senior Senator from Alabama continued. "Do you recall when Cowper speaks of the stricken deer?"

Jimmy's face turned toward the fire in the opposite corner of the room. That part of the poem always somehow touched him deeply, although he never discerned exactly why.

W recited the passage *in haec verba*:

I was a stricken deer that left the herd
Long since; with many an arrow deep infixt
My panting side was charged, when I withdrew
To seek a tranquil death in distant shades.
There was I found by one who had himself
Been hurt by the archers. In his side he bore,
And in his hands and feet, the cruel scars.
With gentle force soliciting the darts
He drew them forth, and healed and bade me live.
Since then, with few associates, in remote
And silent woods I wander, far from those
My former partners of the peopled scene,
With few associates, and not wishing more.
Here much I ruminate, as much I may,
With other views of men and manners now
Than once, and others of a life to come.

He continued, Jimmy marveling at his memory:

I see that all are wanderers, gone astray
Each in his own delusions; they are lost
In chase of fancied happiness, still woo'd
And never won. Dream after dream ensues,
And still they dream that they shall still succeed,
And still are disappointed: rings the world
With the vain stir. I sum up half mankind,
And add two-thirds of the remaining half,
And find the total of their hopes and fears
Dreams, empty dreams. The million flit as gay

As if created only, like the fly
That spreads his motley wings in the eye of noon,
To sport their season and be seen no more.

Jimmy had always thought, perhaps, the deer was symbolic of the risen Lord? He struggled with any new meaning. W's sharp brow furrowed as he wondered to himself at his companion's incomprehension. Finally, in a rare moment of vulnerability, Jimmy was compelled to ask, "Senator, all of this moves me, but I do not understand the fullness of it. I am swept away, but do not comprehend all the comments." He longed for the intellectual quickness to come back with some nuanced observation, yearned for any way to show not only understanding but insight.

W, a natural teacher, was obliged to comply. This fellow was handsome and accomplished, and his sensibilities, and of course his orientation, seem right, but he was perhaps not as bright as he seemed?

The Senior Senator began, "It is quite clear to me that the world views us with repulsion and uneasiness. You and I are both Christians, I know, and yet the church has come up with its theistic dictum, *crimen inter Christanos non nominandum* and has cast out of society those who have committed a crime that has no name that can be spoken. The world has feelings of sadness mingled with disgust, and is somehow humiliated, repulsed and embarrassed by us at the same time."

Jimmy had his own concerns, his whole life long, if anyone had discovered it—the rough boys, his college classmates, his fellow Congressmen, his father. His mother!

"It can only be, Jamie, because they recognize the naturalness of what we do, and their own fear that, contrary to everything that religion and fathers teach, their own different urges are to be condemned. Unable to condemn themselves, they condemn others and almost enter into a panic of punishment. When private and public life were the same, as they were before men left home and hearth to go to factories, shops and legislatures to earn their living, both the internal and the external remained united. Now they are split, and we are the unfortunate progeny of that division."

I am barely getting this, yet it seems so right, Jimmy said to himself. To King, "Do you mean that we are to be different in public than in private?" Even as the question stumbled out, its answer was obvious, and he regretted having posed it.

"Of course," W said without any sign of contempt, "and that is in fact how we live. The secret is to do so in a manner that permits full expression in private, and absolute decorum in public. We must remain in a box. It inside can be a gilded box, resplendent with color and song and texture, even as we venture, sober and gray, on dour streets and chastened lanes. I, for one, want to be separated from that herd and develop my own individuated inner feelings. I must, as you must, be a Senator at day, and in the public functions of the night. We must conform in public and yet can flourish as completely ourselves at home."

Jimmy nodded. He never wanted to be one of the common cattle, and never thought he had been. Now he knew he was in the presence of greatness. He was totally overwhelmed, intellectual and sexual excitement that seemed, as he reddened, to be fusing into a surging, hard coursing freshet watering his very soul.

W now turned to the portion of the poem he read to Jimmy. As he did so, Jimmy remembered the young boy who curiously preferred the company of his sisters and shunned the hard games of the rough boys who paradoxically attracted him. That feeling of what he had come to name to himself his "differentness." He could observe, of course, that it was men and women who married, men and women who had children, men and women who did those things that he had seen his father, after his drunken punching screaming bruising battery of his mother do as she cried and cowered but permitted him to lift her skirt while he watched, horrified and transfixed in distorted excitement, all helpful impulses crippled. How was he now attracted to the transgressor and repulsed by the victim?

Keeping his secret had been no great problem in Mercersburg, where boys and girls, zealously kept apart, were then free, within marital confines, to come together. He had chosen to leave, fleeing as soon as he could. At Dickinson, the drinking, that tavern revelry, made him feel a part of things, and the wenches, sluts and slatterns who partook there were part of a wonderful parade where he could bond with the fellows and be bearded by the young women in the central Pennsylvania town. He had seen some of his classmates slip away into small back rooms or the neighboring woods or, for the wealthier, the upholstered seats of their carriages. They would do, or not do, things that they would relate over ale and whiskey. Jimmy simply listened. He did not have to participate and the different stirrings within him could be drowned. Like the hairless, androgynous, feminized Indian berdaches he had seen and now, in hindsight, realized he had greatly desired on the Pennsylvania frontier, he never had to shave. This odd fact he kept hidden from all, except of course, Pompey. No one was ever the wiser among his classmates. Only the Reverend Lovelace, who had led him to the little room behind the sacristy and opened up the new world as grunt after grunt drowned the cries of angels.

Loveless was found with another, much younger boy, *in flagrante delicto*, and Jimmy's own visits to the chapel, and his overnight stays, led to suspicion and his expulsion from Dickinson. Of course, no one had ever seen the pastor and the college man together in that way, and no one could know for sure.

In Lancaster, it had been permissible, for a while, to lead this life of revelry. In Lancaster, too, it had been possible to bury his desires, to take care of his needs himself, and to avoid the expression of what he continued to view as his distorted and basest desires. Well, he considered, almost always possible...

To advance in law or politics, he knew he would have to take a wife, one with, he hoped, some measure of attractiveness, certainly some breeding, and of course, considerable wealth. It would also help if she were sufficiently younger than he, from a household with a strong father and therefore prepared to do as she was instructed. Someone who would suffer in silence, and in contradistinction to the mandate of the seventh chapter of First Corinthians, agree to be separate from him after the propagation of a child or, at most, two. They could get along, he knew, if she would just do for him and his household as a wife ought, fetch his slippers and coat, cook his food, wash his clothes, darn his socks, and clean his house or, as he made his way, supervise those who did. Let her get wrapped up in the little ones, and keep her counsel as the physical faded away.

Ann met, he thought, all those prescriptives. A bit headstrong, perhaps. That would wane as age advanced and her dependence on him increased. He could not have asked for more in terms of pleasing beauty, societal status, and inheritable wealth. Of course, she had gone and killed herself and taken all that away from him.

At first, he now recalled as W continued, he thought he would have to find another, perhaps someone younger, more distant in age or later someone older, already with children and who would make no such requests of him. He remembered as the sympathy rolled in for him, despite the scattered lies and noxious assertions of his own culpability, that this situation was metamorphosizing into something quite satisfactory. He came to understand there was a way out of this whole dilemma that would afford him, not the future that Ann snatched from him, but something in many ways better. What a strong shield this aspect of distraught eternal bereavement had proved against the Cupidian missiles. He fought off the importunings of young women. He had to counter their mothers, either speaking on behalf of their daughters or on their own. Later, there were other excuses: responsibility of raising the children of his impecunious brothers or the orphans of his dead sisters, demands of his position, and then of course just increasing age and the curmudgeonly ways that could not, despite anyone's affection, easily be tolerated. Always, the Ann stories as needed, providing protection and eliciting sympathy. If he were to marry at 60 or so, it would be to a woman mature enough to be satisfied by position and social place, one who would not require any ardent attention or romantic affection. If to a young woman, it would be someone who could excuse the doting—or perhaps late in life, the doddering— absence of desire in a father figure, and who would make him the elbow-nudging envy of so many.

W noticed that he had lost his dinner companion, although he was not certain how far back. He softly called Jimmy's name, and the younger companion debouched from his reverie.

W continued. It was important that Jamie understand all he was saying. Important if they were to be together, and both be spared the disgusting practices of the streets and alleys, of back shanties and the furtive taverns of the big cities of the East, where Southern Gentlemen were desired yet ridiculed.

"Most of what I have read of this has focused on the image of tranquil domesticity this poem presents. They talk of 'the charms of rural life' and the 'endearments of domestic retirement.' In fact, its significance lies in the intimate private feelings presented, as opposed to the public life demanded of men in our position.

"What you should know, Jamie," W smiled, "is that Cowper remained a bachelor, and by this alone is greatly distinguished among the poets your mother read, or of whom she knew."

Jimmy anticipated the significance.

"I think," W went on, "that this wholly establishes who he was and what his poems mean."

Jimmy hesitated, as he could still not quite believe that Cowper, the poet of his youth, really was "one of them," or, as he now finally let himself acknowledge, "one of us." After all, Jimmy had thought Cowper was only commenting on the beauty of the bucolic, not the ecstasy of the alleyways.

"I don't quite see this," Jimmy said. "With respect, does this mean for certain that he was just as we are? My goodness, the man wrote hymns!"

W went on, "You can read the whole of *The Task*, all 35,000 of its words, and you will see no wife nor child littering its author's rural life, removed from public glare and performance. The few women in the poem flit on its outskirts and soon drift into oblivion. Only the man remains in the center, and his private life is his concern. All else is floss and dross."

As the buzz from the wine rang through his head, Jimmy thought, I am beginning to get it. "We do not need women," he said aloud almost without realizing he had uttered the words. They are mere adjuncts to men. "Why," he said, as he looked at the expositor across the table, "would we want to share ourselves with them when we can have one another?"

Jimmy considered the rumors that surrounded both him and his dinner companion. He was grateful that the exclusive club of men who populated the House and Senate paid deference to the implicit promise not to pry too far into the personal. Wives and children were left at home. The few women in Washington were there to clean and cook in the boarding houses in which they lodged, or provide other services on demand and payment.

Jimmy had a quiver of insight. "W, I understand! Washington itself is the inside of the great public box of the country. It is itself gilded inside. Because it is wholly a masculine city, it can protect us and our secret!"

W smiled at his companion's excitement. He had long known that being a *homme sole* was not in and of itself cause for comment in the masculine swamp of Washington, and if one were discreet, there was never any need to fear discovery or disclosure. If needed, tales of women at home, or in his companion's case, the distant death of Ann, could provide requisite substitutes for suspicions.

W reminded him of something else whose shining obviousness acted to shadow their status. "Most people," W said, "deem the conduct so reprehensible that it has no name that is not dripping with Biblical condemnation or criminal allegation. I have found, as I have achieved an evermore respectable position, it is simply not spoken of. The box we have been talking about, plain on the outside, will be kept, except for private whispers and the occasional boor like Jackson, closely shut. No one will ask, and we do not need to tell. In fact, there is hardly the vocabulary to do so."

"Remember when I was in Russia?" Jimmy said.

W thought, I cannot really "remember" that, but no matter.

"I was able to identify a code that transcended culture and language. I don't even know how exactly, yet I knew those among the royalty who sought this pleasure."

Crimson crept hotly on the back of his neck as he recalled how he cast about on the frigid St. Petersburg streets in search of the quick and anonymous satisfaction that arose from the combination of strong drink and dark alleys. "W, when I was young, it was not about romance," Jimmy said earnestly, concerned he had mentioned too much. Now, he realized, deeper affections were beginning to blossom. "I know of your own career and your service at the same age in Russia. You need not tell me, of course, but I well suspect the reasons for your discharge and your wanderings in the Eurasian wilderness."

King's initial reaction (quite unaccountably, he told himself) was anger, and some embarrassment. He checked himself, "I do know the pain, and the pleasure, of similar experiences."

Jimmy was now convinced that he had revealed far too much about earlier dalliances, quick alliances that had nothing to do with love. "Of course, in Lancaster," Jimmy continued, "I have had to be inordinately discreet."

Memories of how he had studiously stayed away from the one sure source of activity, a small bar down from Strawberry Hill, with its fox hunt motif. Jimmy knew that even in his hometown, men, and sometimes women, met one another and wandered into the night, landing within the back rooms of Water Street.

"Even in Washington," W added, "and even when messages from the complex code of suggestion and manner seem strong, one must be hesitant."

Each pondered, for a moment, his separate trips to Boston and New York, and quick visits to Baltimore, providing greater relief in certain taverns and certain places, the dark deadly delicious city alleys a potent cocktail of relief and danger.

Jimmy told W not of these trips, but of the political fallout from his Philadelphia forays. The City of Brotherly Love ("How apt," smiled W) was only a three-hour carriage ride from Lancaster or the Capital. "My political supporters complain of what they called my, 'comet-like swings' through the city yet never suspected my real purpose. They never knew of the nights at the Metropole and its fine wines and succulent viands. They were unaware of the midnight shoots off of Locust and Sycamore that fed the very tree of my life."

Here they were at Barnum's, in Baltimore, which he was already hoping would become their special place.

"Think about the trauma of the deer," W said, returning to his poetic lesson. "In the passage I recited, consider the imperfect rebound from the shot into a quivering heart. Of course, one cannot discount the Christian symbolism, yet the poet is plunging much more deeply into the despairing loneliness of the words. So very few share this fate and the imperfect salvation received from the shots of an undisclosed hunter as death approaches. Think about the wounded creature who appears to be forced to flee. We are that creature; we have our secret captured deep within us. We have had to run from the temptation that would otherwise overwhelm us. We have had this sense of difference, all our lives, have been overwhelmed by the necessity of an internal life. We have been isolated beyond the herd. If we didn't acknowledge this fact we could not remain intact. Now we have each other!"

They shared a smile. "You should know, Jamie, that people believed that Cowper was writing of his madness, his suicide attempts, yet it is clear to me that it is but the surface. Throughout his life, Cowper acknowledged his bouts of depression, and later wrote of his suicidal tendencies. He always alluded to a particular cause for his depression and ideations, yet as he approached death never revealed it."

W dismissed the whispered assertions that Cowper was a hermaphrodite, concluding that this was the likely product of those who sought to libel him, and perhaps was even a case of mistaken identity.

Jimmy wondered whether to tell W of his beautiful box of letters from Ann, now shuffled under his bed in Lancaster. "I want to tell you, W," Jimmy began, then hesitated. The truth he ended up with was something less forthcoming. "Sufficient to say, upon my demise, I have certain letters that will explain to the world what I now see is the other mystery of my life. All will come to understand me, and the grievous wrong done to me."

In a rare flight of what Jimmy thought of as literary grace, they were the very embodiment of the secret itself, encased in the shrouding box.

What an elucidating dinner, Jimmy thought, on the ride back to Washington. They would have stayed at Barnum's but for the press of Senate business and the need for their votes on matters of common interest. Their hands secretly reached, outside of the driver's gaze, toward each other.

When Senator King suggested, with perhaps one too many sniffles, that Jimmy's quarters were not quite up to the level one should have as a Senator, and that he might wish to move in with him, Jimmy gratefully accepted. They secured a residence on "F" Street, between 13th and 14th Streets, in which they lived together for the next eighteen years. Even when the whispers began to waft through Washington in the next few weeks, and continued into the succeeding years, Jimmy resolved to follow his roommate's example and proceed with a decorum rarely utilized by him in the past. It proved the appropriate closed box for their life together.

He had to bear the brunt now of being called "Aunt Fancy" to his lover's "Miss Nancy." His resolute public propriety and the hesitancy to take direct offense for what was not only a sinful abomination but also a crime appeared to be having their effect. The fear and shame that he would otherwise have felt were strangely absent now, and besides, who would believe such stories outside Washington? When they began commonly to be referred to as the "Siamese Twins," in recognition of the widely known, poker playing, hard drinking, and fecund conjoined new residents of W's native state of North Carolina, Chang and Eng Butler, Jimmy and W both took it, for public consumption at least, as a political allegiance recognized and for a friendship envied. Each knew it was the nineteenth century code for male lovers. Like the appellation "Mrs. Buchanan," increasingly applied to W, the term was simply fluffed off.

It did seem as if everyone in Washington really knew. When the proper Mrs. James K. Polk received a letter from Aaron Brown, a Tennessee congressman and Jimmy's future Postmaster General speaking of "Buchanan and his wife" in referring to Jimmy and W, she apparently found it unremarkable. In a letter marked "Confidential," he wrote the prim future First Lady about an argument between Jimmy and W he witnessed, *Mr. Buchanan looks gloomy and dissatisfied & so does his better half until a little private flattery…. Aunt Fancy may now be seen every day, triggered out in her best clothes and smirking about in hopes of seeing better terms than with her former companion…in the presence of Mr. Buchanan and his wife and some others, I advanced the opinion that neither Mr. Calhoun nor Mr. Van Buren had any chance to be elected. This of course was highly indecorous towards Mrs. B…it would be better of course not to irritate Colo. K—but considering his former course of life, his associations and future aspirations we conclude that silence may not conciliate.*

The more vehement and radical newspapers might accuse one of bigamy or bastardy, one's mother of prostitution, or hint quite directly of a past murder, yet they were shy of brazen allegations of subjects like pederasty, incest or sodomy. Those censures were simply absent from the public discourse. W was right. Homosexuality was the crazy uncle of early 19th century America, and he was in a box in someone else's attic closet. They could conduct business on the Senate floor and retire together at night in the large four-poster bed they shared. They would read Byron and Shelly, and of course Cowper. When W read to him, Jimmy was taken back to Stony Batter and Mercersburg, and his mother's lovely lilting Appalachian voice softly coating the remembered passages. He wanted to have her finger in his mouth, suckling him, and sought its substitute. At times, they would read to one another Byron's words in a little play of love.

First, Jimmy as Manfred, "Away, away, there's blood upon the brim! Will it never sink in the earth?"

and W as the Chamois Hunter, "What dost thou mean, Thy senses wander from thee!"

with Manfred's riposte, "I say tis blood-my blood! The pure warm stream which ran in the veins of my fathers, and in yours when we were in our youth, and had one heart, and loved each other as we should not love."

All in all, it was not that difficult to keep their relationship boxed in. Jimmy was by nature secretive and, as he no longer had to haunt taverns and alleyways, their loving evenings of Madeira and Cubans were enough for him. In session breaks, as they retreated to Lancaster and Selma, each tried to abstain from others, comforted in the sure hope that they would be together again.

For public consumption, Jimmy continued to permit feminine forays but always deflected those efforts before intimations of the altar grew too forceful. Although these imagined romantic liaisons were now as much from lassitude as any attempt to throw up smoke screens, Jimmy realized this was also a way of protecting their shared secret.

No visitors were ever invited to the upstairs quarters on F Street. As with Walt Whitman, who had to invent secret affairs, secret children, and secret mistresses, it was sometimes necessary to create the opaque screen around the gilded box. After all, men had indeed been executed for acts of sodomy; Jefferson himself advocated castration of sodomites, and Leviticus 20:13 was quoted verbatim in the Connecticut statute.

Jimmy, of course, was still haunted by the possibility of Thaddeus Stevens and what he might say or reveal if it were about his carnal desires. What was it? Was it that? Most important, the possibility of proof—did Stevens really have any?—that would, in one crushing moment, lead not only to his expulsion from the Senate and the end of his career, but would land him in prison, perhaps until death. Still, he was able to place such thoughts out of his head, at least during the day. His tortured nights would sometimes lead him to wake sobbing, begging for the steady arms of the Alabamian around him, but he thought it best not to tell him the source of his anguish. Who knew what W would do or, worse, compel him to do? Best to let the sleeping dog lie. Jimmy heard tales of Stevens' shift from anti-Masonry to an unholy alliance with the most rabid of abolitionists, yet paid it little heed. Glad, he thought, that he is otherwise occupied.

It was only through continuing compromise and concession that the constitutional right of slavery, Jimmy knew, would persist. The slow erosion of slavery in the North made its staunch maintenance south of the Mason-Dixon Line, from ocean to ocean as new states were added, even more critical. W used his position as President pro tempore to name Jimmy chair of the Committee on Slavery and the Slave Trade in Washington. The ongoing rights to run public slave auctions, and of course, possess slaves were secured in the nation's capital. Ran Jimmy's logic, one could buy slaves in Maryland and Virginia, so why not in Washington? "W," he promised, "I will remain an instrument of its preservation, and its extension, no matter where our political lives may lead."

Later that year, Jimmy expressed an interest in foreign affairs and W named him Chair of the Senate Committee on Foreign Relations, taking over Henry Clay's post. Everything was going along so well and Jimmy was grateful to his mentor. Perhaps he would not only serve with W in the Senate but perhaps, just perhaps, he would be President and they might even be together in the White House.

Jimmy still did not grasp his ordained role.

Chapter Fifteen
<u>S</u>LAVERY

The last four years, thought Jimmy as his carriage entered Alabama in April 1841, have been the happiest of my life.

His relationship with W was secure. Based on his first year's efforts and surprisingly quick ascension in Washington, the Pennsylvania Assembly had rewarded him with a full term in the Senate by acclamation. He had served with distinction, a voice of moderation and compromise.

The most significant negative, and it was a serious one, was Martin Van Buren's rejection of W for Vice President as he sought a second term in 1840. He still did not understand why van Buren had not chosen to run with Senator King.

He and W had evaluated the situation. W made it clear that he possessed no particular wish to leave the Senate and was concerned about the level of scrutiny that a national campaign might bring. Jimmy persisted, pointing out how W would balance the Van Buren's politics and geography. W would use his firm control of the Southern electors to help the New Yorker secure a second term. Jimmy could use those same voters to propel himself to the Presidency in 1844, with W and his four years of executive experience remaining in the White House as Vice-President. It had seemed so perfect.

Van Buren's first term running mate, Richard Johnson, had been compelled to acknowledge that he had a slave for a mistress and had sired several daughters. Claiming she was unfaithful, the

Vice-President sold the concubine to an owner two counties over and distributed their mulatto daughters among his friends for their use. His public admission of his relationship with the slave led to the refusal of the Virginia electors who supported Van Buren to vote for the Kentucky tavern owner, and the Senate had to affirm the choice. Surely, the President would not run again with such a man?

Jimmy did all he could. The South would still firmly be in the Democrats' pocket, and he could sell a Van Buren-King ticket in Pennsylvania and elsewhere. He launched a press campaign for his roommate, judiciously placing pro-King "puffs" in papers in Philadelphia, Boston, and New York, extolling the Alabama senator's virtues. Other pieces were planted in response, asserting a strong personal motivation for Jimmy to back Senator King and suggesting that he was a stalking horse for Jimmy's own presidential ambitions. Some hinted, as W had feared, that the relationship between the men was more than political.

As his efforts advanced, Van Buren offered Jimmy the Attorney General's post if he agreed to leave his Senate seat. Jimmy saw through the ruse and was disappointed at the attempt to purchase his support and shift his focus. For whatever reason, the President would not accept King as his running mate. Inexplicably, he was retaining Johnson.

The Whigs jumped on the schism Johnson's presence on the ticket created. General William Henry Harrison and "Tyler too," countered the Wizard and the misceginist. Harrison was the hero of the Battle of Tippecanoe, a contest on the Indiana plains to eliminate Indians under cover of the War of 1812. John Tyler was a slaveholding states-righter from Virginia. The Whigs, previously claiming themselves the legitimate descendants of the Federalists, had fully joined with the anti-Masonists and adopted their rhetoric.

"Jamie, notice how vague the platform is," said W. "They are utilizing the General's supposed heroism to rope in everyone who is against wealth and power. That tiny man Van Buren is being portrayed as a pawn of the wealthy, while Harrison has gone beyond his log cabin birth to his military position through good old-fashioned hard work. Ideas are becoming less and less important and personality or, better said, personality as portrayed in the newspapers is now the driving force. It is perhaps Jackson's clearest legacy."

Jimmy took the lesson in as Van Buren, schooled only in the politics of the East, could not counter this appeal or the harsh attacks. During the campaign, Jimmy earned the sobriquet "Ten Cent Jimmy" for suggesting that amount, and no more, should be the total daily wage for anyone who labored in a factory. Although taken out of context, the nickname stuck. After the President lost, W said, "Jamie, you know I did not really seek the post."

"What of us together, as running mates?"

"That is now unlikely."

"What of me?"

W had looked away, "You are still a young man, not quite 50. There will be more opportunities."

As he said the words, W had considered what he might yet do to ensure that Jamie would secure the top prize.

The carriage drew closer. King's Bend was high on the hill. It is the color of snow, Jimmy thought, with its neatly-fashioned shutters framing glass eyes that viewed what must be a thousand acres of prime bottom land, a ripening hill cresting against the spring sky.

The horses pulled across the cross-laced timbers of the covered bridge spanning the sweeping curve of the Alabama River, swollen and snake green. Jimmy's eyes did not register the splintered yellowing bones bobbing below in the mud-laced river, orts of black flesh hanging by bloated tendons to the shattered bones slurping in fallow eddies at the banks' edges. Instead, he focused on the imagined white expanse of spreading young cotton plants emerging fresh and new in front of him. Dark figures bobbed up and down on the greening hills. Odd swooping notes rolled, like rancid butter, toward Jimmy's ears. Waves of black women dug into dirty burlap sacks, plucking small caches of seeds and thrusting them into holes formed by the advancing sticks of young children.

Jimmy bounced up the steps of the double porch threaded across the front of the residence, its white Ionic columns broken only by the second story of the portico. A warm hug, "What do you think, you Old Buck, of my place?"

Jimmy grinned at the name. It sounded both familiar and stately. How good to see W! "It is more than I ever imagined. It combines all that is right and good, stunning vistas, a sound and thriving agricultural engine and so beautiful. You have every right to be proud."

He added, "I like that name, 'Old Buck.' I am getting a bit aged to be called 'Jimmy.'"

"Hardly the case, though I know it is your birthday in but a month. How old will you be?" W winked, "Forty?"

"Fifty and I feel it right now."

"I can still call you Jamie, can I not, Jamie?"

Jimmy smiled. "Of course," and added, "but I think 'Old Buck' might soon do for others."

W ushered him to a large wicker chair on the broad porch. He turned to a large black man dressed in a scarlet jacket, the edges of its dozen brass buttons smooth from a decade of daily polishing, "Caesar, whiskies, long canes. How was the trip?"

Jimmy looked down a stone path shunting from the side of the mansion, framed by pink Pangaean rhododendra and leafy boxwood towers. He leaned back in his chair, wiggling his feet out of his shoes. The tips of his stockings softly moved in circles on the shellacked floorboards. "It was fine, only a dozen days. Sailing around Florida would have taken longer by the time I came upland, and I might have taken a train ride or two and patched it together with a succession of coaches, but it was easier to hire the Cleveland bays. I have to tell you, I just suffered through one of the more ghastly inaugurations you might imagine. You were wise to avoid it. The wind whipped through the crowd. It was freezing, and I was without a good view of the portico and could barely hear Taney administer the oath, the crowd was so restless. There stood, coatless and hatless and gloveless, that ancient General 'No sirrah'," Jimmy winked at the inversion, "and spoke for two hours. I couldn't follow his speech and everyone wanted to leave. I saw Daniel Webster, his head in his hands, surely wondering why he had ever wanted State."

W waited for an opening. "We should consider what all this means. Harrison is already 68 and I cannot imagine he will run again. Tyler is a Southerner and his loyalties are with us. He's really a Democrat, not a Whig. If you are to be President, we must consider how he might be derailed from succeeding the General."

Jimmy braced his elbow on the chair arm and tilted his head onto his upraised fist, his back resting against the wicker, slowly rocking. W was surely right.

W continued, "No Southerner will be President again, unless someone comes from the West, perhaps Kentucky or Tennessee. The Northeastern cities are growing with their factories and all those Irish, Germans and French coming in. Soon, many of them will be permitted to vote and I fear we will see more of those black Irish. Even counting our darkies toward our electoral votes and Congressional representation, the shift is to the North. We must grow slavery to the west, and make sure that the institution perseveres. We will need northern candidates who see things our way. It has to be a northern man with a southerner under him. Obviously, you are the ripest fit for that mold."

"Does this mean Tyler cannot win?"

"Yes. I am sure of it. Most assuredly if he remains a Whig. That is where you can still fit in."

Jimmy was pleased. He had wanted W to take office with Van Buren, and if the little Dutchman had just acquiesced the ticket would have won. Now, they had to deal with Harrison, and Jimmy had been concerned that Tyler was likely to follow. It should have been Van Buren and King in office. Then, of course, Jimmy himself.

"I was in church this Sunday past," King continued, "and the preacher gave me a lot to consider."

"I am sure."

W's eyes tightened a bit, but Jimmy seemed not to have intended the remark as a slight. "I know you come at the issue constitutionally, as do I, but the Biblical support for slavery is considerable as well. Certainly, it is no moral evil. You are familiar, I am sure, with the New Testament verses calling for obedience and subservience on the part of slaves. Witness Paul's epistle to Philemon where he is divinely inspired to write of the runaway slave returned to his master. Many of Jesus' parables recognize the very fact of slavery. They speak only of humane and fair treatment being desirable, which is what I certainly do. We all know there were no black men on Noah's Ark, just some odd business afterwards. Wallace Thurmond, two plantations up the river, quoted Josiah Priestly in our meeting, affirming the idea that the 'tempter in the Garden of Eden was a talking beast, a nigger.'"

Jimmy had moved his chin to the apex of his two arms, his fingers intertwined and drifting downward, his head positioned as if he were a gargoyle at the mouth of two gutter pipes. With the last remark, he raised himself and tilted his good eye toward Caesar. The slave had not moved an inch, but Jimmy thought he saw the negro's jaw tighten.

"Of course, most importantly for our country," Jimmy said, "and I know I need not tell you, the Constitution itself recognizes the institution. In fact, it embraces it. Most of the founding fathers had slaves, or someone in their immediate family did and they wrote the institution into the fabric of the nation's laws and recognized its economic necessity. Even those who cannot afford to own slaves support the property rights of slaveholders."

W nodded. "Those so-called abolitionists who want to take our property away therefore do so without a moral imperative nor a constitutional one. They fabricate stories of whippings and caterwaulings. Each day, my overseer is instructed only to lash the least productive of the men and one at random besides, and another each of the women and children, but it is simply an incentive, and a warning, to the others. It is never done so roughly as to compel them not to work the next day. I have certainly not once personally dragged a wild mountain cat's claws down a slave's back and buttocks while he lays spread-eagled staked in the mud, nor salted the newly-sliced wounds. In fact, I've only seen it on few occasions."

Jimmy's stomach churned a bit as the image gathered like disagreeable storm clouds.

"Further, lest you believe otherwise, I have never had carnal relations with a darky, though my father did believe that southern boys should be introduced to the fairer sex in the shanties. You can imagine, Jamie, how that was…"

Jimmy's head slowly affirmed the pain.

Oddly, the recollection of Ann Coleman's obituary on December 11, 1819 pushed at his brain. He had retained several copies of the edition containing his handiwork, and reviewed it as the spirit moved him. On the same page as the father's brief but competing panegyric, the notices for unclaimed horses and billets seeking the arrest of horse thieves, land for sale, offerings for shares of public companies, various petitions and available brick houses and tenements, there was an announcement about an anti-slavery meeting in nearby West Chester.

Farther down the page still stored in the box beneath his bed, this advertisement in the Lancaster *Journal*:

FOR SALE

The unexpired term of six years (from the 25ᵗʰ of March next) of a young healthy BLACK GIRL. She can wash and iron, and do house work, and was bred up in a family of Friends in Delaware State. For terms, inquire at the Lancaster stage Office of Robert D. Carson who has also to dispose of a strong, active healthy Black Boy of twelve years of age-has fifteen years to serve and has been bred on a farm and used to horses.

As Jimmy was reflecting on the notice, W left his chair, long strides on rosined wood, his shoulders twitching as if to shake off the image of that hot North Carolina night, his daddy silently pacing outside that shanty with a scarred woman whose hair flew in wild kinks into the darkness. Down the hard path at the wood's edge squatted the dogtrot shack, one room for two families, next to a field still awash with August's white harvest. The walls had seemed to collapse upon each other, their essence extracted by soft-bodied ants the color of spit floating in the morning wash basin. He had felt his father's eyes weaseling between the calico tacked to the sides of the shack in its futile attempt to brace the termite-ridden remnants.

It would not, no matter how much he wished it would do so, it simply would not, rise.

Still known as Billy, he dragged the slave girl to the darkest corner. The strands of moonlight skittered only halfway across the dirt. His narrow back shielded what happened next. Billy ripped off Rose's patched and flimsy dress. He forced Rose's whimpering naked body to the floor and tried to mimic the sounds that spurted from his parents' bedroom. Billy knew Camellia, her mama still outside with Daddy, had told her to do anything the master's son asked. His own daddy had said, "You will know what to do. Have her touch you, lick her chest and all the rest will come."

It had seemed like forever to Billy and, he expected, even longer to Rose. He had ended, "Here, take this coin you filthy pickaninny. Don't you be telling anyone or you will be getting a hard whipping for sure."

W returned to his chair and to the present, a hard breath drawing a startled look from his companion. After a moment, he said, "Jamie, slavery will be this country's most divisive and intrusive issue. You have seen how it can dominate public discourse, those zealots appealing to the baser instincts, talking of what they view as horrors. Why should black babies not be sold by the pound? They have no value until they are five or six. Some oppose branding, but what should one otherwise do to help ensure their return? You know I just snip off the left ear and impress a "WK" on the side of the throat. No crude X's scrawled with rusting knives across cheek or forehead. No hot metal thrusting on the inner thighs."

Jimmy nodded, although this talk of branding was adding to the cloudy unsettled feeling. Finally W turned back to their future, his future. "Your brilliance in opposing efforts to limit slavery, especially to keep public slave markets alive in Washington, has not gone unnoticed by others beyond me, and it sets you in good stead for a presidential push, perhaps not next time but soon."

Jimmy considered mentioning the advertisement for the Quaker-raised slave that appeared on the same page as Ann's obituary, but that would link their discussion to her, and W always seemed pained at any allusion to Ann. "Of course, that 'gag resolution' supplies a safe harbor. I was wise, I think," his head inclined a bit more, "when Calhoun called for the absolute rejection of anti-slavery petitions, to propose that petitions be received but contemporaneously tabled. It was more than just a compromise. It allowed their vain filing by Quakers and their friends, but with no hope of fulfillment the process stayed within the Constitution."

"Yes, Jamie, that was exactly the right course," said W, recalling that he himself was the genesis of the concept.

W continued, "You know my constitutional position. I seek to divine what our founding fathers would have desired, and hold fast and true to their vision for America. I don't think we have any need to discuss slavery on the Senate floor. My legislation prohibiting the dissemination of any anti-slavery literature through the U.S. mails was also well-founded. Webster's response that such agitation is protected by the First Amendment and those materials are private property falls of its own weight. States can ban literature intended to destroy them. I simply made this a matter of states' rights. It's a question not of private property but of public safety. Imagine if those mailings were allowed to percolate from the hot opinion factories of William Lloyd Garrison, that colored Frederick Douglass or some Yankee woman? Why, there could be civil unrest and upheaval. We have as little right to interfere with slavery in the South as we have to touch the right of petition. It's fundamental procedural due process. Both are constitutional. Those petitions, and that literature, might as well be stoking our fire back on F Street!"

Jimmy let out a full grin.

Feeling very much like a contented Old Buck, he looked across the field, reached out his tongue and drew it slowly back under his top lip. His gaze took in the lines of dark slaves furrowing and planting the Alabama clay, the mysterious syncopated chanting rising against the gathering gloom, and the wind blowing indistinct words toward the Senators. This, certainly, was life as man was meant to live it.

King's Bend offered so much more than the Coleman house. He recalled his boyhood vow to have a residence that stood above all others, a place of gentility and grace, and resolved again someday to acquire such a plantation home, more in the strain of the music of the South. He had shown all that he had conquered Ann and all the Colemans, punctuating the message by actually invading their environs with his purchase of their home.

His point was proven and his vindication, for at least the moment, felt secure.

Chapter Sixteen
<u>HOMAGE</u>

Up for re-election before the Pennsylvania Assembly in the fall of 1842, Old Buck scurried to find a deterring romantic interest on which the press could feast. He established a relationship with Anna Payne, the teenaged niece of Dolley Madison, and made certain it was well publicized. A scant week after the voting, unable or unwilling to face the young woman, he chose the mode of iambic pentameter to explain why he could no longer court her..

He wrote and declared his "rebel passion." No need to reinvigorate the memory of Ann Coleman this time. He chose, as he had with Mary Snyder the very day after his selection for the first Senate term, the notion of advancing age, ignoring the fact that it was only a few months since the relationship's inception, as predicate for breaking off the relationship.

At the age of 51, in stilted poesy, he wrote the 19 year old:

In thee my chilled & blighted heart has found
A green spot in the dreary waste around.

Oh! That my fate in my youthful days
T'have lived with such an one, unknown, unseen,

Loving and lov'd, t'have passed away our days
Sequestered from the world's malignant gaze.

A match of age with youth can only bring
The farce of 'winter dancing with the spring'.

Becoming nineteen can never well agree
With the dull age of half a century.

Thus reason speaks what rebel passion hates,
Passion,—which would control the very fates.

Meantime, where're you go, what e're your lot
By me you'll never, never be forgot.

May Heaven's rich blessing crown your future life!
And may you be a happy, loving wife.

Another diversion, another heart discarded.

Harrison had died of pneumonia the month after his inauguration and Tyler was now President. The ostensible Whig, true to his roots and social class, had announced that he was more comfortable as a Democrat, and switched his party back. The Democrats had now, via Tyler's transmutation, won the election after all, and there was a great deal of glee in the party. W and Old Buck, however, felt betrayed. "It is worse than we had feared. We had counted on a level field, and now our own party has its own successor in office. Tyler will surely run again and you need to oppose him. By the time his terms are up some new younger star might already be shining."

Jimmy suggested, "What if I do not run against Tyler but support another? I can leave the Senate, take a cabinet post with whatever administration comes in. Even if Tyler wins, he'll need to unite the party and I would be the logical bridge to the other wing. You can arrange the appointment, and see if you can secure one for yourself."

"Perhaps," W said, "that is workable. Tyler cannot win in any event. His Whig flirtation dooms him with our party. I know you have some skittishness about going through that state assembly, and I agree it is never a sure proposition, what with the Philadelphia faction and more legislators from the western part of your state."

Old Buck could not meet W's eyes. He had still not told W of Stevens's threat and yet here W was suggesting a way he might never have to do so. Time's passage was not making it easier to reveal that meeting and the unknown contents of the letter that still stood stark and red against the York sky. Now Stevens was out of the legislature. He was certainly not without influence, but precious little. Just another Lancaster lawyer, worming his way through the streets and courtrooms. He was in no position to harm him anymore. Maybe this would be a good time to tell W? If he did, what would W want him to do? What would W make him do? It was not only the secret, but the withholding of it, that now made divulging it too painful. It might be, he hoped, no longer necessary.

"A cabinet post for each of us," W said as he wondered at the odd whiteness of his companion's forehead, "keeps us together and polishes your prospects. You should make a nominal run, but accede to someone who agrees with our plan."

How wise W is. He has surely sensed something, but is too kind to ask. At worst, Old Buck considered, this will flush Stevens out of his duck blind and see if, after all these years, there is really anything that can interrupt my flight. If so, I can tell W and have him imagine this is a new development. W can help me solve it. If Stevens proves wingless, there can be a fuller flight in the next quadrennium, the 1848 presidential election.

Tyler, as W predicted, was a candidate without a party. W resolved to pursue a gathering plan. The Democrats did not trust Tyler and the Whigs refused to take back their fallen nestling. Although harassed by a fever and the rough reddish-brown rash on the palms of his hands and the bottoms of his feet, Senator King set out for the Hermitage and a visit with its aging occupant.

The journey to Nashville, even in a comfortable coach, was more arduous than he anticipated. Old Hickory, now 77 years old, strode stiff-backed toward the front door of his grand manse. "Why, it's Miss Nancy! You have come to visit an old man."

W had grown accustomed to Jackson's frequent insult. To hear it again, and how it was delivered, it came across as almost a term of endearment. He looked at the strains of gray hair splayed atop the haggard face, angled stubble sprouting from lines more crimson than the remnants of the lips cupped over vacant gums. Still, the man stood erect and his handsome fire still blazed. "It is my pleasure, Mr. President." Looking around, he remarked, "No slaves here to help you?"

"No, let go long ago. Neighbors stop by. Enough company for me."

Jackson sought a chair. His painful twisted descent to its seat put W on edge. Old Hickory's mouth pursed and the wrinkled half-moons of his cheeks rose to cloud his milky eyes.

"No pleasantries needed. What do you want?"

"I just need to know whom you want to be president. Tyler cannot stay, that fat frump Lewis Cass is too old and I know how you detest Van Buren. The Whigs are probably going to try to remold Clay for office. Who would you like to see beat him?"

"What of your good friend?," Jackson asked.

"I can advance Mr. Buchanan, but there are reasons peculiar to him that preclude his serious candidacy at this time."

Jackson stared hard. "I have to admit, Senator, that was simply a test. I do not think the nation could endure your friend. All right, would it be acceptable to have a Tennessee man?"

"Why, anyone you desire," W said, but did not immediately know who Jackson could mean. Surely, approaching 80, Jackson did not intend himself?

"What about Polk?"

W was startled. James Polk had left Congress five years earlier, served one two year term as governor, and then failed in consecutive gubernatorial elections. Why was Old Hickory putting forth a two time loser? Anyone who had newly lost a race in his own state was a hobbled and unlikely candidate for the presidency. Like W, Polk was a North Carolinian by birth, and would not accord with W's contention that a Southerner could be elected, but his childhood move to Tennessee changed the equation. He was also a life-long slaveholder, an endearing trait, but not necessarily for national office in changing times.

"Mr. President, I am not sure how that would work."

"It will work if I say it will. As you said, there is no one of particular ability to consider. You are right I cannot abide that New Yorker."

W read Old Hickory's sidelong gaze into the fire. Surely there would be a place for Jamie?

"What of Buchanan? What of me, if I aid this enterprise?"

"You have, Senator, always, I think, longed to return to the playing fields of Europe?"

King ran his right palm across his constructed curls, one bow tumbling loose revealing a hairless patch, purple crepe draping his ear.

"That can be done, with your friend if you wish. Or I could do something else that might keep him about."

W waited.

"If you ensure Polk is in, you can go to England or, perhaps, France? Your friend can have the other."

W considered the proposition. "I think I should prefer Paris. Perhaps State for Jamie? He's got the experience and he's pierced by the diplomatic arrows."

Jamie? thought Old Hickory, but nodded his agreement, "Place Polk on the ticket. He'll prevail. The Whigs are weaker with each passing winter. Use your friend to front for him and toss whatever support he can gather. I'll make sure Polk abides by the bargain. Are you sure your friend would not accept the Vice-Presidency?"

"Polk may ask him, but I am certain he will decline."

The man who had defined American politics for over two decades took a long look at Senator King. He softened for a moment in a measure that W had not fully anticipated. "With all your floral shirts and satin pants, you have been honorable. I do this for you, and not for your friend. Despite your nocturnal doings, you have always had my respect."

The back of W's hand crossed his moist right cheek before it reached to clasp the General's. Time and the wars of life forge bonds that are not possible in younger men. "You, Andy, have always also had mine."

Polk did not even carry his home state but prevailed in fifteen of the twenty-five others. Old Buck, Secretary of State as promised, was soon far from satisfied. Polk ran his own foreign policy, and quite successfully. He acquired Texas, waged war on Mexico, and set a firm course in diplomatic affairs. The Tennessean made it clear early on that he considered Buchanan, chosen only to appease his mentor Jackson and the powerful Pennsylvania delegation, too consumed by tactical thrusts and parries to grasp the larger strategic battle. Polk was also wary of the cabinet member he viewed as overly ambitious and out to make a name for himself at the President's expense, telling more than one intimate that Old Buck was "the enemy within."

Acting on the advice of W, Old Buck spoke to the President, "Texas should enter the Union as five states, a mix of slaveholding and free, perhaps four states with slaves and that panhandle area without slaves. That would give the South eight more Senators, and ensure its primacy in the upper body."

Polk considered the proposal. He had promised in his campaign to annex Texas and admit it as a slave state. He agreed with Buchanan that slavery was constitutionally mandated, but saw no need to gild the southern lily. Slavery should be available to any new territory that entered the Union, at least ones south of the Mason-Dixon Line. The nation's God-given right of Manifest Destiny would require the incorporation of slave states into the Union to achieve control of the entire continent. No need to take that wasteland to the west and chop it up. Polk considered, too, despite the forefathers' wisdom on composing the Senate without regard for population, Texas had fewer than 30,000 white men in the whole state and almost all of them lived in a few small settlements in the eastern part of the state. They could hardly justify adding five more states to the existing twenty-seven and giving them 10 Senators. What was Buchanan thinking?

He turned to his Vice-President. "George, what do you make of this Buchanan? It seems to me that he approaches compromise not from a position of integrity seeking a resolution, but from the point of view of Compromise as his God, with concession after concession the commandments."

"It has always been a puzzlement to me," Dallas replied, "from my Philadelphia vantage point, that he has ever advanced. You know our rivalry goes back two decades, and his gobbling and hissing have grown no less. His arrogance in instructing the electors to recommend him to you was unashamed. Time after time, he ends up on the Senate floor or in some appointed place. Why did you put him here yourself?"

"I was compelled to do so by honor."

Dallas's hazel eyes hardened and his aquiline nose developed a hitch halfway down. Polk quickly added, "Mine, not his."

Old Buck felt he could not win with Polk. After being criticized for paying too much attention to the little things, Polk told the Secretary of State's Dickinson classmate Robert Grier, slated for the Supreme Court, "Buchanan is an able man, but in small matters he is without judgment and sometimes acts like an old maid."

Indeed, cartoons of Old Buck now began to portray him as a soft-bodied but shrill and senescent granny, clad in an expansive cotton nightgown, sometimes fulminating her underlings, sometimes treacherous, sometimes merely bewildered. He developed a tumor on his nose and wrote Thomas Kittera, *I have always thought it too short, and now they seek to snip it away gradually taking it back, inserting their probes within my passages and extracting my flesh. I worry it shall become flaccid, flopping about my face, if there is but another inch of bone removed.* Kittera's eyebrows screwed toward one another as he read this, well aware of the intended Victorian allegory represented.

Meanwhile, W was not as happy as he had anticipated in Paris. As minister to France, the separation from Jamie was painful, and spawned accusations and fears of other lovers amid concerns about, as he wrote, *the anxieties of love.* W posted a parade of plaintive epistles seeking assurance from Jamie that, *I am still your one.*

Old Buck sought to reassure the absent W, even calling him his *"wife"* in one letter, but fretted about the allures of Parisian men for the Senator. When W wrote him, upon finding himself in the French capital, *I am selfish enough to hope you will not be able to procure an associate who will cause you to feel no regret at our separation. For myself, I shall feel lonely in the midst of Paris, for there shall have no Friend with whom I can commune,* he was not wholly reassured. The use of the word "commune" was intentional, as they had often shared "communion." It certainly should be with no other!

Yet Old Buck did consider other liaisons, as he wrote W, perhaps in an effort to incite trans-Atlantic jealousy, *I have gone wooing to several gentlemen, but I have not succeeded with any of them.*

On the day after he wrote W about his failure at obtaining suitable male companionship, he wrote the widowed Julia Roosevelt, *I feel that it is not good for a man to be alone, and should not be astonished to find myself married to some old maid who can nurse me when I am sick, provide good dinners for me when I am well, and not expect from me any very ardent or romantic affection.*

W lamented, *Why do I not hear from you? Packet after packet arrived but brings me no letter, thus verifying the old adage, out of sight, out of mind,* signing it, *believe me to be as ever devotedly yours, W.*

Senator King decided he could abide the separation no longer and left the Paris legation, sailing back to American shores in 1846, two years early. Old Buck met him coming off the ship at Baltimore's harbor and each coolly appraised the other before warmly clasping. They retired to Barnum's and were ushered to their same table.

"What shall we do now?"

"Jamie, our plan remains in place."

Old Buck's face flushed as he considered again if he should mention Stevens. Ever since his move to Lancaster, Stevens was cutting a swathe through the courts but, as far as Old Buck knew, leaving him to plow the political field. No need to bring up something that probably amounted to nothing.

"I think it is time for you to run," W said, "and in earnest. Start now. You have not only your years in the Senate and as minister to Russia, but now the very cabinet post that spawns presidents. No need to retreat to the Senate and the horse trading in Harrisburg."

Old Buck was grateful for the course W plotted toward the Presidency. He butted against Dallas, Polk's Vice-President, and vied first for Pennsylvania's support at the upcoming convention. There seemed to be, he thought, an inordinate amount of local sniping but W suggested they counter their antagonists with a series of dinners beginning on Christmas Day 1847. The first was a well-laden meal hosted with W in the downstairs of their Washington home. In attendance were nearly all 30 Democratic Senators and several Congressmen, many from the opposition, and anyone who happened to be in Washington from an important state. Liquor was abundant, and some left feeling not only tipsy, but indebted for the hospitality. Stephen Douglas, and his frequent drinking companion Daniel Webster, aware of the manipulation and perhaps chary of the lifestyle, stayed away. Nonetheless, dinners followed in Philadelphia at the Metropole and in New York at a Greek Revival town home overlooking the private Gramercy Park, itself dredged from swampland not much more than a decade earlier. All manner of politicians and financial backers, great and small, mountains and foothills, came to Mohammed.

Dallas prevailed in the city of Philadelphia by three votes after municipal judges under his control threatened to cancel the licenses of tavern keepers who supported Old Buck. By the March state convention in Harrisburg, however, Dallas had mysteriously dropped out of the running. Old Buck and his "Buchaneers" were pitted against his venerable nemesis Lewis Cass of Michigan and two minor players. Old Buck's strategy prevailed with the Pennsylvania delegation, but a motion to make the selection unanimous left the vote 103 Buchanan, 30 holding out for Cass. Old Buck sat down with a little black book, and wrote down the names of all the enemies who had not finally joined his side. He kept this list with him, telling W that he feared these "traitors" would stab him in the "fifth rib."

Despite carrying the Pennsylvania legation, Old Buck ultimately lost the national Democratic nomination to Cass as his support unexpectedly evaporated in the midst of the balloting. It was just as well, he soon thought. The hero of the Mexican War, Zachary Taylor, swept over Cass with Southern and Western support. The electorate was further fractured by Martin Van Buren and his support of the Wilmot Proviso's banning slavery in any territory acquired from

Mexico, running on a platform of "Free Soil, Free Speech, Free Labor and Free Men."

As they sat in their upstairs bedroom while Pompey brought in reports of scattered election results confirming Old Buck's secret wish that Cass and the upstart northern splinter of the Democratic Party be defeated, he tendered his hand. "W," Old Buck asked, "am I yet attractive?"

He felt increasingly epicene and white headed, his piebald skin crowned by hair pulled up with daily repeated strokes into a topknot. To obscure the waddling on his neck, his cloth collar now extended to his chin, and he tied a neckerchief about it. At a time when all America was a half century away from wigs, and the upper classes had moved from the ornate fashions of the nation's colonial days, Old Buck longed for the pomp and purple of earlier dress.

"Yes, of course," said W as he pulled from their secret wardrobe of such fashions and placed the well-tailored coral evening gown on Old Buck's corseted body.

The next presidential election would be the last time, both thought, for Old Buck to ascend to the Presidency. W was resigned that they would not share the White House together, although perhaps he could serve in the cabinet?

It remained surprisingly easy to lure camouflaging young girls into his web, although some targeted widows had grown chary after eyeing the fruitless efforts of others. Old Buck continued to explain why he would not, could not marry. The Ann stories had gotten more elaborate and self-contradictory. At times, Ann had broken off the engagement because her father told her to, at times at the urging of her mother. At times, an interfering friend falsely accused him of being unfaithful. At times, Ann was so distressed by his love of the law, that "jealous mistress," that she despaired of fully fitting into his life. At times, he was away in Philadelphia. At times, west or north of

Lancaster, and returned to find her unwilling to marry him because of some imagined slight. At times, it was just pure out and out mental imbalance that did her in, always asserted with feigned kindness. He even fashioned a completely new story, as subtext, that Ann actually pursued him after meeting him at a luncheon at Mayor Passmore's house, having adoringly watched him pass by so many times on King Street.

What was important was that the death of Ann, now three decades in the past, continued to shield him, as needed, from entreaties by widows and mothers who sought the stately figure themselves or on their daughters' behalf. Old Buck continued to enter into oh-so-proper-from-a-distance dalliances. Once anything might arguably appear to be headed to a committed relationship, Old Buck, by earnest personal entreaty, or conclusory poem, always managed to evade the altar. Now, as he could descry the end of his sixth decade, he hoped that he could finally be left alone on the whole bloody issue. Part of that effort, he reasoned, finally required distancing himself from Ann Coleman and her legacy.

Chapter Seventeen
<u>WHEATLAND</u>

His residence, Old Buck considered, should be finer than any in Lancaster. With the deaths of many of his siblings, and the pastoral poverty of brother Edward, he anticipated the necessity of fulfilling his promise to his mother. He would have to find housing for more of his nieces and nephews. It was not lost on him that even a few such relatives ought to provide an additional sandbar to those who sought to wreck him on the shores of marriage.

Old Buck was soon compelled to take in the son of his deceased sister Harriet, James Buchanan Henry, when the lad was seven. Anointed "Young Buck," the boy was appropriately grateful to his uncle for letting him live at Wheatland and for the opportunity to play in the oaks and wander the property. He chafed a bit at the letter a day and five books a month dictum, as his mother had not been so strict. Yet his uncle was kind, reading bedtime stories, sometimes dusting off the Bible, or regurgitating William Cowper's verse, or exposing him to the works of Lord Byron. Young Buck often fell asleep, in his uncle's embrace, as the reading concluded.

Harriet, age eleven and sister Jane's daughter, moved under her uncle's care one year later than her cousin. Her role in Old Buck's political and personal life would soon grow in importance.

On a late fall day in 1848, when Lancaster's leaves flaked off the trees and were crushed to dust by a new generation of schoolboys, Old Buck sought the visiting W's approval for a house west on Marietta Avenue. Out of the city, but accessible, and surrounded by 22 acres of land, was what Old Buck thought of as a cousin to a Southern plantation, once removed. He did not know what W would think, and fretted as they approached.

Hands touching, they surveyed the property, circling it like wary predators, Old Buck glancing for approval, the key swallowed in his pocketed hand. Finally, "It reminds me of King's Bend and even grander mansions in Alabama. Jamie, you have to purchase it."

Old Buck was delighted. "I know I can never truly be a southern planter with no slaves available, but I have held the image of a country squire since my boyhood."

Oaks, elms, evergreens, groves, and pastures, outbuildings. A gardener's house and an icehouse. Oats, fruits, and berries. This was perfect. It was Georgian, or was it Federalist? In any event, very southern in appearance, with porticoes and pediments, tiny porches and dormers. Symmetrical with arched windows and linnets. Simple columns, drawing more on the Doric and Ionian than Corinthian. They entered, and embraced. A ladies' sitting room to the left as one entered, where he could display his Feuillet china, represented to be from Worcester, in England, enameled in green, black, gray, and red. On the fireplace screen, in front of the marble coal-burner, a comely face. A courting sofa, with room for a chaperone, in the middle of the room. Rococo revival. A table for dominoes would go near there, as Old

Buck had grown to hate cards, at which he so often lost. Gentlemen could visit to the right, with room for 18 at dinner under the six enclosed globes of the massive chandelier. Room for ample stocks of cigars and Sherry, Madeira and rye. A secret, separate entrance to what would be his library and study, with pink dancing trumpet flowers carpeted on the floor. Tiger maple, rose mahogany, walnut, poplar and pine conditioned to look like oak. His reverse oil panting of a Scottish castle made of abalone, an imagined ancestral home, would be well placed at stairs' landing. Three stories. Everywhere, on wallpaper, floor and carpet, a wheat motif. Swirls of wheat everywhere. "Why not," suggested W, "call it Wheatland?". Tiles of brown and green in a sea of gray. Big wooden slatted Venetian blinds, a touch of the Mediterranean, which Hetty would hate to clean, but little matter. A David Weatherly clock, with its big old moon face looking down from the upper staircase like a cherubic vision of an adolescent Old Buck. In the bedroom, hard in the middle, would go a tin sponge bath where Pompey could wash him before he took his clean body to the four-poster bed. Nearby, a commode, for those cold winter nights. Outside, in a flight of hygienic fancy, there were staggered heights and three adult-sized seats, in small, medium and large, and two holes made for children, in the outhouse, its cesspool stagnant 12 feet below.

Connecting all, the center hall was covered with oilcloth pressed down hard. It would have to be hand shellacked each year. Ten thousand tiny white snow flakes danced in the middle of each of its little black squares.

It was, indeed, perfect! With W's approval in hand, he moved in less than a week later.

Soon, he had geese, two horses, a cow, the Affenpinscher Lara and its toy companion, a Coton de Tuléar that went by Mara, as well as Dick, the canary. Someone gave him two eagles, Tippecanoe and Tyler II, who wandered the grounds with their wings clipped, emasculated symbols of the nation. The viable anthropomorphic analogy cut a bit close to Old Buck even in this brief retreat from public life. When Harriet, Jane's daughter joined her cousin, she played the Chickering piano, straight from Boston. Old Buck proceeded to set 1,200 strawberry plants and enjoyed it when Miss Hetty prepared some of her "Pennsylvania Dutch" sauerkraut. Life was not without its other pleasures. His coachman, William Whipper, snapping at the horses, remained on call for clandestine forays into the city to the East when W was away.

On his next visit north, in late November before the session started, W took note of the fading herb garden. With a bow to imagined sagacity, he anointed its owner the "Sage of Wheatland." Old Buck was delighted, and made sure that others knew of his new sobriquet. Soon, the people of Lancaster adopted the moniker, although not always without a hint of barely-disguised humor.

W had not brought enough of a cloak for the weather and had to borrow one from his companion when snow fell early. He wrapped the grey coat around himself and halfway again, feeling too dour and somewhat emaciated in the garment. "Come, W." Old Buck said, "Let's carriage in this winter wonder."

The host hailed Whipper and glided down Marietta Avenue behind a team of white horses, and they snuggling under the same sort of buffalo covers so favored during Old Buck's courtship 30 years past. Even as he shivered, W said," There have been brief furies of snow in Washington, but this interplay of snow and ice is delightful."

Old Buck smiled at the fateful misuse and restrained himself from correcting the Senator.

The men went into the Grape, still true to its original incarnation and still the epicenter of the ruling elite in Lancaster. This time, Old Buck could take the center table. All were curious to meet the Senator from Alabama. When W left for Washington the following day, Old Buck returned with Harriet. Some of the younger patrons now hovered at their table. The aging uncle saw himself young and hopeful, a copier of manners and vices. As they left the tavern, Old Buck turned to his niece. "Harriet, you should not have any relationship with boys at your age and for a good many years hereafter. No good can come of it."

Harriet was silent. She was not surprised when she was obliged to stay in Lancaster and forbidden to visit Washington during Congressional sessions. "This is necessary," said Uncle, "to protect you from the city's dissipations, particularly enticing for one of your ardor for pleasure."

A year later Harriet wrote from Wheatland, *Uncle, may I not meet with you and the Senator this time? It is but one session of each two years and it is so dull with just Miss Hetty about. James has his friends, but they are boys and so much younger than I, and I really do not think Miss Hetty is a sufficient governess to prepare me for my married state.*

Old Buck considered the request, although he was not eager for his niece to explore the "married state." He and W investigated the possibilities in Washington and acted on Mrs. Polk's recommendation. They identified a school near where they had first met, the Visitation Convent in Georgetown, and Harriet was permitted to board there. Still, except for brief visits in the front parlor, the F Street residence remained off limits, as the upstairs did to her and all others. No sense allowing rumor to be enhanced by direct observation. Old Buck continued to fund his surviving siblings and the educations of their 22 children, although their lifestyles might meet with his clucking disapproval. Harriet later wrote in her diary,

October 21ˢᵗ, 1850

It is my relief tho perhaps not Uncle's pleasure that James Henry was finally also permitted to go off to college, in Princeton.

When Dickinson College's entire junior class was expelled, Old Buck felt a certain amount of exoneration in brokering their return to the school, recalling his own concerted efforts at readmission.

Old Buck missed reciting Byron to Young Buck, but enjoyed reading the work of a serializer from England, Charles Dickens. He loved the characters in Oliver Twist and fancied himself a good deal like the plucky young Copperfield from the latest offering. He would soon have the opportunity to share that evaluation with the English writer himself.

Chapter Eighteen
SUFFRAGE

By the spring of 1848, Thad had been in Lancaster for six years, and done what was necessary from this side of the Susquehanna. The time to move forward was at hand.

He had long since determined to take Buchanan's old seat in Congress and move to Washington when he received an announcement from a man long admired, but never met. Veterans of the abolitionist movement were holding a meeting in upstate New York, near Rochester, in a few weeks. Frederick Douglass published a notice in the *Liberator* and sent a general mailing to any he thought would be interested in their discussion. Thad was feeling closeted in Lancaster County, and longed to meet others in the abolitionist fight.

Thad traveled by boat up the Susquehanna to Owego and by train to Ithaca. From Cayuga's broadening southern end, he went by horseback, steep-rising drumlins forcing him close to the lake's western edge. In the distance, the rumble of tumbling water. Thad arrived on a steamy July day at the tip of Cayuga, the middle finger of the lakes that the last ice age scratched from the rich farmland. He was astonished at the number of folks patrolling the streets of the little village of Seneca Falls. More amazing, they were almost all women. What did they have to do with the abolitionist movement? He did not spot Mr. Douglass, but upon inquiry recognized the names that went with several other faces dotting the crowd. Who were all these women, most of whom appeared to be Quakers? Night approached. Thad spied the fiery northern newspaper publisher. The ex-slave stood out in the otherwise all-white crowd. Thad was eager to meet with him but the fugitive slave was awash with well wishers and admirers, and Thad was unable to part that particular sea.

With the local hostelries already full, he found private lodging with John Morris in his recently constructed house about three miles from town. He woke up early the next day and headed to the little Methodist church on Fall Street where the group was assembling in its chapel. Thad canvassed the crowd. Maybe four out of five were women. What was going on?

He did not have long to wait. While many were avowedly abolitionists, the focus clearly was on something called "the rights of women," not on freeing the slaves or their rights. Thad did not know what to make of it. He knew and respected James Mott of Philadelphia, who was leading the group. At least women were not actually running things.

Mr. Mott spoke first. "My wife Lucretia met Elizabeth Stanton, or "Lizzie" as she calls her, at the World Anti-Slavery Convention in London in 1840. Mrs. Mott and Mrs. Stanton were not only forbidden to speak, but were only allowed to sit in one area, cordoned behind a curtain with no view of the stage. Although the speakers there were mostly white men, a few former slaves, including Mr. Douglass, addressed the group. While this did not bother my dear wife, it did set her to thinking about issues of women's rights and opportunities when a black man could speak and a white woman could not even view the proceedings. She and Mrs. Stanton, who is now our neighbor, figured they would at least explore those issues. That is why we are here."

Elizabeth Cady Stanton strode to center stage. What a flowing mountain of a woman thought Thad. With her black curls and billowing cape like ebony snow on the Jungfrau, she looked a very pile of a person. Her voice was surprisingly strong for a woman's. After thanking her friend's husband and acknowledging Mr. Douglass, she began to read from a prepared document that she called the "Declaration of

Sentiments." How quaint, and how like a woman. Everyone assembled immediately recognized its Ur-text, the document from where all that followed originated.

Mrs. Stanton began, "When, in the course of human events, it becomes necessary for one portion of the family of man to assume among the people of the earth a position different from that which they have hitherto occupied, but one to which the laws of nature and of nature's God entitle them, a decent respect to the opinions of mankind requires that they should declare the causes that impel them to such a course."

So far, so good, as long as she was speaking of slaves. He feared that she was not. His suspicions were confirmed as Lizzie continued:

"We hold these truths to be self-evident: that all men and women are created equal; that they are endowed by their Creator with certain inalienable rights; that among these are life, liberty, and the pursuit of happiness; that to secure these rights governments are instituted, deriving their just powers from the consent of the governed."

Well, that's it. Pretty clever, but pretty easy to do. What, exactly, was the point?

Mrs. Stanton proceeded, detailing "a long train of abuses and usurpations," and then speaking of man's "absolute despotism." Why it was too much! She was really going too far. It was one thing cleverly to take shears and paste to the Declaration of Independence, but did she really mean it was the "duty" of women "to throw off such government?" This band of women and their politically cuckolded husbands could hardly overturn the United States government. It was offensive, emotionally and logically, to toss all of Jefferson's words into the mix without a thought to their portent.

The crowd seemed to agree with Thad's conclusions. Muttering moved to catcalls, at least from the back where it appeared a few men, curious farmers and shopkeepers perhaps, gathered. Mrs. Stanton ought to watch herself.

Now she was honing in on her point, "Such has been the patient sufferance of the women under this government, and such is now the necessity which constrains them to demand the equal station to which they are entitled."

"Equal station, indeed!" said Thad to himself. "Why, women have it better in most ways."

Mrs. Stanton continued, speaking of the "absolute tyranny" of man over women, denouncing marriage, and speaking about being "civilly dead." She seemed to be arguing also that women become ministers, doctors, and lawyers! What was this talk about being, "aggrieved, oppressed and fraudulently deprived?" Now the crux, the "denial to women of rights which are given to the most ignorant and degraded men—both natives and foreigners." Where were slaves in this equation and, more importantly, how were the husbands taking this?

After this litany of alleged wrongs, what else could be coming but some resolutions if the template of the text held true? He was right. These women wanted equality with men. They actually sought to compel that they be treated the same, despite their gender. This was not like black men and white men. It was wholly, completely, and irredeemably different. What of black women? Was their goal to sign contracts with men, and separately acquire property? Or was their immediate need not to *be property*, raped and beaten and have their children stripped from them and held in a lifetime of bondage without hope of one free breath of air? How offensive to compare the plight of the Negro to the "rights" of women.

Thad's mouth twisted. He read Emerson and Whitman and Thoreau, and he knew his moral position was right. Slavery's oppression was so much worse, and here they were complaining of their "degradation" as being equivalent to the slaves. How absurd, how against the great weight of history. First, it is simply wrong. Men and women are different. They are not the same, and that is all there is to it. More importantly, and more dangerously, if we get diverted on to the "rights" of women, we, and not just the abolitionists, but the whole anti-slavery movement, will have our entire focus blurred. He had just heard Mrs. Stanton acknowledge the ridicule that would come their way. This would certainly play into the hands of the South and the doughface sympathizers! The movement would be moved to the margin, while history was written down the middle of the page by the pro-slavery forces. This feminine palaver was not only silly; it was downright dangerous.

Well, here come the resolutions. First, citing Blackstone of all people, while duplicitously playing with the noun, "That such laws as conflict, in any way, with the true and substantial happiness of women, are contrary to the great precept of Nature." Blackstone has not been dead 70 years, and his poor bones cannot stand the tumbling. Let the man rest in peace. , Again, the talk of "absolute equality," including equality under the law, and the right to speak in religious assemblies, and the clincher, the "sacred right to the elective franchise." With that, which seemed to the crowd much more understandable and specific, murmurings grew to rumblings. Who was that striding toward the stage, her plain face framed by a transparent bonnet over hair bound so tightly it tugged her eyebrows into the middle of her forehead? Thad knew a Quaker when he saw one.

Lucretia Mott arose, her rigid lips trembling a bit. She had co-founded, with William Lloyd Garrison, the American Anti-Slavery Movement seventeen years earlier. She was used to confrontation but not to the type of fundamental division now required. She now contradicted her cohort. "I agree with thee on all other points, Lizzie," Mrs. Mott began, speaking gently but forcefully, "but this last. Thou hast gone too far. Woman cannot yet vote and there be no support for such a notion. Whether it is right or not, this will indeed make of us all laughing stocks and defeat our whole heavenly mission."

Mrs. Stanton demurred, chagrined that their private dispute was now public.

The crowd began to take sides and Mr. Mott arose to quiet the throng. He urged patience and consideration and glared, a little sharply, Thad noticed, at both Mrs. Stanton and his wife. Thad remained, pacing, as the meeting adjourned abruptly and everyone retreated into the nearby church. He sought Frederick Douglass but could not find him. Perhaps, wisely, he had retreated for a breath of unfeminized air. How could a man, beaten and hunted, who had to take his very name from an Englishman's poem as he was required daily to evade those who would return him to bondage, possibly be enamored with this group of white women?

The opinions of the women seemed to be sharply divided on this point of voting, and the men were almost all against it, save some of the husbands, who apparently could not stand up to their wives. After a prolonged debate, balloting began. Thad was surprised to see Douglass now on the dais with Mrs. Stanton.

The publisher rose. "I concur, as a black free man, with the granting of the right to vote for all women, white and black, property holder and tenant. It is the underpinning for the righting of all other wrongs we seek to redress."

Sixty-eight women, including Amelia Bloomer, editor of *The Lily* and designer of Lizzie's undergarments, and 32 men were chosen as "official delegates." All resolutions passed unanimously, save the one seeking the right of women to vote. Thad's prediction proved true. The provision was far too radical and irrational, even for these true believers, and only eked out a bare majority, undoubtedly pushed by Douglass. If everyone else present permitted to submit a chit, Thad thought, that peculiar position would have received not one more measure of support than it did from the chosen delegates. The whole mess disturbed him, particularly the apparent claims that women could in any fashion be perceived as suffering the situation of slaves. That was poppycock, and destructive poppycock at that.

He returned to Lancaster. The silliness of this enterprise rubbed him raw. Why had Douglass, otherwise a wise fellow and a strong advocate, chosen to be involved in this movement that subsisted on the very fringes of common sense? He was not surprised to read the newspaper accounts over the next few weeks. Stories talked of this *shrieking sisterhood* of immoral *Amazons* who sought a *petticoat empire.* One writer wondered why women were there at all, and neglecting their *more appropriate duties,* noting Lucretia's six children. In a particular affront to the many Quakers, one news article blistered the *drunken women* who sought to forge their unfeminine agenda.

In the Rochester *North Star,* Douglass wrote: *A discussion of the rights of animals would be regarded with far more complacency by many of what are called the wise and the good of our land, than would be a discussion of the rights of women.*

The New York *Herald* did pay a somewhat grudging compliment to the suffragist movement when it editorialized, although opposing her aims, *Lucretia Mott would make a better president than some of the White House's more recent occupants.*

Thad also read that several of the men, upon returning to their hometowns and places of work, were disavowing their support. Gangs of fathers, brothers, sons and grandfathers attacked the tents where Lizzie, Lucretia and others spoke, flinging seats at fleeing participants as the local constabulary looked away. It was 1848 and revolutions were being fought all across Europe and slavery still held sway through the South. These silly marauding women were undercutting the great issue of the age. Why would, or should, anyone pay attention?

Thad sat back. This women's movement was indeed a new aggravation. Still, he had to focus on his greater plan, already well underway.

Chapter Nineteen
P R O S P E C T

When the Missouri Compromise of 1850 passed, Old Buck was wandering among the fowl and spices of Wheatland. Lara and Mara were forced to scamper as the geese took nips out of their furry rumps. He watched and sighed, unable to help either them or the flightless bald eagles as he snipped at red and white roses imported from the Empress Josephine's garden at Chateau de Malmaison. Old Buck fretted about Stevens's decision to take his former Lancaster seat in Congress. What designs did that scruffy abolitionist still possess?

Although frustrating not to be in Washington, he and W agreed that it was best for him to stay away from any other elective office and look toward the 1852 election. He cursed himself for not making a harder, earlier run. Stevens's move to Lancaster had, frankly, scared and upset him. The post-hoc usurpation of his Congressional seat had seemed ominous, and evoked images of his won acquisition of Ann Coleman's house. His 1848 choice to take a cabinet post, indeed all of his skittering and furtive decision making, seemed now to be premised on a phantom fear. There had been nothing to suggest Stevens was actively blocking his way. In any event, it would have been difficult, even if he wanted to, to convince the Assemblymen that he merited a return to those halls. Now Stevens' decision to take Old Buck's former seat and go to Congress representing Lancaster made it simply too perilous to be in the same building as the new Representative. On his few forays to the nation's capital since Stevens went to Washington, Old Buck had been careful to find paths home to F Street that did not impinge on any route Stevens was likely to take. Only at the wedding of their mutual physician, Jonathan Longfellow, had they even seen each other. Stevens had executed an about face at the outstretched hand. Jimmy quickly withdrew it, acting as if he were simply adjusting the stock around his neck as his tormentor walked away.

Old Buck had still hoped that the Lancaster citizenry would extract Stevens from Washington like a bad tooth, but he was re-elected in the fall of 1850 over token opposition. It sometimes seemed to him that his own career had crested over the other side of a hill Stevens was ascending with seven league boots, so effortlessly had he made the transition from Gettysburg's Assemblyman to the emerging Congressional leader of one side of what was becoming the great issue of the age.

The California Gold Rush in 1849 and 1850 had heated the ever-simmering issue of the expansion of slavery to a full boil. No other single issue ever roiled the nation so deeply. Thaddeus Stevens was not shy about tossing a clawing lobster in the pot. He now was a true believer and he never strayed far from his adopted quest to destroy this evil. Much as Cato's cries of "*Carthago delenda est,*" rang through the Roman Senate even as he sought appropriations for more lead pipes to channel water and dispose sewage, Thad pushed the issue of slavery in every speech.

Some tepid abolitionists urged only the limitation of slavery in future states, but most now would settle for nothing other than the absolute elimination of the evil institution. Thad had long been the leader of a group that wanted a great deal more.

Henry Clay came up with a resolution admitting California as a free state, providing for votes on the issue in the New Mexico and Utah territories, abolishing the slave trade in the nation's capital (but not slavery) and reducing Texas's boundaries. Southerners split in their views. President Taylor had died in office and his successor, the new president, Millard Fillmore of New York, supported the compromise.

Old Buck recalled his earlier service as head of the Senate committee convened "to explore the issue of slave trade in the nation's capital." His group determined that there was no sound reason to ban the trade, as the business would simply be lost to neighboring states. It could, he reasoned, lead to a notion at the end of that slippery slope that gentlemen could not bring their slaves with them to Washington. Such an interference with property rights was certainly unconstitutional. No reason now to alter his stance. Although the abolitionists might be pressing their agenda, the Constitution itself had not changed.

He composed letters urging that all southern territories come into the union as slaveholding states. *If the slaves are ever freed they would massacre the high-minded and chivalrous race of men in the South.* He warned, *If the southern territories are not admitted as slave states, the division of the country into two Republics is possible.*

This forced hiatus for the first time in thirty years did not rest easy with him. He longed again to feel the embrace of public approval that had once been his. Avoiding the furor over the Missouri Compromise and what certainly would have been withering attacks on his position, as W had told him, was working to his advantage. Old Buck also supported the new Fugitive Slave Law, and the right of property owners to retrieve their property wherever it might travel, or seek to escape.

Meanwhile, Thad moved easily into the body of Congressmen and found many among its 233 white male members, and some among the 60 Senators, who were like-minded. He met with Charles Sumner, newly elected to the Senate from Massachusetts, Joshua Giddings of Ohio, and others at least weekly. When former Secretary of State Buchanan's name came up from time to time, someone was certain to comment on his views. Thad withheld, for now, even from the most rabid, their target's prospective utility.

Sumner delighted in reminding the others of, "Buchanan's amazing two-faced act, as if he were a doughboy shaped and kneaded at the sideshow. This, gentlemen, is the nature of the opposition. First, he says, 'I am opposed to slavery in the abstract.' Then, in the same speech, 'We will never violate the constitutional compact we have made with our sister states. Their rights will be held sacred by us. Under the Constitution it is their own question; and there let it remain.'" Thad grinned at the summation.

Old Buck was energized for what he viewed as his final fling at the Presidency. He detested campaigning but enjoyed going to his elaborate black book and selecting the potential supporters and influence peddlers as he prepared for the 1852 convention. Caller after caller made the pilgrimage to his new residence, some through the front entrance and others through the side door to his study. Old Buck was enjoying his new stature as an elder statesman, as long as he was not thought of as too old. It was only proper that the nation appear to come to him, rather than he to the nation.

If he left Wheatland's doors, he risked those times, inspired by the rabble, he had been induced to stake out positions not favored by those whose influence he curried. Vagueness was essential in his personal and public life and the lack of accountability was intensely appealing to him. It was important to be able to say one thing to one person, and something quite else to someone else, or at least leave that impression.

After a hard day of letter writing, sometimes as many as two dozen carefully placed epistles, Old Buck often fell asleep at his desk, candle dribbling wax onto the desk and floor. Miss Hetty fretted that Wheatland would be incinerated. "Pompey, it is your place to see he gets well to bed. If that means waiting up to the early morning, do so."

Pompey weighed this against the strong and almost violent advice of his master not to disturb him, day or night, when he was alone in the study. Pompey drilled a small hole just above the kick plate on the library door and bent over hourly each evening, entering only if he could spy that Old Buck had slipped into sleep.

When alone in Lancaster, Old Buck rose and ate, sitting at his desk and writing in his elegant longhand, ate again, wrote again, saw some callers through Wheatland's side door, and spent his evenings first with his friend Madeira, and then his close companion rye whiskey.

His large vaulted wine cellar was put to good use, and he amazed visitors with his prowess with alcohol. One of his political allies wrote, *The Madeira and Sherry that he has consumed would fill more than one old cellar, and the rye whiskey that he has punished would make Jacob Baer's heart glad.* Many remarked on the "headiness" of the wine that "would induce an old British sea captain to weep joyful tears." He was often seen to commence with "a stiff jorum of cognac" and knock off a full bottle of rye. He easily outdistanced his drinking companions. When W was up for a visit, they disposed of the company by simply out-drinking them. Old Buck could imbibe as many as two bottles of wine, post-Sherry, and go through a quart of whiskey without, according to observers, evidencing any slurring of words. One visitor to Wheatland later wrote, *More than one ambitious tyro who sought to follow his extraordinary example gathered an early fall. Yet Old Buck himself remains with no head ache, no faltering steps, no flushed cheek.*

On Sundays, Old Buck waited until Miss Hetty was nearly out the door on her way to the Mennonites. Just before she departed, he called Pompey, "Bring the carriage. I am off to church!"

Miss Hetty looked back and trundled down to Marietta Avenue, met by a maiden lady who traveled in from Columbia, Elizabeth Ellis. As they drove off, Old Buck often turned to Pompey, "No need to spend the time with the Presbyterians. Miss Hetty goes enough for all of us."

Pompey knew not to take him into town but to navigate over to Jacob Baer's where a ten-gallon cask, sufficient unto the day, of "old J. B. Whiskey" was procured. Old Buck always joked, "Your whiskey is fine enough, but it is a very nice touch that you have put my monogram on it." The proprietor still managed a smile.

The prospect of war came close to home. In Christiana, in southern Lancaster Country on the Maryland border, a group of black and white men stopped a federal marshal from serving papers on a fugitive slave. The accompanying slave owner was shot, and several government officials were assaulted. To Old Buck, this was vindication of his fears, and he roundly censured the interference with both property rights and federal authority. Christiana was only 22 miles from Wheatland.

Papers were full of condemnation on all sides of the issue. In Lancaster, the *Saturday Express* headlined *Civil War—The First Blow Struck.* The article progressed in ever more lurid tones, detailing the *murder fruit* of the *tree of slavery.* In the South, the affair was characterized as *wanton* and *atrocious, a most foul and damning outrage.* The shooting of a slaveholder as if he were a *wild beast* would be cause to leave the Union. With this riot, eyes turned toward Pennsylvania. Old Buck was uncomfortable with the scrutiny and hoped it would pass before he took the next step necessary to achieve his goal. If he could only reach the presidency, he could ensure the vitality of slavery and of the country.

The May 1852 Democratic national convention was held in Baltimore. As it approached, W and he set up, as well as they could, their headquarters in the back room at Barnum's. No visitors, but a place to reconnoiter and evaluate. W complained of feeling unwell, but told Old Buck, "Likely just a passing fever. Price one pays for living on a river and working in Washington's swampland."

Old Buck had never seen W ailing, and did not know what to do. Should he get Miss Hetty to come? No, better Pompey. He sent a messenger to Wheatland.

Southern delegates from Mississippi, Tennessee, and Alabama, W's home state, all backed Old Buck. Pennsylvania's delegation, curiously, was divided. Old Buck started a heated letter writing campaign, penning the same letter after letter, summoning troops of messengers to deliver his compositions. He wrote Stephen Douglas of Illinois, *Senator, one must admit that you have fought a good fight but now cannot win. You, at 39, are a very young sprout. I shall however, and Senator King as well, be certain to support you in 1856 if you would suggest that yours come my way now.* Douglas considered the equation and dismissed it.

Baltimore was overrun with self-appointed delegates, most of whom were along for the ride, as their state's votes would not increase with their number. Seven hundred now trampled around the harbor, seeking scarce rooms and drinking ample whiskey. Only 296 seats were available on the convention floor and hundreds rumbled around drunk outside the Mechanic's Institute's walls.

W had not gotten better and stayed in bed in their room. Where was Pompey?

The night before the balloting was set to begin, and his victory feeling far from secure, Old Buck gradually wore down to an uneasy sleep, images of himself as Blunderbore, a giant speaking in ennui-inducing malaprops stalked by Jack the Giant Killer and his magic boots while sputtering ill-constructed truisms, "a stolen roan matters not to grass," "a snitch in rhyme is a knave's sign," "one heard in the band, births two in the wash," on and on, Thad gaining and gaining and gaining, finally butting him off the hill, falling into a chasm.

He woke in Barnum's backroom clutching W. His bedmate was hot and sticky but Old Buck felt alone and damp and shivering despite the swarming hot June night. Time had gone by without its use, but was the object waved before him by Stevens on the banks of the Susquehanna just an unseemly sham or would it be revealed for all the world to see, blocking his nomination? No reason to think anything would be used, no reason to think anything existed, no reason at all except for the plain and simple fact he had himself seen it....

W woke that morning and complained, "Jamie, I do not feel at all well. I will have to remain in bed yet another day. You go on, survey the delegates and report to me how Virginia and Tennessee now look. You will need them in your column."

Old Buck went off alone. At the Mechanics' Institute, floor fights over platform planks delayed the balloting. Old Buck made his way back to Barnum's for lunch, and to see how W was doing. He met Pompey coming out of their room. The negro was carrying bedding that looked soaked with sweat and smelled of all manner of excretions. Before he could interrogate the slave on his whereabouts, Pompey said, "Master, you need to look in on the Senator. He be driftin' in an' he be driftin' out."

Old Buck pushed the door open. Little epithets were exiting into the air, "Damn. Damn. Damn."

"What is wrong?"

"I fear I have caught it."

"Caught what?"

W stared blankly and started to shake, in part, perhaps, from his knowledge that he had kept the disease a secret from his lover for over five years.

Old Buck ran out of the room and made his way to Dr. Longfellow's, the physician whose wedding he had recently attended. "Please come back with me to Barnum's and take a look at the Senator. He seems quite unwell."

What had seemed a short but painful illness when it had started was now diagnosed. Old Buck reeled at the sharp and painful news. W was dying. Early ventures in Southern streets, or perhaps in Europe, spawned the syphilis now coursing through him. Old Buck was distraught, concerned not only for W but also for himself. He had seen no signs, but also understood that perhaps there was nothing to see until the evil scourge rotted through one's insides and invaded one's mind.

"I am so very sorry. You know, don't you, had I known, I never would have exposed you."

Old Buck looked at his companion. Another plan began to form. He leaned over, "I know, W, I know." Aware of the coming answer, he nonetheless asked, "Should I stay with you?"

"Go, go to the delegates. You have to be at the convention. Your goal is within your grasp."

On his way to the floor, he ran into some surplus delegates. "Senator, all is deadlocked. Marcy is up, you are down. Douglas rises, Cass declines."

By the time he got to the convention floor, the delegates were on their twenty-ninth ballot and close to giving up for the day. Round after round, William Marcy, Lewis Cass, Stephen Douglas, Old Buck taking turns, flowing and ebbing but never reaching shore. Based on W's impending death, the nomination uncertain and Stevens looming, Old Buck considered a new direction.. This time, he would put someone else first.

Chapter Twenty
C U B A

U nder cover of night, a New Englander was summoned to Barnum's. At dinner in the corner of the dining room, a final persuasive pitch was thrown and a curious quid pro quo was cast.

For Old Buck, this had now become an opportunity to secure for W the prize that slipped away a dozen years ago. W would have immortality. Old Buck withdrew in fact, if not in form, his own candidacy and furiously offered the delegates—the mayors, state legislators, governors and Senators—their way with a new administration, their votes for a new candidate would be the currency for appropriations and appointments.

Backed in the back rooms by the Sage of Wheatland and the Virginia delegation and whispered across the floor, the name Franklin Pierce of New Hampshire emerged on the 35th ballot. The slave states rose like catfish at the bait of the rapidly emerging candidacy and Northerners embraced one of their own, although they remembered little about the man who had been out of elective politics for a decade, since the age of 38. At the crucial moment, Pennsylvania jumped on the Granite Stater's bandwagon and Pierce, on the 49th ballot, secured the nomination. In satisfaction of the prearrangement with the man whose efforts put him over the top, and to complete Old Buck's promise to the man he loved, Pierce named William Rufus DeVane King of Alabama as his running mate.

In the Republic's early days, the second highest vote getter became Vice-President, leading to some odd and antagonistic combinations that did not work on political or personal levels, the mismatch of the elder Adams and Jefferson, and the subsequent forced alliance of Jefferson and Aaron Burr. Choices were still not made by presidential candidates, but separately by the conventions, and that was why not only Pierce, but the delegates, had to be firmly on board. The deaths of the fugacious aged Harrison and the ascension of the turncoat Tyler, and the vast chasm between Jackson and Calhoun as earlier exemplar, caused many to desire uniformity in an administration's approach to governing the country and a well-qualified vice-president. On the other hand, the great and growing divide between North and South mandated a geographical and political balance between the candidates. All major party tickets, from 1820 on, offered such balance. It was hard, Old Buck thought, to get much farther north than Concord, New Hampshire and difficult to be deeper south than Selma, Alabama. In addition, W was, with a tenure of 28 years, the second longest serving Senator in the nation's history and in all ways deserved the post. Pierce, who had resigned from the Senate at his wife Jane's mystic insistence without serving one full term, needed the steady hand.

It was not, however, on any of these bases that Old Buck had approached the Democratic nominee. W was dying, and his death was imminent. If he ran with the Senator from Alabama, Old Buck told Pierce, he could have the presidency all to himself without worrying about a Vice President yapping at his heels on policy, or posturing for the next election. The independent Pierce had taken a long hard drink of whiskey. He considered his wife's hatred of Washington and her belief that God himself opposed his political ambitions, yet needed little convincing.

Although he knew the diagnosis of tertiary syphilis complicated by alcoholism, Senator King, in his sporadic lucid moments, put out the story that he contracted tuberculosis in the hot swampy morass of Washington. Old Buck grieved as W wasted, and they shared this further secret.

Old Buck considered his valedictory present to W. W would have been with him in the White House had he been successful in 1840 in securing him a place on Van Buren's ticket as he sought a second term, to be followed by himself as President. Although W had suggested that would have been more for him than for the Alabamian, certainly he would now appreciate it. W had counseled and advised him for nearly twenty years. He loved him. While, he would perhaps have been more pleased if he had seen him in the highest office, that was not to be. Without W's guiding hand, the nomination had slipped away from Old Buck. At least, W now would have the strong respect that history, in Old Buck's fervent hope, would afford a Vice-President.

At age 48, Pierce ran against the last Whig standing, General Winfield Scott and John Parker Hale, the Free Soiler who also hailed from New Hampshire. Daniel Webster, earlier a Congressman from the same state but now a Massachusetts Senator, who stood as the Union party banner-holder, died before the ballots were cast. The Free Soilers' platform, drafted in large part by Thaddeus Stevens, had as its centerpiece the tenet that, "Slavery is a sin against God and a crime against man." The party was vociferous in its opposition to the extension of slavery in the western states but oddly silent on the issue of slavery elsewhere.

Old Buck broke his usual practice and ventured forth from Wheatland to support the Pierce ticket and help secure for W the nation's second highest post in his last opportunity for the national office. Pierce campaigned on the promise of a transition from the old to the new, anointing his vision for the future as one of a "Young America." America responded, awarding him all but four states' electoral votes, a crushing defeat for blundering Old Fuss and Feathers. The Whigs' smoldering ashes were soon re-lit as the Republican Party.

The deaths of Harrison and Taylor had caused a disjunction in the numbering of the nation's two highest offices. W was elected America's unlucky thirteenth Vice-President and Pierce the fourteenth President, and its youngest. Old Buck had hoped to serve in the administration with W during his last days but the new Commander-in-Chief categorically rejected any cabinet holdovers from prior administrations.

Seeing the handsome Pierce with his wavy hair, dark eyes, strong brow and chin, and wide slash of a mouth, Old Buck was suddenly deeply aware of his age. His paunch now mandated vests with ever stronger buttons and his hair, pulled and tucked into an upright topknot, was all snow and noticeably thinning. He wrote to one of his Pennsylvania friends, *I am surely becoming an old fogy and have got far behind the rapid march of age.* His anxiety attacks increasingly overwhelmed him, and he retched in the back acres of Wheatland and tossed in refluxive pain as he sought sleep. His teeth ached. To another acquaintance, he wrote, perhaps seeking an obligatory contradiction, *I have become a petrification.*

Old Buck needed to spend time with the rapidly-failing W before he took office. Both were over 60 and the earthly union of the Pennsylvanian and the Alabamian was, he knew, soon to be sundered.

Washington was not the right venue for their dénouement, Old Buck thought, with its secrecy, subterfuge and compelled clandestine conduct. They needed an open place where the two of them could "just be themselves." Nowhere in this country was safe from prying eyes, and Europe was both too public and too damn cold in February. From somewhere came an idea, immediately communicated to King who was attending to affairs in Alabama. On the letter in excited script was only one word, repeated. *Cuba*, Old Buck wrote, *Cuba!* He followed it up the next day with a more specific itinerary and secured the rental on the plantation Ariadne, in Matanzas, about 60 miles east of Havana.

On Valentine's Day of 1853, Old Buck set sail from Baltimore to the Caribbean island. W was already there via passage from Mobile. The defeated candidate for the Democratic nomination met the soon to be inaugurated Vice President of the United States. Amid the palm trees, pounding surf and sweet sweltering spring sun, Old Buck and W took long halting walks on the strand. Old Buck propped up his companion, tolerating the racking coughs and spouts of delirium. When the American Consul to Cuba, William Sharkey arrived at their peninsular retreat (as Old Buck joked with W, he "must be a fine swimmer") to administer the oath for the only time on foreign soil in this nation's history, he was surprised to see Old Buck there, but soon fully comprehended the situation. At their best estimation of the time that Franklin Pierce completed his inaugural address, Old Buck witnessed W's ascension to the nation's second highest office. He swore Sharkey to secrecy.

With the end fast approaching, Old Buck clutched the pyretic W in his arms. Through the mind of the Alabama Senator wandered images of an unshared boyhood and the words he uttered, to Old Buck, seemed to ring of roses and camellias and shanties. "I must tell you something, W."

W seemed as if he had been brought back to their tropical present. He took the second pillow and pulled it under his head. His eyes were failing and his bones ached as if they had been invaded by a hundred angry worms. "I have long feared, Jamie, that there is something you have not shared."

Old Buck looked into the now clearer eyes. "There is a reason, beyond this recent gift of national office to you, that I lost my nerve. Perhaps I never could really have run for President. Or, perhaps, if I had told you sooner, we might have been able to resolve the matter. You are aware of Thaddeus Stevens, the Congressman from Lancaster?"

W nodded, or at least it appeared to be a nod, as Old Buck sometimes could not tell as W's body moved like the very waves of the Caribbean out their door, convulsing in rhythmic patterns that began at the top of his now nearly hairless head and extended in rapid rolling tics to his discolored toes, only to commence again. Still, he now appeared to hear and this must be told.

"One late summer's day, now nearly twenty years ago, he confronted me on a bluff over the Susquehanna. I was prevailing against him in court, and he needed some way to stop me. Stevens took out an envelope and would not let me see its contents, but showed just enough to assure me that it had been addressed to him. The hand was Ann Coleman's."

Old Buck paused just enough to make sure this had sunk in. W took both his elbows and thrust himself into a sitting position, his stomach muscles crying at the effort. Jamie had not spoken to him of that woman in years, yet he knew how helpful the invocation of her memory with others had been in preserving their mutual secret.

"I have known something led you away from standing before the voters. That is why…" The words sputtered, almost drowning in the spittle as they sought their way, "That is why I went to see Jackson."

W's head tumbled back to the pillows. "I fear that I have made some decisions without full knowledge and therefore we have made mistakes in your path."

"It is I who am ashamed not to have told you. I do not even know what the letter says, or if he still has it. It was the fear of what it might have that drove me and I don't..." Old Buck began to cry. "I don't even know what it says."

W had fallen back into his delirium. Old Buck took W's index finger. He lay beside his companion and placed the digit between his soft teeth.

"Jamie," the word emerging like an indistinct crackle in the night. Old Buck was already snoring, W's still damp finger lying just beyond his lips. "I hope you know I have done all I could for you."

Old Buck seemed to nod gently, and his mouth again sought the older man's finger.

The next day, a ship left the littoral paradise for the short sea journey to Mobile, the rough steam driven tumble up its river to the confluence of the Tombigbee and the Alabama, and to Selma. A tiny neap tide of life still ran through King's body but only his ragged breath gave evidence that he was still alive. He lay belowdecks while a graying sexagenarian, his face the color of day-old avocado, roamed above.

On April 18, 1853, the boat docked at King's Bend. W was already dead. Slaves gathered and a few neighbors made the short pilgrimage. The shortest tenure of any Vice-President of the United States came to an end. W was laid in his grave, never having returned to Washington nor commenced his official duties.

After a few perfunctories by a local pastor, the northern visitor arose. All considered the Senator's choices curious as the Pennsylvanian read from Chapter Seven of the Book of Micah:

Who is a God like unto thee, that pardoneth iniquity, and passeth by the transgression of the remnant of his heritage? he retaineth not his anger for ever, because he delighteth in mercy.

He will turn again, he will have compassion upon us; he will subdue our iniquities; and thou wilt cast all their sins into the depths of the sea.

Then, yet more oddly, from some poem by someone named "Cooper" that they did not know, about a "stricken deer" and the following passage:

We turn to dust, and all our mightiest works
Die too. The deep foundations that we lay,
Time ploughs them up, and not a trace remains.

We build with what we deem eternal rock;
A distant age asks where the fabric stood;

And in the dust, sifted and searched in vain,
The undiscoverable secret sleeps.

Chapter Twenty-One
<u>LONDON</u>

Old Buck quickly made his way to Washington and received word via post forwarded by Miss Hetty that there was a place for him in the Pierce administration after all. A week after W's interment, Old Buck met with the new President. His heart felt ripped from every artery and he could hardly concentrate on what might now lie ahead. Sitting on what he felt was the wrong side of the desk in the presidential office, Old Buck accepted Pierce's offer of the position of Minister to the Court of St. James.

The President proceeded to lay out his duties. Old Buck again grew queasy. Should he backtrack on his acceptance? Secretary of State Marcy appeared to be pulling the strings, and he felt like he had been "Punched." Marcy remarked to Edward Everett, the future orator of Gettysburg, when Old Buck appeared to be vacillating on his agreement to serve, "Old bachelors as well as young maidens do not always know their minds." There were no real options. Burdened by his deep loss, and without W his desire to remain in the prior haunts having fled, it did not matter much anymore.

Pierce was beset by memories of the ragged beheading of his only surviving child, eleven-year-old Bennie, in a January train wreck as he and his wife Jane watched in horror. All her foreboding about Washington and the Oval Office was validated. She dredged the depths of melancholy while her husband simply drank. Pierce did not like Buchanan, his wife found him a living anathema, and the President was happy to be rid of the aging politician. Mrs. Pierce insisted that Daniel Sickles of New York, a young married man and presumably a good influence, accompany Old Buck to London as his chief aide. Sickles responded by leaving without the 16-year-old wife he had married the year before. Instead, he brought his then-current mistress and soon found others.

It was not until early August that Old Buck actually left Lancaster for London, departing quietly without even a bon voyage dinner, slinking out of a nation where he was not so much yesterday's news but a fish wrapping. He placed his financial affairs in the hands of others, made arrangements for Young Buck and Harriet (he promised her, if duty allowed, to have her visit), and went to New York without any farewells at all in Lancaster or Philadelphia. From New York, Pompey was his only companion on the voyage to London. It stormed the full ten days of the passage, and Old Buck was often seen bent over the railing of the first class deck, his white hair blowing in the sharp breeze as he watched evening's after evening's meal form a swollen waterfall to the sea.

The new ambassador's arrival coincided with the departure of most members of the upper classes in London for Cornwall, Devon and the Continent. The Parliament was newly adjourned for the year and there was not much to do. London was, as far as any Westerner knew or cared, the largest city in the world. In the midst of the reign of Queen Victoria, the capital's 3,000,000 worked to convince themselves they had re-achieved a cultural era to rival the nearly tercentenary old Virgin Queen's, Shakespeare's, Bacon's and Spenser's. He and Pompey secured quarters and the slave became something of a hit, poking about Fleet Street and Mayfair, his color a spring of attention and his accent a well of amusement. For Old Buck, this was at least a diversion from the shuttle between Lancaster and Washington, and he began to enjoy the old town.

He did run into some early difficulties as Secretary Marcy, dictating from Washington, ordered him to appear in a business suit as parliament reconvened. The honored convention required traditional attire of gold lace, ribbons, jewels, and patent leather boots. Old Buck was much in favor of such dress, and W would have loved it, but he could not buck his new boss. Old Buck therefore stayed away from the opening ceremony of the British legislature entirely and was condemned by the *Times* for his *ill manners*. There were calls for a formal investigation into the situation, but the attention of the Houses of Lords and Commons was soon diverted to the war in the Crimea. He thereafter adopted standard business attire, but carried a black sword with him at all times, not certain whether it was a symbol of postcolonial deference or deference.

London would also be, Old Buck hoped, a place to find solace after W's death. Not that he desired another relationship right away but, as their favorite poet had also written,

> *Hence summer has her riches, Autumn hence*
> *And hence even Winter fills his withered hand*
> *With blushing fruits, and plenty not his own.*

He poked around Regent Street and dallied in Mayfair. The rotting stink of sewage was familiar to him, but certainly more intense than in little Lancaster or even the larger cities, where sanitation issues were not compounded with the decay of this ancient settlement.

As Pompey drove him around, the protohistoric town seemed a confusing jumble of poor and rich, groveling hovels and grand mansions, mendicants and the meretricious. Slaughterhouses, full of sheep bleats, pig squeals, and cow bellows, filled the air and ears. Yapping dogs circled in endless loops through the streets. Although the train began running in the 1830's, spawning further development outside of the great city, the thousands of hackney cabs and the new-fangled horse-drawn omnibuses coursed the crowded crooked tumble. Legions of street sweepers could never quite conquer the mountains of excrement. Hundreds of oxen and sheep hung at Snow Hill and Warwick Lane, recent denizens of adjoining abattoirs, blood and entrails dripping from eviscerated bodies. Their remains flooded adjoining streets, joining great cascades of feces, urine, ale, washday soap and industrial waste, as urchins and beggars, inured to the pungent pastiche of the morass, waded through. Above and among all this, petty thieves, hawkers of goods and flesh, beggars and vagrants. Old Buck read in the *Times* that one-quarter of the female occupants of the city were prostitutes and, judging from what he himself could discern with a now practiced eye, a goodly number of the males. Places named Marshalsea and Coldbath Fields held bits and pieces of families as workless fathers lost footing in swamps of debt.

Even at mid-day, London's already legendary fog obscured the infrequent sun. Choking flues led to sodden chimney pots. Scattered pieces of soot and ash rose just a bit above the city's rooftops and, like adventurers losing heart, retreated to the puffs and plumes whose eternal rebirth camouflaged the city.

Drinking water was extracted, bucket by bucket, from the overburdened Thames into which all this flowed. Disease after disease called upon the capital, cholera the most chronic visitor, as skin lost its turgor, kidneys failed, muscles cramped, diarrhea exploded and death, often within the merest breath of time, conquered.

Set in this seeming Seventh Circle and its eternal shambling on the stretching sand, Old Buck was making his way, early in his mission, in a phaeton, faithful Pompey at the reins, to Tavistock House, home of a writer whose unfortunate and unperceptive portrait of his home country merited his reproach.

Old Buck was escorted to a dark study. He was fully prepared to meet the man whose peregrinations from Boston to Richmond, to Pittsburgh via Harrisburg (unaccountably by-passing his beloved Lancaster), and west to Cincinnati and St. Louis a decade earlier spawned an unfortunate journal reflecting perspectives on vagrancy, slow-mindedness, hypocrisy, xenophobia, and jingoism. The author's scathing attack on slavery and what he termed the "bestial" practices of the South were particularly noxious and deserving of censure. Unlike the earlier reports of the too harsh Frenchman Alexis de Tocqueville, this gentleman's caustic observations were unrelieved, in Old Buck's mind and those of most of his countrymen, by any suitable aversion to the glories of American democracy, the nation's blasting factories, and its burgeoning greatness.

What did he mean writing, as he had in a letter later leaked to the New York papers, *This is not the Republic I came to see. This is not the Republic of my imagination. The more I think of its youth and strength, the poorer and more trifling in a thousand respects it appears in my eyes. In everything of which it has made a boast—excepting its education of the people and its care for poor children—it sinks immeasurably below the level I had placed it upon.*

Old Buck was here, in his private capacity of course, to call him the author to task.

The minister to the Court of St. James looked about the study. Full of Scott and Shakespeare and, he noted with approval, Hawthorne, Cooper and Irving. Other names and titles—a new book called "Poor Folk" by a Dostoevsky, recent works by the oddly named Stendhal and Balzac—he did not recognize. Fine, he had a lot of books. A man after his own heart. For his part, Old Buck enjoyed the recent story of the little crippled boy and ghosts.

The Victorian Gentleman walked in unannounced as Old Buck was fondling various pieces of brass and crystal on the author's desk. Charles Dickens cleared his throat. The product of Stony Batter awkwardly juggled and almost dropped a delicate Limoges swan whose neck he was stroking, a gift from the French Senat. Scurrying to the visitor's side of the author's desk, the American nearly tripped on his swaying sword. "I am so sorry," as Old Buck extended his hand, "for prying into the knick knacks, but they appeared so delightful."

The head cocked in apparent deference, the eyes twitched, and the little mouth pursed. He took the proffered hand. Dickens was stunned. Standing before him was his own Elijah Pogrom, a "poltroon and a coward," straight out of Martin Chuzzlewitt. He had seen this curious flourish of a man at David Barnum's in Baltimore when he stopped through in the spring of 1842 and overheard the whispered conversation of this fellow and a prim, meek man, someone named King who seemed much more by virtue of dress and manner, thought Dickens, like a Queen. In any event, as he watched the two and overheard their discussion, he had enquired of his waiter as to the identity of the corpulent cockatoo, and was informed that it was indeed a United States Senator, although the server had not been certain of his name. Nonetheless, this proved to be just the fellow to model poor Pogram upon and he had, after an evening of careful observation, done so.

The author repressed his amazement that this new Minister to Great Britain should be this silly fop whose path he crossed in that harbor city. Rarely had he had to embellish so little to create any character. "My dear Mr. Buchanan," began England's foremost man of letters, only to be immediately interrupted.

The words flowed in a giddy torrent. "Mr. Dickens, it is with none of the self-imposed restraints which generally accompany the opportunity to encounter one as wholly noble as yourself that I do find myself here. In short, a pleasure."

As he assessed the intruder, Dickens said to himself, "Far too good to be true." Ideas were already tumbling as this cornucopia of a character smiled his eager little smile.

The visitor started lobbing sentences at him. "Although I understand there were great currents of prostitution and vice in some of your earlier works, I was, sir, you will be quite pleased to know, I am absolutely enthralled (and I speak here for most of my countrymen) enthralled I say, with 'little Tim' from your wonderful book setting forth the evils of those who fail to appreciate the celebration of our Savior's birth, that is, in a word, Christmas. Surely, little Tim shall live, with the whole Crackpot family, with all his associates and remembrances, as the model of boyish good nature and pluck to the extent of this whole generation. I also advise you that I do find some great bit of myself in your young Copperfield, at least the parts of the serial which I have read, although I do see a good deal of myself placed in the manly young Steerforth as well."

Simply not possible, Dickens thought, something more like a chubby Mr. Dick without the charm or insight. He did not know where, exactly, to insert a reply. The visitor reeled into what he said was the "real purpose" of his visit, why he bothered to go into the streets and visit the author at Tavistock, rather than simply summon him, as perhaps he ought.

"Enough of that," Old Buck said. "I was sorely distressed, sorely sir, as were again my countrymen, upon the publication of The American Journal and the references and inferences, criticisms and calumnies, aspersions and allegations contained therein. Your Martin Chizzlewizz, or whatever that was called. I confess I have not read either, but I seek remonstrance of you. Surely you could draw a more accurate, and therefore a far kinder, portrait of our fair land?"

Old Buck reached for air. "Mr. Buchanan, I do acknowledge that you are a fair and true example of what in America is considered its best."

Dickens risked a pause to let the comment find its bottom. "I was compelled of course to write what I observed. I confess I was distressed at the state of your Republic, and the objects of its veneration."

"I must say," Old Buck replied, " your writing was simply unacceptable. I am here only to lodge this protest, and the kind words about your books were my own addition. You are aware that most of my countrymen, and certainly its finest, sprang from this very soil?"

Dickens acknowledged he was at least that much of an ethnographer and made a mental note that he had been right to dispatch, at least those characters he loved, to Australia, as he did not like to imagine any but his scoundrels expiring in this man's America. Perhaps he should have shipped the late Heep there?

"Mr. Buchanan," he replied, "perhaps if you actually read my books…" but apologized, although he could not help but recall his description of Pogrom, his rude exaltation of all things material and American, and his *sotto voce* Anglophobic mutterings. "I have respect for many who are right now in your native land, and once it settles a bit and its institutions mature, it may prove a most propitious country."

"If the kind gentleman would but stop by, rather than inexplicably ignore, my delightfully representative town of Lancaster? It is named, I should remind you, for a city in your own country. It would certainly confirm the best of your opinions."

Dickens thought that was perhaps the last place he should want to see, but muttered something agreeable in response.

Satisfied that he had heard the apology it had been his mission to secure, Old Buck took his leave. Pompey waited outside, the deep dreck of sooted rain falling all about him. The servant pulled the team away, straining to avoid the detritus of London's streets. Unfortunately, after two months not yet fully familiar with London's web of streets, he went left on Oxford Street rather than right, and the carriage ended up in front of Newgate Prison. Two pilloried souls, their heads and hands each secured in one wing of a four-flanged frame, trudged counterclockwise.

A group of about 60 women milled in front of the scaffolding, and a throng of men and boys stood behind them, pressing the womenfolk against the hamstrung bodies. The hisses and jeers of the crowd crashed into the gathering darkness, daylight strangled rather than extended by the wisps of moonlight piercing the soot and fog. As Old Buck and Pompey watched in astonishment, large globs of mud shot through the heavy air. A great melee of stone and soil hailed on the stockaded bodies. Nor did it stop there. Apparently provisioned by local markets, and supplemented by an assiduous search of surrounding streets, other volleys began. Rotten eggs, molded turnips, fish whose stink assaulted every pore, potatoes with great fibrous growths. The matted hair, desiccated eyes, and drawn mouths of alley cats soared awkwardly to their targets. Buckets of blood and sewage and an occasional brick. Old Buck could stand no more. He leaned out of his window toward a lad of no more than ten, "What, exactly, is the nature of these fellows' crimes?

The boy's face congealed into a case study of contempt, "Guv'nor, 'ere be a conspiracy to commit the Biblical abomination."

Old Buck looked at Pompey, who was already lashing the horses. Only a block distant, "Pull over!"

Leaning over the noisome sea, and as carefully as he could in a vain attempt to avoid the backsplash, Old Buck made his own substantial contribution to the turgid morass in a nearby alley. He learned only later that this was near the very spot where Philip Hot and the man called "Pretty Harriet" were imprisoned and hung for their crimes against nature when the White Swan was raided and the Vere Street Coterie arrested.

Alighting again and retreating on Oxford Street, the drapery of concern settled over both of them. The carriage made its way past Tottenham Court Road, Pompey pushing the horses at as fair a clip as possible, Old Buck still shaking. With a short jolt up Portland Place and a shot toward Marylebone Road, they arrived at their lodgings near Cavendish Square. That night, Uncle penned instructions to have Harriet withdrawn from her convent school and shipped to London.

Meanwhile, back at Tavistock, Dickens, whose own love, in this time of cholera, and marriage to Catherine were disintegrating, carefully made notes to employ this otiose fellow in some other small way for his upcoming book. The name "Pumblechook" came to mind for this speechifier, this curious amalgamation of fish and swine, this roe-eyed, obtuse and porcine fellow, whose once sandy hair still stood curiously erect atop his head. "Great Expectations, indeed!" Dickens congratulated himself.

Chapter Twenty-Two
THANATOPSIS

O n December 8th and 9th of 1853, the year of W's Cuban inauguration, Congress, Senate, and Supreme Court reconvened and sought to honor the departed Vice-President. On a London Christmas Eve, Old Buck finally secured a copy of the speeches designed to elevate W's memory, and carefully scoured the paeans to his lover. He was struck by the seeming esteem reverberating through the speeches. After a few pages, he saw something deeper.

Old Buck read the lead remarks of the portly plantation born and bound Senator Robert Mercer Taliaferro Hunter of Virginia, while wondering at the Southern propensity for four names, *It is a happy thing for a country when the lives of its public men may be thrown freely open to the world, and challenge its closest scrutiny, with a consciousness on the part of the friendly critic that there is no blot to be concealed, and no glaring fault which a love of the truth forbids him to deny, and his own sense of right scarcely allows him to palliate…He trod the difficult and devious paths to political preferment long and successfully, and yet he kept his robes unsoiled by the vile mire which so often pollutes those ways.* Good stuff and true, Old Buck thought.

He read further, imagining the intonations of the planter from Virginia, *Although gentle and kind in his intercourse with others, he could be stern enough when the public interests or his personal honor required it. He was a man, sir, whose whole soul would have sickened under a sense of personal dishonor.*

Old Buck reflected on their relations and on W's unflagging efforts to put forth that very image. Indeed, he would have been personally repulsed if that secret part of him had ever been opened to the scrutiny of the greater public. Their shared life was kept by W in some secret compartment separate from himself. Neither visited it except under dark and it was not spoken of outside their upstairs room in their home on F Street.

Senator Hunter turned to W's short tenure as Vice President, *that much-prized honor was to him the Dead-Sea fruit, which turns to ashes on the lips. It came, but it came too late. The breath of public applause could not revive the flame which flickered in the lamp of life.* Tears formed at the Senator's description of his last days with W, *The balmy influences of neither sea nor sky could revive or restore him. When the public messenger came to clothe him with the forms of office, his chief early wish was to see his home once more, and, in the midst of familiar scenes to die among his friends.*

Senator Hunter closed with a resolution that the chair of the President of the Senate *be shrouded in black* and that the members of the Senate, in respect to the deceased, would wear *crape on their left arm for 30 days.*

Old Buck was now sobbing. Pompey looked in on him in his room, but just as quietly as he had ventured to crack the door, resealed it on his master, uncertain as to the source of his unshared grief.

Old Buck trembled a bit with nascent anger as he read the words of the august and patrician Edward Everett of Massachusetts, who resigned as President of Harvard to serve as Millard Fillmore's Secretary of State and only lately ran for this post, *It would hardly be expected of me to attempt to detail the incidents of the private life of the late Vice-President,* and was greatly relieved as Everett snowed his usual blizzard of generalities. He thought it a bit gratuitous of the classical scholar when Everett said of W that, *he rendered a service to the country, not perhaps of the most brilliant kind, but assuredly of no secondary importance.* How imperiously back-handed! Everett spoke of a *mysterious…disease, for which the perpetual summer and perfumed breezes of the tropics afforded no balm.* Enough, Senator Everett, thought Old Buck. You might well realize that it was not tuberculosis, with all your learning, but that was unnecessary and ungracious. Were there others who guessed the nature of the illness?

The equally rotund Senator Lewis Cass of Michigan arose to speak, the new President pro tempore in W's place. Old Buck imagined his hand, as so often, thrust under his opened vest and kneading his ample stomach. The Democrat held W up as an ideal, *in the whole range of American statesmen there are few, indeed, to whom our youth can better look, when seeking models of imitation and encouragement.* That was more like it. The public man was assiduous in fulfilling his duties and the private man, Old Buck reiterated to himself, was the private man. No one knew, as he did, the struggles, the great and glorious effort, to keep the shroud of 45 years in public life draped over the necessary secret of the private existence. His tears came in great spurts as Senator Cass went on, *In all the relations of private life he was loved and honored, as well from the amenity of his manner as from the kindness of his heart, and in the social circle he was the very model of the accomplished gentleman.* That one remark of Lewis Cass, Old Buck thought, should ensure him a position of honor.

He approached Senator Douglas's speech with caution, but realized that he had not known W well, as he was relatively new to the Senate floor. The remarks about W's *public duty and private intercourse,* and the happiness of those who knew him in both ways, were nonetheless well taken.

The elusive epigram of Senator Clayton alluded to what Old Buck felt was perhaps the key to it all. He had a sense that it encapsulated, despite the ribald comments of some in times past, what W was about. Yet he himself could not quite get the Latin. It seemed to indicate something that struck at the heart of what all the other remarks had skirted. Did they all know? There were indications, veiled allusions. What did the Delaware Senator's foreign phrase mean? Old Buck strained to be certain that his Mercersburg Latin was sufficient to the task as he read,

"Nec male vixit, qui natus moriensque fefellit."

Let's see, "male" is of course not referring to a man, although clever that he used it. It meant something bad. That "nec" in front of it—that means "not" or "nor" or "no," and so "not bad." "Vixit?" A verb, not a vixen. Its meaning out-foxed him. What was "natus?" That was like birth, or nativity, like Christ perhaps? "Moriensque?" Old Buck recalled the "que" meant "and" like SPQR, the Senate and People of Rome. Here, it was the Senate and People of America, Old Buck thought with a little dash of self-congratulatory cleverness. "Natus" and "vixit" had something to do with living, and "moriens" something to do with death. Well, that makes sense. This "fefellit," that threw him a bit. It was a verb, of course, he knew from the third person singular ending and placement. How obscure was this though? Certainly not *requiescat in pace* or something traditional. Why was this quotation chosen?

Old Buck halted his review of the obituaries and called to the hovering Pompey. Well-nested in a phaeton, with Pompey flying through the fog and liquid streets, they alit at Redbreast's. a bookseller on Bloomsbury Square. A fluttering figure peeped from behind a cage of thick blue leather volumes and asked if he could help. In what Old Buck hoped was a sufficiently learned but mysterious mien, "I have not come to acquire anything temporal. I seek something immortal, a translation and a source."

The bookseller reviewed the Latin script carefully copied by Old Buck, and slowly scratched his tufted head. The arthritic claws drew dust. "I have some immediate recollection of the source, and am easily able to effect the general translation. Let me be certain."

He went hopping into the stacks, almost flew up a rolling ladder and fetched a volume high on the shelf. He flitted to the seventeenth epistle of the Epistularum Liber Primus by someone named Quintus Horatius Flaccus. As Redbreast explained, the author was likely better known to the American in front of him as Horace. After pecking away at the text, he read from its tenth line, and provided a stunning translation.

Old Buck's head jerked backward, his nape disappearing in two soft folds of skin. No better or further proof of W's success existed! Therefore his own, of course. Senator Clayton's words, carefully chosen from this obscure text, seemingly out of place and with no meaning except in the context of the Senate's shared knowledge of the private relationships of its departed President pro tempore, were as follows:

"He lived not in evil, who in life and death deceived."

They knew, they knew, they were acknowledging they knew!

As he and Pompey retreated to their quarters near Cavendish Square, Old Buck pondered the amazing, curious, and otherwise inexplicable thing to say about someone whose entire life from the age of 19 to death was lived wholly in public. W had served with just a few score of other men in the Senate for over three decades, and a Congressman before that. How could they begin to pretend they did not know anything about his private life? Why, everybody knew everything, names of wives and children, what they drank and ate, where and how they lived, their other sources of income, where they went to school, what their biases and prejudices were, their successions of mistresses and, yes, yes, their secrets. This phrase therefore only made sense if one suspected to the point of sure knowledge what was transpiring in private. How clever a way to reveal that to all in the know, while keeping it in the box of the upper chamber of the American government, like a broad conspiratorial wink that only the cognoscenti would understand and appreciate.

Milton Latham of California, citing the encouragement that Senator King provided him, almost gave it away, Old Buck thought.

How had he known of his time with W in Cuba? Known he had, as the Congressman spoke of the friend who *had followed him abroad.* Everyone knew, but at least they were not speaking of it directly. Old Buck's lip started to pull against his lower teeth as he realized this would be as close as he might ever come to having his life together with W publicly acknowledged.

There was perhaps another close call, as Representative Taylor of Ohio acknowledged, *I had the pleasure to know him for many years as a public man; and to meet him often in the social circles of this city... with the incidents of his private life and history I am not so familiar as to speak advisedly.* Mr. Philips of Alabama quickly arose and asserted that Senator King, *had not only preserved his reputation intact, but freed himself even from the breath of suspicion.* Old Buck exhaled in relief.

These eulogies, the vicarious fear of discovery and the pangs of absence, made Old Buck feel as if he had ridden a fast steed over rocky ground. With all knowing eyes upon him, it would have been too much to have added his own graceful farewell. He would have been sick for days before and after!

Old Buck concluded his reading with the remarks of Chief Justice Taney, who, upon the motion of Attorney General Caleb Cushing, adjourned the Supreme Court's session in honor of W. All in all, a most fitting tribute.

As the baton of paeans was handed by the House to the Senate and to the Supreme Court, not one mention of family, nor of any personal legacy at all, and no direct allusion, Old Buck saw, to him. Not that he expected it, but he felt as if he did not exist, that W passed to the ages with his greatest personal bond left loose and flapping in the spectral wind. Of course all the property would go elsewhere, but that was of no moment. What was most important was that W had succeeded in taking their secret to his grave. Old Buck considered, he must do the same..

He was pleased that not only the Senate, but also the House, and even the Supreme Court, adjourned for the day. The black armbands and the crape-draped chair were a nice touch. It struck Old Buck, with W's place in history secure, where would he himself stand in the pantheon? He hated the thought that his career appeared destined to end on these green and foggy shores of Anglia, and could not escape the image of himself, in but a few years, gently being plowed, alone and ill-used, into the Pennsylvania farmland.

Other words of Cowper's echoed in his ears, as he recalled W's recitation at their fireside, and the nearly two decades they passed together:

> *...no longer young, I find*
> *Still soothing and of power to charm me still.*
> *And witness, dear companion of my walks,*
> *Whose arm this twentieth winter I perceive*
> *Fast locked in mine, with pleasure such as love,*
> *Confirmed by long experiences of thy worth*
> *And well-tried virtues, could alone inspire—*
> *Witness a joy that thou hast doubled long.*

Old Buck soon turned again to his official duties. With British attention focused on the Crimean war, a great contretemps brewed in the Caribbean and he was called on to secure the purchase of Cuba from Spain. In the freshness of his personal experience on the island, Old Buck found it an odd coincidence that he should be sought to explore the acquisition of this land of sugar and slaves, but soon began to view it as a personal opportunity to honor W's memory. The Republican revolution in Spain and its impending international bankruptcy made this the time to strike. Best not to wait until after Cuba's slaves, sensing the lack of control from Iberia, might themselves seek to take over the land in a bloody revolt.

The United States Congress was diverted in arguments over the Kansas-Nebraska bill that sought to toss the issue of slavery to the voters in those territories. Old Buck, as in Russia, received only sporadic guidance from the President.

The minister to England also had enough of young Sickles and his aide's adulterous escapades. He dispatched him to Washington to seek approval for a course on Cuba. When Sickles arrived, he found Pierce sunk in a deep funk, not eating and often refusing to read his mail. The President had gone horseback riding that fall and, while intoxicated, run over an elderly woman crossing Pennsylvania Avenue. Despite his position, he was summarily arrested and charged with assault, but the indictment was later mysteriously dropped. Pierce finally dispatched Sickles back to London with instructions that Old Buck meet with the Spaniards in Paris and utilize legates from England and the host nation in the quest for Cuba. Old Buck rejected this as improvident, and implored the President and Secretary of State Marcy to convene the meeting at some more remote location.

Ostend, in the Netherlands, was agreed upon, but the press soon found the delegates there, and all retired to Aix-la-Chapelle and adopted what was nevertheless known as the Ostend Manifesto. The plan was to purchase Cuba, return Spain to solvency and to do so with the approval of both Britain and France. The aversion to the possibility of military action if a sale were not effected was subtle. Newspapers in America, with the assistance of supposed inside information from Sickles, clamored for the acquisition of Cuba by whatever means necessary. The public, erroneously, believed that Old Buck split from the Pierce administration and was an advocate of the use of force, despite the repudiation by Marcy and the administration. Nothing could be more unlike the Pennsylvanian's view, but it nurtured what appeared to be an otherwise sourceless but germinating sense in the American public that Old Buck was someone who would fight and seize, asking any questions later. The dough-faced boy also felt the stronger embrace of the South, seeking not only Cuba but also other slave territories and states.

At home, the Kansas-Nebraska Act had destroyed the Whigs. The Democrats were divided and decimated. A new party, the Republicans, was emerging, and the Know-Nothings were sapping strength from everyone, vaulting in only a year's time to a position of startling power. A political sea change flowed through America.

A party, and a nation, would soon unexpectedly turn to someone whose absence from the country kept him apart from and above the fray, who appeared to prove his worth as a statesman, and who had ties to the South and support in the North presumed sufficient to avoid the gathering menace of war. It soon seemed, to paraphrase a quotation already wrongly being attributed to Lincoln, that someone can fool a majority of the people some of the time.

Chapter Twenty-Three
TRIUMPH

A year before Old Buck's return to American shores, a series of "puffs" began appearing in newspapers all over the country, most often in small towns and little cities. These short news articles spoke of political disarray and the economic and social schisms that were driving North and South apart. Each ended with the hopeful prescription that someone from earlier times, now far above the divisive fray, could provide the stability of a calm hand in treacherous times. The unattributed articles curiously hinted at, but did not directly name, the current ambassador to England.

That was not all. Old Buck hosted a dinner in London and casually mentioned his admiration for the Archbishop of New York.

Word quickly got back to the prelate and, in pulpits across the Northeast and down the seaboard, homilies on the virtue of a man who could save the country from its growing rift were delivered to a Catholic population ignored by the Republicans and attacked by the Know Nothings. Contemporaneously, Protestant churches in the South began to speak of the need to have a sympathetic northern voice "at the highest national level" to ensure that their way of life would be protected within the Union.

Old Buck embarked on his return to the port of New York unaware of these stirrings. He had almost secretly slipped out of the country not three years earlier, on April 9, 1856. Cuban cigars in hand, and cupping a glass of Madeira, he settled in for his return voyage. Old Buck reflected on his absence from Congress during the four career-crushing, have-to-take-a-stand, issues of the first half of the 19th Century: the Missouri Compromise; the struggle over tariff nullification and its implication of the battle over state's rights to ignore or countermand federal law; the Compromise of 1850; and now the Kansas-Nebraska Bill. His only conclusion was that he must be living right and could now retire in peace, a good job done.

The trimmer, the compromiser, the back door player, did not realize he was about to be the beneficiary of a most unusual moment in history when absence from power and advancing age could be fashioned as attributes in an uncertain land.

The engaging Sophie Plitt had traveled to London to share with her friend Harriet Lane, now all grown, in the social swirl and intrigue of Queen Victoria's court. Sophie and her husband George had many of Old Buck's nieces and nephews farmed out to them for varying periods of time, including Harriet. The couple accompanied the Minister and his niece on their return trip. Sophie showed Old Buck a newspaper clipping claiming the prodigal diplomat was going to disembark in New Orleans and make his way to Tennessee, and there marry the erstwhile Mrs. Polk, arming himself with a wife as he re-entered the presidential fray. With a wit that brought a great smile to the punster's face, and in full knowledge of the absurdity of the suggestion, she dropped her doughy shipmate a note clipped to the article. It stated that she found it "interesting that you have discovered an agreeable way of Polking your way into the Presidency." Old Buck was surprised at the talk of higher office, but appreciated that a strong lode of appreciation still existed in the America he had mined for so long.

In contradiction to both the news article's purported travel and marriage plans, the Aragoa docked in New York on April 24, 1856, the day after Old Buck's 65th birthday, and ahead of schedule. Particularly given the circumstances of his departure and his eclipsed and ancient political star, Old Buck realized his secret imagined hopes for a return to native soil rivaling Caesar's, stirred by the article Sophie had shown him, were not within reach. With the early berthing, he doubted anyone would meet the ship. Still, he hoped for some representative from Pierce's office, or perhaps at least the city's Deputy Mayor. He went down the gangway hoping for a familiar face, but saw no one.

He was resigned to slipping as quietly back into America as he had withdrawn. When he reached Philadelphia, however, Old Buck was surprised, then delighted, and then overwhelmed. Cannons boomed and an official escort took him to Center City. Richard Vaux, the city's incoming mayor, met him at the juncture of the very streets on which Ann fled her life. Old Buck made what should have been about a three-minute speech. His extemporaneous effort was interrupted by rounds of applause and his remarks about the country's future extended to a quarter of an hour. Wave after sweet warm wave of approval swept over him. That night, from his hotel balcony, Old Buck watched a parade, delighted in a fireworks display, and oversaw a serenading band. All for me, he thought, all for me. Why? Who?

A specially outfitted train festooned in bunting and bearing the legend "Welcome Home, Pennsylvania's Favorite Son" embarked on its stop and go journey to Lancaster, providing Old Buck the opportunity to wave to his admirers and stop in Gap for quickly-consumed champagne. Joshua Jack, Jacob Zechner, Samuel Reynolds and Captain George Sanderson met him at the Lancaster train station. The streets were lined ten deep with people who poured out to see the local boy made good. Mayor John Zimmerman led the parade which the *Intelligencer* reported was full of, *sparkling eyes, pleasant smiles, and waving handkerchiefs.* Old Buck had to bow repeatedly as he catapulted his extemporaneous hour-long speech into a cheering crowd. At the Grape, as he later described it, he "partook a beautiful collation," fully sating himself on liquor and approbation. Who had backed this apparently spontaneous celebration? No one seemed to know.

Home at Wheatland, the "Old Buck Cannon" was fired, and the city enjoyed a two-day celebration of bands, torchlight processions, and fireworks. Old Buck, only a little begrudgingly, paid the $809.65 liquor bill presented for the two days' of comestibles he provided.

Leaving Lancaster, Old Buck stopped in Baltimore on his way to report to the President in Washington and intoned, "disunion is a word which ought not to be breathed amongst us even in a whisper. Our children ought to be taught that it is sacrilege to pronounce it," adding the declaration, "There is nothing stable but Heaven and the Constitution." The crowds that greeted him were unaccountably large.

Within a few days of his arrival in Washington, Old Buck should have gotten a strong whiff of where the country was headed. Congressman Preston Brooks of South Carolina took his heavy cane to the Congressional floor toward the end of May. He proceeded to beat the Senior Senator from Massachusetts, Charles Sumner, nearly to death, following the staggering abolitionist around the chamber as he struck blow after blood-gushing blow with his steel-tipped weapon. Sumner had accused South Carolina Senator Butler, cousin to the Congressman, of taking "a mistress who, although ugly to others, is always lovely to him; though polluted in the sight of the world, is chaste in his sight." Sumner paused for effect as he looked around the Senate floor, from which Senator Butler was absent. "I mean," intoned the Bay Stater, "that harlot—lavery." It took three years for Sumner to recover sufficiently to resume his duties.

Two days after Brooks's attacks, a fearsome radical with a name dripping in normalcy and six henchmen approached the doorway of one James Doyle, a Southerner, at his Kansas home. John Brown split the heads of the father and two of his sons with a broad axe, hacked open their sides, sliced off their fingers and laced their brains with bullets. The dead man's wife and his youngest child screamed into the dead, vast Kansas plain.

Mr. Brown then proceeded to the home of Allen Wilkinson. Morning's light found Mr. Wilkinson's skull chopped into broad mismatched pieces, his eviscerated intestines spewing red across the black clay.

Another homesteader, Bill Sherman, was located the next day in the dribbling little Pottawatomie creek, its waters parting across its rocky bed as they flowed around his open head, carrying his brain and severed hands downstream.

None of the dead owned slaves.

Democrats denounced both the Congressman and the zealot. Republicans, mindful of the abolitionists within their number, condemned Brooks but were muted in their response on John Brown's Kansas foray. The tacit and sometimes explicit approval of Brown's grotesqueries engendered a Southern riposte. When Preston Brooks appeared at a public function in the South, he was often presented a further complement to his growing collection of walking sticks.

The Democratic convention was set in Cincinnati, the first time any party conducted its quadrennial ritual west of the Monongahelas.

Franklin Pierce, wholly misreading the national mood and over the strenuous objections of his sheltered and now mentally unbalanced young wife, was running again, as was Stephen Douglas of Illinois. Out of nowhere and unbeknownst at first to its beneficiary erupted a "spontaneous" effort on behalf of Old Buck, now sipping Sherry at Wheatland. Four senators, Slidell and Benjamin of Louisiana, Bright of Indiana, and Bayard of Delaware, hurried to the Queen City. Their instructions were to breech the camps of the New Englander and the "Little General" from Illinois.

They were quickly successful in getting a Buchaneer, John Ward of Georgia, appointed as permanent chairman of the convention. As instructed, Ward admitted all competing delegations, who warred within themselves which of them had the right to cast the state's ballots. Deals were floated with Douglas supporters. The 43-year-old could certainly run in 1864, or even 1860. Old Buck would secure the path for his ascension. Other Buchaneers promised jobs to everyone overlooked by Pierce.

A dozen ballots kicked off the voting. Two-thirds of the votes were required to secure the nomination. Pierce, on the thirteenth go-round, finally withdrew, tossing his support to Douglas despite Old Buck's assistance to him four years earlier. By the sixteenth ballot, with divisions in every section of the party evident, Douglas withdrew. Buchanan's supporters again promised they would back the young man in 1864. Despite the uncertainty of political promises, he took the deal. Surprisingly, Old Buck's support among the delegates was lagging behind Douglas in the South at the time, but the sexagenarian was unaccountably trouncing him in the East. When the news found its way to Wheatland, Old Buck was mystified. Why now? He soon convinced himself he was finally receiving his due reward. W would be so proud...

John C. Breckinridge, a relative unknown, and half Old Buck's age, was selected by the convention to vie for the vice-presidential post vacant since W's death. He was the youngest man in the nation's history to run for the vice presidency, and his running mate was to that date the oldest first term candidate. When Breckenridge campaigned against Lincoln four years later in 1860 as a "Southern Democrat," thereby helping ensure Abe's election, he was still in his thirties.

The nascent Republican Party selected the brash swashbuckler and self proclaimed "Pathfinder" of the West, John Frémont as its inaugural nominee. Frémont fancied himself an adventurer and a romantic, a combination of Lord Byron and Daniel Boone. He was the youngest man to run for president to that time and over two decades younger than Old Buck. He was guaranteed, the Democrats thought, only to bring the Know Nothings with him, and precious little else. The Republicans had no infrastructure, and no history of allegiance. The party's platform evoked mid-century radicalism, and proposed as its hallmarks the eradication of those "twin relics of barbarism, polygamy and slavery." The Pierce administration was directly attacked, with accusations of murder, robbery, arson, and constitutional subversion fired its way. Frémont and the Republicans sought a "sure and condign punishment" for the perpetrators of such crimes, meaning, Old Buck supposed, all those who opposed them on the admission of Kansas as a free state.

Frémont was born in Georgia and raised in South Carolina, but now espoused an anti-slavery view as a Senator from the new state of California. He was portrayed as a self-aggrandizing explorer, a devourer of "frogs, lizards, snakes, and grasshoppers" and soon proved the perfect foil for the seemingly sure and steady Old Buck. Frémont ran on a five point slogan, an alliterative attempt to be all-inclusive that was both too cute by half and twice too long to be memorable, "Free Soil, Free Labor, Free Speech, Free Men, and Frémont." Sophie Plitt, in a letter to Harriet Lane, summed the Pathfinder up as a *poor ignoramus* and labeled the election a *farce* and a *burlesque*.

It did not take the newly re-horned Old Buck long to realize that the road to the White House lay in one issue and one only: The

Republicans would rip the country asunder, and he and the Democrats could keep it together. Statements from radical Republicans seemed designed only to aid his cause, lifting his cocktail of compromise and moderation to the lips of Americans averse to war, who seemingly would drink any elixir to stay out of an armed conflict between the States.

Other voices had other views. Ohio Congressman Joshua Giddings, representing Ashtabula and environs across the Pennsylvania border, proclaimed. "I look forward to the day when there shall be a servile insurrection in the South; when the black man will wage a war of extermination against his master; when the torch of the incendiary will light up every town of the South." He added, "though I may not mock at her calamity, nor laugh when her fear cometh, yet I will hail it as the dawn of the millennium."

Horace Greeley editorialized that the South should just be let go, echoing many abolitionists' themes. Others, like Thaddeus Stevens, joined Giddings's call for punishment and retribution. Thad was curiously silent at the prospect of his neighbor ascending to the presidency although he did state, with characteristic derision, "There is no such person running as James Buchanan. He is dead of lockjaw. Nothing remains but a platform and a bloated mass of political putridity." Thad also learned of the speech of a fellow Congressman, given above Humphrey's Cheap Store at a state convention in the West held to strengthen the new party. Its author was no abolitionist, and his exact words had gone unrecorded, but the speech had moved all present with its emphasis on the purity of America's principles. Abraham Lincoln of Illinois might prove to be the fellow they needed when Buchanan's work was done.

Amid this tumult, Old Buck stayed on his porch in Wheatland. He had not gone to the convention, and he was not going to "campaign." If they wanted him, they knew where he was. He did not make a single speech during the months leading to the election, and adverted in any public statement only to the need to avoid "disunion." Democrats hinted Frémont was secretly a Catholic. Millard Fillmore and the Know-Nothings, with their opposition to not only the Roman church, but to all immigrants steam boating in from Ireland, Italy, Poland and other undesirable locales, stood to benefit.

Meanwhile, the swashbuckling Frémont was enjoying running about the country, stirring up passions and seeking to secure the northern vote which, with its majority of all electoral votes, could still determine the presidency on its own. Old Buck was sanguine that he had a solid South. He was moved by the little campaign ditties that sprang up as if from nowhere all over the country supporting his candidacy, including one that ran:

> *No braver one his country serves,*
> *Thus honored everywhere;*
> *None, none of all so well deserves*
> *The Presidential Chair.*
>
> *The talents we appreciate*
> *With little more comment*
> *We humbly beg to designate*
> *Thee for our President.*

Another, pithier rhyme was forbidden at meetings of Democrats:

> *"Who ever heard in all his life,*
> *Of a candidate without a wife?"*

HUNKERS, ATTEND!
FIRE AWAY!!

The above is a true likeness of "ten cent Jimmy" Buchanan, the "Damed-Black-Rat's" candidate for President.

OLD BUCK'S SONG.

Old Jimmy Buck goes in for to win,
But we go in for to beat him,
We'll hit him on the head
With a chunk of cold lead
And land him on tudder side of Jordan.

FREMONT'S SONG

Ye friends of Freedom rally now
And push the cause along,
We have a glorious candidate,
A platform broad and strong.

P. S. "Jimmy" you cannot win!

Freedom's Office, FREMONT'S PEAK, Rocky Mountains.

So went the scattered tracts and handbills, ranging from the somewhat benign, to more explicit allegations of a sexual nature. Little saw light in the legitimate media. The whispers about Old Buck's sex life were too astonishing to be reprinted. His private conduct was protected by the great Victorian sensibilities of the time that would not brook, in public print, rumors too horrific, even in the context of a political campaign, for public consumption. Moreover, what if they were not true? Libel suits were common at the time, and this one would be a behemoth.

Unlike those scurrilous rumors, when Old Buck got wind of the allegations of "murderer" that still emanated from some lips, he sought to confront those canards still arising like tiny Hydras from Ann Coleman's death. In a story he placed in *Harper's New Monthly Magazine* and published just before the election, the saga of his engagement was re-spun. He spoke with a a *most amiable and accomplished lady* who related their conversation. With the death of the principals long past, and only scattered nieces and grandchildren about, this latest, verifiably false iteration of the "Ann story" went unchallenged. No longer had, as in some of his previous tales, Ann herself broken off the engagement, leaving him with a grieving heart, based on a "misunderstanding." No longer had he spent too much time with another young woman or "neglected" her. No longer had her father Robert ended the betrothal, in fact he was now retroactively interred prior to the whole saga and her mother was the evildoer. No longer had he been too much of a "fortune hunter," but was victimized by *spies and agents* and Ann's decision, at her mother's insistence, to wed another. Sometimes, in Old Buck's prior stories, her death was immediate, at other times delayed by days or months. This time, she had died of a drug overdose at an uncle's house. Her dead hand clutched the only token of his love that Ann, after his angry demand that everything sent to her be returned, had withheld as a keepsake. The uncle, of course, blamed Mrs. Coleman for his niece's demise. The allusions to Ann's mental instability proved to be particularly helpful.

As Old Buck conversed in the *richly furnished parlor* as *Harper's* described, he recalled the dark rivulets of her hair, her deep eyes, the cheeks bloomed red by wind and cold, and her full lips and strong nose, but all that was now fully reduced to an abstraction, a construct, a false shield to many sabers.

Old Buck had to write down the tales that served him well in an effort to keep them straight. Now, however, all with direct knowledge, were gone, save perhaps that skulking Thaddeus Stevens. No harm to construct yet another yarn to excuse his marital state. Thad's image still occasionally coursed his brain, but he had not surfaced yet, and why would he now? Anyway, he would soon be President and that would be the final nail in the coffin of Thad's empty threat.

Frémont and the Republicans, their party only two years old, were not even on the ballot in 12 southern and border states. Yet the election was not without its surprises. Although Congress had tried in 1845 to standardize the date of federal elections, Maine still voted in September. While the Democrats could not expect that they would prevail throughout New England, the Pine Tree State went surprisingly heavily for Frémont. Could they possibly lose? Fillmore, running on the American Party banner with its anti-papist platform, was sure to siphon off needed support. Perhaps Frémont's father in law, the estimable Thomas Hart Benton, who had by now forgiven the adventurer for eloping with his 16-year-old daughter, was working behind the scenes. Even Pennsylvania, so seemingly securely in Old Buck's pocket, appeared in play. The Democrats stepped up their electoral efforts, seeking to put out fires while Old Buck sipped Madeira at Wheatland. Old Buck could already hear the cries of his campaign supporters, "Get out there, Senator!" and the broken metaphors, "put your hand fairly to the plough, and play the game. You must drive through!"

The southern states were in an uproar. If they were not strongly for Buchanan-Breckenridge before, they damn sure were now. California, Frémont's current home state, was important. Old Buck's supporters were astonished when it turned out their candidate had not bothered to ask Pierce or Douglas for their support, and the former president and leading Senator were making no active effort on his behalf. Surrogates hastily sought to mend fences in the face of the wave of upcoming state ballots.

Stephen Douglas himself became so alarmed at the Republican prospects that he sold some land and donated the proceeds to the Democratic cause. Old Buck's thank you note, drawn in an increasingly less steady hand, was perhaps purposefully misaddressed to "*the Honorable Samuel A. Douglas.*"

Pennsylvania went to the polls in October and Old Buck prevailed, although the margin was scarily slim. When all states finally voted and the ballots were tallied, it was Buchanan with 174 electoral votes to Frémont's 114. Fillmore had captured only Maryland and its eight electors, despite the fact that nearly one in four Americans voted for the New Yorker. Frémont ran third in his adopted home of California and took no state south of Ohio. Old Buck, at a time when no women and precious few who were black could go to the polling places, garnered less than half of America's votes. He was proud that he carried states he had never even seen.

Increasingly, not only sons of the South, but scions of the North, called for secession. A convention in Cleveland debated the voluntary secession of the North, but reached no resolution. In Worcester, Massachusetts, after the election but before Old Buck's inauguration, Wendell Phillips and others sought the same Northern departure from the Union. William Lloyd Garrison declared, "We must have an anti-slavery Constitution, an anti-slavery Bible, and an anti-slavery God." The Radical Republican tossed a copy of the United States Constitution into a bonfire, vowing, "So perish all compromises with tyranny."

Chapter Twenty-Four
<u>PRESIDENT</u>

O ld Buck delighted in his hand-tailored inauguration suit, the product of honored German *Wertarbeit* as conducted on King Street, not far from his first lodgings and the Coleman house. While it gave every appearance of being a regular black coat, it was wonderfully lined in a deep purple hue. Thirty-one golden stars, with Pennsylvania's in the center, were worked into its satin lining. Complete with a flowered silk vest, Old Buck thought how pleased W would be, and felt fully and rightly dressed and ready to lead his country. The clenching snow-drenched seeming eternity of the Pennsylvania winter was coming to an end.

He knew he had to prevent disunion. All else was secondary. He reassured himself and Harriet, who grew tired of his refrain, "I am the man for this job." Old Buck recognized that not only Southerners wanted to leave the country but, as the abolitionists in Worcester so plainly revealed, Northerners did as well. Perhaps two sides pulling hard against one another, though divided against themselves, would discover that it was better to stay together? In any event, his skill at compromise would surely triumph.

Hundreds of visitors a day undertook the pilgrimage to Wheatland in the six months that separated election and inauguration. Most were office seekers; a few were friends. The press chronicled everyone's comings and goings, trying to discern the shape of the upcoming administration. Lancaster and its newspapers strutted with the speculation, and the whole town was full of self-congratulation for its native son. On February 21st and 22nd, less than a fortnight before the inauguration, the local press noted that the President-elect was mysteriously missing from Wheatland.

Upon his return, Old Buck refused to answer questions about his whereabouts. In fact, he stopped seeing any visitors and lay in bed until the day before the trip to Washington, fevered and vomiting. Miss Hetty was kept busy carting out buckets, tossing their contents east of the privy.

His new obligation, easy to do but hard to stomach, plagued him even more than forming the cabinet and dealing with office seekers. He missed not only W but his advice. His coterie of cabinet members in waiting, cobbled together with equal parts of North and South and sprinkled with some middling spice, was already tasting undercooked. He could not resist the mixed metaphor. W had blown him southward; now he felt rudderless.

He had campaigned on the promise that he would prevent the country from falling apart, but he had no certain plan. Perhaps the country could put the whole issue of slavery behind it, as long as people were reasonable and permitted slavery to expand into the territories and new states in an orderly fashion. Or would the Supreme Court perhaps bail him out?

Dred Scott, a slave living in Missouri, had filed a lawsuit eleven years earlier in St. Louis County Court. He contended that, although his deceased master's wife in that slave-holding state now claimed to have inherited him, his years of traveling with his master to Illinois and the Wisconsin territory effectively freed him from bondage. The case had taken on a life of its own, wending its way over the course of a decade to the United States Supreme Court. Scott and his wife Harriet lost their initial lawsuit in St. Louis. They prevailed in front of a jury on re-trial, but he was returned to slavery by the Missouri Supreme Court. Backed by abolitionist money and with a legal team from New England, the Scotts instituted another suit in federal court in Missouri. They again lost. They again appealed, and the oral arguments before the Supreme Court were made in early 1856.

The impending high court decision needed to be announced soon. Old Buck invited his college roommate and fellow Mason, Robert Grier, to Wheatland in late January. Old Buck came right to the point with President Polk's Supreme Court appointee, "I have a small favor to ask."

Grier had expected as much. Not only his own reputation, but the soon to be President's rested on their shared secret.

"Jimmy, you have not kept in touch since my elevation, but I just wanted you to know that all is safe with me."

Old Buck eyed him. It was obvious his old classmate was reflecting on earlier days. Grier had as much to lose as he did and he needed to press the advantage.. "I am not of course seeking anything untoward, but simply a bit of foreknowledge."

"You must be speaking of that slave's case. I thought perhaps you had another concern." He paused and looked away, "I think you can be certain that the decision will be as you expect."

"Do not play me like some Pythia, Robert."

Grier missed the Delphic allusion, but decided to be transparent. "The Constitution's plain meaning is obvious. Slaves are property, wherever they are or wherever they may run to. It's just like a suitcase. It travels with you but you don't lose ownership of your valise when you cross from Maryland into New Jersey. Still, Justice Taney and I have found a simpler way of getting to our destination."

"That's good to hear. I hope you will issue an extensive opinion, covering all aspects of slavery and perhaps forever finally putting the issue of the legitimacy of involuntary servitude to rest."

"The thing of it is, the plaintiff is not even a citizen. He has no standing to sue in the first place."

"I agree that is obvious to anyone," said the President-elect, "and he will have to be returned to his mistress. Perhaps the Court can find, at least in dictum, but better yet in its holding, that Congress had no power whatsoever over slavery in the territories? That would make the Missouri Compromise unconstitutional and placate the South."

Robert nodded and returned two days later. In his hands were key portions of the balance of the opinion, copied by hand. "I will make certain the Chief Justice will not issue the opinion, and its damning dictum, until after he swears you in."

"I appreciate that. I can make good use of this. You should be sure to vote with the majority, so that any appearance of a North-South split on the issue may be avoided and that all know the North supports this view as well."

Grier agreed, driven by the demons of forty years earlier and pleased to be relieved of any current concern. Why, he wondered, had not anything arisen concerning his classmate?

Old Buck crafted his entire March inaugural address around the decision. The opinion was as expansive as he urged, venturing far beyond a simple decision that Dred Scott did not have standing to sue because he was not a citizen. Instead, Justice Taney's opinion gratuitously held that slaves were property, like cows, geese, or rakes, wherever they might escape. As chattel, they could always be returned to their masters. Further, the Missouri Compromise was unlawful and unconstitutional. Old Buck would act surprised, and appear wonderfully prescient, about the forthcoming eight-to-one decision.

It snowed on March 2, 1857 in Lancaster, as it has on many March seconds in that city's history. Pompey bathed his master in the tin tub in the bedroom, and Old Buck puffed around Wheatland in his fine black coat with the secret lining and prepared to head to the train station in the gray nether-dawn. By six in the morning, a crowd of wintered Germans and weathered Scots was already gathered at the train station. Marshals with batons pranced about. When Old Buck's coach did not arrive as scheduled, the assembled farmers and tradesmen, wives, and children began a march toward Marietta Avenue, slipping on the snow and ice as boots and shoes made more for show than service lost traction. Several citizens tumbled on Chestnut, Orange, and Plum but dusted off the detritus of winter and continued their unlikely procession in the gloom. One of their own was going to Washington as President, and they were not going to miss this opportunity to snatch a bit of history.

The band, too cold to play any longer, and the townspeople arrived at Wheatland with no president in sight. Finally, as toes began to lose feeling and fingers seemed to disappear from the sensate world, the carriage appeared, Pompey driving. Old Buck and Miss Hetty and Harriet along with his brother's son James Henry Buchanan, "Young Buck," stepped in from Wheatland's miniature portico. The parade was off.

At the station, the slave, the housekeeper, the flirtatious niece and the favored nephew boarded with the pater familias of the curious agglomeration. At a moment that begged for wife and children, there were none. The specially decorated train, replete with images of Wheatland and the nation soon to be thrust under his care, tooted and left the station.

A big luncheon awaited at Barnum's Hotel, a short walk from the Baltimore station. Guided by cavalry with long swinging scabbards, the party entered Old Buck's old haunt. By the time the entourage arrived, however, the knowledge of his first presidential decision made him too sick to eat He removed his star spangled coat and lay in his underwear, unable to sleep, twitching and turning on the back room bed. While the rest of the party dined, Old Buck spent three hours in agonizing fits of fear and pain, vomiting and sweating.

The party arrived in Washington and checked into the National Hotel. The incipient President was friends with the proprietor, and the report of an epidemic of illness at the hotel would not deter him. Besides, the story of rats scurrying through the plumbing, their feces freezing in pipes and disgorged into the morning's pancakes just sounded like the kind of thing they might make up at the Willard Hotel down the way. Old Buck worked on his address, floating out bits to some of his visitors to see if they had support, carving and cutting the document to meet everyone's expectations. All around him, the hotel's guests were sickened, and he could not shake his own fever, now complicated by food poisoning.

The Fourth of March in the nation's capital was beautiful, clear and bracing. The approaching spring reaching a gentle arm back into the fold of its gelid predecessor, and the promise of the soft calls of birds, the opening of blossoms, and the scents of the season seduced the President-elect. What a propitious day, Old Buck thought. This city, its quaggy streets and tangled tumble of half-finished edifices, was now his.

Vice President-elect Breckinridge came by the National Hotel at the appointed time, but Franklin Pierce was unaccountably late. Was he, yet again, visited by the *Katzenjammers*? Harriet looked at the lobby full of members of the incoming administration. Was no one going to take charge? She turned to Pompey, "Run down to the Willard and find the President. Have the clerk remind him, if you have to, that today is Inauguration Day and we need him."

Pompey returned with the President in tow. Pierce, his head still throbbing from last night's imbibing, joined his successor in the barouche. Behind a float drawn by six white horses and a real live "Goddess of Liberty" on top, portrayed by one of Harriet's convent classmates, the 14th President and his successor paraded down Pennsylvania.

Old Buck turned to Franklin Pierce, "What, sir, do you plan to do after your presidency?"

Still saddled with his addled wife and lacerated by grief over his son Bennie's death, he replied, "There's nothing left to do but get drunk."

A remarkably unliterary statement, Old Buck thought, from the man who married the daughter of his Bowdoin College president and who claimed as college classmates not only Nathaniel Hawthorne but also Henry Wadsworth Longfellow. He made a mental note to do better with his final comments when he departed office.

Chief Justice Taney, a Maryland native and the plantation-born scion of slaveholders, was also a graduate of Old Buck's alma mater, Dickinson College. Unlike the man who stood on the cusp of the presidency, the faculty did not reject the recommendation of the Belles Lettres Society 62 years earlier. In 1795, Roger Brooks Taney was the class valedictorian. Buchanan grasped the jurist's head and moved his lips to the ancient ear. A few words were whispered. Taney's long curly gray mane tossed and he seemed to snort, the deep pillow of skin under his left eye drawing toward the socket. He returned to his seat and kicked it two feet further away from the speaker.

Old Buck faced a crowd fortified by 1200 gallons of ice cream, 500 chickens and 800 gallons of oysters, "Fellow Citizens, I appear before you this day to take the solemn oath 'that I will faithfully execute the office of President of the United States and will to the best of my ability preserve, protect, and defend the Constitution of the United States.'"

He recalled the February visit to the Metropole Hotel. The joy of this day was robbed again as he contemplated the mandate he would now be compelled to spew out to the crowd.

He had been instructed to take the room on the second floor, toward the back and at the corridor's end. It was the suite, Room 214, his personal choice on his "comet-like swings" to Philadelphia. That is to say, he had been told the room, and had known what was meant, although the number itself was not written.

He remembered waiting in that room after a night-long ride on the Philadelphia pike begun from Wheatland's back stables as dusk closed upon him. There he sat fully clothed on the outer ridge of the bed, his feet not quite reaching the floor and his hands clasped between his knees, arising, pacing to the window, looking toward Rittenhouse Square, going to the door, timidly pushing it ajar and peering down the empty hallway, returning to the bed's edge. He must have repeated those actions forty times while he waited for his interlocutor.

The letter, received at his study's side door two days earlier, read:

Mr. Buchanan

I have something to discuss that is of grave import for you personally and the country. You recall York and the bluff and the letter.

You have gotten this far but I can assure you will proceed no farther unless we meet. It would be at your peril if you were not to attend.

The 21st. The Metropole. You know the room.

Thaddeus Stevens

When he set the missive on his study desk, it was already stretched and creased, its cotton fibers separating from his jittered twisting. Why now? All these years, and now on the lip of glory! How fearful to be without W and his counsel. He could not meet him! Yet he must...

The knock had finally come.

"I do not desire," Stevens began, "to spend any more time here than necessary."

Old Buck needed to sit down. He returned to the bed. Stevens remained only a step inside the room, his frame filling the doorway.

"I have a single demand. Your activities on the bed on which you now so primly place your bottom are not unfamiliar to me. You will do what I ask, or their existence will be the lifeblood of every newspaper in the nation."

His shoulders had shuddered, the shiver racing between them an uncertain safety net for the sweat falling from his neck.

No presidency. No Wheatland. Perhaps, indeed most likely, prison. Still, he had to ask, "What of the letter?" His eyes could not face Stevens and one thumb was drifting back and forth on the other palm as if he were a nervous supplicant at the confessional.

The dark hard voice. "It is, for the present, of no moment. Sufficient, I would think, is what I have just told you."

Sufficient for what? He had mentioned Ann's letter when he wrote, fairly promising to reveal its contents. In the light of Stevens's apparent sure knowledge of this room and its visitors, however, that girl's epistle might as well be the ephemeron he had almost convinced himself that it always had been. Simply a bit of imagination, a wild guess. Who would even dare print what Stevens suggested? Yet if even one person did. If word somehow got out…word of Thomas…word of Robert…word of others…

Stevens had made only one command, and he had agreed to obey it.

• • •

Now that stonier face in the audience was dominated by nostrils that closed in on themselves. Stevens's cheeks bunched like red cabbage, forcing deep wrinkles in repeated radii from his slitted eyes to the wisps of his tangled black wig.

It had to come to this. Each word of the inaugural speech traveled like a bacterium up his ear canal.

"Having determined not to become a candidate for reelection, I shall have no motive to influence my conduct in administering the Government except the desire ably and faithfully to serve my country and to live in grateful memory of my countrymen."

Well, there he had said it. Buchanan would be completely compromised throughout his administration, a lame duck unable to flap his wings, destined to be fluttering in a swamp of malversion and ineptitude. What a stupid statement, and how important for the abolitionists' goals. Thad had disclosed more than he ought, perhaps, to achieve this commitment, but it and the inevitable consequences were well worth it. Thad thought he saw a hint of relief in Old Buck's face when he conceded the quest for a second term. He certainly would have been advanced in years if he were to run again, but even Old Hickory had been about his age. Men grow old at different paces, Thad considered, and Old Buck and his fussy, fawning, punctilious ways, was ancient long ago. His announcement at the inception of his administration that he would not run again was and would remain, Thad expected, unparalleled in American history.

"We have recently passed through a Presidential contest in which the passions of our fellow-citizens were excited to the highest degree by questions of deep and vital importance; but when the people proclaimed their will the tempest at once subsided and all was calm... and instant submission followed." As if, Thad thought, any issue dividing the nation had been mystically strangled in the polling places. Old Buck's election would revivify those differences, not assuage them.

Now, to the heart of it, the supposed veneration of the Constitution above all else, above human liberty, above the law of the God he supposedly served. Old Buck perorated, "What a happy conception, then, was it for Congress to apply this simple rule, that the will of the majority shall govern, to the settlement of the question of domestic slavery in the Territories."

Old Buck further dismissed the entire issue of the extension of slavery as, "happily, a matter of but little practical importance...Besides, it is a judicial question, which legitimately belongs to the Supreme Court of the United States, before whom it is now pending, and will, it is understood, be speedily and finally settled. To their decision, in common with all good citizens, I shall cheerfully submit."

What had Buchanan and Taney whispered only moments before the President-elect started to speak? Surely, Taney had not disclosed the Dred Scott decision. To do so would be unethical, and what would Taney have to gain? Of course, he reminded himself, Buchanan was hardly capable of extemporizing based on some just-shared confidence. Still, if the Scott decision were going the way Buchanan was clearly indicating, it would only hasten Thad's goal for this presidency.

Thad noticed that Justice Taney was also listening very closely to this portion of the inaugural address. The audacity of Buchanan's attempt to get him to divulge his carefully considered opinion, the capstone of his mighty Supreme Court career, was egregious. Buchanan knew better. His request had an air of seeking confirmation, not disclosure. The Chief Justice's opinion that the Scotts remained the personal property of Mrs. Emerson was curiously, as Taney listened, fully anticipated as part of the inaugural. Because they were slaves, the whole case was void *ab initio*—neither Scott nor his wife were entitled to sue in the first place because they were not citizens. He had been curious as to why Justice Grier, a Northerner, insisted on going well beyond the mandate of the facts of the case and traded his vote for a ruling that the Missouri Compromise was unconstitutional. Now any congressional limitation on the right to decide to become a slave state or not was forbidden as a matter of law. Each territory, wherever located, could vote on this issue itself. The Constitutional language, inserted by slave owners, that *all men are created equal* was obviously inapplicable to *the enslaved African race, beings of an inferior order, and altogether unfit to associate with the white race, either in social or political relations, and so far inferior that they had no rights which the white man was bound to respect.* Therefore, *the negro might justly and lawfully be reduced to slavery for his benefit. He was bought and sold and treated as an ordinary article of merchandise and traffic, wherever profit could be made by it.* So had he written, and so should all soon know the law of the nation to be.

Taney's eyes drew closer, one eyebrow ascended, and two furrows formed on his nose's bridge when he heard Buchanan say he would "cheerfully submit" to "whatever" the Supreme Court decided. Of course he must, Taney thought, but my legal conclusions seem suspiciously no secret to him. If Buchanan had somehow purloined a transcription, or the opinion was divulged, there was a problem on his court, an unforgivable action that would end at least one career. Should he stop this right now, and refuse to administer the oath?

Thad, as he listened to the speech, was struck by the number of times that the assemblage had to hear the words "happy" and "cheerful" when human slavery was the subject of discussion. Old Buck's only goal seemed to be to make the people—the white people—of the northern and southern states feel good about one another as if this would keep the union together, intoning, "Under our system there is a remedy for all mere political evils in the sound sense and sober judgment of the people. Time is a great corrective." Thad looked to the clouds forming above the capitol. The beaten man actually believes time is with him, with our country. He thinks that what we are talking about is just "politics." Not human liberty. Not vengeance.

Thad could not contain his revulsion as Old Buck went on and on, "I feel an humble confidence that the kind Providence which inspired our fathers with wisdom to frame the most perfect form of government and union ever devised by man will not suffer it to perish until it shall have been peacefully instrumental by its example in the extension of civil and religious liberty throughout the world."

This was too much. The Commander-in-Chief, the only President ever to serve in the armed forces of his country and not reach the rank of officer, was declaring America the New Jerusalem, the shining city on a hill, and the beacon for all to see as a model of "civil and religious liberty!" "For whom?" Thad muttered, perhaps too loudly as several women dressed to the very ends of their wardrobe looked his way, eyes and noses raised. For whom? Certainly not for anyone whose skin tone was not fleshy pink, not for anyone who was black, and not for anyone who greeted the Scots-Irish forbears of the speakers on these shores and, Thad thought of Lucretia and Lizzie, not you, you hissing women.

Tippling on, the happy state of the economy, the great surplus in the treasury, despite "wild schemes" of "speculators and jobbers." All the better, Thad said to himself, that there are monies in the public coffers for what needed to be done.

Immigrants were welcomed by Old Buck, "a hardy and independent race of honest and industrious citizens…who may seek in this country to improve their condition and to enjoy the blessings of civil and religious liberty." Thad worked his way out of the crowd, occasionally bumping, perhaps just a bit too hard, some of the more obviously southern members of the assemblage. Those words, meant to apply to those who willingly came here, and not on whose backs the South was built.

Thad's mind raced as he thought of what he would have said to all assembled. He would not ignored in that group the black people wrenched from their native lands, thrown into nets, dragged and bloody, cast into the dark holds of ships where, in squalor and a mix of every liquid excrement that emerged from their incarcerated bodies, they endured the prospect and fulfillment of daily death, the decaying corpses of their fellow Africans removed as morning broke, only to be cast upon these shores to spend their lives sold and enslaved, and watch, if the families were not irreversibly sundered, as their children and their children's children were offered no hope of anything more than beatings, rape, and eternal earthly subjugation. Thad battled his mounting fury, but had to keep tongue and temper in check. He had no problem with immigrants, but to place them, as soon as they lit on American shores, above those whose conscripted sweat had filled the pockets of the South was really, as he thought about it, horrific. Where was, in Old Buck's lugubrious verbiage, their "civil liberty," their "perfect equality," their being, "kindly recognized?"

Thad leapt on his waiting mount, Cobbler's grandson, and rode toward the Potomac, galloping along the river's northern bank until both rider and horse, sweat-soaked even in the late Maryland winter, were fully exhausted. He had not remained to hear the despicable Taney administer the oath of the nation's highest office to the more despicable Buchanan, but at least the game was afoot.

Old Buck was grateful for the pre-speech brandy that fortified him and especially grateful that he managed not to throw up before the assembled multitude for the two hours the ceremony lasted.

Harriet enjoyed the inaugural ball, under gold stars and bunting, her white pearls and artificial blue flowers appropriate for the occasion. Reports later emerged that some of the revelers, overcome by wine, had to be locked up behind doors festooned with red, white, and blue bunting. The final president born in the eighteenth century only stayed for a little while, and retired, febrile and inanite, early to his new home.

Chapter Twenty-Five
HARRIET

ROTATION IN OFFICE

Harriet Lane wrote in her diary:

March 11, 1857

We are well and truly in, all my old dresses now must be replaced. Ball after inaugural could not have been more wonderful, tho Uncle was not well and retired very early to his room, where he remains. He greeted all in the Blue Room but then went behind the gold draperies & was sick yet only a few saw and Pompey was on the spot.

Of course no dancing since Mrs. Polk said No so adjourned to the Hotel. But it was a Dazzler, with nearly three hundred there swirling and lots of gallant men, most of whom quite old. There are those who say my gown was a Scandal but it would not have been in Queen Victoria's court and she is no one to be avant garde. In Paris, it would be de rigueur to show décolletage! It was far less than at my Presentation to the Queen, where I had one hundred yards of lace and a diamond crown and Ostrich feathers!!

I am looking forward with great joy & much Anticipation to our stay here. Everyone now calls this the White House. I would have preferred President's Palace as at least it was once called or Mansion (or as Dolley Madison liked President's Castle!) but I do not mean to be too full of puff. In London it is so wonderfully Ceremonial and it is otherwise quite like living in an office building with bedrooms and no great rooms as at Buckingham. I do love the South Portico and having Tea. If it were named otherwise, as it once was, it could perhaps be expanded a bit and have a proper ballroom tho again grateful for President Washington and his Insistence that it be enlarged from original Plans. Still, it is quite crowded with all manner of people, some simply having Wandered in.

Buckingham Palace has so much that is new and Grand and this is not so much so. (Perhaps I should call it the Buck House now as Uncle did to the Palace with a wink!) It had all pinks and blues and much Scagiola and Chinese Regency in some rooms and plastered panels on the ceilings with such beautiful gardens and the Royal Mews not as those here which run to Pasture, nor do we have anything such as the open cour d'honneur and the marble Arch from times of Constantine. Still, it is far from Wheatland and I am Fortunate to be here and Grateful to Uncle. I hope we shall have as much music as at the Palace, with Costume Balls and composers with their Symphonies, tho we have no Music Room for that as at Buckingham and no Rembrandts or van Dycks or Rubenses are here and of course no Throne Room and no dancing in the White House since Mrs. Polk and Uncle has kept her dictate. Imagine, if Uncle were upon a Throne!!!

Pompey has been given his own room in the East Colonnade by the stables and laundry, and John Henry and I have been ensconced in *quite serviceable bedrooms in the family quarters, down the hall from the President. My brother Elliot has come with me and he will be Secretary to Uncle & read all the mail, routing it and digesting it as needed.*

April 11th, 1857

Uncle has retched and sweated through all of March and now into April. It is approaching 40 days and 40 very disagreeable nights. Now I must not only imagine, but execute, the social functions. All say I am youthful and Gay, and I learned much from Queen Victoria's courtiers. Miss Hetty is simply in the way, poking about and acting as if she is in charge ! No imagination and no grace. I do think, however, that this may be too much for me as I have hardly any staff of people and must decide on who sits Where at every dinner, oversee the kitchen (if I can block Miss Hetty from entering!) and must keep those who are Foes apart. If only Uncle had married, but scarcely possible… How far easier in London, when all I needed was to appear and my just being American was the ticket to success, with Queen Victoria treating me as if I were the ambassador's wife! Uncle found that quite amusing but it was good practice for all the challenges I now face.

Gottlieb Vollmer is making us new furniture as much that is here is quite old-fashioned, tho some is still quite serviceable. I think it is only in comparison that I am a bit Disappointed as if I were only coming from Pennsylvania all would seem quite Grand.

Every mid-day after luncheon, Uncle walks alone up and down Pennsylvania, and I have spent many afternoons riding sidesaddle on a large white horse given to me as a moving-in gift. In all, when not vomiting, Uncle seems to feel good about where he is but he must pace himself better if he is going to attend to the nation's business.

May 9th, 1857

Today I am 27, but it is not a happy day, tho Uncle does try. Elliot has died of a fever and John Henry has come to be his Secretary.

Wave upon wave of supporters come claiming their "rewards." Uncle spends all his time, when he is not en toilette, seeking ways to accommodate not only his friends, but also friends of friends. I see him out on the lawn among President Jackson's magnolias musing his way about as he leaves them Frustrated in his office. All these holdovers from Pierce refuse to leave. I think of Uncle, broom in hand, going to their offices and shooing them out! Not really, diary, but it is funny to think so.

Uncle fears his strongest supporters and oldest friends may turn against him, but each Cabinet Member has his share to appoint and what should Uncle do? I do not think he lacks Consideration or Gratitude, but Uncle says the whole Administration cannot come from Lancaster and Philadelphia! Many from the South seem to find their Posts.

Uncle cannot just dump them out into the street and replace them, but each Holdover is permitted to serve out his four years and that New Hampshire sot (I am sorry, but everyone knows this, maybe only because of his boy's death) appointed a whole passel of friends and Surrogates as the sun set on his administration, and now Uncle's opportunities to reward his own followers are eclipsed. (I am perhaps too proud of that description, but it seems right, as Uncle does have quite a moon face and it is becoming a moon body!)

June 21st, 1857

When not ill, Uncle meets with his cabinet almost daily, usually for four or five hours. I have little idea what they discuss, and my new good friend Henry Johnston (who I hope will be my beau) says it is better that he not discuss the country's finances with me, owing to my position!

September 2nd, 1857

George Plitt, Sophie's husband, was removed by Uncle from a minor post in 1846. Now, Sophie says the promise was that Uncle would take care of him "as soon as he could" but Uncle has not done so & now should.

September 30th, 1857

This swamp is horridely steamy and beetle-ridden but social life is on an upswing. Uncle chastised poor Thomas Hall for delivering spirits in bottles that were too small. He told him, "Pints are very inconvenient in this house, as the article is not used in such small quantities." Then smiled at me, yet he won't let me imbibe. It seems quite wrong that he may drink so much and yet I (supposedly) not at all.

Yet another widow, Elizabeth Craig, has set her sights on the President. I expect, as with all Others, she shall perish in the attempt. Mrs. Craig is a good friend of the Georgian Secretary of the Treasury Howell Cobb and his wife Mary Ann & had come to visit her friends from Athens. Mrs. Cobb told me that Uncle is "the greatest man living" and said Mrs. Craig had her arrows set before her arrival and wrote Mrs. Cobb, "nothing short of the first man in office will answer." She is but 36, and Uncle seemed pleased by her attentions. Mr. Howell is his favorite cabinet officer. Mrs. Craig is tres charmant, but she shall have no particular Success in trapping dear Uncle.

October 4th, 1857

They are starting to call this the Panic of 1857. Uncle tells me he is reminded of a time when he was a young man in Lancaster in 1819 only, of course, this is much bigger. Nearly 1500 banks went under in September and masses of unemployed are roaming the northern cities. Mills have closed. They are prowling the streets chanting "bread or blood." Uncle seems quite disturbed and has taken to bed. As best as I can piece together in conversations with Mr. Cobb, who is quite generous with his time, and what I overhear, there are so many things that have caused this, a trade imbalance with Europe, overextension of credit, overexpansion of rail lines in the northern states, land speculation, stock market manipulation. Uncle says he has "inherited a firestorm."

I spoke to my friend Mr. Johnston. He thinks Uncle should do more than just announce that there will be reforms in the future, but agrees it's not the job of government to provide any form of public relief. "America will just have to ride this one out," said Uncle.

November 16th, 1857

I did not know that finance was such a part of the presidency, with all the other issues of foreign affairs and domestic ones and the slavery question and everything buzzing about. Uncle has now decided we will stop issuing paper Notes for less than a $20 denomination. All workers will have to be paid in hard coins. Uncle says, and Henry Johnson and Mr. Cobb agree, that those who had not proceeded with prudence deserve punishment anyway. Still, Uncle has instructed Mr. Cobb, "We are going to have to use some deficit financing. I do not care about the Democrats and their two decades of hard money policy. We have got to meet the federal needs."

Now, I hear that thousands of Northerners are fleeing into the new Republican camp. The Dred Scott decision has seemed to alarm and energize abolitionists, but Uncle says the South is still unhappy. Mr. Cobb and the South speak of the Value of agriculture and "King Cotton." Uncle misses Senator King. He read me from the Selma paper which still arrives by post, "We are but put upon by the speculators and swindlers of the North. Our dollars go to Washington and disappear into grimy industry and corrupt cities."

December 1st, 1857

Miss Hetty has lost our battle. Uncle has asked her to leave and I understand she shall return to Lancaster. Triumph!

January 3rd, 1857 I mean 1858

Uncle likes the Southerners in the cabinet the most, it seems to me and has the Northerners around to "balance" the cabinet yet seems to have a particular affection, but not in any untoward way, for Lewis Cass, the

Secretary of State. This is peculiar as they are old rivals, but Uncle muttered something about "kind words said" and "an homage to the Senator" and I expect he means Senator King, tho I cannot be sure. I cry for the Indians and their treatment but even Jacob Thompson, who should at least from his position in Interior care, does seemingly not.

January 11th, 1858

Uncle's old guard is mostly dead or gone. He is already the very last surviving member of the 17th Congress. He is both proud and sad therefor, and talked of an era that seems more and more distant with the younger generation that surrounds him. He and Jerry Black were talking about "the giants of the Senate," Clay, Calhoun, and Webster, all dead and buried and the Attorney General suggested that Uncle be included there along with Senator King, and Uncle nearly seemed to blush. It seems to me that there are already myths surrounding our nation's founders. People are saying Uncle and his administration are out of touch with the country, with no one from a big city, no free-Soiler, no one identified with the younger wing of the party, full of a rural and southern outlook. It was only just after we got to Washington that I heard Mr. Black talking with Isaac Toucey and he said, "Old Buck is stubborn and old and "very fond of having his own way, and I don't know what his way is." I was angry at the time, but I am beginning to think that is true. I do think that it is good not to be part of all those big cities in the North, although Mr. Johnston is from Baltimore, but that remains Uncle's and my favorite "big city" if that is really a big city. London was a big city. I don't think Baltimore is.

Uncle is very adamant that I not marry, but I am nearly 30 and I hope that I soon may, perhaps after this term is done?

February 2nd, 1858

Postmaster General Brown has scandalized Uncle. He wrote some time ago to Mrs. Polk, who many had falsely said would marry him. Mrs. Polk is an upright woman, and Uncle says there were no dancing, liquor or cards when her husband was President and that is why there is no dancing yet there is plenty of card playing and liquor! (or at least none of which Mrs. Polk knew, as Uncle does not now know of Sophie and I and Champagne in the Kitchen, or Henry's coming to the back door !!) (and that is Miss Plitt, shall I ever forget in an addled old age and need some prompting! and I shall be I hope married to Mr. Johnston!)

Anyway, when he was but a Congressman the Postmaster General wrote Mrs. Polk about Uncle's "relationship" with the Senator and called them "Mr. and Mrs. Buchanan" !!!! Uncle is furious and seems a bit at sea, beside himself about what to do. He has not ever had any executive experience, never a governor nor even a mayor, and I fear for him and his health.

February 14th, 1858

There is trouble brewing in Utah. Those Mormons have found their promised land but Uncle does not want to give them title. Apparently President Pierce sent out federal judges opposed to marrying more than one wife at the same time ! ! Brigham Young's people are charging the judges with land Fraud. The Judges tell a different tale, and Uncle believes them. He told me, "I am in utter abhorrence of the notion of men with wives scattered all over the dessert. The Bible speaks clearly of Adam and Eve, and not Eve and Eve and Adam."

Uncle had sent out orders to replace Brigham Young as governor but now the Mormon claims they were never received, and he blames the fact that Pierce stopped all mail service to Salt Lake City and the entire territory, so perhaps it's true. Uncle is going to send a posse of 2,500 federal officers to Utah.

March 11th, 1858

Uncle proclaimed at his inauguration, "no nation will have a right to interfere or complain" if the United States sought to expand its territory. He now is driving the Europeans out of the Caribbean and seeks to fill in the open spaces in the continent with red blooded, but not red skinned !,

Americans. He is considering colonizing Alaska with the Mormons, and has sought to purchase it. Congress seems opposed—not to the refrigeration of the Mormons, but to the purchase of the icebox itself!! Uncle has declared war on Paraguay and the country has almost come to blows with Canada in the Curiously named "Pig War" over the boundary of the Oregon territory. Uncle likes his foreign policy, I think, more than the economy or Slavery, which he wishes would just go away, meaning of course the issue not the practice!

I was called in the paper today "Our Democratic Queen" and I think that is because I do care for what happens in our country and not just because Uncle is a Democrat. The Chippewas have called me "Great Mother of the Indians" but I think that I am not old enough for that!! Tho I do care for the Indians and think that there is much to be done to Reform our hospitals and prisons as well.

June 1ˢᵗ, 1858

The government men were ambushed by a Mormon militia, trapped in the Western snow, and routed, but not before the Mormons burned most of their own homes and businesses to keep them out of the clutches of the invading federal forces. Uncle has now sent the message that he will not interfere with polygamy as long as there is "general decorum." If only everything were that easy....

No parties right now as Uncle must spend all his time trying to figure what is best.

July 23ʳᵈ, 1858

Kansas. Slave or free? This is dominating all of Uncle's time and attention. The Nebraska Territory is set to come into the union as two states and who knows whether they will be slave or free. Certainly not Uncle.

That 1850 compromise has spawned a tempest worthy of Antonio. Senator Douglas seeks to outlaw the very emigration his bill triggered, thousands of New Englanders and sons of the South are pouring into

Kansas. There are several Governments, one at Lecompton under southern control, another at Topeka with Northerners, and six others scattered about the plains. Jayhawkers in some, Slavers in others. Open warfare has broken out.

Murder is the order of the day. New Kansans are killed in bars and taverns, in duels and ambushes, on streets and the open prairie. "Border Ruffians" they are called coming in from Missouri. Uncle says many so-called "settlers" from the North are there because they are paid by abolitionists to transplant for the moment. Mr. Black says many Southerners are there only for a little time as well, to vote and return to Alabama or Mississippi or Texas.

Horace Greeley, in the safety of his New York newspaper office, has anointed the state, "Bleeding Kansas." Uncle worries how the electoral process can work in the midst of open Warfare!!

August 4ᵗʰ, 1858

If the big issue is Slavery, the subtext, Henry says, is land, who controls it and who distributes it. Uncle's enemies, the abolitionists do not even want to vote anymore on the issue. Not only should there be no more slavery anywhere, they argue, it certainly should not be expanded, and certainly not north of the Mason-Dixon line.

Uncle says he is sworn to uphold the law. I know he will do so, at least as best as he is able. He does not like the Free Soilers, and recognizes the Government at Lecompton.

November 30ᵗʰ, 1858

The Republican Party sweeps into office around the country. Uncle is disarmed and blames Kansas. There are open fistfights in Congress.

January 4ᵗʰ, 1859

Uncle is increasingly Nosy. He gives his associates scorching tongue-lashings. Now all are employed (me included!) even cabinet secretaries poking about in everyone's private affairs, always trying to find out information. It is apparent that he not only wants to have one up on them, but sometimes simply seems to do it for the Delight he takes. He makes sure that all Mail comes to him first, and employs James Henry to help him sort out what might be Interesting.

Uncle appears Stung and maybe scared by the words of Harpers Magazine, "Mr. Buchanan ceases to exist as a private individual. He becomes an institution—the Executive—and he has no more claim to privacy.... a public functionary for the time being, and has no more claim to exemption from the inseparable inconvenience of publicity." He tells me that Senator King would not tolerate the suggestion that it is permissible to strip away the walls of what he calls his "private box," as if we were at the opera! Uncle was perhaps always overly sensitive to imagined slights, but he now sulks around the White House, all Fearful and scattering as he Shambles along, often dropping to his knees and feigning prayer. He despairs despite all efforts of disunion and fears the South will leave despite all his concerted efforts at compromise. People seem not to hear his pleas. I know he loves the country, wants slavery, and desires Peace. Why is it not working to achieve those things which otherwise all seem to agree upon? Is there no Remedy?

February 18ᵗʰ, 1859

I am tired of these new restrictions on dancing and card playing! Uncle had no problem with that before.

I have now begun to call him "Nunc," and told him that it was short for "Uncle." Sometimes, with others, I call him Old Pub Func, that being short for "Old Public Functionary," but not ever to his face. Old Pub Func was once seemingly so concerned about public knowledge of his private affairs & now opens all my mail, sometimes writing "opened by mistake" on the unsealed envelopes! I tell you, Diary, "Nunc" is not short for "uncle" it is actually short for "quidnunc," that is Latin for "busybody."!!!! Mr. and Mrs. Cobb, who are so nice to me, seem agitated as his investigations into their personal affairs, and especially financial matters.

March 3rd, 1859

Nunc's eye problems seem to be balanced by a Keen sense of hearing. It is not unusual to find him squinting his eyes in an effort to hear what is intended to be Private.

Now Sophie and I, being tired of Nunc's scurrying flurries into our privacy, have begun to communicate by placing notes in the butter kettle that arrives from Philadelphia! to avoid presidential snooping. My notes, "Signed, your Hal" to Sophie and hers to me all conveyed with the milk products!

March 13th, 1859

John Henry has now fled Washington. He has gone to New York to marry without securing Uncle's permission! The President was not even invited to the wedding! I do not want to speculate on why that might be…..

Mrs. Elizabeth Craig, the Cobbs' widowed friend from Georgia, has finally given up her quest and returned to her native State, disgusted by many things.

October 31st, 1859

John Brown, tho traveling with a band of negroes and men, has not been caught for his the Kansas murders. He now has led an Insurrection at Harper's Ferry in Virginia just a fortnight past. The first victim, Hayward Shepherd, was a negro porter! Killed by Brown. Reports are that the dear toasted one of the abolitionists lived there throughout the summer and into the fall under the nom de guerre Isaac Smith. He must have counted on slaves, and perhaps the poor whites of the Appalachians, to join him. Instead, the townspeople took aim fire at Brown's party as they tried to swim across the Potomac! Maybe a dozen people were killed, mostly Brown's confederates, but including the Harper's Ferry mayor. All in all, quite horrific!

December 4ᵗʰ, 1859

Nunc has dispatched a party led by Colonel Robert E. Lee that includes Lieutenant J.E.B. Stuart (who is quite an unhandsome man) and they have come back with their Quarry. Uncle told me (again!) the story of the Whiskey Rebellion and Lee's father, Lighthorse Harry, and his quest to Quell the Pittsburghers. How long ago that was now, the cooper and Mercersburg and my grandmother. Brown has already been hanged for treason, and his henchmen will be as well.

Sic semper tyrannis.

Uncle is furious! He says that New England abolitionists funded Brown's raid. The Northern press, and Radicals everywhere, are glorifying his Exploits, with allusions to martyrdom and Christ on the cross. Walt Whitman and Henry David Thoreau are praising his actions. It particularly upset Uncle when a certain Congressman came out in favor of John Brown's actions. Of course, I could not talk about it, as he has sworn John Henry and me not ever to mention the name T_____ S_____. And he is "our" Congressman from Lancaster, tho of course not really. Uncle has never had Mr. S_____ to the White House and I don't think ever will, especially now. Uncle also does not like another Whig gone Republican, who has in any event lost to Senator Douglas, himself defeated by Uncle, Mr. Lincoln of Illinois, but at least we may say his name!

Frederick Douglass, the slave who kept Brown in his own home, but says he declined to join the Raid (perhaps because he might have been recaptured!), wrote in the rag of a newspaper, the Liberator:

"He has attacked slavery with the weapons precisely adapted to bring it to the death. Moral considerations have long since been exhausted upon Slaveholders. It is in vain to reason with them. One might as well hunt bears with ethics and political economy for weapons, as to seek to 'pluck the spoiled out of the hand of the oppressor' by mere force of moral law. Slavery is a system of brute force. It shields itself behind might, rather than right. It must be met with its own weapons."

Even Henry Wadsworth Longfellow has joined in this evaluation,
if not the tactics. The New York papers got hold of his private journal,
where he wrote, "This will be a great day in our history; the date of a new
Revolution, - quite as much needed as the old one. Even now as I write,
they are leading Old John Brown to execution in Virginia for attempting
to rescue slaves! This is sowing the wind to reap the whirlwind, which will
come soon." People about are muttering (and when I write this People I
also mean the afore-not-written T_____ S_____) that there are those
who wish such a result. Traitors they must be.

Old Pub Func had always thought Longfellow a reasonable man
and liked his Poetry! He now fears that the name "John Brown" will
became a rallying cry for southern opponents of what they view as "northern
fanaticism." It could make it easier to secede from a North containing such
men, and Uncle fears that deeply.

January 17th, 1860

Uncle seems rapidly aging and only on rare Occasions leaves the
White House. At times he travels to Baltimore with a smaller group of
friends usually at the Barnum Hotel, yet drinks in his usual manner, with
wine at ten dollars a bottle. That would be one hundred times what he
thought a good daily wage for a laborer!

On one other occasion, Jacob Thompson and he left Baltimore by
boat and went to Raleigh and Chapel Hill. Newspaper reports were that he
was "gay and frisky as a young buck." Uncle seemed pleased.

Herr Vollmer's furniture has finally arrived and it is no longer a la
mode but we must of course pay for his three years of work and Uncle is upset.

Sophie has written me. Her husband, loyal to Uncle to this day,
and Nunc has found no place for him. "I don't care who is President. I
worked for one nearly all my life—my husband removed from office &
we have been ever since counting every dollar to keep our home. I despise
politics. There is too much ingratitude in political men & I am not a

spaniel." The last phrase Sophie has heavily underlined with a sputtering fountain pen.

April 23rd, 1860

Uncle's birthday. 69! Who would have imagined that age? Why, of course, he has been nearly that old for many years now. Still what a horrid present. Representative John Covode from our own state claims to be "alarmed" at Uncle's "ineptitude" in handling the Kansas crisis. Henry Johnston tells me that the national deficit is now $100,000,000 and that is very serious. I would not think for that Covode to call for Uncle's impeachment! He will be out of office in less than a year anyway. Are these people simply shameless?

Uncle says that these are "false and atrocious charges" and that there is a group of radical Republicans that practices "filthy politics." I must agree.

May 3rd, 1860

The Japanese are coming to the White House! I must prepare for them, and there can be no women at the Reception so I shall not be able to attend.

Good news! The Prince of Wales is to visit in September, and I wish to have a large ball. I am worried about Uncle. He says he is not up to it anymore. I would do all the planning!!!

He is growing quite Grumpy and it is getting to me. He even has already had my picture removed from the bedroom in which Prince Edward will be sleeping! I think I shall teach Edward Albert bowling!

May 27th, 1860

Cabinet members are threatening to leave. They and their wives say much bad privately and I hope I have not fueled that. Mrs. Thompson, and I cannot but believe that the irony was intended, has anointed Uncle "The pride of the Christian World."

Mr. Lincoln of Illinois is now talked of as if he might win the Presidency, but he has no office and no following, so no one here in Washington whose opinion I should respect thinks so.

Japanese have left behind many Objects with plum trees and blossoms and long birds with great beaks all in gold leaf and they are quite Beautiful. There is much now that is Rococo and I think they may go well together but I feel somewhat silly going on about these things as I think Uncle is not aware of the flaming Passions in the country and is Withdrawn, speaking with Jerry Black and no one else.

September 4ᵗʰ, 1860

Uncle tells me he is working hard on his legal position on the Question of keeping the Union together. It would be unlawful, of course, for any state to secede. Contrarily, it would be unconstitutional for the Union to prevent the succession.

It is Independence Day and Uncle paces the White House halls, carping at all around him. He stops and cries. After the crying, and sometimes during,, he prays. All scurry out of his way as if not to block his words that spring ever Louder from his lips.

He stubs out lit cigars in his palm. !!!

I am going to see Sophie and do not expect to be back.

November 21st, 1861

All results are in and Uncle must of course go home in six months. I am sure it will be a far better time for him at Wheatland, and I shall plan to visit.

Chapter Twenty-Six
<u>DISUNION</u>

THE OLD SCHOOLMARM IN TROUBLE.

Old Buck had to replace the carpet in his office yet again. It was the fourth time since he took office and the flayed bleached threads could not stand the pounding.

Congress vilified the President as a "Southern tool." Why would a northern Democrat allow himself to be so used by the South?

Congressional investigations in 1859 and 1860, and months of secret testimony by disappointed office seekers, found no direct links by the President himself to corruption. Some witnesses spoke of a "deep relationship" with Vice President King, but he was long dead and no one, when pressed, had anything specific to recount.

Old Buck continued to speak of the need for a united policy on the importation of slaves, mentioning that "our domestic slaves" experienced "advancement in civilization" that "far surpassed that of any other portion of the African race. The light and the blessings of Christianity have been extended to them, and both their moral and physical condition has been greatly improved."

He feared that if trade with Africa were reopened, it would harm the interests of slave masters because of the "introduction of wild, heathen, and ignorant barbarians among the sober, orderly, and quiet slaves whose ancestors have been on the soil for several generations. This might tend to barbarize, demoralize, and exasperate the whole mass and produce most deplorable consequences." The native-born slave, he continued, "is treated with kindness and humanity. He is well fed, well clothed, and not overworked. Both the philanthropy and the self-interest of the master have combined to produce this humane result." He extolled, "The feeling of reciprocal dependence and attachment which now exists between master and slave."

Quite unexpectedly, the new Republican Party had achieved a plurality in Congress in 1858, but could not get a bill past the southern bloc or the President's veto, or both. A former congressman from Illinois, loser in the last Senatorial election, was a frequent visitor to Washington. Thaddeus Stevens and he were seen caucusing, according to reports Old Buck received. What kind of friendship, what kind of intrigue, existed there? His concerns grew as Lincoln emerged from the Republicans' convention in the western state of Illinois in 1860.

Who would vote for this defeated man, without an office, from the far recesses of the nation? Why had the Republicans selected him?

Old Buck's Vice President, John Breckenridge, ran as a Southern Democrat in 1860, splitting the vote with the Northern Democrats led by Stephen Douglas. The Republicans did not run an anti-slavery or even an anti-secession campaign. Instead, the party's slogan, emphasizing the desire to expand the United States through western territories, was "Buy yourself a farm." Old Buck backed Breckenridge, who fled the North, and traveled through Florida to Cuba when he lost. Lincoln won, and where he won, he won big.

There was still, Old Buck thought, time to preserve the Union. If only he could have run again, he surely would have defeated Lincoln. He had been compelled to swear he would not, and it was perhaps just as well. His stomach could hardly stand it, and he would be glad to enter a peaceful retirement, a reward for a job well done with the country preserved and its constitutional institutions, such as slavery, still in place. He sent Caleb Cushing as a secret delegate to South Carolina's state convention, but the Massachusetts native was not well received. On December 20th South Carolina seceded and turned its guns toward an island in Charleston Harbor, its fort still manned by federal troops.

Old Buck took to bed. His country had needed him, and needed his skills. Had he failed? No, it was those northern Congressmen and Senators, those Republicans and the abolitionist element, those antislavery females, indeed the North itself. The North acted unconstitutionally in refusing to follow the Fugitive Slave Laws. South Carolina, if left alone, would come back. Now what to do about Fort Sumter?

Old Buck wrote the incoming president,

Washington, in the District of Columbia

December 31, 1860

Mr. Lincoln,

I have done what I, in the spirit of union and as God would will, can. This country needs a national constitution convention, but I fear my call for one will not be heeded.

Will you join me in this resolution? I have of course sent this correspondence with Jeremiah Black, who has the particulars. I know you will extend him all courtesies of my Office.

Very sincerely yours,

James Buchanan, Esq.

President of the United States of America

Jerry Black, now Secretary of State with Lewis Cass's resignation, arrived in Springfield. William Herndon met him at the law offices he shared on the west side of the square facing the state capitol building. Black's report to the President went by special courier to Washington, *I was immediately cast in a world of dilapidated furniture, a small desk sat on an unscrubbed floor, a lounge that looked unfit for repose, and a scattered Collection of hard backed chairs. Some Blackstone, Coke and Kent, but scarcely a library. Mr. Herndon took me in, and bade me sit on one of the wooden seats. I brushed off some dried mud that I can only imagine was the remnants of the booted Lincoln, who remained in absentia.*

Herndon sat to the side of his partner's desk. Had he been behind it, he could not have peered over or through the distorted pile of papers, dust crusting upon them. A piece of script stood atop the bundle, 'When you can't find it anywhere else, look in this.' I would have done so, had Lincoln been entombed in the papyrus, but he was not.

Herndon informed me that the 'President' as he already was calling him, had gone on a vacation to the West, and was traveling by railroad train with a companion to something called the 'Dells.' In any event, he was not there to be met, and I shall return to your Offices as soon as practicable.

Frantic, uncoordinated compromise efforts to avert war flamed up like so many ragtail fires all over the country. In New York, frightened financiers sought to enforce compromises at almost any political price because they stood to lose $150,000,000 in notes to the South. A particularly virulent strain of abolitionists, with representatives from Massachusetts, Ohio and a Congressman from eastern Pennsylvania, was working to scuttle these efforts. Republicans realized they directly benefited from secession of the southern Democrats elected to Congress and the Senate, and their party would therefore control Congress. Many of them thought it was simply good riddance and were prepared to proceed with a smaller, more cohesive country without the southern states and all the problems they created. The future for those southern states that did not secede was one of weakness, certain legislative losses, and emasculation.

In his Annual Message on December 3, 1860, a month after the election of Lincoln, Old Buck commenced in his written submission to Congress, "Since our last meeting the country has been eminently prosperous in all its material interests. The general health has been excellent, our harvests have been abundant," and, continuing with the odd leitmotif of jocularity constructed in his inauguration, went on to say that there were, "plenty of smiles throughout the land."

Old Buck pulled back the curtain. It was the North, not the South, that threatened the Union. The "agitation" of the "public press" and "abolition sermons and lectures" and the time Congress "has been occupied in violent speeches on this never-ending subject," as well as the "intemperate interference of the Northern people" were the cause of the disunion. Not slavery, it was the talking about slavery that was the problem. Yet there was an even greater "impending danger" that he had "long foreseen and often forewarned my countrymen" which itself would cause the South to secede. Thinking of his own dear mother and sisters, Old Buck asserted that Southern women were in "immediate peril" of physical assault by negro slaves who had been inspired by "the incessant and violent agitation of the slavery question throughout the North." They had been given "vague notions of freedom" and therefore, "a sense of security no longer exists around the family altar…Many a matron throughout the South retires at night in dread of what may befall herself and children before the morning. Should this apprehension of domestic danger, whether real or imaginary, extend and intensify itself until it shall pervade the masses of the Southern people, then disunion will become inevitable."

Thad sat in the back row of the gallery as a surrogate read the message into the record. The President was now reduced to defending slavery as the last bulwark to preserve the chastity of southern women. Old Buck had as much as invited war. Thad thought, he could not have asked for more. His hand covered the small grin born of prescience and delight. Lincoln, he thought, Lincoln will not be enough to stop the sure march of history.

South Carolina began its siege of Fort Sumter in December. Virginia explored a compromise at a convention with chaired by former President Tyler. Most southern states declined to participate and nothing came of the sound and fury. Senator John Crittenden of Kentucky proposed an amendment, supported by Old Buck, preserving slavery and permitting its expansion south of the Mason-Dixon Line all the way to the Pacific Ocean.

Lincoln sat silently in Springfield.

Rumors spread that Old Buck was in league with the secessionists, and Senators began muttering about impeachment of the "cowardly old imbecile & traitor." He was publicly compared to Benedict Arnold, the husband of Peggy Shipton, the esteemed belle of Old Buck's early Lancaster days. Horace Greeley of the New York *Tribune*, reacting in part to reports of the Commander-in-Chief wandering White House hallways in alternating fits of loud prayer and louder crying, periodically escaping into anterooms to vomit, ran an editorial that held that the President was, in fact, "insane." Edwin Stanton became Attorney General and was appalled at the fading President's conduct and his paralytic ineptitude in crisis. At one of the many cabinet meetings which now went by without Old Buck in attendance, Stanton mocked, "The President's policy appears to be that 'a state has no right to secede, unless it wishes to, and then the government must save the Union, unless somebody opposes it.'"

State after state did secede. Senator Louis Wigfall of Texas, author of the "Southern Manifesto" urging immediate secession, hatched a scheme to kidnap Old Buck and put Breckenridge in charge of the nation in his stead, delivering the whole country to the South. By the time of the inauguration of his successor, seven of eleven of what became the confederate states were gone, and the others were but a ratification of the vote away.

Lincoln would soon be in place. I was right, Thad thought, just right, in how I played it. Although only New England and spots in New York and Ohio were hotbeds of abolitionism, the movement prevailed. The South was trapped. Ultimate defeat and deserved and condign punishment waited. Let them secede; let them do what they want. Let them go straight to Hell. War is necessary, war is inevitable, and victory will be ours. We will avenge John Brown and set men free. Already, the anonymously authored song was coursing through the north:

> *John Brown's body lies a-mouldering in the grave…*
> *But his soul goes marching on…*
>
> *Glory, glory hallelujah*
> *His soul goes marching on…*

He's gone to be a solider in the army of the Lord…
His soul goes marching on…

John Brown's knapsack is strapped upon his back
His soul goes marching on…

John Brown died that the slaves might be free…
But his soul goes marching on.

The stars above in Heaven now are looking kindly down
On the grave of Old John Brown.

Old Buck believed, as the carriage he shared with the incoming Chief Executive went by the few passersby lining Pennsylvania, he had been caught in a web not of his own making. He felt like a moldering toadstool next to the spidery six foot four inch Honest Abe, his size 14 feet and his attenuated arms and arachnidan fingers. Miss Muffett-like, in a distorted metaphor of the nursery rhyme, he was being scared, or rather thrown, away. Old Buck remarked to Lincoln, thinking he was doing far better than poor Pierce and his naked lust for the nearest saloon, "My dear sir, if you're as happy entering the White House as I shall feel on returning to Wheatland, you are a happy man indeed."

Lincoln countered, "I do not enter this sacred trust with pleasure, but shall do what I can to maintain the high standards set by my illustrious predecessors who have occupied it." The superannuated lawyer riding with him did not fail to note the use of the plural, and its indefinite antecedents.

The President sat to the far side of the portico, the soon to be elevated Hannibal Hamlin and several justices of the Supreme Court blocking his view of Lincoln. It was, in contrast to his own hopeful inauguration day, cold and whipping, the wind scourging his aging pores.

Why did the South say they feared this man? Why had he been used as an excuse to flee the Union? Old Buck listened closely, as did

Thad who took the same post in the crowd's far reaches that he held four years earlier.

Lincoln cited one of his earlier speeches as proof he was not against slavery, "I have no purpose, directly or indirectly, to interfere with the institution of slavery in the States where it exists. I believe I have no lawful right to do so, and I have no inclination to do so."

Where was the Lincoln he had been warned about, thought Old Buck, the man who opposed slavery on moral grounds, who would plunge the nation into war, if necessary, to eradicate the institution?

The Republican platform supports, Lincoln said, that each State had the right "to order and control its own domestic institutions according to its own judgment exclusively." He promised that the federal government would not initiate war against the seven southern states that had seceded, "we denounce the lawless invasion by armed force of the soil of any State or Territory, no matter what pretext, as among the gravest of crimes."

Thad fumed in the back of the crowd. This was hardly the stuff designed to punish the South. This was the stuff of appeasement, the stuff of Buchanan. That platform plank was there for public consumption, not for Lincoln's private digestion and post-election regurgitation. Lincoln reiterated support for the Fugitive Slave Law in what seemed to Thad like an endorsement of not only slaves' hounding, but their whipping and beating. "It is scarcely questioned that this provision was intended by those who made it for the reclaiming of what we call fugitive slaves; and the intention of the lawgiver is the law."

Was Lincoln not going to abide by their convention bargain? Over the strong objections of Giddings, Garrison and Douglass, Thad had not only delivered the abolitionists' support to Lincoln rather than to Salmon Chase, but ordered thousands of counterfeit passes to pack the convention and keep William Seward's supporters out. On the second ballot, at the crucial time, all of Pennsylvania west of Plymouth

Meeting slid into Lincoln's column. With that one act, the public expression of so much that he and Lincoln had agreed would remain private, Lincoln was in. Now, he heard Lincoln conclude, "One section of our country believes slavery is *right* and ought to be extended, while the other believes it is *wrong* and ought not to be extended. This is the only substantial dispute."

Lincoln asserted the constitutional heart of his argument, that a country's "perpetuity is implied, if not expressed, in the fundamental law of all national governments," and the near tautology, "the Union will endure forever, it being impossible to destroy it except by some action not provided for in the instrument itself."

Thad listened, a drop of blood dangled from his lower lip, caught by the edge of his anterior teeth. Lincoln seemed pastured within narrow hand-wringing arguments, munching on the same grass as the current President.

Thad looked at Old Buck, whose white-capped head bobbed like a waterlogged buoy in silent approval. How, Thad wondered, how, if in any way, did any of these positions differ from the soon to be former President's? Had Lincoln decided that he was now invulnerable by virtue of his office? Would he let the southern states slowly slough away wit no reprisals, no war?

Thad recalled last Wednesday's meeting. Lincoln handed him what he had called the "final draft" of the inaugural address. Obviously, someone had gotten to him. Lincoln was supposed to end his remarks by challenging the South. "Shall it be peace or sword?" He was now talking about "the better angels of our nature" whatever the Hell that was.

Both Old Buck and Thad listened as the ancient wisp of Chief Justice Roger Taney's voice curled around the words that swore in the country's new President. Old Buck concluded, "There is no damn difference between Lincoln and me."

Thad was thinking the same thing. He was also resolving that he had to do something about it.

Chapter Twenty-Seven
<u>RECONSTRUCTION</u>

C hristmas Eve. What he was going to do, what he felt he had to do, disgusted him.

Back in March, Old Buck had turned to Jeremiah Black as they watched Pompey pack up the last of the former President's possessions, "I expect I will be the last Commander-in-Chief the whole country ever has."

He had returned to Lancaster on March 10, 1861 in the same elaborately appointed train car that carried his bilious body to Washington four years earlier. When he arrived at Penn Square, the "Old Buck Cannon" boomed, 34 guns saluted, and St. James's bells dropped their raucous notes over Ann's grave. How happy, he thought, to leave Stevens and Lincoln behind him. A welcome at the train station, an exultant carriage ride home, its wheels sowing circles on Orange, Lime past Chestnut, west on Walnut, again north on Mulberry to Lemon and, finally, home. The unused smells of a new spring drifted over the clusters of citizens strewn on the roadways. Plain folk, shopkeepers, veterans of the War of 1812 leaning on rotting hickory sticks and clad in tattered blues dragged from attic trunks, factory workers let loose for the spectacle, all grasped one another in germinating civic congratulation. Ladies, in their finest, spun red and yellow against the sapphire sky. Another short speech from Wheatland's front porch and, as fireworks flew like transcendent seraphim across Marietta Avenue, a good night wave from the upstairs music room.

The next morning, Old Buck read the accounts of his successor's inaugural address. Newspapers were calling it *strong, straightforward, plain, terse, all bone and iron muscle, clear as a mountain brook,* even *manly.* Within days, Lincoln advocated a national constitutional convention. This, Old Buck thought, from someone who had been silent as a puckered radish after Old Buck sent Jerry Black out West to urge that same approach as his presidency painfully passed away. Now, Lincoln was using his well-conceived ideas as if they were his own!

• • •

For Lancaster, the next few months were an extended party. Old Buck sat on Wheatland's lawn or gazed from his study as bands came to serenade. He drank from the deep spring out back, sat before the fire, smoked his Cuban cigars, and sipped his Madeira. He moved Ann's picture from above the mantel in his bedroom to his study. Miss Hetty was kept busy shooing visitors from the front yard. "Mr. Buchanan, I have seen several intrude into the backyard, and one was pawing at the study window, peering between the drapes."

"That will not do. Let them gather across Marietta Avenue. Be alert for those among the rabble whom we know. Have Pompey escort them to me."

. . .

Meanwhile, Thad felt like an unharvested vineyard, his overripe grapes bursting. If Lincoln abandoned Fort Sumter, it would delay, and might avert, war. A constitutional convention might preserve slavery and keep the country intact. He conferred with Wendell Phillips, William Lloyd Garrison and the Senators and Congressmen they controlled. The message needed to be strongly delivered to Lincoln. Thad went to Lincoln, "Mr. President, do not withdraw. It is pure weakness and you will lose our support. Now is the time for firmness, the time to supply the federal troops. If you pull the forces, it is the same as giving into the South, and tantamount to recognizing the Confederacy."

Abe weighed his choices. "Thaddeus, if I reinforce the troops, I am inviting conflict."

Thad said nothing, searching Lincoln's eyes. Had he so misjudged him?

"If there is fighting, it may last for much more than the few months most believe. Nevertheless, at the end of the campaign, the South will just come back on what they might agree to now, preservation of slavery in the South, restrictions on its expansion. I was elected to keep the Union together, not to abolish slavery."

"Mr. President, you do not seem to apprehend the nature of your agreement. You are President. You did not get here without the northern vote. Indeed, had Breckinridge not split the South away from Douglas, we would not be speaking in this office."

Lincoln had done his own analysis, and that was not so. He would have won anyway if Breckinridge had not run, but no matter. No abolitionist had been or ever would be elected President, and he was certainly not going to go down to defeat four years later by adopting their rabid rhetoric now.

"I am not unaware of our bargain. I am President now, and more than my own ambition informs my decisions."

Thad considered the absence of character that statement reflected, how Lincoln was seeking to disavow the conditions precedent to his Presidency. He looked at the magnolias beyond the president's office, at the unfinished Washington monument against the cinereal late winter sky, and at the Potomac, slowly shivering through the last of its serrated ice. He imagined the South's magnolias consumed by crimson, its rivers flushed with sulfur. He was not going to let Lincoln slither down his private passageway to his private library. This was a public matter, and it needed to be resolved.

He decided to appeal to the politics of the situation, "Your party, our party, can control the whole country, the entire Union, if Sumter is attacked. I agree this conflict might be prolonged, and the country could even still be fighting when the next election arises. As a wartime President, and with southern electors on the sidelines, however, your re-election is assured if the war is going reasonably well, and probably even if it is not. The country will not swap horses when crossing the stream."

Lincoln made a mental note of that phrase, and waited for Stevens to conclude. "The war can be blamed on Buchanan and the Democrats. The electoral fruits of the conflict can then be plucked by Republicans."

Stevens was certainly right, thought Lincoln. The abolitionist sometimes seemed to be driven solely by his odd notions on slavery, but his political analysis, despite the shabby summation of last fall's election, was compelling.

Lincoln was also not proud of that part of his spirit that was on the verge of reneging.

"Mr. Stevens, I will re-provision Fort Sumter."

On April 12th, three days before the supplies reached the federal soldiers, and not yet five weeks after Old Buck returned to Wheatland, the star spangled banner was shelled in South Carolina.

In mid-July, at Manassas Junction, Virginia, Washington society, stretched on picnic blankets and sipping good wine, watched what they expected to be a quick and easy victory over what some called "those damned nigger drivers." Instead, General Thomas Jackson stood like a stone wall over the little rill of Bull Run and left 500 northern dead, over a thousand wounded and 1300 missing. There was hell to pay, and hell came to collect at Wheatland.

Lincoln, with clear intent but without using his name, accused Old Buck of a litany of wrongs. "Someone" sent federal muskets and rifles to the South on the eve of the war, transferred monies to southern banks, left funds in southern mints, had the Navy "scattered on distant seas," and used some sort of "quasi-armistice" as the excuse not to reinforce southern forts. Thad ensured that abolitionist papers published that it was Old Buck whose failures and flummery had torpedoed the nation; his quavering inaction had left Lincoln with no other choice but war. Now they were in it, and the war could not be fought in halfway measures. Garrison's *Liberator* wrote that Old Buck was even now sending secret missives, urging foreign governments to recognize the Confederacy, and perhaps ship arms to it. In ordinary times there were multiple newspapers in even the smallest cities. They vigorously competed in an atmosphere of freedom of the press and sanctity of the First Amendment. It was now wartime. With only one mass medium, control of the press was control of public sentiment. A scapegoat for a war far uglier, bloodier and likely longer lasting than anyone had believed was needed. Newspapers that did not regurgitate the administration line were threatened with being shut down completely. The Fourth Estate cratered. The agony of a widening war was soon understood by all to be the mephitic legacy of the Lancaster exile. William Flynn wrote to his boss and mentor, *Fear of Lincoln's and Seward's penitentiary has greatly weakened the power of the pen*, concluding, *Power and patronage have a wonderful and mysterious influence on men.*

Miss Hetty arose before the sun broke and headed to town, banging on newspaper offices to see the early newspaper editions, scanning them all and cutting out the sentences and paragraphs that asserted her master's duplicity or treason. Soon, whole issues were not brought to Wheatland. She was finally confronted. "Mr. Buchanan, I only bring back those that do not echo one another, and many days now some do not publish at all. There are also articles that you need not bother with, they are so wrong-headed."

"Bring them anyway!" He scoured each issue and ordered the Philadelphia, New York and Washington newspapers by expedited post.

Miss Hetty began to make sure she looked on both the front and back doors, on the steps and on the windows before she left mornings. Violent and insulting notes were daily slipped under the back door at Wheatland, and tacked to the front door. Threats of arson kept her wakeful and wary. Finally, she approached Old Buck. "I am thinking, Mr. Buchanan, that we might have some of those Masons stand guard nights here. There are still many who seek to intrude and need to be kept away. I am too busy with other matters and need my sleep. Pompey does not seem able to do this task, as he has taken to sleeping later each morning."

When Katherine Ellis, W's niece, wrote that hordes of *negroes broke into my home and committed outrages in my sight—I was protected by an officer, but others were not.* Old Buck did not have to let his mind wander very far to have a clear and disquieting picture of what those negroes had done, imagining their hard black bodies pressed against the soft white flesh of the daughters of the South. This was just what he had warned the country would occur! Grateful for Katherine's role on her side of the family, as Harriet's on his, in destroying his correspondence with W, Old Buck promised, *I shall meet with you at the War's conclusion.*

The charges might be bricolage but they stuck to Old Buck's ample mortar and he felt immured. He cowered in his study and Pompey peeked in at his old hourly intervals, seeking to assure that Wheatland did not catch on fire from some smoldering cigar. It was often two or three in the morning before he could enter, retrieve his master, take him to bed and finally catch some sleep himself. Old Buck felt like a sand crab surprised by a tide that had never reached so far up the shoreline. Was it Stevens again? He could not prove it. Throughout the summer and into the fall he lay in bed, etiolated and afraid. The anticipated sweet cream of retirement had turned dreadfully sour. He arose only to relieve himself and to troll about in his backyard. His nose's festering tumor, seeking further calcified growth, was clandestinely flayed and emasculated by a team of surgeons, shaved small and inert.

Young Buck, married without his blessing, stayed away with his bride. Harriet was always in Baltimore, or with the Plitts. Only Hetty and Pompey were with him still. He started to write the agonizing defense of his administration, seeking to counter the Republicans', and the country's, principal charges. Old Buck sought $1209 as his cumulative per diem for his earlier English mission. His query to Secretary of State Seward received no reply. He tried to sell the Mercersburg farm in exchange for a cellar full of whiskey, but the price was too dear for the distiller. Jeremiah Black finally purchased the homestead, overpaying out of loyalty. Old Buck kept all the funds as family executor, "for services rendered." Bills for medical care from a decade earlier were received for the first time. Old Buck was furious, and sought to sue the offending doctor for *abusing and vilifying his Commander-in-Chief.*

Hetty would look through the peephole Pompey had fashioned in the study door. The old slave knew enough not to question why she was prone on the floor. Quill in his hand, she watched as Old Buck wrote that any course other than the one he chose would surely have been incendiary, that he was trying for a compromise, or at least a convention. The navy had not only not been scattered, but actually grown in his administration, he had not sent guns anywhere, and he had not thought to transfer monies. His failure to ban southern sympathizers from his cabinet or in government posts or the military had to be viewed in the context of the times, he argued, not in hindsight. Certainly, in 1856, no one foresaw the war, and he had done all any President could to avoid the conflict and the dissolution of the Union. Who could have foreseen this mad rush to war?

Four years earlier, Old Buck left for Washington in triumph. Less than twelve months earlier, he had returned to acclaim. Now, his name was a scourge. He learned that his portrait, ostensibly to protect it from vandalism, was removed from the Capitol rotunda. He read the papers. Now, he must go into town. What were his townspeople really saying about him? He feared he knew, but he had to know.

It was Christmas Eve, 1861, the war eight months old. Old Buck trundled to the attic, this time not to forage for finery but to dig for disguise. He must be bundled, unrecognizable. No mutual dance of delight with W but a dark and furtive walk lay before him. He rummaged, tossing aside what was too delicate, too bright, too revealing. He was distraught at the prospect and somewhat horrified at the result. At the bottom of the leather-girded trunk, Ann's letters, the now shabby bow tightly laced around the gift box. He had let them sit there for decades in cloistered exile, swarmed by clothing bequeathed to him by W or worn by Ann once or twice, the legacy of his closeted life.

Dressed in a flowing dark cape, a scarlet muffler around his face, Old Buck left by his study door on the side, as soon as night fell. He slipped, nearly sprawling, on the ice.

He set out on foot toward the center of the city and made his way down Marietta. Smells of purity and newly formed ice dissolved. There was no longer any element of his own life in town, he considered, his decayed youth irrelevant. He passed Gundaker's, DeMuth's, afraid to enter any establishment. Old Buck did not notice that most of those on the streets were women. Already, many of the men whose faces filtered through his veil were sixty years or more.

The whole town was not of the young and firm but the old and soft. No laughter. Darkness crumpled harder. He passed Race, walked down Columbia, turned on Orange and ended on King. He went near one of his old haunts, but the Leopard had changed its spots and was now a dry goods store. He looked at its shuttered windows and recalled his father's establishment in Mercersburg. I wonder, he thought, if there is a lad who works here that seeks to return people the money they are owed?

In the window someone had placed a "banknote" with Old Buck's simpering caricature, gallows in the background, his eyes red and bleary, a rope around his neck and the word "Judas" slashed in blood across his forehead. This would not do! Old Buck went farther down King, away from Penn Square, toward streets not even on the plat when the town was his. Small wretched houses all in a row. He passed the crushed Grape, and shuffled off to the stoop of what had been the Widow. Few seemed to notice, and none to care. He pressed his eyes against the Widow's leaded glass and saw a young woman at a back table surrounded by old men, their tongues hanging on her words, curling on her syllables, rolling them back into their gullets and swallowing until they became part of their very innards. As if from nowhere, a stranger's hand, perhaps a child's, tossed a Christmas coin. The old York shilling plopped into his dress, sinking in the spread of the billowing cotton sea, spinning obverse reverse obverse into the gray folds between his parted thighs, drowning it. Old Buck looked up, but could not see its source. Had it been that young girl, flouncing away? Muttered words floated by. "Damn that Old Buck, it has surely been his doing. His treason done plunged us into this war. His whole life slurping at the public trough, and now fat and happy in his mansion. My son is someplace God knows where, his life every day in danger."

Old Buck arose from the Widow's steps, shambled into the darkness and went home.

• • •

The next year, in Washington and across the nation, all were aware that the tide of war was flowing against the North. Thad watched for his moment as Lincoln grew more desperate. Despite the ten to one advantage in factory production, the greater superiority in iron, the complete dominance in coal and with three times the farmland and two and a half times more railroads, the North was losing, or at least not winning fast enough. As corpses piled up, and coffers dried up, public support was precarious. Lincoln had not found a winning general, and his army was being stonewalled and leed at every turn.

A hypochondriac and so suicidal that he did not allow himself to carry a penknife, Abe was trying to find any way possible to motivate his country, and his troops. On September 17, 1862, one out of every four soldiers at Antietam, Maryland was wounded or killed, including ten generals. The 12,000 Union casualties had helped stop General Lee's thrust into the Union, and kept the wavering Maryland as part of the country on the eve of Congressional elections. At least a Pyrrhic victory could be claimed despite the bloodiest day in American history and General McClellan's inept leadership.

Thad went to the President, "You must seize this moment. There is another cause, new to the conflict, that will invigorate the nation, and provide us with secret troops in the South, already garrisoned and ready to punish the Rebels."

Lincoln considered his wife Mary Todd and how she spoke of missing the "delightful niggers" from her Kentucky upbringing. He himself had pledged as his inauguration not to disturb slavery where it already existed, and had remained open to its westward expansion. Perhaps, however, Stevens has gotten the winning issue right. God knew, something was needed. Thad pounded him with the notion that Southerners were war criminals. Lincoln did not reveal he had read the Lancaster *Intelligencer*, which wrote, *Nobody doubts that Thaddeus Stevens has always been in favor of negro equality, and here, where his domestic arrangements are so well known, his particular recognition of his pet theory is perfectly well understood... There are few men who have not given to the world such open and notorious evidence of a belief in negro equality as Thaddeus Stevens. A personage, not of his race, a female of dusky hue, daily walks the streets of Lancaster when Mr. Stevens is at home she presided over his house for years. Even by his own party friends, she is constantly spoken of as Mrs. Stevens.*

Believing he knew his advisor's motivations, Lincoln remained uncertain. Was the country ready for him to free any slaves, even if it were only a phantom gesture waved by a wand over those whom he had no jurisdiction? Lincoln considered the thousands of dead and his country's wavering will for war. Finally, Lincoln said, "Mr. Stevens, you and your friends shall have their cause. Threadbare sloganeering and my current generals cannot preserve this Union. The moment has come when slavery must die so that the Union might live. Understand though that only those in the rebelling states are freed, and I will exempt all states loyal to the Union. The North can keep its slaves until, and if, the states themselves decide otherwise."

He caught Thad's eye and raised his hand. "I hope those negroes do what you say they will. We certainly need their help."

Thad realized Lincoln now feared for even his wartime re-election if he could not motivate the troops to at least a few battlefield victories. Thad has already considered how unlikely that word of their "freedom" would even reach the slaves' southern recesses, but it would certainly put the whites on edge. If people like Buchanan really believed that they might rise up, rape the women and bludgeon the children, certainly southern soldiers away from home would be agitated, even scared, with a proclamation that their property was emancipated, despite the fact that it had no legal force or effect. At least, the slaves might look on this as cause to flee to a more welcoming North and leave the plantations' crops rotting in the fields. Thad's own harvest had never seemed closer.

Lincoln proclaimed, without any authority to impose the edict on what was now a sovereign and foreign country, the emancipation of all slaves in the South, effective that following New Year's Day. Slaves were still owned in parts of the North, although a majority in Congress, its southern members gone, had finally abolished slavery in the nation's capital nearly two years into the war.

Lancaster received its only real scare of the war as Confederate troops, trudging toward Gettysburg, came within 10 miles of Wheatland as Old Buck fled to Philadelphia. He later learned that the troops did not lay siege to Lancaster only because they could not cross the demolished Wrightsville Bridge over the Susquehanna, the same one under whose trusses he had sat as he watched that legless trio issue into the night. How long ago that was, and how small his troubles were then.

He had not enjoyed the trip to Philadelphia. He was now sagging and soft, and the search for relief in alleyways and bathhouses had lost much of its appeal. He was delighted to learn upon his return that the Confederate General Jubal Early had diverted some of his troops for the express purpose of burning down Congressman Stevens's Caledonia iron works, but quickly discounted Pompey's retelling of his own sweaty fears as the smoke of the destruction drifted heavily into Lancaster.

On November 23, 1863, after nearly two years in Wheatland's penitentiary confines, shooting out mostly unanswered missives to friends and enemies, Old Buck strayed away from his homestead for the first time since his foray into Lancaster and set out with Pompey for Gettysburg. At least, he could view Lincoln's failure, his feeble excuses for a futile war. The freshness of the bodies disturbed him. Worse, the feeling of intellectual superiority he had finally clasped at the afternoon's end was stolen by Thaddeus Stevens. The tramping jackboots of history overwhelmed him. The smells of the day pierced the carriage on the way home. It was as if he could see bits of deserters' blood falling in a sanguinary mist against the snow torn by the carriage wheels as he fled back home. The taut brevity of Lincoln's speech, in the estimation of so many of the papers he eagerly ordered Miss Hetty to procure, seemed actually to enhance it. No wonder he had not set out again.

The Lancaster *Examiner and Herald* intoned later that fall that Buchanan's conduct was treasonable. It editorialized that *manifestation of the popular indignation against the man who might, had he the will or the pluck, have nipped the rebellion in the bud, as Jackson did before him* was amply justified. It all hurt, but the comparison to Jackson wounded Old Buck most deeply.

• • •

In Washington, faced with Lincoln's April death and the ascension of the Tennessee tailor Andrew Johnson, Thad confronted the painful proof of his own mortality. He authored bill after punishing bill. There would be, Thad proclaimed, "plagues on the nation" for the "oppression of a harmless race of men inflicted without cause and without excuse for ages." He recited his mantra at every turn: "Hang the leaders, crush the South, arm the Negroes, confiscate the land." William Lloyd Garrison echoed those sentiments, writing in the

Emancipator, Hail ye ransomed millions, no more to be chained, scourged, mutilated, bought and sold in the market, robbed of all rights, hunted as partridges upon the mountain. Thad's legislation included a loyalty oath as a condition for return to the Union; the striking of compensation for the taking of slaves; what became the 13th Amendment to the United States Constitution freeing all slaves; the powerful 14th Amendment which guaranteed all citizens, black or white, equal protection under the law; and the 15th, which granted all free men, black or white, the right to vote. "I did not hesitate, in the midst of bowie knives and revolvers and howling demons upon the other side of the House, to stand here and denounce this infamous institution. I claimed the right then, as I claim it now, to denounce it everywhere."

President Johnson, many others in the Republican Party and almost all Democrats, nevertheless sought to provide financial compensation for the taking of slaves, and most opposed permitting former slaves to vote. Johnson summed up his views on black suffrage by asserting that, "negroes possessed less capacity for self-government than any other people. Wherever they have been left to their own devices they have shown the constant tendency to relapse into barbarism." Johnson issued pardons to all Confederate leaders, a good many of whom promptly returned to Congress in a series of specially-called elections. Thad foresaw his Reconstruction efforts slipping away. When the new Congressmen showed up in December, Stevens conspired with the clerk of the House, Edward McPherson, not to call their names in the roll. Thad moved to "consider them for membership." The motion was passed, tabled and never revisited. The southern legislators were, for the time, unable to reenter the Congressional chambers.

Seeking a way to punish the Tennessean for his attempted scuttling of northern spoils and Negro rights, Thad found his lynchpin in the President's eviction of Secretary of War Edwin Stanton in violation of a hastily adopted piece of legislation called the "Tenure of Office Act" requiring congressional approval to remove Lincoln's former lieutenants. Thad knew the law was likely an unconstitutional abridgement of the separation of powers, but strongly backed the bill. Here was a way to get rid of Johnson and all who stood with him.

Thad soon took on almost mythic proportions, a modern Colossus bestriding the roads of Washington, the leader of not only the Reconstruction effort, but the Manager of the team seeking Johnson's impeachment. The decision on how to treat the defeated southern states was not for the executive branch nor the judicial, Thad's words fairly strutting, "the government and final disposition of the conquered country belongs to Congress alone. The whole fabric of southern society must be changed, and never can this be done if this opportunity is lost."

On March 23, 1868, so ill that he had to be carried into the house chambers, the 76 year old began his valedictory trial of the detested seventeenth President.. Thad argued English and American law. He quoted Latin, and railed against repression. The House and the country were galvanized. The impeachment resolution passed overwhelmingly, 126 votes to 47.

Thad went to the Senate. Reduced by illness to a post as one of the seven managers, no one doubted where the power and fury resided. On March 4th, eleven years to the day since Old Buck ascended to the presidency, proceedings commenced. Chief Justice Salmon P. Chase, Lincoln's Treasury secretary and a Radical Republican himself, presided. The proceedings dragged into April. Thad at first stood with the support of the Secretary's desk near the Senate president's rostrum. He then had to seek permission to continue, quite literally, from the floor. Senate pages sat at his feet as he hunched up from the carpet, his back resting against the rostrum. The whole Senate gallery, and all Senators, rose, not only to see and hear him but out of respect. His voice emerged, strained perhaps, but pure and clear. "To me this seems a sublime spectacle. A nation not free, but as nearly approaching it as human institutions will permit has sought to punish the treason of the South."

Of the fifty-four Senators, 36 were necessary to impeach. Any more than 18 in opposition and Johnson stayed in office. After seven weeks of trial, the roll was called. Thirty five voted to convict; Johnson remained in office by virtue of a single ignoble vote.

Thad withdrew, in physical and psychic pain. As Death approached his doorway, he headed to Lancaster for the last act that his life compelled.

Chapter Twenty-Eight
<u>R E D E M P T I O N</u>

O n the third Saturday of the fourth month in 1868, Thad's journey to Lancaster in spring's still coldness would be, he knew, his last. Hoarfrost dug its early morning teeth into the sleeping grass. Robins pecked at scrabbled earth. Red maples' golden boughs fought to flower. The cold, the growth, the rebirth went unnoticed. After he accomplished what was necessary, he would return to pursue, until his body gave out, the nation's Reconstruction effort. Thad was old, aching, gaunt, and ghastly. He was well past any vanity and wrote a friend, "It is not my appearance, but my disappearance, that troubles me."

No longer able to ride his horse, he had to rent a carriage for the pilgrimage. Its seats, torn leather and crushed velvet, provided little comfort. The tumble of the trip bruised his bones. His club foot, now fully captured by arthritis, exploded pain up his leg and into his groin. As he sat in the carriage for the 100 miles or so up from Washington, skirting Baltimore, Thad had the impulse to ask the driver to head a bit east, and jog over to Bel Air. One last time, he wanted to see the house where he pounded Madeira, played fiploo, and passed the bar, to revisit a time when life seemed limitless. The Federalist edifice was sagging and paintless, surrounded by a spotted sea of sooted snow. Defeated blooms and angry seeds swarmed in frozen islands ambushed by winter's last gasps. The spent orchard out back grappled its sterile arms around last fall's frigid plunder. The realization came dark and strong that General Winder, Hopper Nicholson, Theodoric Bland, and Zebulon Hollingsworth were long in the deep hard ground, and he felt like a voyager to prelapsarian times.

From Bel Air, the driver crossed the same bridge on which Thad almost perished. It was now sturdy and long established. As they clumped north to Lancaster, Thad reflected on his years in courts and Congress. Couldn't soldier, couldn't run, couldn't jump, couldn't play. Now, can't even ride. Immobile except for the painful carting of this useless limb.

Words. His weapons and his refuge. Words. Strong words. Hard words. Clever words. Words and words. Words upon words. Words against words. Squabbly, wobbly words rising into the rafters, competing in the air, dancing into the ceiling, drifting out the door, sneaking through the cracks and crevices of court and Capitol. Had they been, would they be, enough?

Thad approached the city that so intimidated him nearly 50 years past, and directed the driver north on Queen, west on King, north on what would soon be called President Avenue, and west on Marietta. The carriage rattled up the streets of the town that seemed so divorced from Danville and Caledonia Notch, but where he had chosen to live his life. There, in front of him, was Wheatland and the occupant with whom he had not, for but one time in twenty years, spoken.

He wrenched his leg toward the small porch in front and thought he saw late spring snow gathering toward the Susquehanna. The unmistakable notes of the German's little Bagatelle in A minor, *Für Elise*, wandered from the upstairs window. Thad knew that must be Harriet, back on a visit to her uncle. Perhaps the upstairs curtains stirred as he approached; he was not quite sure. Thad kicked off the traveling mud on the front sill. The piano kept playing. Hetty must have been off in town as it was Pompey who came to the door. "Mr. Pompey," Thad began, not knowing if the former slave had a last name, "I am here to see Buchanan."

Pompey recognized the Great Commoner and let him cross the threshold. He bade him wait in the room to the right, and went to the study, knocked tentatively and, in a few minutes, returned. "Mr. Buchanan will see you now."

Thad struggled toward his object, hauling his bad leg over the patterns of dancing snowflakes pressed into the hallway. His rebellious pain did not drown the imagined echoes of Ann's little voice imploring her father, while snow swallowed Christmas Eve, to let her stay in town just a bit longer.

In the study, the ragged remnant of the 15th President rose from behind his mahogany desk. Thad looked at him, at his burnt and decaying pastiness, at his imploding body carved and scarred as if furrowed by the deep hard Coleman-fired iron of a hundred Amish plows, and thought about the great leveling effect of age on all men.

"What, as God is my witness, is your purpose in coming here?" Old Buck demanded.

Thad fixed hard on the dying heap of a President. These bones had certainly dominated much of his thinking as, he expected, he had invaded the waking and sleeping concerns of the Old Buck before him.

"I have come, Buchanan, to explain a few things, and to set some things aright."

No response.

"I think, at times, you have been greatly afraid of me?"

A nod, in grudging assent.

"At other times, perhaps until our meeting now over a decade past, of the false belief that I had nothing which could do you harm?"

Old Buck nodded again, recalling his now vanished times of uncertainty before Thaddeus Stevens's February visit right before the Inauguration. Even then, no certain proof, but enough fear to lead to his peculiar declaration.

"I have come here to share the letter."

Those words, half of Old Buck longed to hear, if only to answer the mystery. More than half of him feared this moment. At the end of this tumult, he believed he had achieved some measure of equanimity.

Old Buck was therefore surprised at his antistrophe, by its vehemence and by its strength, and the voice that sputtered, "Out with it man, damn it!"

"Not so fast. First, I need to provide some predicate for the information."

My God, Old Buck thought, he sounds like me.

"I was disgusted at your effrontery, Ann's fair body not a year in the grave, and you running for Congress. I had a mind to halt your efforts then, but had obligations to my client and her father and let your little dance play to what I thought would be its certain tuneless demise. Of course, you continued on, and by the time of Mr. Coleman's death in 1825, I well knew how you might be useful."

What did that mean? Of course, Thad had that letter before he even ran for Congress, obviously he had it all along. He had not used it then, and what was meant by "you might be useful?" Useful to whom? Old Buck countered, "Yet I was victorious in my Congressional race, well before I had any knowledge of you, let alone that unseen letter. I did that all on my own. It was my quest, and my success."

"Hardly, sir! Were it not for Mr. Coleman's early deal with you that propelled you to the Assembly you would not have even been in the game."

Stevens was right, even on this, Old Buck realized. Perhaps he might have sought that modest office at some point, but only if it aided his only desire at that time, a substantial law practice, some real estate ventures, and a fine home. Why had he not settled for that? It was true that Coleman had arranged all that for him, but that was, he was certain, as far as either expected it to go.

Thad continued, "Consider your decision to run for United States Senator. I had been in the Assembly for but a few weeks when your candidacy was proposed. Although that was your next logical step, the antipathy of the members against you was so intense that I could not convince any to vote for you. I took some pleasure in the ignominy of your defeat. I am sure you recall, you were booted out with but five votes. More delightful is the memory of the way your crest fell as you spied me and scampered out the hall. In many ways, I should have been content, perhaps, to let that be the end of your political forays, but your potential usefulness could not go unplumbed."

That word again, "usefulness." Old Buck countered," What of that next year? I won, on my own and despite your opposition."

"Hardly so, sir. There was, in fact, a great deal of work to be done. With the resignation of Senator Wilkins to go to your beloved Russia, an appointment that must have seemed to you mere fortuity, I knew you would be back at the trough. It was not easy feeding, but I was able to turn sentiment around and dispatch you to Washington. Did you fail to notice that many of your votes came from my side of the aisle, and that members of your own party supported, to the very end, your opponents?"

Old Buck considered the names in the black book, his list of enemies. Thad was right.

"So my running for the Assembly a month before your consideration," Thad continued, "and the reasons for your subsequent victory, are now clear?"

Old Buck nodded, but still did not comprehend this errant knight's early moves on his life's chessboard. It was clear, he thought, clear he had won, but how was all this managed, how monitored?

Thad was on his own flight. "There was some potential delight in clipping your wings at the outset, but knowing I could always shoot you down in mid-ascent made my pleasure often sweeter. I had the letter, and I could use it whenever I needed. In its hovering unknown presence, there was power. Although it grinded at me to see you enjoy what you perceived as your own success, your useful fear after the York bluff made all a little easier to tolerate, knowing I could swoop down on you at will."

"What," Old Buck stammered, "what of your move to Lancaster?"

"I had to consolidate my power, and my own prospects. Gettysburg served its place. Through my offices and my calculated withholding of what would have scuttled you at any point, your career was well begun. You were not returning to the Assembly's devices. I could not resist taking your own seat to the Capitol," Thad said as he recalled Old Buck's similar but surely more ignoble grasping at the Coleman mansion, "and there assure the next steps."

Old Buck looked at Thad, and away as Stevens continued, "Do you not recall the abrupt decision by George Dallas to drop out of the running in 1848? Though it was still too soon, it had been the thought of some others of us that 1848 was not too early. I did not agree, and needed to maintain control and therefore was off to Washington with the idea that the next election would be your time. You of course were busy burnishing your little career as the result of your friend's agreement with Jackson, but you did little harm as Polk was wiser and my presence in Congress made it easy to oversee your time at State. It was King who kept you going. I had all I needed in a pouch within my pocket, but scarcely had to use it. How painful it must have been for you," Thad nearly smiled, "to know I was in the Capitol corridors having taken your very seat. I expect you must have made all efforts not to waddle across my path on your way back to your little F Street nest!"

Old Buck cupped his forehead in his right hand, the heel of his palm working the ridge above his eye in small circles, his little finger mimicking the movements over his left eye. He had, he thought, as his pupils were pressed with pain, not been able to see near, nor far.

"There were, by the way, others we could have used, though with different mechanisms, but you proved the most enduringly useful when one considered that it was only the ultimate goal that mattered. That next election did not go as I had thought, and I must admit feeling a bit outfoxed by the Pierce maneuver, which in light of your overweening ambition was a bit unanticipated, but it was still, as events proved, too early.

"It would perhaps been good," Thad added as he watched the soft splotches of white now harvested by Old Buck's other hand, "had it happened sooner. Many were concerned as you failed from time to time despite our efforts to advance you. Yet we had no organized apparatus to accomplish our aims until 1856. Some others among us were content with Pierce's stumbling around, if he could have been re-elected, which I doubted. In any event, Pierce's Yankee heritage, his more expansive view of the Constitution, even the uncertainty of his wife's mind, made him open to other influences and others' control. Only with you could we be certain of hand-wringing inaction. More importantly, there was no trump card with Pierce as I held with you, and his mere drunken ineptitude was not sufficiently reliable for our aims."

What were these aims and goals they were talking about? Who was "we?" Old Buck was struggling to comprehend the swirl of words and images. Why was his "inaction" more important than someone else's action? "How, and why, did you not simply assure Frémont's election from your own party in 1856?"

"That, sir, should be obvious. The Whigs self-destructed in the previous election, paving the way for our Republican party. We made no effort, however, even to place our sham upstart of a nominee on the ballot in twelve states. With those electoral votes already in your pocket, how could you lose? Frémont was a wild unnecessary ride with no certain destination. With you, the end was clear."

Old Buck's chin twisted upward and the channels carving his neck ached to burst. What end? What had he done?

Thad reflected on what would, he thought, be obvious to anyone not quite as dense as Buchanan. While some among them thought it simply good riddance to the South, others were determined to place the nation in a position to punish the southern generals and politicians, the slave owners and all their myrmidons. They needed Buchanan, or someone like him, to ascend to the presidency to ensure the paralysis of the executive branch, a weak-willed response that permitted southern states to depart without early force being used to permit them to return them to the fold with their slaveholding intact. Many, like Greeley and Garrison, might have stopped there. Thad knew that only once those states fled and reconstituted, could war, born of that attrition, be spawned. Damn those compromises. 1820. 1850. Only delaying the inevitable. Only with war, terrible cleansing necessary war, could there be the retribution and ultimate redemption the Radical Republicans sought. He let loose the unshared truth, "You old fool, we were just using you to exacerbate the contradictions that already existed, and to accelerate the inevitable. You were our means to an end, and that end was war."

"War? I was opposed to war!"

"You, sir, you made it possible."

"I do not believe it. I did all I could to stop it. It was only under Lincoln there was war, not me!"

Thad's thumb and forefinger went to the bridge of his nose and his left elbow sought the arm of the deep leather chair across from

Old Buck's desk. His breath traveled in an exasperated burst down the interior of his forearm.

"Mr. Stevens, if you did all you say you did, exactly how did you make me President? How is that even possible?

Thad's shoulders went to the barnacled brass nail heads lining the back of the chair. He stared as Old Buck. "It should be obvious, one would think. It was simply a matter of a few well-placed puffs and some closed-door leaning on editors. There is only one medium in this country and we were direct with its message. We explained the plan, careful not to share our goal with those whose uncertain allegiance might let the wind blow all the way to California. There were already plenty of others whose stomachs could not abide the pitiful Democrats seemingly arrayed against you. With a Republican camarilla and your own party in disarray after four piercingly bad years, we were able to orchestrate a triumphal return from England for you, on what in all justice should have been the fare-thee-well of your career. Hardly anyone even noticed you had gone, and all the sudden you return from a foreign nation to all manner of ceremony? The rest fairly flowed. The elevation of the straw man Frémont as the Republican Party's first standard-bearer was easy to arrange and ensured your victory. Anyway, it is now of no moment."

No moment? No moment? The skin cracked around his eyes as they stretched toward his forehead. It is only all he ever thought he wanted, his life's one true goal, and now to find that none of it, none of it, was truly his.

Thad misapprehended. Was it not yet clear? "Mr. Buchanan, did you not consider it a bit unusual that you, having taken French leave from the country less than three years prior, returned from abroad, having accomplished nothing, as if a conquering hero?"

Old Buck's head was attacked by a jumble of concerns. He had to acknowledge to himself that he had not understood it, had not grasped why a country that had no use of him in the three prior elections suddenly conceived, in his absence, a veritable oratorio of adulation. Why had he been rejected before? Polk had come from nowhere in 1844, the nation's first dark horse, as Jackson and W had agreed, so that Old Buck could advance without standing again for office. He had been motivated by fear. What had been W's motivations? Had he known of Stevens? Had he just sensed his fear of going before the Assembly again? What of the maneuverings in '52 and the decision, his alone and his gift to W (he thought at the time) of the Vice Presidency. His own subsequent hopes gone as age and W's death prepared him for nothing more than the uncertain leisure of retirement, contemplated from the vantage of England. Far better, far better than this exile! In 1856, to the surprise of all, he emerged as the nominee with Pierce the victim, the only time in history a sitting president was ever denied his party's nomination. While sitting at home creating little rondos of letters and sipping Sherry, he was played into office. Why?

"You were," Thad went on, "the chosen one, the man I was able to convince the others best assured the election of a Republican in 1860, the necessary predicate for our goals. Some had wanted a more rabid abolitionist, say Salmon Chase or William Seward who had spoken of the upcoming 'irrepressible conflict,' but those candidates faded after the first ballot. I was damn sure he did not want that crook Simon Cameron as Chief Executive. Although Lincoln appeared to be a third ballot compromise, he had been my choice all along despite his weak words on slavery. Simple pragmatics. He was the most electable candidate. You do not find it a coincidence, I hope, that I orchestrated the selection of the far western city of Chicago for the Republican convention, as an additional fillip to ensure the Illinois lawyer's nomination despite his recent electoral defeats?"

Understanding began to rise as if it were the sun dawning through the mist. It was not the placing of him in office, it was the sure prediction of his presidency's result, that had mattered to his adversary. Old Buck's own goal, the one he had sworn with his circling bleeding palm on the top of his oaken desk, had transmogrified into his enemy's plan. His own symphony of ambitions, his own clever craftings, his own posturing as he sought the first chair, was what Thad and his cronies wanted all along. Only a few nudges were necessary, and he had wrung and slithered in political and personal fear of exposure all this time, feeling now like a mole that had burrowed in some prairie's buried labyrinth, emerging blinded and uncertain. He was, *nolens volens*, bequeathed the presidency by a cabal of abolitionists, and only because he so vigorously opposed them!

"Only a few times did I simply want to say to Hell with the consequences, and to expose you and what you did to Ann, no matter where it placed our goals. The latest, of course, was in August, right before the election. It was already too late but as bad as your circumlocutions and twaddle were throughout your public and private life, your damn and obvious lies to that magazine boiled my blood. That lying liquid pouring forth, drowning the truth. 'In her dead hand the little keepsake of your love.' I hope, sir, you are now finally ashamed of the ways you used that girl!"

Old Buck, spider veins engorging in radiated array across his nose and down his cheeks, recalled the spun web of a story he told that made its way to *Harper's* right before the election, the conscious transposition of people, places and events, the outright prevarications he thought so clever and so beyond discovery with all other participants decades dead.

He had not thought of Ann, except every day, since his return to Wheatland and now looked again at her portrait staring down at him. Before his church and his God, he was convicted of his still unknown role in her death. Most especially, his manipulation of the event for his own purposes finally emerged from deep patterns of denial to trouble a conscience whose chief attribute was its disuse. How he had debased the poor girl's memory, how cavalier in the ways he employed his tales. Only now, for the first time, did he appreciate how detestable and disgusting his post mortem conduct would have been to a young woman of her background, station, and sensibilities. It was one thing to use the tale to keep other women at bay, but trading on it to win the nation's highest office left him with a raw sense of shame and a dry draught of mortification, admittedly made the more so by the paltry prize the presidency proved to be.

Old Buck wept.

Slowly, but palpably, another presence seemed to hover in the room.

Thad looked at the blubbering pile in front of him, and began to consider the farrago of his own life. The secrecy, the posturing, the posing, the deceit. He was angry, and should be, and yet…there was a growing sense of pity, no, better yet, compassion. Nonetheless, he unfurled, slowly and tantalizingly, the faded epistle, carved in a young girl's hand nearly a half century earlier, all the time thinking, or perhaps saying in a voice that sailed above the pounding music into the empyrean, he did not know, "Damn your soul, old man. Damn it to Hell."

Old Buck began to tremble.

Thad read:

My dear Mr. Stevens,

I fain know where to begin as I sit here preparing to breathe my last.

You are now fair and well and forever my lawyer? I beg you do not reveal to any while my father and dear mother live what I here disclose, and then only after if needed, and only even then to protect the fortunes of any young girl as may seem to cross the path headed toward matrimony with James Buchanan, Esq., of Lancaster.

Old Buck, as he heard the words that echoed her speech of five decades' past, mewled bitterly. Thoughts, defensive and uncomprehending, played through. *What caused her to write this, and indict me? What had I done? I may have neglected her, been untrue to her in his saloon ramblings, but I was never with another woman. I may have wanted her fortune, and not her love, but why had this led to her death? Surely, surely, she could not have known…*

Thad continued with the words, exhumed from a half century of dormancy, re-imbued with power, made brand new as they were spoken for the very first time,

You may, sir, know of him. He is a lawyer here, well known to my father, and until barely a day ago, engaged to me.

My very pen shudders as I relate to you what I saw on yesterday's eve, the 8th of December, in this year of Our Lord.

Old Buck became his mother's Jamie again, drawn to the tale. He was twittering, his whimpering body moving in a spasmodic rhythm.

Thad continued,

I thought well to surprise my Intended (my heart does claw at me even as I set that word to paper) upon his return from what I thought to be some triumph of the law.

He had indeed come back to town, I learned, but not sought me, rather adjourning to his office.

It being but across the street, above the Widow's Tavern, I thought perhaps to make an appearance there and excite the senses of Mr. Buchanan (who, withal, to that time seemed to me too much of a man not given to what is beyond the prescripted realm).

As I relate the next, I can feel the slow creep of God across my skin and deeply reconfirm that I cannot return, with shame and anger, to my family or my town.

I made slowly my way up the stairs of the Widow, careful despite the covering noise of the tavern not to creak the steps as I, eager to see anew my Betrothed, thought I would fling open his door, and he, looking up from his heavy old law books to see me, would reveal his deep delight. Yet I could only crack it, as it was unlocked but chained.

There, Mr. Stevens is what I saw, if I can proceed.

The pen seemed to pause at this point, and a large black blot punctuated the end of the sentence.

Thad read what must have been, he knew, not only for the abnormality of the act, and Old Buck's participation, but also due to the nature of the relationship of the actors, most horrific for Ann and, fairly said, most disgusting,

Mr. Buchanan had his trousers dropped and, like a hairless white eagle spread, was as if staked to the floor. Upon him was his dark slave Pompey, and Mr. Buchanan thereon inverted, as their heads, black and white, bobbed to and fro upon each other.

Mr. Stevens, I do not need to tell you, sir, how diabolic was this sight, and how unnatural to me. You can imagine, sir, the picture and my feelings and I pray you, sir, well understand the act I now make as the only one left to me. Forgive me, blessed sir, my implication of your professional and personal offices, and my great need to reveal this to you, as I do not myself comprehend it, even as I return to my good Maker.

I remain (but not for long),

Sincerely,

Ann Coleman

Old Buck was now prostrate on the pink-trumpeted rug. He rolled and twisted, clutching his hands to his ears. Thad heard the scuffle of echoing motions outside the study door, muffled by even more aggressive playing from above, but clear nonetheless. "Pompey," Thad spoke firmly, "come in."

The slave, his ancient eye to the augured pinhole, shambled in. "You, sir," said Thad, addressing Pompey with a formality previously unknown in the course of his 75 years, "I know you have heard this as well."

Pompey joined the general ululation. It was a good thing, if anyone thought of it, that Miss Hetty was out. Thad looked down in contempt. Harriet's now stentorian playing had switched from Beethoven to Brahms and the powerful notes of *Ein Deutsches Requiem*, "siemlich langsam und mit Ausdruck" flooded Wheatland.

Against his own will, as he looked down on the pitiable sight of the duet writhing on the floor, black and white, unintentionally echoing the portrait Ann so graphically described, Thad's mind went elsewhere, back in time to Caledonia Notch. His thoughts drifted to Sarah, his mother, bereft of husband and funds, on the edge of the White Mountains, scrubbing floors to raise her boys, two deformed, all by herself only to see her favored one flee Vermont and seek the destiny that now confronted him. Small waves at first, but then great, crushing, overwhelming tidal bores of insight and regret compassed him. My God, how hard for her, and how hard for all women! My mother was every bit as bright, every bit as hardworking as I have ever been, and she could never expect to do anything except clean privies, wash the kettles of others, and empty their filthy chamber pots. It was not only, Thad realized, the black man who was kept down, it is women like my mother and dear Lydia, restrained at least as much by her sex as her color.

He felt the creeping pain of failure, the awareness of his own discrimination, as he realized that the female suffragists were right. They had not been slaves, but they had been enslaved. They had every right to own property, to divorce, to work, to vote, even to hold office. Maybe, someday, that would be so. What of people like Old Buck, whose sexuality dominated his entire existence, never knowing who might condemn, and who might respond, risking criminal sanction and career-ending exposure. He had contributed directly to that. This bag of a man, who in human terms accomplished so much, was never able publicly to love, never able to disclose his affinity, never able to be wholly who he was. The great champion of black men felt that he had been far too meager, far too myopic, in his approach and efforts. And then, quite suddenly, he felt the sharp dagger of own culpability in using and manipulating Ann's memory. It had been for a greater good, but it still twisted in him that he had done so.

Old Buck turned to Thad. From his supine position, he looked up the fearsome mountain in front of him, "Why, sir, why, sir, why did you wait so long?" he implored.

Thad started his reply, as if by rote, "the fulfillment of the abolitionists' dreams and goals…" He blurted, "Damn it, I am ashamed but I enjoyed the power of the knowledge, enjoyed your squirming. More than that, and bluntly, I was disgusted by you and your conduct, not only by the denial of rights to black men, but your wifely ways and the prissy path of your prinking southern King. Followed by your pretense and falsity and story after story, excuse after excuse. The way you let those women think you actually might marry them. By God, you milksop, at least you could have been a man!"

With those words, more than that, the way they were formed and spoken, the hectoring fulmination, the peculiar look on Thad's beaten face, Old Buck was thunderstruck. It was more than politics, and it was rooted in Thad's being. His soul had opened and swallowed his very essence. Old Buck looked back, wrinkles radiating from the squinting white-rimmed turnips of his eyes. Startled but direct, his eyes conveyed to Thad that Old Buck now knew. Thad's secret expired, twisting its death agony in the study's dust. Perhaps for that reason as much as any other, Thad had not revealed the letter's contents. True, there were the legal bonds, the political goals, but the major chord was the personal restraint that played through his veins more strongly. Thad loathed the way Old Buck conducted himself in his public life, loathed his softness, loathed everything about the ossified voluptuary before him. He himself fought, fought hard, fought very hard, the desires he too shared, but had not, had not, save for short rare bursts that filled him with post-coital loathing, given in. He had not, damn it, had not had not had not given in. Now, envy stalked his soul. Before him, this dubious mark of a man, this puffy doughface, this fetid gimcrack, he had known it, he had known it. He had known what Thad had never known. He had known love.

Just like me, Old Buck realized, just like me. The man he feared, the traducer with the trump card of his life always buried in his paw. Thad's own delusive life and affairs finally made sense. Whether scored from birth or simply following life's notations, the bars and clefs had been the same. Strong and loving mothers doted on each. For Elizabeth and Sarah both, their smart and good son was the universe's center. In Old Buck's case, a father whom he could never please, who abused his wife and her favored little boy. For Thad, a father who fled when he was five. Alone, apart and wandering as children. Each took in the offspring of siblings. Neither could bring himself to join a church, until Old Buck, weary and finally regenerate, or perhaps just fearful of damnation, had done so as his life dwindled to the end, Thad feeling pulled toward his Mother's God but despising how he was used, in the hands of men, to foster evil. Both Thad and Old Buck, activating some vague uneasiness and dislike in classmates and faculty alike, were denied academic honors at their respective colleges, despite achievements that merited that distinction. Each expelled for reasons that are steeped in mystery, just as W had to flee his native North Carolina, where he already held high public office, for Alabama to start anew. Each never married, at a time when nearly all men, and certainly all those who enjoyed the opposite sex (and many who did not) and could afford to, married. There was the total immersion in public life, as if that were an excuse to have no family. Why, there had never been a president without a wife, and nearly all Senators and Congressmen were married. Not that it necessarily had anything to do with it, but Old Buck hereditarily hairless except for the top of his head, Thad ultimately glabrous from disease. Old Buck had to come up with sham after sham, fable followed by myth. Old Buck reflected that it was so much easier to believe it about him than Thad, that Thad's constructed box was more fortified, and his gruffness, his well-burled wrestler's physique more of a barrier than Old Buck's public eagerness to please and his private fears. Even W's flamboyant dress served to insulate him in its very obviousness. His own formal attire never seemed to protect quite as well. What a flourish for Thad to have Lydia Smith move in to his home! Why, that was sheer, wild, diverting, stunning genius. Speculation about his relationship with a black woman, such tasty food in the simmering sauce of scandal, extracting all possible steam from any other stream of thought.

As he was thinking this, Thad, a squall rising in his own eyes, leaned over and, while he could not bring himself to kiss Old Buck but on the fading few tufts that still dotted his head, held first him, and then Pompey, long and tight in his arms.

The three men now looked at one another, in some peculiar way almost equals. Each experienced separate regrets and each knew the bond that linked them. Without a further word, right hands were extended. First, on the bottom, Pompey's gnarled gray fingers. Old Buck's soft palm embraced Pompey's and, capping them both, Thad's dark and fearsome hand.

Thad left by the open front door. Harriet switched to the hymn conceived by the redeemed slave trader and published as part of the Olney Hymns by John Newton, its author, and his friend William Cowper. The strains of *"Amazing Grace"* floated down the walk. Thad dragged his leg to the waiting carriage. He would return to the arena. It had not been snowing after all.

In the wink of three fortnights, his kidneys gone, Old Buck lay deposited on his dank and chattering deathbed. His last words, thrown into the fading light in a faltering voice doused with the unstaunched drench of tears, were perhaps as much for the American public as for W, "I am grateful to have once been loved."

At his internment at Woodward Hill following his June 1st death, attended by a few score Lancastrians culled from the several thousand who thronged the streets, Old Buck's rise from a log cabin in Stony Batter was compared, without any apparent sense of irony, to Lincoln's. His burial plot was by charter available only for the "burial of deceased white persons." A Masonic seal is embedded in the ground next to the grand granite stone, on which there are engraved the dates of birth and death, and a notation that the body below was once the Fifteenth President of the United States.

Thad soon followed, dying the same summer on the midnight of August 11th. At the end, he was attended by two black pastors, one of whom told him, "Mr. Stevens, you have the prayers of all the colored people in the country." The men of God sang a spiritual, with Thad's consent, its canorous words unfamiliar to his northern ears:

O, blow your trumpet, Gabriel,
Blow your trumpet louder;
And I want dat trumpet to blow me home
To my new Jerusalem.

De prettiest ting dat ever I done
Was to serve de Lord when I was young.
So blow your trumpet, Gabriel,
Blow your trumpet louder.

O, Satan is a liar, and he conjure too,
And if you don't mind, he'll conjure you.
So blow your trumpet, Gabriel,
Blow your trumpet louder.

O, I was lost in de wilderness,
King Jesus hand me de candle down.
So blow your trumpet, Gabriel,
Blow your trumpet louder.

The ministers withdrew, knowing they had seen the last of the Great Commoner. They waited at the door as Lydia, armed with her Catholic faith, attended to Thad, whose eyes only opened intermittently and blankly. In his oneiric state, black nuns garbed in flowing dark habits poked and fluttered about the deathbed like tenebrous African mantises. The gloom that had stolen into the room exercised its domain. One of the sisters asked Lydia if she could baptize the unregenerate Congressman. Lydia assented readily, feeling only a little guilty for sneaking Thad into heaven. Some words were intoned and some water sprinkled. As the clock moved from one day to the next, the powerful advocate for the rights of all men, surrounded by the people to whose freedom he dedicated most of this life, expired peacefully.

•   •   •

Accompanied by eight pallbearers, three white and five black, the embalmed body of Thaddeus Stevens was escorted to the nation's capital. There, in the Rotunda of the Capitol itself, on the very bier where President Lincoln had lain in state, thousands upon thousands of Americans paid their respects. On the body's trip back to Lancaster, a mournful public besieged every train station on the way. On Queen Street, under Lydia's watchful eyes, three days of visitors, 20,000 in all, swarmed to view the open casket. The funeral that followed included eight Protestant ministers and a Catholic priest. The nation's supply of black bunting was depleted to obscure both public buildings and private residences.

The towns and cities of the North mourned, and the hearts of ex-slaves everywhere wailed. Flags were flown at half their normal height and news accounts of Thad's life and death were published under black-bannered headlines. Articles in newspapers in New York and Philadelphia proclaimed that only the deaths of Jackson, Clay, and Lincoln in the current century produced similar displays of grief. Abroad, even papers sympathetic to the South reported his passing. The *Times* of London, the most vociferous of pro-Confederacy papers abroad, stated, *America has lost one of its foremost men.* The obituary proceeded to call Thad *fanatical, self-willed and most bitter in his animosities* but conceded, *there was neither meanness nor deceit in his nature* and praised the *iron will* that drove him on the *road he had chosen.* Southern papers were not so charitable, but their reactions were understandable. Later in the House, a long-time adversary compared him to "an eagle, perched alone upon a blasted oak in sullen and defiant majesty, scorning alike the chatter and the screams of other birds around him…That proud and defiant spirit, often fierce, sometimes unforgiving, and always bold and honest, has passed away."

Thad was owed, at the time of his death, the principal amount of $100,000 for loans provided over the course of a lifetime with no expectation of repayment. His will established a school in Lancaster open to children of all races, colors, religions and nationalities. Lydia was given a small bequest. His nephew Thad, for each five-year period in which he abstained from liquor, was entitled to one-fourth of a large legation, and could also draw an annual income of $800. Thaddeus Stevens wrote in a codicil, *out of respect for the memory of my mother to whom I owe what little prosperity I have had on earth, and which, as small as it is, I desire emphatically to acknowledge,* the Baptist church received a thousand dollars.

Thad composed his own epitaph, which graces a headstone in Shreiner's cemetery, known as Concord cemetery until two years before his death, in his adopted Lancaster, a graveyard where most of the deceased inhabitants are people of color:

> *I repose in this quiet and secluded spot,*
> *not from any natural preference for solitude,*
> *but finding other cemeteries*
> *limited by charter rules as to race.*
> *I have chosen this that I might illustrate in death*
> *the principles which I advocated through a long life,*
> *Equality of man before his Creator.*

EPILOGUE

A lmost all of the people and all of the significant dates and historic events in this book are true. Only minor characters are not "real." The Bauschultes hosted me during my studies on the land-locked island that used to be West Berlin; my children's names are portmanteaued and pop up periodically, as do those of friends; Ebenezer Franklin, and Judges Tulkinghorn (with apologies to Dickens) and Mannliebe are invented. In what I hope they will regard as a modest tribute, the names of my college's Athletic Director, men's basketball coach, women's lacrosse coach and its women's track and field coach are used. Pompey is a construct. The Coleman family in fact owned the *soi-disant* Little Dick, although it is likely that he continued to slave at the Elizabeth Forge, and not in their home.

Curtis Root and Luke Sweatt were adult contemporaries when Thad was a child in Danville. Samuel Merrill (1792–1855) was a native of Peacham, Vermont. He attended Peacham Academy, and spent a sophomore year at Dartmouth College in 1812-1813. For the next three years he lived in York, Pennsylvania, teaching school and studying law. It was his teaching position that he offered to Thad, and which Stevens filled. In 1816 he moved to Vevay, Indiana; the following year he was admitted to the Indiana bar. Merrill befriended Henry Ward Beecher and later bought an interest in a bookstore and started a publishing concern. His company evolved into Bobbs-Merrill.

Importantly, all of the correspondence concerning the relationship of King and Buchanan is presented verbatim, whether authored by others about them, or the letters exchanged between the two men. Buchanan's letter to Robert Coleman and his awkward poem to Dolley Madison's teenaged niece, the "Colebrook" letter in Chapter Six, and most of the other letters used are rendered as written, including Buchanan's mother's plaintive request that he decline the Russian ambassadorship. All quotes from the Senate floor and the halls of Congress concerning Senator William R.D. King, President pro tempore and Vice President of the United States, are in the Congressional Record. The letter conveying Buchanan's expulsion from Dickinson is created, although the expulsion, as with nearly every significant event recounted, was real. The letter from his father reacting to the faculty decision to deny Buchanan collegiate honors still exists.

I have to confess to having fun with the Dickens chapter. The description of Uncle Pumblechook in *Great Expectations*, "a large hard-breathing middle aged slow man, with a mouth like a fish, dull staring eyes, and sandy hair standing upright on his head, so that he looked as if head been all but choked, and had that moment come to," was simply too accurate a depiction of Buchanan, and too good to pass up. Dickens was, in fact, at Barnum's in Baltimore on his first visit to America in 1842. He found it the most refined hotel at which he stayed. It is certainly possible that he saw Old Buck and W some evening in hotel's dining room. My description of London of course draws heavily on Dickens's own view of his adopted city. There are other allusions for literary detectives, some admittedly more facile than others, to the works of James Joyce, Thomas Mann, Wm. Shakespeare, Robert Heinlein, Nathaniel Hawthorne, e e cummings, Herman Melville, Marcel Proust, Alfred Tennyson, John Steinbeck, Dylan Thomas, Dante Alighieri, O. Henry, Lewis Carroll, Larry McMurtry, Percy Shelley, and Gabriel Garcia Marquez, as well as the Bible.

Robert Coleman was in fact one of the wealthiest men in America, and a skillful and rapacious war profiteer. During the Revolution, with most of those in Lancaster and surrounding areas conscripted, Coleman convinced General Washington and the Continental Congress to permit him to use 70 Hessian prisoners to man his iron works. He quickly turned them into skilled ironworkers, compensating Congress with the small sum of 30 shillings a month offset from the price he charged the government for their work. When the number of Hessians available failed to satisfy his needs, Coleman's power became even more evident. Congress quickly passed the required legislation: young men in Lancaster and surrounding counties were exempted from the draft. They found themselves instead compelled into service at Coleman's Elizabeth Furnace and other outposts of his growing holdings, receiving only military pay.

Slavery officially ended in Pennsylvania shortly after independence for the colonies was declared, but was grandfathered by state legislation for many in bondage until 1828, the year Andrew Jackson was elected president. The Colemans and most of their friends, including judges, legislators and cabinet ministers, owned slaves. Even after they were "free," most continued as servants, usually with no pay, as dis slaves throughout the South well into the 20th century. .

The precise particulars of Ann's death are lost in the mists of history, as is the full story of the predicate. What is known is that she broke the engagement with Buchanan, that she fled to her sister Margaret Hemphill's house in Philadelphia, and that she died of an overdose of laudanum, an opium derivative commonly prescribed at the time. It is highly unlikely that she did so accidentally, as she was in fact attended by the two physicians named in the text, including the mysterious and wonderfully named Dr. Philip Syng Physick. Dr. Chapman was later quoted as saying that no one in Philadelphia, to his knowledge, ever died of "hysterics," the condition for which he prescribed Ann a moderate amount of the drug. Dr. Physick has been called by some the "Father of American Surgery." His grandfather, a silversmith, designed the inkstand that held Jefferson's pen as he wrote the Declaration of Independence. When Dr. Physick accompanied Dr. Chandler to the Hemphills', his patients already included Dolley Madison and Chief Justice John Marshall. He would later treat Andrew Jackson. He moved into a house built by Henry Hill off profits from the Madeira trade, Buchanan's favorite beverage. The word "Sherry," an Anglicization of Jerez, Spain, is capitalized as it was in Buchanan's time. Hill's house still stands. It is one of the few freestanding homes in Society Hill (so known not for any elitist pretensions but as the result of its guild background) and is now known as the "Physick House." My thanks to J. Del Conner, Dr. Physick's multiple-great grandson, for his graciousness in giving me a personal tour when I arrived there at an hour when it was closed. It's worth a visit.

Most accounts have Ann dying in bed "under peculiar circumstances," but there is no independent verification of that. Thomas Kittera, Buchanan's friend and likely lover from Philadelphia, wrote in his journal on December 8, 1819, that he saw a seemingly healthy young woman fitting her description that afternoon on the streets of Philadelphia, and that she had died that evening. The rough and watery passage to the spice filled Bartram's Garden (developed by a highly capable self-taught naturalist and visited by Washington and Jefferson among others) and to the mulberry and the oleander are of course allusions to the myths of Pyramis and Thisbe, and Hero and Leander, with a bit of Ophelia thrown in. Incidentally, family, friends, and newspapers spelled her name as both "Anne" and "Ann." Although Buchanan employed the former in the obituary he composed, I have chosen to go with the orthography of her headstone.

The letter as set forth in Chapter Six was so written by Buchanan and rejected unopened at the Coleman residence. It is also the fact that Robert's will was designed to slash Sarah's inheritance if she married William Muhlenberg. The St. James vestry was bribed by her brother Edward Coleman with a $5,000 donation conditioned on Muhlenberg's expulsion. The young pastor never returned to Lancaster. It is also true, and somewhat chilling, that Ann's younger sister Sarah, thrust into despair by her father's opposition to her possible marriage, his ex-sepulcher limitations on her future and fortune, and the departure of her intended, went to Philadelphia almost six years to the day after Ann's suicide, and died of what was called "pulmonary affection." When she plunged into the icy waters of the Schuylkill, Sarah Hand Coleman was precisely Ann's age.

Elizabeth Speer Buchanan and Sarah Morrill Stevens were estimable women. Elizabeth did spend long hours reading her son from Milton, Pope and Cowper, and the Bible, and raised a succession of children in challenging circumstances. Sarah was likewise a heroine, caring not only for her four sons after Joshua fled one early day, but running the farm, cleaning homes, nursing the ill, ensuring the best education possible in backwoods New England, and pushing her boys toward notable success, although her husband's namesake Joshua, cursed with two club feet, died a drunken death.

The rivalry and mutual disdain of Thaddeus Stevens and James Buchanan was at least as intense as portrayed here. There is every indication that they actively hated one another. Why Stevens, who was strikingly successful as a landowner, lawyer and politician in Gettysburg and Adams County, relocated to Lancaster, is best explained for the reasons suggested in this book. There is, in fact, evidence that Thad's planned elevation of Buchanan found support among the more radical abolitionists. The estimable suffragist, Jane Grey Swisshelm, editorialized in February of 1858 that her paper, the *Visiter*, would become, *an Administration organ, to support Mr. Buchanan's measures and advocate his re-election. ... Now, good friends, do not be so angry, but that if you strike you will also stop and hear us.*

Mrs. Swisshelm set forth her reasons for taking this curious position in support of a President she and her readers and political allies despised. Meeting Buchanan on his own turf, she stated that the Constitution had become the *Magna Charta of a Southern gentleman's right to whip women, rob mothers of their children, and sell upon the auction block the souls for whom the Lord of Glory assumed humanity and laid down his life upon the cross. ... We believe the Democratic party is likely to succeed in reducing all the poor and friendless of this country to a state of slavery.* With Buchanan as president, she opined, the country would quickly reach a point where conflict was inevitable, *the point which shall answer to that 'good old time,' the middle of the thirteenth century, when kingcraft ad* [sic] *priestcraft shall be triumphant, and the masses shall be provided with masters to exact their labor and furnish them with their peck of corn each week.* She promised to support unequivocally Buchanan's reelection, if necessary, so that conflict would be accelerated. She may, as did Stevens and others, have read Marx and Engels and the analogous communist thesis of permitting capitalism to run its inevitably crushing course toward flagrant oppression and therefore rebellion.

Susan B. Anthony, in an interpretation that demonstrates the broad power of Stevens's 14th Amendment, relied on it as constitutional authority for her attempt to vote in the 1872 presidential election.

Tellingly, she urged the removal of all secrecy for the support of Buchanan, echoing Thaddeus Stevens's manipulation of the electorate by placing Buchanan in the presidency. Although she noted that Buchanan's adherents would now become aware of the abolitionist scheme and *will not all approve of our plan of aiding its measures, but we think a little reflection will teach such that there is* **no longer any occasion for concealment**. (emphasis added)

American giants Jefferson, Clay, Marshall, Webster and Calhoun preceded Buchanan as Polk's Secretary of State, a post he held, as he did so many others, without distinction. It is a mark of the great progress of this nation that two of the last three Secretaries of State have been women, and two out of three African Americans. One can only imagine Buchanan's reaction to President Obama!

When John Eaton died in 1856 after penning Jackson's authorized biography, Margaret O'Neill Eaton (as she took to calling herself, transfiguring her maiden name) had a small fortune. That same year, at the age of 59, the still vivacious widow married her granddaughter Emily's 19-year-old dance tutor, Antonio Buchignani.

His name was not, she assured all, Italian for "Buchanan." Five years later, the dance instructor took off for Italy, accompanied by both her granddaughter Emily and the residue of Peggy's fortune. Her colorful life long past, she breathed her last in 1879, at the age of 83, dismally ensconced in a home for destitute widows; perhaps her bony, blue-veined hands still desperately sought the kindnesses of strangers.

There is also a contemporary footnote to the legacy of the now largely unknown Vice-President William Rufus DeVane King. The King County commissioners, seated in Seattle, Washington, voted in 1986 to change the designee of the honor of its namesake from the former Vice President. King was denounced as a slaveholder, someone who, "earned income and maintained his lifestyle by oppressing and exploiting other human beings." *Ex post facto*, in a bit of historical thaumaturgy, the Reverend Martin Luther King was substituted for the honor. If the Senator's sexuality counts for anything among the thinkers who initiated the historically revisionist motion, this was itself an unintentionally discriminatory action. Just south of King County in the State of Washington is Pierce County, first populated on the eve of the Pierce-King administration and named for the 14th President. Three American counties are named for Buchanan, in Iowa, Missouri, and Virginia.

King is the only Alabamian ever to hold national office, just as Buchanan holds the demographically-surprising distinction of being the only Pennsylvanian. King's long service as President pro tempore of the Senate, and the quoted eulogies, signify the respect in which he once was held. Although he was installed in 2003, along with a local grocery and drugstore magnate, as a member of the gender-segregated Alabama "Men's Hall of Fame," King is disproportionately unknown for a man of his accomplishments. The eulogies cited are available in the Congressional Register and are bound in one book, O*bituary Addresses on the Occasion of the Death of the Hon. William R. King of*

Alabama, Vice President of the United States, delivered in the Senate and House of Representatives, and in the Supreme Court of the United States, eighth and ninth December, 1853.

The translation of the phrase, "Nec male vixit, natus et moriensque fefellit" is accurate. Relying not on Mercersburg Latin, but on my own public high school's courses, I was astonished and delighted when I came across the epigram, whose enlightenment still resonates as at least secondary support for the then-widespread Washington knowledge of King's (and Buchanan's) homosexuality. Not trusting my own rusty four years of high school language study, I contacted my Latin teacher, Dr. James Greenberg, now with the University of Maryland, who confirmed the translation. The head of Maryland's Classics Department, Dr. Judith Hallett, also added an unexpected fillip that my faltering facility had not produced. "Fallo, -ere" does not only mean "to hide" or "make secret," it has the additional connotations of fraud, falsity and deceit. Its related noun, "falsum" and adjective, "falsus" directly bequeath the English "false." This obviously further empowers Senator Clayton's inspired choice of a linguistic capstone. A possible alternative translation, "he has not lived badly who lived and died in obscurity," also has no resonance when one is talking about a man who held the Senate's highest post unless one is, in fact, speaking of the very secret so desperately maintained.

My thanks also to Andrew Elfenbein of the University of Minnesota for his insightful analysis of William Cowper's verse that provided the shoulders on which I stood in utilizing his poetry.

Some further historical notes. Until 1914, with the passage and ratification of the 17th amendment to the Constitution, United States Senators were elected by state legislatures, rather than a direct vote of the citizens save for efforts in Wisconsin, Oregon and elsewhere to modify the dictate that Senators "be chosen by the Legislature" of each state. The framers of the Constitution were clearly concerned about the passions and prejudices of the people (then of course only white males) and placed not only presidential electors as a buffer, but also devised, in Article I, Section 3 of the Constitution, this mode of Senatorial election. It was therefore possible for Thaddeus Stevens, or any state legislator with political power and shrewdness, to orchestrate the election of a United States Senator. The movement toward reform of these elections began in earnest in the 1850's, and there were numerous cases of bribery and extortion, nine of which were brought in front of the Senate, and scores of deadlocks, before the constitutional amendment finally passed.

The President's Annual Message has become better known, but only since 1935, as the "State of the Union" address. The custom of delivering it orally, rather than as a written statement, was resumed by President Woodrow Wilson in 1913 after a century's lapse.

As an odd end to the Dred Scott decision, Mrs. Emerson, widow of his master, remarried the next year to a husband opposed to slavery. He ordered his wife to return Mr. and Mrs. Scott to their former owner, Peter Blow of North Carolina, who promptly freed them. Unfortunately, Dred Scott died within the year.

Pennsylvania has been described by the sparring pundit James Carville as "Philadelphia, Pittsburgh and Alabama in between," a particularly provocative phrase given the Buchanan-King/Lancaster-Selma connection. More of Pennsylvania's residents live in rural areas than do those of any other state. The Commonwealth is only the 32nd largest state in square miles, less than half the acreage of Oregon. Until 1960, Pennsylvania was the nation's second most populous (with a corresponding number of electoral votes); it is now sixth and falling fast. Although young people increasingly flee its borders and its job creation is among the lowest in the nation, Pennsylvanians conversely live and die in their home state at the highest rate in the country, making its population older than any state's except snowbirded Florida. The Keystone State's growth rate lags behind even similar "Rust Belt" states because relatively few choose to move there. Pennsylvania has had the largest net loss of inhabitants in the country for many of the last twenty years. When Buchanan stood for election in 1856, Pennsylvania had over 11% of all federal electors. In 2008, it had less than 4%. Incidentally, Maine with eight electors had more than Texas and Florida combined when Lincoln was elected in 1860.

Lancaster is not without its shaded charms. In nooks and crannies around Penn Square, in the heart of the city, down King and Queen and Orange, there are homes and mews that date from the time of Robert, Ann, and Old Buck. For the most part though, the winds that drove it to colonial prominence have long since blown out, and the attributes that made it a vibrant city have faded. Lancaster continues to drift along, as it has for two centuries. Big box stores and chain restaurants encircle a decaying core. The area now survives in substantial part off the curiosity of New Jerseyites and other Northeasterners about the increasingly arcane and, if recent news reports are to be credited, abusive Amish way of life. The town of Mannheim has long since changed its spelling to eliminate the middle "n" but is now again the home of some of Lancaster County's more prominent families, fleers of the city proper.

In Ann and Jamie's time, the precise and regular plats of Lancaster were designed to accommodate the neat rows and well-maintained trellises of the gardens the Germans cultivated behind nearly every house. Streets were paved with brick and stone. Its regularity of design, its location among the wooded hills, and its pleasant farmland drew favorable comment from almost all who came upon it, although one visitor wrote, "Lancaster is for the major part sluts and slovens. They place their filth (when they, as seldom, clean their houses) right outside their doors." Swine were, however, forbidden to run in the streets by municipal ordinance.

Lancaster's once proud road to Philadelphia is now an overburdened two lanes, slowly trod by Mack trucks and mini-vans. Agrarian interests, and those who fear the influence of the big city, resist the extension of a direct route to Philadelphia. The metropolis to the east is reachable only if one heads north for nearly 20 miles to the Interstate, or proceeds on a back road, a large part of which is now named the "Lincoln Highway" in honor of Old Buck's successor, through towns like Paradise and Gap, and the tourist traps that line the roadway. Even those basket, quilt, bric a brac, and tee shirt stops are premised on a fundamental, but heavily fostered, misapprehension. There is no historical antecedent for the tulips, windmills and wooden shoes, and the whole fraudulent construct of "Pennsylvania Dutch" is just a corruption of "Deutsch," or German, the nationality of many of Lancaster's original settlers. The town's principal industries have gone or gone under.

Most Lancastrians have only a vague notion of James Buchanan. He remains, despite his shadowy uncertainty and his virtual eclipse in Lincoln's light, the city's most famous son and Pennsylvania's sole United States President. Thaddeus Stevens, truly a giant of 19th century America, is similarly locally obscure. His name is known principally because of a trade school that bears his name.

Dickinson College, in a town now most notable for its annual Corvette rally, has not fared much better. Although ancient by this country's edificial standards, it has never lived up to the promise of contemporary or even much younger schools, and remains mired in the morass of middling liberal arts colleges. It draws 70% of its now majority female student body from within a two hour drive. The school has made recent strides to attempt to return to at least the local prominence it once held. It competes with later founded similar schools, such as the merged Franklin and Marshall, where Old Buck first chaired the Board of Trustees, and Gettysburg College, originally funded by Thaddeus Stevens and greatly aided by state appropriation bills he authored and pushed through the legislature. Many students still come to Carlisle from surrounding communities, including Mercersburg, Gettysburg, and Lancaster. Dickinson has had a law school for over 170 years. Recently merged with the state school system, it historically has sent its lawyers mostly into Pennsylvania's small towns and rusting cities. Many have become local politicians. In the nearly 200 years since Roger Taney and James Buchanan attended, no other graduates of the college have attained national political prominence, nor particular distinction in any other arena.

Jeremiah Atwater's administration at Dickinson instituted a series of reforms curtailing student misconduct. Without sufficient funding, but with an abundance of internal squabbling, the school in fact closed from 1816 to 1821, and again in 1832. Buchanan later wrote of Dickinson's *wretched condition* and, in hindsight, his considered great wish that he had been schooled elsewhere. Reflecting on this foreshadowing of a life of hard drinking and esurience, he summed up his Dickinson experience, *chiefly from the example of others, and in order to be considered a clever and spirited youth, I engaged in every sort of extravagance and mischief.*

Wheatland is maintained by a dedicated staff, but little visited except under the compulsion of local elementary school trips and the promise of an afternoon away from the classroom. Its docents are not well versed in the political milieu of the nineteenth century, and some are aggressively defensive of the memory of the benighted President they serve, especially against implications of Buchanan's complicity in Ann's death and increasing questions about his sexual orientation. Tours are better designed for those who want an understanding of nineteenth century dining and bathroom habits. Buchanan is a sketchy figure who retains no especial fascination to a visiting public largely unfamiliar with, save for the iconic Lincoln, any of the series of then-westerners, increasingly Ohio born, who populated the White House in the mid to late 1800's.

The Chamber of Commerce in Mercersburg, grown from Buchanan's childhood 300 to only 1500 today, proclaims the town his birthplace. While hardly the stuff of the Kentucky-Illinois rift disputing which has the better claim to Lincoln as a native son, little Cove Gap, five miles away, was certainly the site of his birth. In fact, a log cabin from that small spot was transported to Mercersburg and anointed the 15th President's birthplace, although the veracity of the claim for that particular dwelling is suspect. Cove Gap does itself have a small state park commemorating itself as Old Buck's birthplace, with a stone pyramid marking the site from which Mercersburg purloined the cabin.

James Buchanan told many, time and time again, throughout his lifetime of the box of letters, once under his bed, but later secured at the Bank of New York. He represented to others that they were moved there out of fear for the possible consequences of a Civil War battle in Lancaster. These letters finally would "explain all" about his relationship with Ann. Upon his death, a subsequent letter from Old Buck instructed his executors to burn the box without reading the letters. With respect to the "Ann letters," one could speculate that natural curiosity might have driven someone to read at least the ones on top of the beribboned pile. Perhaps someone's eyes even saw that some missives were not exchanged by Ann and Old Buck, but an individual named "W" and the President, drawn in a masculine hand. If the letters in fact revealed something negative about Old Buck's role in Ann's death, it is reasonable to suppose, after this bit of poking, that the executors would have had no reluctance in adhering to the testator's instructions.

We are fortunate that Buchanan's self-indulgent letter to Robert Coleman after Ann's death survives, as we are for the few extant letters between Old Buck and Senator King, although we are also helped by third party letters and the reports of handbills that referenced their liaison. Unfortunately, both the President and the Senator, themselves and perhaps through the offices of their devoted nieces, destroyed almost all of their correspondence. Still, evidence for Buchanan's and Stevens's relationship based on extant correspondence and contemporary statements of Andrew Jackson and others has to be regarded as conclusive.

Mary Snyder soon married someone else and ended her life in Snyder County, Pennsylvania, named for her grandfather, penurious and alone in a small wooden house in Beaver, surrounded by towns named for Washington, Adams, Monroe and Jackson.

Mrs. George Blake married again, and Dolley Madison's niece Anna Payne quickly wed a well-situated gentleman nearly as old as Buchanan.

If further proof be needed, the *Harper's* article from August 1856 on the eve of his election seems clearly to have been placed there to counter rumors of his sexuality, much as his hasty alliances with handy females were entered right before earlier votes, and sundered upon his election. It is replete with obvious, self-aggrandizing, and not particularly carefully- crafted, lies.

According to this article, Senator Buchanan visited a married woman in Washington. There followed a conversation on the reasons he had remained a bachelor and not married. The woman proposed that Buchanan seek the attentions of an attractive young friend of hers. He reportedly became agitated and stated *to love he could not, for his affections **were in the grave**.* The emphasis is in the original article.

Curious, the woman *with the blandishments only know to the sex* derived what she was led by Buchanan to believe was the truth about his relationship with Ann. Buchanan started, *It was my good fortune, soon after I entered upon the active duties of my profession, to engage the affections of a lovely girl, alike graced with beauty of person and high social position. Her mother, her only living parent, was ambitious; and, in the thoughtless desire to make an alliance of fashion, opposed the union of her child with one who had only his talents and the future to give in return for so much beauty and wealth. The young lady, however was more disinterested; mutual vows of attachment were exchanged, a correspondence and frequent personal interviews succeeded, and the further seemed to promise a most happy consummation of our wishes.*

Buchanan related that he *was engaged on a suit of importance before one of the courts holden in the city of Philadelphia.* This would, he anticipated, compel his absence for not more than two weeks, *The law's delays, however, detained mea month beyond the anticipated time; and, although I succeeded beyond my most sanguine expectations, and established myself in a position before the highest court of my native State, my triumphs were dashed that in all the time thus engaged I had not received a line from Lancaster, instead of which, the atmosphere was filled with rumours that the person upon whom I had set my affections had been seduced into the ambitious designs of her thoughtless parent, and that I had been discarded.*

As soon as his six weeks of argument were over, Buchanan sought to travel by stage to Lancaster, *The idleness consequent upon traveling gave time for my consuming thoughts, and my suspense became painful to the last degree.* He was *unable to bear the slow pace of my conveyance,* and he bolted the stage, acquired a *fleet steed,* and galloped toward his intended. As he approached Lancaster, *the animal from some unaccountable cause, sprang from the road, threw me with force, breaking my arm and otherwise injuring my person.* He was then *conveyed, helpless and full of physical and mental agony, to my home.*

A surgeon came to treat him, and it was only then that he learned that Ann, while he was away, had become engaged to another man. Buchanan, as he told it, *&concealing my wounded limb under a cloak, probably pale and haggard, I presented myself at the mansion of the mistress. I was received by the presence of the mother.* **She** *confirmed my suspicions. The young lady stood by, the picture of despair, yet silent as the grave. Desperate at what seemed this bad faith, I returned to my house, wrote a hasty letter demanding my correspondence, and returning, at the same time, every once cherished token of affection. I received all I sent for, save, perhaps, some forgotten flower."* (emphasis in original)

That same night, according to Buchanan's revisionist saga, Ann and a female servant went to Philadelphia to visit her uncle. Upon arrival, Ann said she was fatigued and retired to her room. *Complaining of some serious pain, only soothed by narcotics, she sent her faithful but unsuspecting servant and friend to a neighboring drug-store for laudanum* and went to sleep. *The following morning not making her appearance, the family became alarmed, broke open the door, and found the young lady dead—in her hand the little keepsake retained from my correspondence.*

The unnamed uncle took her coffin back to Lancaster and charged Mrs. Coleman to gaze upon, *the result of her work.* Mother sent a messenger to hail Buchanan. *Over the remains of the daughter, she revealed the particulars that led to the awful result. My letters and hers, by untiring industry, the command of large resources, and paid agents, had all been intercepted. The reason for my prolonged absence explained as the result of the fascinating charms of city belles. All this while the victim had been full of hope. She had heard of my arrival in Lancaster, but not of my accident; for long weary hours she was in the parlor waiting my presence, yet doomed to disappointment. Here was seeming indifference, a confirmation of all that she had heard. On the other side, I was made the dupe of the mother's arts, and the friend who had poisoned my ear was merely the agent to carry forward the great wrong.... The result was death to one party, and the burial of the heart of the other **in the same grave** that closed over tone who could not survive the wreck of her affections.* (emphasis yet again in the original)

Harper's, in its "Editor's Drawer" segment closed, *Many years have passed since the incidents idealized above in the above sketch have transpired. But the country strangely becomes interested in the event, from the fact that the "White House" may possibly have a bachelor for its occupant; but one, not so because of indifference to woman but really from the highest appreciation of one of the loveliest of the sex.*

As all readers of this book know, this self-serving tale well reflects Buchanan, in tone and his conspiratorial incantation of *the command of large resources and paid agents.* In fact, Mr. Coleman was alive in 1819 (and for six years more) and Buchanan did not break his arm that year or, as far as is reported, ever. There is no reason to believe Ann was ever engaged to anyone else; or that she went to an "uncle's house" in Philadelphia and that "uncle" accompanied her body and confronted the evil Mrs. Coleman, charging her with Ann's death; or that Buchanan was absent for six weeks at an argument before the state's highest appellate court, a contention that any lawyer would know is beyond improbable on its face. He was involved in a case involving financing for the Columbia bridge, and may have had to go to Philadelphia for a few days, but the whole story of frustration at the slow stage, the acquisition of a fast horse, and the subsequent tumbling from the horse's back are Buchanan at his lurid and self-centered best, embellishing a story for his own purposes when he believed it would not be countered. Not to mention the melodrama of the dead hand encasing a last small token of their trammeled love…

There is corroboration from many sources that Ann and Sarah visited Philadelphia together in December and stayed with her sister Margaret and her husband, later an undistinguished Congressman (who held the sobriquet "One Note Hemphill" by virtue of his making but a single speech) from Philadelphia, residents of Chestnut Street.

Buchanan's friend Thomas Kittera, the bachelor who lived with his mother and niece in Philadelphia and was frequently visited by Buchanan, ostensibly in connection with a "romantic interest" with Kittera's niece, Mary Snyder, supports this conclusion.

Kittera wrote in his journal, *At noon yesterday, I met this young lady on the street, in the vigour of health, and but a few hours after her friends were mourning her death. She was engaged to be married, and some unpleasant misunderstanding occurring, the match was broken off. This circumstance was preying on her mind. In the afternoon she was laboring under a fit of hysterics; in the evening she was so little indisposed that her sister visited the theatre. After night she was attacked with strong hysterical convulsions, which induced the family to send for physicians, who thought this would soon go off, as it did; but her pulse gradually weakened until midnight, when she died. Dr. Chapman spoke with Dr. Physick, who says it is the first instance he ever knew of hysteria producing death. To affectionate parents sixty miles off what dreadful intelligence-to a younger sister whose evening was spent in mirth and folly, what a lesson of wisdom does it teach. Beloved and admired by all who knew her, in the prime of life, with all the advantages of education, beauty and wealth, in a moment she has been cut off.*

Suicide by laudanum was common in Philadelphia in the early 1800's. Dr. Chapman routinely administered opium to treat the waves of hysteria. Opinion against Buchanan was intense, one woman writing, *I believe that her friends now look upon him as her Murderer.*

There is ample and, in my considered view, conclusive evidence of Buchanan's sexuality, despite his deathbed destruction of not only the letters to and from Ann but most of the correspondence between him and King. Stevens is more of an enigma. There is no hint of any adult relationship by him with a woman, save for the fact that Lydia Smith was his housekeeper (certainly not in and of itself sufficient to conclude a sexual relationship between James Buchanan and Miss Hetty, for example) and a series of unanswered charges of adultery. The only credible anecdote concerning any female companionship extant has him scampering away from a young woman named Sarah Sargeant who reportedly joked about the purchase of a wedding ring. Stevens fled the relationship.

It is not too great a stretch to believe that his great sympathy for the black race was derived in part from the feelings of discrimination he himself experienced as the result of his disability, and perhaps his sexuality.

In Fawn Brodie's felicitous phrase, refulgent with Christian iconography, Thaddeus Stevens was indeed the "Scourge of the South." Always angry and always in search of a machine against which to rage, his seemingly instantaneous tergiversation from anti-Masonry to anti-slavery, and the resultant active antipathy to the South and all things southern, informed his life. Sarah Morrill Stevens taught all four of her sons to read by the light of the cabin's only fire. One would become a doctor, another would teach, and Thad a lawyer. The oldest son, born with two club feet, followed his eponymous father's descent into alcoholism and an early death. In the light of Thad's later notoriety, stories abounded that a similarly afflicted French diplomat, Count Talleyrand, must have sired him but it is now known that Talleyrand did not visit Vermont until after Thad's birth. Stevens was even less successful than Buchanan as an uncle raising his nephews, his uneasy mixture of Calvinism and angry ambition not translating well to ersatz fatherhood.

Uncle Tom's Cabin was published in 1852, with its tale of Little Eva, Topsy, Simon Legree, and its strong Christian imagery. Over one in eight white American adults snapped it up. In its first year of publication alone, more than half the citizens of the northern states read the book. Its melodrama raised a country's consciousness and changed the views of many concerning slavery and helped propel Stevens's abolitionist agenda.

Many abolitionists would come to permit, or even encourage, the departure of the slave states from their country. Others secretly welcomed secession as an excuse to punish the South through war and any other means necessary. Thad Stevens always stood with that group and may have pursued tactics, as suggested earlier in the discussion of Jane Swisshelm, espoused by Karl Marx, whose writings were certainly known to him, of creating conditions so hostile that revolt is the inevitable result. Marx, by the way, was reportedly a strong admirer of John Frémont, the candidate Buchanan defeated.

At his death, Coleman bequeathed Stevens not only the ironworks the lawyer named "Caledonia" after his birthplace, but two others as well. They were perhaps not the best performing of his properties, but it was likely more due to their mismanagement by those Stevens put in charge than any niggardly intent by his client. Thad's later aborted plan to run the railroads at public expense on a zigzag Gerrymandered course stretching like a tapeworm across eastern Pennsylvania had to be concocted to try to resurrect their success, but it did not pass legislative muster.

Only when Lincoln had named Simon Cameron, the governor of Pennsylvania, as his first Secretary of War was Thad truly upset with the administration to which all his efforts had pointed. He knew Cameron to be corrupt, something that was only gradually realized by the trusting Lincoln. In one meeting with the President, after a particularly caustic comment, Abe asked Thad about the character of his fellow Pennsylvanian, "Why, Mr. Stevens, you do not believe that the Secretary would steal, do you?" Thad replied, with characteristic understatement, "Mr. President, I don't think he would steal a red-hot stove."

Cameron got wind of this remark and, in what became a staple in the retinue of stories of both President and Congressman, confronted Stevens and demanded that he go with him to the White House and retract his calumny. Thad agreed to do so. In the oval office, looking directly at the President but keeping an eye on Cameron, Thad complied with the cabinet member's request, "Mr. President, I believe I was in error. I regret that I told you that your Secretary of War would not steal a red-hot stove. Upon thinking it through, I now believe he would." Within days, Cameron was out of the cabinet. It was on his ill-constructed railroad, work parceled and piecemealed in a crazy quilt of corruption and bribery, that the governors of eight states later traveled to the Gettysburg battlefield on the 40-mile trip that lasted eleven hours due to breakdowns of equipment and derailings.

The Great Commoner's sardonic wit expressed itself often, in exchanges where he feigned an inability to recognize another legislator who "adheres by his own slime" to his seat, and another in which he concluded, after learning that a debating opponent had children, "I was in hopes, sir, that you were the last of your race." Yet again, "You must be a bastard, as I knew your mother's husband, and he was a gentleman and an honest man." He was also quoted as frequently saying, "all men are mercenary and all women are unchaste," withdrawing the remark fully and finally when someone implicated his mother in the evaluation.

Stevens's actions blocking the seating of the southern delegation after the Civil War certainly accelerated what might have otherwise taken decades. The Congressmen never took office, and Reconstruction continued without southern voices and votes until after his death. Without this maneuver, it is likely that nothing like the 14th and 15th amendments would have been passed for several more years. Even with those amendments, however, their *de facto* effect, disregard by certain of the individual states for a century was certainly not what Stevens envisioned. Nevertheless, by living beyond the Civil War, Stevens was able substantially to lay the groundwork for Black civil rights. He achieved a venerable status among all abolitionists, leading the charge against Andrew Johnson and fighting for punishment of those he viewed as southern war criminals and their aiders and abettors.

It was nearly two years after the Union victory when Stevens spoke in Congress on January 3, 1867. "Since the surrender of the armies of the Confederate States of America a little has been done toward establishing their Government upon the true principles of liberty and justice; and but a little if we stop here. We have broken the material shackles of four millions slaves. We have unchained them from the stake so as to allow them locomotion, provided they do not walk in paths which are trod by white men. We have allowed them the privilege of attending church, if they can do so without offending the sight of their former masters. We have imposed upon them the privilege of fighting our battles, of dying in defense of freedom and of bearing their equal portion of taxes; but where have we given them the privilege of ever participating in the formation of the laws for the government of their native land?

"What is Negro equality, about which so much is said by knaves and some of which is believed by men who are not fools? It means, as understood by honest Republicans, just this much, and no more: every man, no matter his race or colour; every earthly being who has an immortal soul, has an equal right to justice, honesty, and fair play with every other man; and the law should secure him these rights. The same law which condemns or acquits an African should condemn or acquit a white man."

Lincoln was of course not himself, nor when he took office, opposed to slavery in the South or North, despite the false gloss of history. His post-dated proclamation announcing the freedom of slaves in the rebel states was done out of desperation, not personal conscience or commitment. He was well behind the leaders of history's march. Stevens and others had to convince him of the necessity of this tactic to provide some moral basis for a bloody and unpopular war that extended far beyond anyone's earlier assessment. He might be a "gorilla" and "coarse and clumsy" but he was an excellent lawyer, a strong tactician and a superb strategist. It is certain he disdained abolitionists like Wendell Phillips and the derisive moniker he hung on him as the "slave hound of Illinois."

At the conclusion of the Civil War, 19 of 24 northern states did not allow freed black men to vote, in 10 states they could not testify in court, and none were permitted to serve on juries anywhere before 1860. It was not until Stevens's sweeping reforms that these issues began to be addressed in North and South. President Johnson kept trying to veto the measures most offensive to his sensibilities but, for the first time in the nation's history on any measures of significance, the Senate overrode those vetoes.

Stevens died, perhaps mercifully, before the active retreat from Reconstruction and into the descent into the Jim Crow era was fully realized. In D. W. Griffith's paean to the South and the rising Ku Klux Klan on Appomattox's golden anniversary, *Birth of a Nation*, the character of Austin Stoneman, patterned directly on Stevens, might be a better barometer of his public persona. Stevens was lionized at the end of his lifetime. He is now little remembered by a public whose appetite for historical heroes is sated by only one or two icons per era. When he died, his Dartmouth roommate, Joseph Tracey, was invited to offer a short remembrance for the college magazine. Tracey declined, stating, *Perhaps I knew him quite as well as any person who was in the College with him...He was then inordinately ambitious, bitterly envious of all who outranked him as scholars, and utterly unprincipled. He showed no uncommon mental power, except in extemporaneous debate....He indulged in no expensive vices, because he could not afford them, and because his ambition so absorbed him, that he had little taste for any thing that did not promise to gratify it....It seems proper that the Dartmouth should take some notice of him, and that notice should be prepared by some one who never knew him so thoroughly as I have done.*

Harriet Lane, who served as her uncle's first lady, finally married at age 36. She had two sons, but lost them both as teenagers to rheumatic fever. Her husband, banker Henry Elliot Johnston, also died early of pneumonia. She turned to art collecting and willed her holdings to the Smithsonian; they formed a substantial portion of the collection of the National Gallery of Art at its inception in 1906. Johns Hopkins University maintains the Harriet Lane Outpatient Clinics in recognition of the Johnstons' earlier endowment of a hospital home for invalid children.

James Buchanan Henry, "Young Buck" went to Princeton, served his uncle as secretary until he could not stand it any longer, became a lawyer and co-wrote a book on college life.

Edward Buchanan, the President's brother, was married to Stephen Foster's sister and presided at Harriet Lane's marriage ceremony at Wheatland in 1866. The couple honeymooned in Cuba, perhaps at the suggestion of her uncle.

Daniel Sickles, the young man who left his teenaged wife behind and took his mistress to London with Buchanan, returned to run for state senator in New York. In 1859 he shot the United States Attorney for the District of Columbia, killing him outside Dolley Madison's house on Lafayette Square for alleged "intimacy" with his wife, then only 22. After a month-long trial with Edwin Stanton as his attorney, he was acquitted.

Sickles later led a disastrous and insubordinate charge at Gettysburg which he spun, in a public relations masterpiece, into a story of heroism although it took him 34 years of lobbying to receive the Congressional Medal of Honor. At Gettysburg, he lost a leg, which he donated to the Army Medical Museum and visited in its glass enclosure each year on the anniversary of its loss.

Sickles continued unabashed in a life limned by scandal, and served as Minister to Spain under President Ulysses S. Grant (where, rumor has it, he have had an affair with the deposed Queen Isabella II), held prominent positions in New York and was elected to Congress at the end of the century. In 1871, at the age of 52, he married a young Spanish noblewoman. The couple had two children. His wife refused to return to the United States with him, later relented only to separate from him once again, finally reuniting at his deathbed along with his son, named Stanton after his successful advocate. Rumor has it that he skimmed funds off the top from the Gettysburg Memorial commission he chaired. He lived until the United States entered the Great War, perhaps still clamoring for a battlefield commission at the age of 94.

Buchanan's Vice President, John Breckenridge, became a candidate for President in 1860. He swept the deep South and added

Maryland and Delaware to his column, finishing a strong second to Lincoln. Despite popular perception, Stephen Douglas did not just "lose" to Lincoln, who had only 40% of the popular vote but dominated in electoral votes. Douglas actually finished fourth in the electoral college, also trailing Tennessee's John Bell and the ubiquitous Edward Everett of Massachusetts of the Constitutional Union ticket, a one-shot party composed of the remnants of Whigs and Know-Nothings. Breckenridge soon fought for the Confederate States of America against the country whose second highest office he held only months earlier and whose presidency he came close to winning.

What of the public Buchanan, the only Pennsylvanian ever to be president (although neighboring, smaller Ohio has produced seven), and widely regarded as among the nation's worst presidents? It is almost impossible to overstate, after reviewing his significant letters and addresses, his love for things southern, his belief that slavery was morally justified and "good for" slaves, his condemnation of abolitionists and the whole North itself for interfering with the institution and therefore fomenting disunion and war, and his straight-jacketed constitutional interpretation, how historically out of step he was.

Buchanan retreated into outright prevarication, which came smoothly to him, when matters that might reveal his orientation were raised. Although he thought history would redeem him on the issue of Ann's death and otherwise, its verdict has been unrelentingly unkind. He now provides the3 cushion on whom any other occupant of the White House may rest as his or her presidency drifts to the bottom of historical estimation.

The man who asserted, "What is right and what is practicable are two different things" thought it an easy thing to resolve the issue of slavery. The North just had to keep from sticking its Victorian nose in the South's business. Buchanan's solution was simple: keep the North out of the issue altogether and let the South, and any new states that voted to be slave holding, remain so without interference,

"All that is necessary to accomplish the object, and all for which the slave States have ever contended, is to be let alone and permitted to manage their domestic institutions in their own way. As sovereign States, they, and they alone, are responsible before God and the world for the slavery existing among them. For this the people of the North are not more responsible and have no more right to interfere than with similar institutions in Russia or in Brazil." Unless the various northern legislatures repealed their "obnoxious enactments" that "unconstitutionally" repealed the effects of the Fugitive Slave Law and the Supreme Court decision, "the injured States, after having first used all peaceful and constitutional means to obtain redress, would be justified in revolutionary resistance to the Government of the Union." History now views these positions as abhorrent, but it is important to remember how close the elected Lincoln adhered to these sentiments and policies.

Even Cabinet members who could refute the most important calumnies declined to do so. Lincoln had wisely and defensively hired most of his predecessor's former appointees. Although now positioned in various inferior positions, they were nonetheless jobs for men used to government service. The sinecures restrained further ambitions. Others were silenced simply by public sentiment and fear. In an environment where *habeas corpus* was suspended, prison could be a long and lonely time without trial or the opportunity to mount a defense if they were implicated in the alleged treason.

Others "looked scared and began to chaw" when asked to assist the former President in his response to the charges. Jerry Black acknowledged the *fictionist* nature of the charges against his friend and replied to his old boss's entreaty, *this request is more than I can comply with at present* when Buchanan offered 7000 dollars to write a favorable biography. Buchanan apparently regarded this as further evidence of cowardice, and told Black, "I have always felt and still feel that I discharged every public duty imposed on me conscientiously. I have no regret for any public act of my life, and history will vindicate my memory." He was, as always, notably silent about private acts.

The ex-President wrote to Howell Cobb, even as his former Treasury Secretary was constructing the South's prisoner of war dungeons at Andersonville where 13,000 Union soldiers would die, that these reactions by those still holding onto office, *are the grossest insult... they are willing to profit for their new masters by the slander, rather than speak a word of truth in justice to the old President.* He concluded, *I was going to say, such is human nature, but I will not say it because the case is without parallel.*

On December 15, 1862, almost two years after he left office but in a country whose war was going very badly, Senator Garrett Davis of Kentucky, a Democrat and the successor to Old Buck's Vice President, now fighting for the Confederacy, introduced a resolution in the United States Senate:

Resolved, That after it had become manifest that an insurrection against the United States was about to break out in several of the Southern States, James Buchanan, then President, from sympathy with the conspirators and their treasonable project, failed to take necessary and proper measures to prevent it; wherefore he should receive the censure and condemnation of the Senate and the American people.

The resolution did not pass, but the "censure and condemnation" were already about the land. Buchanan started a letter writing campaign trying to defend himself, but this only invited more opprobrium and, fearing greater scorn, he ultimately decided not to file actions for libel.

The former president completed his memoir in 1862 but no one would publish it. Its limp third person singular preface asserted, *Mr. Buchanan never failed, upon all suitable occasions, to warn his countrymen of the approaching danger, and to advise them of the proper means to avert it. Both before and after he became President he was an earnest advocate of compromise between the parties to save the Union, but Congress disregarded his recommendations.* By the time it was finally issued at war's end, it found few readers.

When Lincoln was assassinated in April 1865, Buchanan wrote that, *my intercourse with our deceased president* convinced him of his good intentions. It would nevertheless be unsurprising if he felt a touch of Schadenfreude, and some genuine anguish and fear for his own well-being, when Millard Fillmore's house in Buffalo was splashed with bright red paint by Lincoln adherents who thought the thirteenth President was not sufficiently solicitous over Abe's passing.

On September 23, 1865, the war over, after "putting himself in the position of a little child, and asking questions in the simplest terms" and seeking to understand "how a man might know what he believes," Old Buck found himself in the dark basement of the First Presbyterian Church on Orange Street. He undoubtedly felt as if a stranger in a strange land, a "prophet without honor" in his own hometown. Old Buck was ready and, as one of those present later wrote, "old and broken with the storms of state." As such, in front of the four others present, D. W. Paterson, C. S. Davis, and J. S. Miller of the vestry, the Reverend Walter Powell, and his God, James Buchanan, Jr. was "admitted to the communion and fellowship of the Church."

Old Buck was appalled at the conduct of "reconstruction" after the war, and hastily endorsed Johnson's approach, an encomium that did nothing to raise the esteem of donor or recipient. When the thirteenth amendment passed, he still tried to hold some ground, stating, "emancipation is now a constitutional fact, but to prescribe the right and privilege of suffrage belongs exclusively to the States. This principle the Democracy must uphold." He also was beginning to recognize that Stevens's methods might provide the Democrats a chance to rebound. He echoed the increasingly popular view among Democrats that whether ex-slaves could vote was a matter for the states, to be determined in elections in which of course only white men could vote.

At his death, and as a marker of how far he had fallen, the *New York Times* buried President Buchanan's obituary deep in its June 2, 1868 issue, on page 5. It was one of many obituaries that attacked the president, out of office for less than a decade, but nearly forgotten. Noting that *his decease was not unexpected* the paper told of Old Buck's rise from *what was then a comparatively wild part of Pennsylvania* and noted that there was *some doubt respecting the exact date of his birth* and that he never himself mentioned his age, and might be two or three years older than the 1791 date typically fronted. The obituary expostulated his political ascent, but did not mention Ann Coleman, nor Senator King, and described Old Buck as *naturally timid and cautious* and wrote of his stance on slavery, *Mr. Buchanan took a very decided ground against the agitation of the slavery question. He was afraid of its ultimate political consequences, and desired to prevent them by an act of Congress which should shut out the question of slavery from the deliberations of that body [and advocated] a declaration that Congress had no power to legislate on the subject.* The Times noted, *time has proved how vain and shortsighted* his policies were.

The *Times* writer attributed a statement to Old Buck, which actually was an ellipsis of President Lincoln's interpretation of his predecessor's views, as offered by Secretary of the Interior William Seward, "The South has no right to secede, but I have no power to prevent them."

Although only a teenager, the Gray Lady's astute summary view of the late President was as follows, *Temporizing in this pitiful manner with the gravest crisis that ever fell upon a nation, he did nothing to prevent the accomplishment of secession.* Upon retirement to Wheatland, the *Times* noted, he was *followed by the ill-will of every section of the country* as he maintained the *strictest privacy* and made a *feeble and inconclusive* attempt to justify his course on the eve of the rebellion. What Old Buck viewed as his unfair vilification continued, although the *Times* stopped short of terming him a pro-slavery conspirator and traitor.

Other roughly contemporaneous views were not much kinder to the man who trusted in history for his vindication. Horatio King, erstwhile Postmaster General, published a collection of letters in 1883. They reveal an inflexible adherence to strict construction of the Constitution that led to an inability to punish secession, but also show that Buchanan was no traitor. They portray a sick and besieged man, often too ill to attend to routine business as his transient occupancy of the White House expired. Richard Nixon's last days, beset by war and Watergate slightly more than a century later, come to mind.

In a review of James Ticknor Curtis's early and sympathetic biography of Buchanan, the unnamed author in the November 1883 Atlantic Monthly provides insight 15 years after the President's death. The reviewer writes, *The same qualities which made Mr. Buchanan beloved at home made him popular abroad. He offended no one, and every one was glad to help him forward... There is something very pitiable— something almost tragic— in the figure of James Buchanan during those last months of his administration. The smooth, plausible, wary politician, having touched the summit of his ambition, was caught at the last moment between two greater factions, bitterly excited and just ready to spring at each other's throat...At bottom Buchanan was weak and timeserving, but he was not a villain...Buchanan failed miserably at the great crisis in the nation's life.... Treason was rife in his cabinet, and he allowed the traitors to depart without a word.* The writer next tells of Buchanan's *cowardly panic* and concludes, *The fact was that Buchanan was a very weak man, who had been a tool of stronger forces all his life.... he found himself drifting helpless and alone on the seething waters of the secession and civil war. He quivered and shook and made some constitutional arguments, and failed utterly, hopelessly, and miserably. He served slavery all his life, and when the crash came, he had no courage and convictions to fall back upon. He sank out of sight, and the great national movement swept over him and all his kind...no art or argument can rehabilitate him, or make him other than he was. He was not even a great failure, for he showed in his downfall that with all his ability, adroitness, and industry, the essential qualities of greatness were wholly lacking.* Curtis's biography, by the way, alludes to the charges of what was by then just on the eve of widely being known as "homosexuality" but dismisses the rumors as too disgusting to be worthy of exploration.

Curtis had earlier prepared a full account of the relationship with Ann based on first person interviews. He ran the draft by a Samuel Barlow, a Buchanan family heir, for criticism. Barlow wrote the biographer, *I am clearly of opinion that you should not print any considerable portion of what you have written on the subject of his engagement to Miss Coleman.*

He suggested that Curtis simply mention the engagement and that it was ended by her death. Further, implored Barlow, Curtis should only indicate that her death was the impetus for his entry into politics, that Ann was his first and only love to whom he was true all life long, and that he kept all her letters but on his death bed commanded that they not be opened, but instead burned. He ended, *And this is all. In this view Mrs. Barlow agrees fully.*

Unhappily, Curtis followed these dictates and his original draft has never surfaced. In his book he states only that, *it is now known that the separation of the lovers originated in a misunderstanding, on the part of the lady, of a very small matter, exaggerated by giddy and indiscreet tongues, working on a peculiarly sensitive nature.* What those "giddy and indiscreet tongues" said would, of course, along with talk of same-sex liaisons, now be the stuff of tabloids and so-called "entertainment news."

Buchanan is incessantly portrayed, by metaphor and in political cartoons, as a woman. Several examples are within this book. Many others are extant. While the dithering befuddlement he exhibited in crises might be viewed by some as the basis for such representations, these portraits do not simply reflect nineteenth century notions of feminine weakness. The constant and consistent use of such a symbol is telling with respect to Buchanan's homosexuality and the widespread, but encapsulated, awareness of it.

• • •

Jimmy and Old Buck, boy and man, trimmer and compromiser, was void of empathy, emotionally disconnected and unavailable. One cannot but have sympathy for the struggles bequeathed by his upbringing and the shadowy nineteenth century duel with his sexual orientation. He was not always the passive fool of history. Any activism, however, was informed by a blind veneration of Constitutional provisions that had become artifacts, an ultimately unrequited love of the South, and a devotion to one particular Southerner. His great show of projecting punctilious honesty and grandiloquent piety in small things was overwhelmed by his overweening inability to share the pain of a race of people, or to recognize the jackboot of history. Whenever a crisis of body or soul, public or private, arose, he suffered in physical agony and retreated into narrow legalism. This posture might have preserved him for posterity as an inconsequential president had he earlier held the post. It was insufficient for dangerous times and led James Buchanan, perhaps with Thaddeus Stevens's guiding hand, into historical oblivion and the nation into its bloodiest war.

ACKNOWLEDGEMENTS

My deep thanks to all who have assisted on this endeavor.

In particular, David Goehring of the Harvard Business School Press provided early encouragement, as did Peter Carfagna. Those who read this book in any of its many drafts, and therefore took on an especial burden, include Robert Rizzi; Tracey Sherman; Ron Dayton; Michael McDonough; Jean Stayman; my mother, Louise Evans; my brother, Christopher Evans, David Parker and, of course, my skilled and generous editor, Sally Kemp. There are others who made this path easier in other ways, some unknowingly, including Pete Briscoe, Beck and Randy Mathis, Lewis Lapham, Harland Cass of South Windsor High School, MSNBC's Chris Matthews, Professor Arthur Miller of Harvard Law School, Professor Will Provine of Cornell, Robert and Judy Rawson, Joseph "Skip" Ryan, Rita Carfagna, Doris Kearns Goodwin, Jess Wittenberg, Debbie Kovacs, Dale Godby, Jonathan Dowell, John Minna, Friedrich and Ruth Bauschulte, and my late father, David Longfellow Evans. Again, to each, and the one who knows who she is, my great appreciation.

Of course, all errors are mine and mine alone, including any as the result of my stubborn insistence on points of grammar, orthography, vocabulary and literary style.

1950232

Made in the USA